Mrs J Ramsay
Listowell

Read in Calcutta May. 45.

THE FRENCH PRISONER

THE
FRENCH PRISONER

by

PHŒBE
FENWICK GAYE

THE REPRINT SOCIETY
LONDON

FIRST PUBLISHED JUNE 1943

THIS EDITION, 1944

PUBLISHED BY THE REPRINT SOCIETY, LTD.
BY ARRANGEMENT WITH JONATHAN CAPE, LTD.

PRINTED IN GREAT BRITAIN IN THE CITY OF OXFORD
AT THE ALDEN PRESS

CONTENTS

CHAPTER I

JOHN VANDERVORD BECOMES PARTY TO AN ADVENTURE

... Time does not exist! There exist no perpetual and eternal appearance of phenomena, no ceaselessly flowing fountain of ever-appearing and vanishing events. Everything exists always! There is only one eternal Present, the Eternal Now, which the weak and limited human mind can neither grasp nor conceive.—P. D. OUSPENSKY

THIS tale is not going to be easy to believe. If it were, it would not be worth the telling. But in so far as it has a certain artistic completeness from the beginning to the end of the circle of small time it compasses — here it is for what it is worth.

It concerns chiefly the year eighteen hundred and one. That is to say, the protagonists in it reached their grand climacteric in the Autumn of 1801. Strange things come to pass in the lives of the humblest amongst us, as they happen in the lives of seas, trees, nations, mountains; and they go for the most part unrecorded save by the people or substances concerned. This particular climacteric — one amongst a million million — would certainly never have been recorded or even remembered (once those to whom it had occurred were dead), had it not been for the singular experience that befell a certain young American on a visit to East Anglia exactly a hundred years after 1802. Yes, 1902.

Exactly how or why the tale has never come to light until now, over forty years later, is one of the secrets that cannot be disclosed. But the fact must be accepted that it *is* a secret, as much as the fact must be accepted that what has been here recorded seemed to that young man at the time to be sober truth, however incredible. He wrote down what happened to him at the time, without explaining the whys or wherefores — and he did the same with what was told him (whether by word of mouth or by other less explicable means) with an absolute lack of question or suspicion. There was, he afterwards confessed, no time to feel either, with the impact of such happenings pressing upon his consciousness. And though he did not disclose anything about the affair thereafter (until now, that is), he drew subsequently a certain amount of comfort from the writings of certain distinguished physicists and mathematicians about the elastic properties of space and time; and also from the extraordinary account of the adventures at Versailles, early in this century, of the Misses Moberly and Jourdain. These all convinced him, but particularly the last-named, that if he was crazy then a great many intelligent and serious-minded people were crazy likewise.

The Versailles episode may be recalled as the experience of two English ladies who, visiting that royal estate at the beginning of this century, found themselves suddenly and inexplicably transported into the Versailles of Marie Antoinette. The most noteworthy fact about this happening is, of course, that two people suffered it together and one was able therefore to witness and confirm what the other experienced and recorded. Think what you will, dismiss it as offhandedly as you please, this unique Versailles experience of a certain trick of space-time remains obstinately in the mind — disturbing to some, delightfully liberating to others. Why should it have happened? Why should these two ladies, seemingly so securely well-planted in the space-time groove of the early twentieth century, be slipped suddenly as a gramophone needle into another groove altogether — so that the tune they knew and were was abruptly changed into something like and yet curiously un-like? It was, they recorded, exactly like walking into a dream — yet both were wide awake — painfully so, indeed, after the first few shocks. And it occurred, this transition — not once, but twice.

Or recall instead the experiences of those two Welshmen, Mardinn the Prophet and Enoch Lake, who — thirty years before the French perpetrated their abortive invasion of Fishguard, *saw* foreign soldiers drinking from a certain stream, called Finon Cribb, *saw* them cutting down a hazel tree and a whitethorn, *saw* other soldiers landing on Carig Gwasted Point — and heard them sounding their drums.

These fragments of prophetic vision were borne out later by the

8

actual happenings; There and Then became Here and Now without a shadow of doubt. How did it occur? Surely Finon Cribb and Carig Gwasted Point, for these two men, had slipped out of their own peaceful place-in-time groove long enough, *and strongly enough*, to show them a more intense, passionate, deeply-felt place-in-time — although this was before (according to our reckoning) the events had yet occurred . . . Does it not appear as if, to the percipient eye, the French invaders will be for ever hastily wetting their lips with the waters of *one* Finon Cribb, for ever splashing ashore at *one* Carig Gwasted Point? As Versailles — or one Versailles — must be for ever part of the urgent forebodings of those last fated days of the French Court?

Young Vandervord, for such is the name of the medical student whose experience is about to be described, never gave his own slipping into another groove a chance to be repeated. He spent a week in that particular corner of Suffolk. He had never been there before. He never went back afterwards. Indeed, he never returned to this country at all but thereafter took his vacations (being wealthy and well able to do so) across the Pacific instead of the Atlantic Ocean. You may have heard of him as an expert on early Chinese art. He has lectured extensively and has donated a very fine example of its best period to the particular New England Art Gallery of which he is one of the principal Trustees. Yes — Chinese art belonging to a particular dynasty which flowered and faded long before the Christian era. He chose it, he said, because its colours were serene and faded, its rhythm lively but static. Nothing murky here — nothing to catch you by the throat. It was something perfectly and completely dead — or completely immortal, whichever way you liked to look at it. And it was a longish way away in space *and* in time — far enough away, anyway, to be healthy. The Cristo-dophoulos Collection of Greek Art in London; the Vandervord Collection of Chinese art in Maine; now doubtless you understand why the name seemed familiar in the first instance.

And if you had been in a position to tell anyone in Maine that, however well Dr. Vandervord understood the early Chinese artists, there was a particularly murky year in Napoleonic Europe the implications, experiences and state of mind of which he knew as well as his own soul, and with the same awful certainty — he or she simply would not have believed you. And if you had said that there was no secret corner of the human heart for a passion or a love or a hope left to hide in, which Dr. Vandervord could not have met and greeted with trembling recognition, they would not have believed you either. For it was well known that Dr. Vandervord was a singularly self-possessed bachelor with no experience of, or interest in, passion of any sort.

But to the tale; in the late summer of 1901, this young student was to be found holidaying in the Eastern Counties. He had ridden down from Northamptonshire and now was leisurely making his way from small town to hamlet, hamlet to watering-place, watering-place to small town again. A legacy from an uncle had financed this vacation, after a year spent in the stiffest cramming the studious Vandervord had ever tackled. Three weeks of it had already passed, and he was now in the fourth and final week before being due to sail again for home.

It was the end of Summer, as well as the end of his holiday. The young man, riding on his hired mare, was tired but happy. (Physically tired, he insisted later. The *mental* tiredness had largely faded away on the voyage over — though some aftermath of it, some residue of cerebral fatigue, may have accounted partly for his subsequent lack of scepticism, of complete physicianly balance.) He had started from Northamptonshire because his great-grandfather had had associations with that county a hundred years earlier. John Vandervord the great-grandson knew little more than this bare fact — that there was a great prison near Peterborough, a famous prison, that had once housed his great-grandfather as a French prisoner of war. The sentimental journey there had proved more satisfactory in prospect than in reality; the place seemed to him bleak and flat, the inhabitants dull and unenterprising as the landscape. He sketched the church, as a good American should do, he leaned over the bridge and pondered on the advantage the water had of being able to hurry away underneath it; he gave ha'pennies to little boys. But it was idle to pretend that any of this benefited himself or his great-grandfather, and soon he was ready to resume his travels, glad he had come but not sorry to go, and was making his way eastward to the coast and then south again, through Norfolk and the fen country, until he had reached Aldeburgh in Suffolk.

It was while riding inland from Aldeburgh that his adventure began. He had done himself well with high tea at the local inn and after that, well satisfied with the meal and with the day, had called for his horse Cherry and mounted, his light luggage on the crupper behind him, and begun to ride towards the setting sun. Half a dozen miles or so, he reckoned, would see him well on his way towards Woodbridge, one of the first signposts on his return journey to London. If the evening stayed fine, he might ride on to Woodbridge; if not, then he would stop at the first likely inn or lodging that took his fancy. And that was that.

To those who do not know that sparse heath-like stretch of Suffolk coastland, it must seem insufficient to say that, by the waning evening light, it looked uncommonly bare and lonely. If a desert could be furnished with stretches of gorse and heather, rising and dipping ever so little, and by an occasional oasis of pines, then here was an English desert, or so it seemed to young Vandervord. This was odd, since his eye was used to distances far bigger, emptinesses far vaster, than any of these environs. He reflected upon the fact with interest, telling himself that it was doubtless something to do with riding into the setting sun, a sun still warm from summer. This sun seemed to blaze between his horse's ears and into his eyes as if its sole purpose in travelling millions of miles was to pierce into the eyes of a certain John Vandervord travelling at that precise moment at infinitesimal pace across a minute stretch of the crust of the earth's surface known as the Woodbridge Road.

Because of this fierce *personal* intensity, it blinded him to all forms of other movement, and particularly to other houses or other people that might be also along this stretch of sandy road. Afterwards, he found it incredibly difficult to recall to himself any particular feature of this part of the journey. There was nothing left of that gentle ride but the remembrance of the sound of grasshoppers whirring ceaselessly in the scrubby land about him, that inevitable mechanical accompaniment to the heat of the day; the sound of the mare's measured pacing, with the tawny-pink light streaming between her ears and flowing along the curved mountain-track of her hogged mane and blazing warm from thence upon his hands and face.

Now, staring into a light, or any bright, unwinking, steady blaze, is apt to produce a trancelike state of mind. Young Vandervord was not ignorant of that. In fact, taking together the pendulum tick-tock of his horse, and the steady glare of the sun into his eyes, he does remember that these between them produced a sense of great drowsiness and that he slipped momentarily into a kind of waking dream. But only for a moment — and awaking with a start of perplexed awareness to wonder if he were still on the right road or not.

To make sure, he drew rein at the first hope of discovering. There was a hedger-and-ditcher, a melancholy man with a long face and a billhook, tending, very slowly, a growing heap of brushwood beside the road. Vandervord demanded if he were right for Woodbridge, and was told to go on until he reached an inn called The Happy Man; after that there was a small birch plantation which would lie on his right, then there was heath again for a matter of a couple of miles, and then, said the hedger-and-ditcher, he was to go straight on until the Burnt House lay back to his left again. Vandervord asked if this were another inn, thinking the name strange enough for one, but was told no. It was just the Burnt House. It had been burned down a good many years since — before the hedger-and-ditcher's day certainly, but he would know it by the great chimneys still standing and the grassy expanse before it that had once been handsome parkland. What else lay beyond? asked Vandervord. Farmlands, said the hedger-and-ditcher, and another wood, and then farmlands again. After that there was — but Vandervord's memory was full. Another item and it would spill over. He threw his informant a couple of coins which surprised him into complete immobility, and once more urged on the mare with his heels and tongue.

By now the light had drained from the sky completely and a chilly twilight wind began to blow. It bent the birch trees of the small plantation that he passed, bowingly before him, and for the first time he began to regret his gloves, left carelessly behind the previous day. Leaning forward to clap the mare's neck he was almost surprised to feel it warm beneath him. Good girl, he said. But Cherry was either too tired or too bored by now to flick back an ear in response.

The plantation past, the scene merged back into scrubby heath again — curiously cold, curiously grey, the grasshoppers suddenly silent that had been so vibrant; nothing to break the line on either side of the road, no heaving hill, no copse, no wind-bent bushes; only this low, almost level sea of gorse and shrubby umber-coloured heath, as if it went on like this for ever, round the whole circumference of the world.

Then he came upon the Burnt House. On his left, as his guide had stated, but with something wrong about it nevertheless. For it was not burnt, as far as John Vandervord could see, at all. It stood well back from the road, just where the fringe of heath receded, a long brick house with stout chimney-stacks at either end, the whole structure no more than a shadowy mass behind its own parkland in the grudging light that was left. He pulled his mare in off the road on to the sandy roadside, leaning low in the saddle as she paced past and peering low to see if there were a name on the iron gates or the stone pillars that flanked them.

There was neither, he recalls, but there was the figure of a woman not far inside the closed gates, a bowed figure with her back to him and with a red shawl over her head. She appeared to be running, creeping along beneath the avenue of elms with the curious effortless motion of an animal — mole or badger, or some such wild thing. He hallooed her, thinking that here was a caretaker who might give him the confirmation he desired.

'Is this the Burnt House?' he shouted. But the figure only melted further into the twilight, running and running away from his voice. He stood in his stirrups then and hallooed again, louder and more desperately, though precisely what he felt desperate about he could not afterwards have told you.

'Is the name of this place the Burnt House?' he shouted again.

The vigorous challenge of the cry seemed all wrong there. It was as if its very vigour stopped the bent creature in her silent tracks, and turned her round and brought her back slowly towards the closed gates, drawn on the cords of that strong young voice.

She still kept the dark red shawl drawn closely about her head and shoulders and — just when he was beginning to lose patience with her:

'No,' she said. 'It was once called Redonda, Redonda Farm —
'Redonda Farm?'

The woman came closer in the failing light — failing so fast now, running away from Vandervord's eyes as the last teasing fragments of a dream runs away from the waking mind. She gripped the iron bars of the gates as a prisoner might hold prison bars. When she spoke again her mouth was a black square in her shadowy face — terrifying, grotesque — a bad dream in all truth.

'Redonda,' she repeated. 'But for a long time — oh, a very long time now, it has had only one name, and that is Désolée.'

CHAPTER II

DÉSOLÉE

Ah, once I loved thee, Atthis, long ago.
The fields about the farm are silent now,
Where in the windless evenings of the Spring
We heard Menalcas singing at his plough.

Ah, once I loved thee, Atthis, long ago.
I shall not see thy face nor touch thy hands.
The empty house looks seaward; far away
The loud seas echo on the level sands.

ELIZABETH BELLOC: *Translated from the Latin*

WHO was it said a word was like a knell? Certainly no knell ever struck with a more shuddering insistence upon the ear of young Vandervord than those three syllables of *Désolée*. Again it seemed to him that he was caught up helplessly in the net of a dream not of his own imagining and — as if in a dream — in some weird way re-tracking (not of his own volition but under some nameless compulsion) a path already traversed timeless times before. The hands clasped the bars, the black shadowy mouth had opened and his apprehensive ears had known what was to issue from it. Not, *I have been here before*, but *What I am about to hear I have already heard before, long, long ago. Somewhere, somehow, that despairing name of Désolée has chilled my blood and deadened the tempo of the beating of my heart*. Nothing moved. The figure stood still after the word had been uttered, the huge trees above her stood still; far behind her the shadowy mass of the house itself made a hole in the dusk like the hole of the bottomless pit. Everything was dun-coloured, static — of a fabric to be sensed rather than felt, exactly the fabric of a dream.

Vandervord bent lower in his saddle towards the woman waiting behind the gate — in deference to the mood and hour.

'I beg your pardon, Madam,' he said, 'but am I still on the road for Woodbridge? I must find somewhere to sleep and a stable for the mare. Is it far to an inn?'

'Van —,' said the woman. The mare's withers shivered silkily against his knee. (They say horses are sensitive to atmosphere — can smell blood shed long ago, cannot be made to pass trees by the roadside that have been used as gallows.) There was no room left for surprise in Vandervord that she should know his name — his pet name to familiars — nor that she should address him by it; only he became conscious of a great and compelling lassitude. The Burnt House. Redonda Farm. Désolée. All were one. All merged into a reality present, potent and terrible — far more real than any nebulous inn upon any road to Woodbridge.

All at once he knew that he was to go no further that night. He was to stay here. Against his will or with his will — there was no question of his will at all, only of inevitability.

It was not long after this that he found himself dismounted and, without another word, walking up the long drive towards the house with his companion. He never recalled the gates being opened to admit either him or his horse; for all he knew, he went through them. But he was not conscious of surprise — only of this lassitude and of a vague hope that they should reach the house before the complete darkness of a moonless night enveloped them. It was a long drive. The mare lagged behind him, her neck extended full-length to the pull on the bit, in that seemingly provocative way of a horse that follows only to please you but considers the whole expedition unspeakably foolish. Her hoofs were as silent on the drive as his footsteps and those of the woman. Why?

The drive was thick with leaves, the coarse gold-yellow leaves of elm trees, and the trees above them were already half bare, as though it were early October, not late August. This was ridiculous! Summer had only just begun to die and the leaves elsewhere only begun to turn — certainly not yet to detach themselves. He looked questioningly upwards. . . .

'They were like this when he went—,' said the woman, answering part (at least) of his unspoken question, and as if what she said explained completely any unseasonableness. (Again he had the sensation of hearing her answers in his own mind before they issued from her lips.)

'When did he go?'

'On October the third, eighteen hundred and one — '

Some last element of Yankee caution and horse-sense shrieked *Nonsense!* in Vandervord's brain at this; bidding him pull himself together, be a man, do a simple sum of arithmetic to dispute this statement. But how dispute the evidence of his own heavy eyes, and the bitter smell in his nostrils of leaves that had not just fallen but were clammily fibrous from the rotting of a hundred years? How would this scene look in Spring? He could not imagine it in Spring, nor yet in deep Winter. It was a place speaking for ever of October, and it exuded the sad smell of dead leaves and dissolution because bitterness and dissolution were the spirit of Désolée now and for evermore.

He did not guess this; he knew it. And all at once, too, he knew the woman's name:

'You are Harriet, then? Harriet Bromewell, of Redonda?'

Their feet lagged, dragging through the leaves side by side. (Hard work going backwards into Time like this, like walking through deep water.)

'I am Harriet Vandervoord, of Désolée.'

Pettishly he cried: 'No one ever called it that but you!' — yet astounded a little at himself to hear such words coming out of his mouth, which his brain, as far as he knew, had never formed.

She stopped then in her tracks and turned to face him. The shawl was still over her head, yet somehow he knew that if it were pulled backwards, beneath it the hair would be folded sleekly backwards and upwards in two sweeps from the brow — blue-black as a starling's wings. Hands his yet not his (were not his deep in his pockets, from the cold, with the reins tugging at one elbow?) reached out now to her shawl, and swept it back tenderly from her head — and found all as he expected, the hair sleek and warm and smoothly swept back in two wings.

They were standing very close together now. As hands his yet not his explored the shape of her head, holding it firmly yet tenderly, so her hands crept up in the dusk and passed searchingly over his bowed face.

'My poor love,' she said. 'Your spectacles. Where are your spectacles?'

It was sweetly, anxiously said. Still holding her head between hands his yet not his, the voice his yet not his answered, just as gently — half-laughing, half-wistful:

'It's no use, Harry. Your breath blurs them and then I can't see!'

Again the Yankee part of him, the common-sense part, protested (but as if gagged and struggling, from ever further and further away): Are you crazy? You never wear glasses. You never have! And how the devil did you know her name was Harriet, just now? And what gave you the right to call her Harry? And how is it, even before you have kissed her, that you knew that the kiss is coming, and it will be the sweetest and the fiercest that you have ever known?

How answer? Events lapped over at this point, submerging each other, as the leaves lapped over each other beneath their feet. Locking her arms round his neck, she pulled his head down in the darkness and kissed his closed eyes slowly. He felt the tears start under his eyelids, weeping for a grief already long, long dead in another and yet resurrected without reason or explanation in himself. But sweet, sweet the kiss on the eyelids, on the wet cheeks (his or hers?). Sweetest of all the kiss upon the mouth — lasting while the world reeled about them for ever — rushing through black-dark space after its own fiery tail. . . .

The leaves shirring over their feet grew lighter, less resistant. They must have been walking hand-in-hand, and now utter darkness enveloped them. Yet when they reached the front of the house he knew, without her pressure on his arms, that there were three steps together, then a pause, and then two; and he reached out his right hand to rest it, with absolute certainty, upon the head of a little leaden statue, still leaning against the stone balustrade at the top of the steps.

The head was there, and his fingers relaxed over it, remembering these cold curls, and the pipe at the lips, and the cold fingers upon it.

'Still here?'

'Still here.'

'Ah, the poor *Petit-Petit*,' said the voice his yet not his, 'you should have had him put to rights.'

But she was up the steps ahead of him, negotiating the door, and said only:

'Turn the mare loose in the park; she won't take any harm.'

'No, she's tired. Give me something to cover her.'

'I have nothing.'

'There's my coat in the hall.'

He was slipping the bridle off Cherry as he said it. The mare shook her head, as if a ponderous weight she could not have endured for another moment had been removed and — dropping it — began to snort suspiciously at the carpet of leaves round her hooves.

. . . Perhaps she found the stables of her own good sense, or perhaps her master's sleep-walking feet led her there — round to the left past the morning-room window, past the dairy — and into the farmyard of Redonda. Still by touch alone, he slipped open the half-door — encouraging the mare forward into its shelter — loosening the girths, slipping off the saddle. . . .

I shan't need the coat after all, he told himself, taking down instead the horse-cloth which was hanging over the adjoining partition,

18

and ladling out a feed of oats into the bin with the sure touch of a man who knows his own place and the things in it. The coat . . . What coat? Why, the military greatcoat, of course, which he had purloined once from Clancy — with its six silver buttons (the top left-hand one was a trifle loose from so much twiddling between impatient fingers)..

Across the farmyard Redonda opened a square pale eye upon him — a light shining through its dairy door. The servants would be there — or would they? Ivory, Susan and the goosefeather girls. Round to the front of the house, past the morning-room window, he might catch a glimpse of Clancy and Clement — Harriet's brothers. With experienced fingers he felt his way lightly round and past the morning-room — to the front of the house once more which looked eastwards over towards Aldeburgh and the coast. A whiff of sea air mingled with the smell of Autumn now caught his nostrils — saltness and bitterness together, engendering a pulsing and inexplicable excitement, so that the blood drummed in his veins.

Something was wrong, strange, disasterful. The names just recalled — Ivory, Clancy, Clement, Susan, the goosefeather girls, *Petit-Petit*, the greatcoat with the silver buttons, the steps three up and then a pause and then two — *Great God, what were they all part of?* How did he come to be amongst them (or amongst their memories) and why in Pity's name, if they were part of Redonda, did they not materialize as had Harriet herself? *Who goes there? A Memory. Advance, Memory, and be recognized, but in God's name (again) advance!*

His heart thumped, the only noisy thing in a world of utter silence.

The steps at least were there. He made his way cautiously up them once more, found the door ajar, entered the huge cold hall. The dining-room lay, he knew, to the left, in total darkness like the rest. He would go in and light the candles. It would surprise Harry — and yet not surprise her — that he should know his way about so well, after a hundred years.

The candles, too, were still there, in brass sconces, at either end of the mantelshelf. They sputtered under his fingers and burned reluctantly, sending up a strong stench of tallow before settling down into slender petals of flame, sufficient merely to lighten the darkness a little, not to illuminate the room.

Vandervord shivered, feeling for the table behind him and relaxing upon it, swinging his booted legs and rubbing his hands together against the cold. The great curtains hanging at the two tall windows swung too, in the draught from the open door — swung still more as Harriet swept in, eyes panic-filled, crying:

'Van! The shutters!'

The candleflames curtsied as she passed, their reflections danced in her dark eyes, animated, too, by the swiftness of her entry. And as surely as both candleflames curtsied, dipping down before that speed, so surely his heart dipped down too, momentarily — all but panicked. Afraid of whom? Of what? Why the shutters?

The shutters. Their cold hands met as the great iron bars came downwards over the shutters, slid portentously into place.

'My dear, had you forgotten we look out over the sea?' Harriet said.

The candles had recovered their equanimity. Their flames wriggled upwards undisturbed once again, two sinuous points of light and life with two nimbuses, in the black pool of the room. Harriet drew the curtains across the shutters with a wide sweep of the arm that again — to Vandervord — had a whole world of familiar custom in it. As if the secret had been hiding behind the curtains until then, together with that sense of inexplicable dread — and as if both chose now to expose themselves with a graceless bravado, they bounded into the open with one single word between Harriet's parted, panting lips:

'Bonaparte!'

CHAPTER III

VANDERVORD COMPLETES A JIGSAW

With what I bear, my senses fraught,
Till what I am, fast shoreward drives.
They are the vessel of the Thought,
The vessel splits, the Thought survives.
MEREDITH

THE single word Bonaparte is the last clear word-picture concerning his adventure that John Vandervord can recollect. People in a high fever suffer from the same inconsistencies of recollection. Phantasmagoria crowd and hustle in the sick brain's waiting-room, chattering and muttering; they drift or rush, singly or together, across the mental retina; the rhythm of approach and retreat, their dimensional qualities, their reality or unreality, vary with the temperature and the disease. There is about all the inconsistency of these phenomena only one consistency, and that is the prevailing belief that if the spectator could survey them all *en bloc*, each fragment would somehow have its rightful place — would 'make sense'; broken up, they are only meaningless fragments of a jigsaw puzzle; pieced together, a flat picture from memory or premonition — a perfect whole.

It was as if young Vandervord, during the first part of his retrospective adventure, had been presented with a coherent picture — tiny and isolated though it was — a small filled-in corner of the whole jigsaw in which the façade of a house, the figure of a lady, the head of a leaden statue, the buttons on a greatcoat, the horizon (though distant) of the sea — interlocked inexplicably but correctly upon the table before him, suggesting the whole colour and contents of the completed picture. A jigsaw, too, that he had solved once before, long ago, and now could approach again as a comparative novelty, since so long a time had intervened between.

He held one key-piece in his hand — himself. Yet not himself.

21

Once he could discern where that piece fitted in — and the precise significance of the self-not-self problem — then the various other fragments would, he believed, interlock about it until the whole finally became plain.

It took him a week to complete the jigsaw. At least, it seemed to him to be a week in length at a time — you must remember — when time itself had turned topsy-turvy. How can one reckon the passage of minutes and hours when the day that contains them is one that itself appears to have been torn off the calendar of a hundred years ago? Still, measurements of time do not alter, and therefore he always afterwards estimated that it took him about a week.

Not that he could have outlined clearly how the week passed. His approach to Désolée (or Redonda), his meeting with Harriet, his entering the house up to the incident of the shutters and the word *Bonaparte* — all these linked together fairly coherently like the completed corner of that jigsaw the other pieces of which still lay jumbled together, half-concealed under each other, upon the table. But after that, nothing came plainly or step by step. He finished the jigsaw eventually, as meticulously as he finished every job he ever undertook — but by what process, beyond that of 'great elation and great suffering', neither he nor anyone else can ever know. Perhaps the best clue to the process lies in those words of his, 'Great elation, and great suffering'. The tale he told, the story he walked into, had to be lived by him, felt by him. It was not enough that Harriet Bromewell should tell it to him as an episode finished, concerning a relation he had never known.

How unsatisfactory, barren, all this conjecture must seem! Yet whenever we enter the world of pure feeling, we drift more easily than at other times beyond the normal barriers of space and time, and into the common whirlpool, for ever turbulent, of human hates, hopes, loves, fears. These do not change and — where they are felt with sufficient intensity — they exert, it would seem, a personal and *eternal* hold upon the time and the place where once they had their being.

It has been suggested before that one reason why the temporal Versailles of Marie Antoinette manifested itself again round the two Englishwomen over a hundred years later was that the emotions

aroused by the news of the Revolution in Marie Antoinette and in
her court were so tremendous that they overflowed their own particular groove in time and in the human heart, and splashed over,
as it were, into another groove altogether, and into other human
hearts. Such grooves would not appear to run parallel side by side,
beginning or ending in a way the mind might be capable of con-
ceiving; they are not some nearer to us and some farther; it seems
that they must exist simultaneously and eternally, charged with the
fury of atoms, the velocity of light, the immutability of planets.
Not Never the Time the Place and the Loved One all together, but
always the Time and Place and the Loved One all together — or if
not the Loved One then the Loathed One, or the Feared. Inseparable from their surroundings because of the transcendent emotions
they once experienced or inspired — if others enter those surroundings they run a great risk (as did the Versailles visitors) of slipping
out of their own shallow groove of time and feeling and of
encountering therein these dead persons and their passions.

So John Vandervord had encountered Harriet Bromewell in
her surroundings. So, during the subsequent week, he absorbed the
story begun so abruptly out in the darkening park. He was not
told it; he *lived* it — not only the life allotted to him simply by
relationship of blood, but also the life of the youthful Harriet, of
Susan Shattuck, of Ivory, of (rest her soul!) Sabrina, of Clancy and
Clement — of the whole gallery of associated ghosts. Yes, there is a
good old-fashioned word for it. Harriet Bromewell was simply
a ghost that would not be laid — and as soon as she had told her
tale to John Vandervord (and by doing so perhaps expiated her
crime), she stopped rattling her chains and dissolved obligingly into
thin air. Peace, peace, perturbed Spirit!

If you prefer it that way, certainly part of the story subsequently
may be made to bear out such an interpretation — but that comes
later. The question meanwhile would still seem to be: was Harriet
a ghost wandering in that deserted park on that night, *and that night
alone*, or does her encounter with John Vandervord in 1902 exist
as permanently and independently (in its own groove, of course)
as her parting from Jan Vandervoord in the same place in 1802?
So that (if you follow me), if you and I were to pass the Burnt

House to-night, or any night, and look through those same iron gates, we should stand as much chance of seeing one couple together as the other?

Sooner or later, in all metaphysics, we must come to precisely such uncertain and boggy ground; better turn back where the foothold is firmer! One returns with relief to the postulate that, where any passion has been felt by any person with intensity, both passion and person wear a groove in the intangible but nevertheless *real* substance of Time, much deeper than the average. In the Versailles story one of the recurring moods felt by both Englishwomen was that of foreboding, with the sound of a messenger's running feet in the background and the terrible cry *They are coming!* Turn this mood inside out (retaining the foreboding), and surround Harriet Bromewell instead with the words *They are going* and she, too, like that unhappy Queen of France, will never unlock her hold on time or place concerned. She *cannot* do so, because both mean so much to her. For ever will Harriet love, and for ever will Vandervoord flee her. For ever the word is Désolée.

For about a week, then, the young man stayed with his companion — until she became (shall we say) his familiar; until, through her, he had relived the lives bound up once so intimately with Redonda before it became Désolée. Afterwards, years afterwards, he recounted the whole experience (though the doing so took much longer than a week). And when there was no more to feel (better, more accurate, to put it that way than to say no more to *hear*) he saddled the mare Cherry once more, mounted, and moved on to Woodbridge.

This perhaps you have already guessed: when he got to Woodbridge, he found, somehow or other, that he still had that week in hand, for the boat he had intended to catch was still in dock at Harwich. He also found, through tactful inquiry, that he never could have stayed at any Burnt House near Aldeburgh, for it had not been in a condition to receive guests since it was gutted by fire on a certain July night in 1880. You must have noticed the chimney-stacks still standing, they told him. Nothing else, just the chimney-stacks. Quite a landmark.

Yes, young Vandervord agreed. Quite a landmark.

Used to be a lovely ole' park, too, went on his companion. O' course you couldn't know that. Ellums. Wholly beautiful ole' trees ellums, but treacherous. That's dangerous to furnish a park wi' em. Oi reckon they larned that, time arter they fell, two on 'em, and killed a passel of heifers sheltering under 'em, in my grandfather's time. So they cut 'em down, soon arter the fire — those that hadn't been blown down by the nor'easters. Are you a stranger to these parts?

A *stranger!* How say to such a man that — if he had lived 'in these parts' a hundred thousand years he could not know more about them or be more a part of their very kith and kin? Vandervord never did say it. He left Woodbridge instead — left Harwich, setting out upon the wastes of the sea in his homeward-bound vessel, and seeing in the tossing lacy wake she left behind her the ceaseless script of *Désolée* appearing, disappearing, reappearing, as surely as the bubbles and beads of foam, all the way home. A name written in water, and salt as tears or sea-water, and to be seen by John Vandervord for evermore, in the Pacific as in the Atlantic — a part of his life.

The chief difference the adventure made to his outlook, he confesses, is that after it he ceased to regard man so much as a creature of free-will and inclined, sometimes quite dogmatically, towards predestination. What other explanation could there be, he would say, of the fact that he — out of all England — should have chosen Suffolk to travel through, and out of all Suffolk that particular road leading out of Aldeburgh on that particular night? Or — again — he would revert to the 'groove' theory. I was young and careless, he would say, and in a very shallow groove of feeling — loosely attached, that is, to my own time and place. Consequently, when Chance directed me to take that particular road I fell without difficulty — you might almost say was pulled by the law of gravity — into the adjacent, much deeper groove of feeling and of time-and-place — the Harriet-and-my-grandfather one. (You'll remember she claimed his name as her own, thus making of the episode a Vandervord returning to a Vandervoord — the whole of time coming full circle again, altogether without John Vandervord's knowledge or consent.)

An odd story. You were warned, remember, that it would be hard to believe. But if it has interested you, read on. The 1902 part — John Vandervord's part — he always claims was merely the preface. The pages of time must be turned backwards now, for we are returning to years before he was ever born.

CHAPTER IV

THE BIRTH OF HARRIET BROMEWELL

'... To plunge into this far-away and yet so intimate ghostly past, where everything and everyone lives again but to become lost over again, and what seems most to come forth are the old pains and sufferings and mistakes ...'   HENRY JAMES

CAPTAIN BROMEWELL returned to Redonda House in 1770. It was called in those days Debenham's, since a gentleman farmer of that name had built the place and lived there until, during a period of great peace and consequently of shockingly low prices for the farmers, he had hanged himself one evening in the Great Barn. Captain Bromewell's lawyer, Mr. Marsham, and Captain Bromewell's agent, Spens, had been on the look-out for some time for an estate of some grandeur and of good acreage for their client and master; had bullied Debenham's executors into parting with the property by brandishing before their eyes a great many papers with the magic words West Indies upon them. Whereupon, as aforesaid, Captain Bromewell left Redonda (in the West Indies) and proceeded to establish a new Redonda about him on the estate near Aldeburgh. Thus Debenham's Farm became Redonda House.

The Captain did the thing as thoroughly and noisily as he conducted all his operations. He had been a noisy young soldier in the Militia, he developed into a noisy buccaneer and plantation owner in the West Indies, and he returned to East Anglia to become one of the most audible gentleman farmers that that neighbourhood had yet known. The din he made, however, was a rich-sounding one and it is extraordinary how people will forgive commotion and shouting if they come from the right quarters; the right quarters being, of course, any part of the house except the attics and the servants' quarters. Besides, the man was competent. He turned from breeding Barbadoes slaves and sugar to English horn and corn with the greatest ease in the world, and he and his assiduous agent between them speedily built up Redonda into one of the most prosperous estates in the district. Money breeds money, so they say. Money certainly flowed into Redonda. Add to this that the Captain was a local product — family known in Suffolk since the Middle Ages, father a Bury man, and that he had married a Miss Clements, the daughter of a Suffolk squire of high repute, before he ever partook himself to the West Indies. He had taken a bride out there with him, with a great deal of bravado and energy, some particularly sharp cunning and not much else. He returned with a wife and family, a fortune and the usual accompaniment of livestock and servants, including Ivory, a black butler with a fine silver collar which he wore round his neck with his master's name and address on it, just as the dogs did.

None of this, you may say, was very extraordinary. The country was full in those days of prosperous gentlemen home from the East or West Indies who, not liking the look of the way things were going in the Americas, sold out while they could do so advantageously and brought their accumulated assets home to work for them in England.

Sweat and blood and tears soon enriched the soil of Redonda in Suffolk. His own sweat and Spens', his agent's, and his farm-people's, the blood of the livestock killed on the premises, and the tears of his wife Sophy, who had not relished a homecoming nearly as much as her husband. The West Indies had suited her, whereas the dank air and sea mists of the English Redonda turned her into a permanently pettish invalid. Weeping became her private pleasure. She lay all day on an ottoman in her upstairs drawing-room, with a tremendous fire blazing in it and both windows shut tight, weeping for the life left behind them, weeping because she could not manage her two sons Clement and Clancy, weeping above all because she was pregnant again and dreaded the coming ordeal of labour. The house inside was consequently as ill-managed and untidy as outside it was a model of prosperity and order. The rough meadows before the house where Farmer Debenham's cattle had fed were raked over, levelled and planted out with an avenue of young elm trees. Iron gates of handsome and expensive design barred the wide sweep of the entrance. Ten tons of clean shingle brought up from the beach at Aldeburgh was dispersed over the drive, the forecourt and the paths round the farmyard and stables. Life and vitality were everywhere. Calves called from the corner of the field nearest the farmyard. Their mothers lowed back to them from the cowsheds. The bull, hock-deep in his own manure, bellowed back at them from his private and perpetual prison. Maids banged stairways and doors as they swept, chattering like starlings below stairs with the labourers. They giggled and bickered in the attics, scurrying over the bare floors like mice in the cold dark. All the lively din of a farmyard, shrieking birds, clattering pails, banging doors, creaking pumps, swish of water, expostulations of cowman or horseman, rose round the house all day like the hum of bees round some huge hive. Footsteps on the shingle shirred hoarsely all the way from the gate to the door that first summer, and the lord of the manor, with a voice as loud as his own bull's and a whip he was not above using on anything he was displeased with, human or animal, made the rounds of his property, infusing with his own tough vitality and prosperity the whole acreage of Redonda. Things went well. Except with Sophy, his wife, things went very well indeed; and pregnant women were always difficult, though not as difficult as pedigree mares in the same condition. At least Sophy did not kick her children to death if she was irritated. He made this joke to Spens, who laughed more than was necessary, before they set off together on one more of their interminable rounds of the estate.

Sophy Bromewell was brought to bed one November evening in her bedroom where the fire was banked up so high that it would have illumined the scene without any lamps, and which was so hot that the doctor sweated as he worked. He was a little drunk, too, but Mrs. Bromewell was above caring about that, though it did not render the confinement any easier. Her husband had been all for having a midwife, but what was the use of being Mrs. Captain Bromewell, late of Redonda, W.I., if you could not command the best medical attention when you needed it? She cried silently into her pillow all the time between the pains, the only cold person in all that inferno.

Outside, the mulatto girl Sarah, with the little boys Clem and Clancy clinging to her skirts, sat on the stairs and waited with awful joy for the baby to be delivered. She strained her ears. Mother and grandmothers and great-aunts had taught her that to hear the first cry of a new-born child was a lucky thing. What luck constituted she did not know, never having had any, but if it was something different from her present experience she was all for trying it. She was fifteen, but a lifetime of sadness had compressed itself within that tender span. Born of slaves, brought up in a communal kitchen of slaves, she had become attached as accidentally as a burr to the skirts of Mrs. Bromewell and been subsequently whisked across the seas to Suffolk with the family's other appurtenances.

Sarah sat on the stairs. Down below a good humoured uproar disclosed that the master was at dinner. As the dining-room doors opened and shut continually behind Ivory on his errands, so the waves of noise advanced, receded and were shut off completely. Above it, and through it, Sarah strained her ears for the birth-cry, the magic sound. The little boys, tired of the waiting, were playing about now on the staircase, scrambling about on all fours on the landing, or thrusting their chubby little legs through the balustrade so that their slippers dangled over Redonda's hall.

'Iv'y! Iv'y! Guess who this is!' they shouted to the black butler. 'And guess who this is!'

The busy servant stopped, grinned, tickled the dangling toes, rolling his eyes upwards and wriggling his fingers inside their bronze slippers. They shrieked with joy.

'Sarah do it, too!' they shouted.

She begged them to quieten, for her own sake chiefly. She begged and prayed them. At any moment the bedroom door might open and that thin wail come through, to be lost in the general din. She must not miss it for the world.

'Sarah do it!' they commanded, louder and more imperiously.

To quieten them (anything to quieten them) the little servant dropped down beside them, slipping her slender coffee-coloured legs through the banisters so that now three pairs hung downwards over the hall instead of two. The red slippers dangled from her toes, which with casual and un-European dexterity kept them some-how suspended safely there. So she swung her feet with the little boys, the red slippers between their bronze ones, back and forth, back and forth.

She wished to hear the birth-cry more than she wished for any-thing else in her life.

Blind and deaf with pain to everything else in the world except the dampness of the pillow under her cheek, Mrs. Bromewell writhed on her bed. Beads of perspiration, rolling off the doctor's forehead and down his nose, damped the sheets as well as the pillow. The fire roared unappeasedly in the grate. The whole place — as he told his wife afterwards — steamed like that African jungle the Bromewell couple had come from. (He was a very ignorant fellow who knew no geography.) Sitting back for a minute, more exhausted (he told himself) than his patient could possibly be, he ran his fingers over his dirty wig before applying himself again to the struggle, pull devil, pull baker. No, by God — this was cer-tainly not an easy birth! Why didn't the woman yell? Especially when one was a little tipsy it was a comfort to hear the yells. They signposted, as it were, the progress of pains and delivery.

'How do you feel now?' he asked.

'Thirsty,' said Mrs. Bromewell, through lips so muscle-bound by pain she could hardly articulate the syllables. He looked round for a bell and rung it, hanging on to the cord with owlish solemnity long after it had sounded below. Mrs. Fitchet, the wet-nurse in waiting, leapt to answer it, congratulating herself on the shortness of the wait.

'Brandy!' commanded the doctor over his shoulder, once more at the tug-of-war.

Brandy must be procured from the decanter. Impossible to do this without descending again, and acquainting the Captain, still at table. It created quite a commotion with his roared interlocutions and her whinnying replies, and the agent and Mr. Marsham, the young lawyer, ever so mischievously interested. She was so put out by it all that scurrying out with the bottle clasped to her bosom she forgot to close the door.

'Ivory!' roared the Captain. 'Door! Draught!'

But before the butler could comply, Mr. Marsham, who was the least tipsy of the three, caught a glimpse of the feet with the dangling scarlet slippers on them, hanging as it were from some invisible ceiling outside. By tilting his chair back — yes, by tilting back his chair just a leetle, he could follow those delightful contours right up to —

The door shut, and the Captain kicked out at Ivory's shins as the negro went past the table, for not shutting it sooner. He was at the all-but-choleric stage. Spens, the agent, was singing 'All in the Downs'. He was at the cheerful stage and if nobody listened — as nobody did — he was not the man to mind.

'To whom would those pretty legs belong?' asked Mr. Marsham of the chandelier, grammatical even in his cups. Ivory's eyes rolled upwards to the ceiling. If the chandelier had answered the question he would have been hardly surprised at all, so many inexplicable things had happened already in this inexplicable land.

'Legs?' said the master of the house, his tilted chair falling forward with a jerk. 'Where?'

'Oho!' crooned Mr. Marsham, still tilted, still gazing amorously at the chandelier. 'Such pretty legs, with such swelling calves, such slender ankles! Hock bottles aren't in it. I give you my word!'

'Hanging from the ceiling,' he added after a pause.

Spens did not like anyone to speak of hanging. There had once been an incident in his family connected with Tyburn. He stopped 'All in the Downs', gazing reproachfully at the tablecloth.

'You mean the *light* is hanging from the ceiling,' concluded the Captain, tracking down the lawyer's meaning with — he felt — indescribable cunning.

'No — sir,' said Marsham, mellifluously as ever. 'Legs.'

'Legs?'

'Beautiful legs, I assure you —'

'Talking of legs, sir,' began Spens, and they all took up this delectable topic. The bottle went round once more. Upstairs, life and death fought a silent battle for the not-yet-emerged body of a girl child. More than a single floor seemed to separate the three men below from the striving woman upstairs. Outside on the landing were Clem and Clancy and Sarah, the nurse-girl, still swinging their feet over the dark hall, to and fro, to and fro, the little boys singing tunelessly, Sarah's head tilted ever backwards, still listening for the magic cry.

Half-way through the legs discourse, action overtook the Captain. He rose and rushed at the door, bursting it open with both hands. Immediately he perceived what Marsham had perceived, the little swinging legs of his sons, the slender coffee-coloured ones of their nurse.

It wasn't fitting; it certainly wasn't, considering the circumstances upstairs.

'Hi, you there! Sarah!' he roared.

The dangling slippers, scarlet and bronze alike, withdrew with the celerity of a snake slipping into its private quarters. Instead, over the top of the banisters, Sarah's face peered, eyes as large and white-ringed as Ivory's, the little boys clinging to her skirts and peering, too, through the bars. If he had been a lion at the foot of the stairs and they Christian martyrs the scene could not have presented a better picture of intimidation and respectful terror.

He opened his mouth to roar again, but was stopped in the act by the gentle pressure of young Marsham's hand on his arm.

'By Hector, Bromewell, that's a pretty piece of goods!'

Both men stood staring upwards at the girl, ignoring the children. How much? was the thought in both their minds. How much does he want for her? queried Marsham's. How much could I get him to do for me in return, echoed the Captain's. There were, he knew, endless legal quibbles and formulae still to be got through, if an energetic and purposeful farmer were to squeeze the very last ounce of benefit out of his property. If Marsham were kept good-tempered, then his fees would stay reasonably low and his advice be permanently on tap. Besides, there were certain tricky corners still to be negotiated, the sort of corners that a resourceful and not too scrupulous legal adviser might manage very comfortably for one, if he had a mind to do so. Spirrell's Corner, for instance, which needed not only draining and dunging to turn it into good soil, but clearing of human encumbrances as well. One took a harrow and rake and dung-cart to the first part, but for ridding oneself of the human encumbrances and their little shacks there was nothing so efficacious he knew as an *annunciamento* with swinging seal attached, and a plethora of Latin phrases.

Spirrell's Corner would be an addition, a handsome addition, to Redonda's ever-enlarging estate, there was no doubt. The poor, cleared out of it and losing, as they would do, the common rights of feeding geese and cattle upon it, would come all the more readily to work at Redonda, for this was the obvious alternative to starvation.

But the procedure was tricky, he knew. Even Spens the agent admitted that, and Spens had never lost a fight with anyone but his master yet. But with the Law to back one, to draw up the petition, to present it to the proper quarters, how much would be made easy — and legitimate!

Spirrell's Corner, in the fraction of time that the two men stood at the foot of the staircase that night — Marsham's hand still soothingly on Bromewell's coat-sleeve, Bromewell's hand closing over the great carved pineapple that topped the balustrade post — assumed suddenly vital proportions in the Captain's head. He must have it, and Marsham was the man to get it for him. It was worth a mulatto servant.

During the same fraction of time, Marsham was fingering his stick and guessing (with his eyes still fixed on the girl) the price the Captain meant to charge him. He'll give the girl to me, he told himself, but by George he's going to get his money's worth out of me in return! I'm useful to him. I'm well connected. I've friends at Westminster, and the crafty rascal means to take full advantage of my influence so as to add to his acreage here. Enclosure of Common Lands — of — what is it he and his factor call it? — of Spirrell's Corner in particular. Patriotic motives, of course.

Tucking his chin deeper into his stock, Mr. Marsham permitted himself a smile at the thought of Captain Bromewell being actuated by motives of pure patriotism. The purest thing in the house, Mr.

Marsham could have assured his host, was the Jamaica rum. And, perhaps, the expression of pure terror in the face of Polly here at the top of the stairs.

'Hello, Miss. What's your name, eh—Polly?' Mr. Marsham made his inquiry in a voice of real blandishment. The mulatto never stirred, her round eyes fixed immovably upon him and her master. Some of her apprehension must have communicated itself through her trembling skirts to the little boys, for they began to whimper.

'Silence!' roared their father. 'Your mother's ill, you young imps. Can't you be quiet, even a minute?' but their whimpering rose to a roar as their father's wrath rose. It was always thus. If he bellowed they bellowed, if he growled they growled — proper cubs of such a tiger. Mr. Marsham fell back a step. His ears (like his host's) buzzed slightly from all the wine and reverberation. Nevertheless his eyes still roved appreciatively over Sarah.

What of her? She was aware, of course, that these two below her boded no good. She was terrified by the children's outcry, knowing that that later would bode her no good also. But half her attention was still given, through all this, to listening for the cry of the newly-born child. A wild cat cornered and ready to spring upon its pursuers will still spare a muscle to flick an ear back if another, more interesting, sound than their growls and snarls breaks the silence. If she were to die this very minute, she would still be saved and somehow made happy — provided that sound of good fortune should overtake her in the act.

'Hush, hush!' she implored Clem and Clancy, half because of the wrath of their father, half because she could not, through such a pandemonium, hear a thing — and her chance might be lost for ever. This consideration finally became predominant. She ignored the men, bent all her energies instead on the roaring children, dropping on to her knees between them, consoling them, crushing their hard, knobbly little skulls against her tender, frightened breast, her own head still thrown back listening for the cry.

The light from the lamp in the hall below glinted upon her eyes, her hair, her teeth, the swinging ear-rings in her ears. Mr. Marsham pictured the vision as it might appear amongst his other *objets d'art* at home at Blackheath, for he was, in a modest way, a collector. He

34

could not provide the children, of course, but he could provide a parrot for her to look after every bit as good as the Captain's parrot, and as picturesque as herself. Monkeys also, possibly. Bromewell would tell him where to get them; he knew all the dodges.

'Come away out of the din!' commanded the Captain, swearing and turning back on his heel to the dining-room and bottles again. Women and children signified din to him — no other loud noise did.

But the next noise to be heard — which was not loud at all — stopped them in their tracks. It was the quavering wail which had previously announced the arrival of his sons. Action followed precipitately. The doctor, still tousled and with wig awry, flung the door open on the landing above them to announce what needed no announcing. The mulatto girl jumped to her feet, her hands clasped together, smiling quite divinely. Clem and Clancy stopped in their sobbing, turning to gaze with the rest at the strange man coming out of their mother's room.

'It's a girl, Captain!' the doctor announced.

It is Good Fortune, said Sarah to herself. I have heard it. Happiness is about to be showered upon me. My mother bore me in the southern wild and I am black, but O my soul is white. Hallelujah!

'Splendid!' said Captain Bromewell. 'Congratulate me, Marsham.' He flung his arm round the younger man's shoulders. 'Mrs. Bromewell has done it this time. We shall need a girl for the dairy, eh? And to break the hearts of the young men at Aldeburgh and Woodbridge!' and he pulled Marsham back into the dining-room with him — out of the din. Spens was asleep, chin sunk on chest, over the spilled wine and empty walnut-shells.

'You've a fancy for that girl, eh?' said the Captain, filling the glasses again. 'You like the colour?'

'She's a gem,' agreed Marsham. 'Such sparkle, such spirit!' Holding his refilled glass against the light, he might have been speaking of the wine instead of the girl.

'Take her,' the Captain commanded, draining his own glass at a gulp. 'You've done well by me, Marsham. I'll do well by you, never fear. Glad to do you any little service.'

'My dear Bromewell — I can't.'

'Rubbish,' said the Captain, continuing generously though inaccurately. 'Dozens of 'em about the place, lazy good-for-nothings. Look well, I'll own, but damned lazy. You'll have to make her work!'

The lawyer's tongue flickered round the rim of his glass, savouring the idea of making her work with the last rich drop. Both were intensely pleasant.

Upstairs in the night nursery Sarah was putting the boys to bed, her heart being full all the time of the stroke of Good Fortune awaiting her. What could it mean, she asked herself as she tucked them up. To go home, to be sure! How or when she knew not, but what else could Good Fortune mean but to be home again in Redonda in the sun? Nothing else signified Good Fortune; nothing else could!

In Mrs. Bromewell's bedroom the tidying of the patient was completed at last, and the dressing of the infant who, continually addressed in a whisper as a lucky girl by the doting wet-nurse, still shut her eyes resolutely against all premature congratulations. Six pounds at most, she seemed to shrink into a still smaller weight beneath her voluminous wrappings. The mother's tears had momentarily ceased and the daughter's, after that first protesting wail, had ceased too. They were both of them making the best of what was nevertheless a bad job all round.

The doctor had clattered his things together in his bag, run his fingers over his greasy wig again and gone down to congratulate the Captain in more detail. He was in time — as he had hoped — for something out of a bottle. They drank to the child, to Redonda, to the King, and the more they drank the lower they sank in their chairs until, like the agent's, most of the gentlemen's chins were at table-level, and snores succeeded congratulations and toasts.

As they sank, so Mrs. Fitchet rose. She was not a Suffolk country-woman for nothing, and she knew that, according to local lore, if a child is to rise in the world she must go upstairs before she ever comes down. Consequently the wet-nurse rose with the baby, mounting the attic stairs with the pomp of the Queen of Sheba and addressing the baby appreciatively all the while: 'You'll not need to come up here when you're a grown girl, my Treasure!' Attics were for mice, bats, stored apples, servants — not for the Daughter of the House!

The fact that her own swarming family of little Fitchets might have found these same attics magnificent quarters after their own rickety barn never entered the simple woman's mind. The barn was all the family had ever known and constant intermarriage between Fitchet relations had resulted in a weakmindedness which, it must be admitted, made her children incapable of appreciating subtle differences in degrees of comfort. Poor children, God help 'em! ejaculated their mother, with piety but without hope. And then her thoughts reverted to herself. At any rate for the time being she was to live here amidst plenty and splendour—sleeping in a superior kind of cupboard off Mrs. Bromewell's apartments, fed on good food at regular hours, and nursing the dear baby.

Her own baby, who was at that moment taking exceedingly unkindly to the spoonsful of goats' milk proffered him by his grandmother in a corner of the barn which was his home, protested vociferously but unheard, since the old lady was deaf and his mother beyond earshot. It was to be some time before he could bring himself to stomach it, but hunger is a stern and successful nurse, as the grandmother knew. Besides, it was no good pitying the child; it was in the order of things that the gentry should have what they wanted.

As for that other baby — the baby of gentlefolk — all through the dark chill-breathing November night she slept that intent and undisturbable sleep of the newly-born, asking nothing of this life in which she found herself except that it should leave her alone to recover from the exhaustion of the journey there.

The next day Mr. Marsham went back to London by the Woodbridge coach. His luggage, his manservant and the young mulatto travelled outside on the roof. The mulatto girl might, of course, have thrown herself off, except that Mr. Marsham had seen to it that she was strapped on as firmly as the luggage. However, since she froze to death during the journey (deliberately, no doubt), Mr. Marsham's foresight proved insufficient. (The manservant merely caught a cold in his eyes.)

CHAPTER V

THE BIRTH OF SUSAN

O thou poor Widow, who in dreams dost view
Thy husband's mangled corse, and from short doze
Startst with a shriek; or in thy half-thatched cot
Waked by the wintry night-storm, wet and cold
Cow'rst o'er thy screaming baby! Rest awhile,
Children of wretchedness! More groans must rise,
More blood must stream, or ere your wrongs be full.
Yet is the day of retribution nigh;
The Lamb of God hath opened the Fifth Seal;
And upward rush on swiftest wing of fire
The innumerable multitude of wrongs
By man on man inflicted!

COLERIDGE

THREE years of intelligent energy on the part of Captain (otherwise Farmer) Bromewell and Spens his agent produced excellent results. Redonda prospered, enlarging its borders on every side. Spirrell's Corner, incorporated into it with the aid of Mr. Marsham and the necessary legal procedure in the parish and at Westminster, had ceased finally to be common land and was now enclosed by a handsome fence of split chestnut palings to keep out the geese, cows, pigs and human beings who had once found food or firewood on it. This brought another twenty-two acres under Captain Bromewell's control, and certainly the land did well under him. His foresters tidied up the wild little wood, cutting out the undergrowth and staking the saplings; his farm-workers, under the agent's direction, drained the boggy side of the common-no-longer-common, and hedged it with quickset to a ploughable size. Some pasture-land was left, too, and derived much benefit from the harrowing and dunging which turned its turf from olive-green to a rich emerald in a wonderfully short time.

The little hovels which had backed on to Farley Spinney (the thinner side of the wood) were not difficult to demolish, and grass soon grew over their cold hearthstones. Their hedges of quickset and bramble were speedily grubbed up by Captain Bromewell's rakes and picks and burnt on Captain Bromewell's bonfires. The brambles, it is true, came up again later, throwing long sprawling tentacles out over the cleared turf, as if seeking for the things so recently vanished — the dog's kennel, the toy wooden horse which had stood under the apple tree in all weathers, the potato patch, the wild plum trees with the washing-line dipping between them. All had gone on to the huge continual bonfire; all been melted down to good flake-grey potash to feed the indifferent earth.

As to the cottagers who had inhabited these hovels — like water running down a ditch they followed the line of least resistance. The able-bodied amongst them went, as Captain Bromewell had desired they should, into his dairies, mills and barns (except for a few of the more adventurous, who struck out for the North to find work in the new manufactories there — travelling by night to avoid the officers of the law, since they broke the law by the mere act of moving out of their own parish). The aged and infirm amongst the cottagers, and the women and children, went into the other cottages provided by Captain Bromewell on the edge of his estate, and the able-bodied returned to be with them at night, and to share the tea and potatoes which formed the bulk of their meals. It is doubtful whether they lived any worse than they had done on their own, before the enforced exodus — since a skilful system of pilfering from Redonda's teeming fowlyards and piggeries soon gave them that occasional variation in diet which before had been found on the common land. But a certain enthusiasm and hopefulness — yes, and dignity—disappeared inevitably from life. Perhaps part of their spirit was enclosed, as well as the land they had once lived on. However it was, they soon felt that there was no use in planning to extend their boundaries — since their boundaries had been fixed by Captain Bromewell for all time; there was no use in hoping for the future—since the future, too, was ruled over by Captain Bromewell as much as the planting and mating and harvesting seasons of the year.

Some few rebelled. These were the daring young spirits who still intended to get their kindling, as of old, out of Farley Spinney. The chestnut-pale fencing did not stop them but the mantraps did, and after half a dozen mauled and broken legs and arms had been dragged home at night, they soon learnt to leave ill alone lest it should become worse. The foolish geese who flew over the fencing to regain their lost feeding-grounds had a way of disappearing into Redonda's pies or Redonda's fattening-pens.

As for the older rebels, who were more proud than spirited — though they had spirit too — there was nothing to be done with them. They had, according to their own view, tottered along pretty comfortably in the old days, on their own bit of ground, with a pig and a goat and a fowl or two between them and starvation, and they now refused Captain Bromewell's charity cottages and the misery of being no more than another mouth to feed in a younger relative's house. These few went defiantly 'upon the parish', living on, six miles or so away from their old homes, with (it would seem) a dogged determination to revenge themselves upon a Government that had so wantonly permitted the destruction and confiscation of all that had made their life worth living.

Yet on the whole Captain Bromewell was fortunate. There had been two cases only of open rebellion when the petition for the enclosure of Spirrell's Corner was set in motion. One was a stout young yeoman-farmer with a truly excellent eye in judging cattle — sick or well. He had clung to his rights as to his own pitchfork, standing square in his low doorway and refusing to listen to a word that Mr. Marsham had to say concerning the legalities of Captain Bromewell's enclosure and his own eviction. All he knew was that though he made the most of his good arable land, as well as the pasture on which his bullocks ran, it was to be taken from him. The farmhouse would be left, it lay outside the proposed new boundary lines, but what use was the house without the farm, the snail-shell without the snail, the hive without the bees? Very well, said Mr. Marsham, folding away the crinkly parchment of the Deed of Enclosure inside his capacious waistcoat pocket; very well my fine fellow, you have your remedy!

Remedy? The man glared dully at him — frowning eyes under a

curly forelock of hair. Really, thought Mr. Marsham, these yokels grow to look absurdly like their own beasts!

The remedy was to present to Mr. Marsham, or to Captain Bromewell's agent Spens, or even to the parson by a certain date, 'A clear and correct statement of his rights and his claim to a share in the Award'. Not to his farm or farmland, which he and his father and father's fathers had held since land was ever farmed in England, but to some mythical share in some incomprehensible Award — that was all.

Mr. Marsham smiled as he left, picking his way delicately over the puddles which lay along the path to the farmhouse. To ask for a clear and correct statement from a person who can neither read nor write was no more extravagant than to ask him for a very thin slice of the moon on a golden plate. . . . So the stout young farmer, floored by weapons of pen and ink as he never would have been by any other weapons, had no alternative but to sell his cattle, and his own particular 'way' with calving cows, to Captain Bromewell — who did extremely well out of all these, needless to say — as well as out of the extra acreage of farmland.

Shall it be admitted that the thought did once cloudily cross the yeoman-farmer's mind that, since he had been a good churchgoer and God-fearer as his fathers before him, the parson might come to his aid, now, and help him over the business of stating his case on paper? He paid a visit, therefore, to the parson, and found that worthy tremulously grateful to his patron, the Captain, for a munificent gift to the church — enough not only to repair the roof but also for a new rood-screen and a splendid stained-glass window to replace the one ruined in Cromwell's days, all to be built round the text 'The Lord loveth a Cheerful Giver'. It had been, in fact, hardly worth the while of the young farmer to get off his horse, certainly not to tether it to the stable door of the rectory and to stand and argue at the door. He found himself defeated by Church as well as State.

The other case concerned the brothers Anderson, a trio of them — hungry-looking men of huge stature who inhabited a tumbledown shack at Spirrell's Corner and conducted a gypsy-like trade there in wood-selling, wood-getting, wood-chopping, clothes-props, broom-handles and clothes-pegs; with the aid also of a donkey and cart and a two-handed saw. The Andersons had mastered reading and writing (being the offspring of a schoolmarm mother), and they might have succeeded in supplying the 'clear and correct statement' if they had been able to fulfil the other hard condition in the necessary time. (For the law was cunning enough to cut both ways; if you could read and write, it argued, you could hardly be handy and quick over physical labour — and *vice versa*.)

The second condition set the Andersons, and all others like them, *was to fence the entire circumference of the land they claimed*, with wood of a certain height, thickness and length and within a specified time — or else to forfeit it. This was what defeated them, for the spinneys, copses and woody corners wherein the Andersons had done their business and lived, as casually and freely as the squirrels, badgers and woodpeckers which shared such places with them, were scattered variously over the parish. They were no inheritors of a fair and square acreage, like Redonda, but of little odd green tracks and brambly byways, oddments which nobody else wanted or could do anything with. They sharpened pencils, licked them, drew maps by rushlight with unsteady axe-scarred fingers, squabbled furiously between themselves as to what led from here to here and how to bridge the stream ... meanwhile time passed, inexorably. Their pile of stout staves for the necessary fencing lay ready, but by the time they had agreed upon the way to do it, the time to do it in had vanished. The day came, the hour struck. The shack they had all been born in went down on its knees with a kind of apologetic sigh before the labours of the demolition gang employed by Captain Bromewell, and the work of the Andersons' hands, including the staves for fencing and the two-handed saw, were carted away with the aid of the small donkey to be incorporated into Redonda; together with Farley Wood, the spinneys and open spaces of Spirrell's Corner and the hazel copse. Sound of axe and saw was heard no more 'up at Andersons'; sawdust no longer lay like snow over their well-head and yard. Instead the plough, much heartened by the lightening qualities of the plaster rubble which used to be the shack, drew its clean fangs across their late garden and common. Mud returned to mud, therefore, and in the Spring green wheat sprang up from both.

42

The Anderson brothers put up their two-handed saw, perforce, in the Great Barn at Redonda. It found much work to do there, in the shape of logs for the house, wheels for the tumbrils, ladders for the lofts, sties for the pigs. The Andersons worked well when sober; when drunk (and they had seldom been drunk in the old days) they slept noisily in Redonda's haystacks and quarrelled with everybody else they met. Captain Bromewell and his agent Spens suffered such behaviour, since, on the whole, the Anderson labour was a cheap enough bargain.

These two cases were the only troublesome ones in the whole period of the acquisition and enclosure of the common lands near Redonda. Captain Bromewell was fond of saying that he had the whiphand of this as well as of every other situation. Certainly the whip was never far from his hand, though he conducted himself tolerably well towards his employees, taking the period into consideration.

As his acreage grew, so the respect of the county grew with it. Popular with his neighbours and with the Lord-Lieutenant, Captain Bromewell hunted, drank and took his pleasures with the best and worst of them. The young elms in Redonda's plantation changed from saplings into small trees and took sturdier root every year. The house stood fair and square amongst its ever-increasing farm-buildings, with life as busy about it as swallows about a mud nest. Like its owner it seemed to echo, staring out over the flat horizon towards the grey shingle coastline: *I have the whip-hand*.

But just as in the best-regulated barns and outbuildings there is always a corner where one field-mouse will contrive to get in and to bear away its unpaid-for grain of barley, so there was a corner in the Redonda estate where for once Captain Bromewell was baffled and the whip-hand failed, and this is how it was.

Farley Wood had been enclosed with a vengeance — partly to conserve its timber for Redonda, partly to provide coverts for game. In the wood there were occasional clearings and towards one of these clearings, one early morning in September, three years after the birth of Harriet Bromewell — the Little Miss at Redonda — came a man bearing a great bundle upon his back and a woman heavy with child. The man had the robin-bright eyes of the consumptive;

his wife was ashy-pale. Both were gaunt and famished, with shoes worn through with much travelling and clothes mossy-green on the shoulders from fading and exposure. This was not strange, for the Shattucks, man and wife, had not only slept in ditches for the past three weeks but had crept along and fed and rested in them as well. The law of the parish, as they knew, was particularly harsh on pregnant women, lest the offspring, once born, should prove a burden on the parish for the rest of its life. Besides, the man was breaking the law in wandering so from place to place. There had been work for him in his own parish, and that being so, he must seek employment in no other. This was good English law and by such processes the magistrates strove to stabilize population and to keep down the rates.

But Shattuck was no longer fit to work anywhere, as anyone could see; and his wife was not to be hustled by rude hands out of any more parishes as she had been out of the two last. Consequently, recalling Farley Wood as a place known to him in his youth, and as a kindly hiding-place where an unwanted couple might take refuge, they had been making their way thither, by dint of hedges and ditches, during the past week.

Nell Shattuck felt ill. She had borne the heat and burden of the day and of her unborn child well enough, until the hustling she had received at the hands of the constable in the last parish. He had given her a push at the boundary crossroads, which had sent her stumbling down on to her knees in the dust. And the baby had stirred uneasily — ominous portent of what was to follow.

Shattuck contented himself with helping her to her feet again. To have struck the constable would have been madness, would have engendered that separation from each other which they feared worse than death.

Once the constable had been left well behind, and the echo of his abuse had died down together with the dust he had raised, Where shall we go now, she had asked, with such a perfect trust in Shattuck's wisdom that it wrung his heart to see. She was so obedient, so uncomplaining, she would go wherever he said, though several times already he had taken wrong turnings and lengthened their pilgrimage in the most cruel way. He comforted her, hitching his

44

great bundle upon his back once more, minimizing the distance. Only a little way now, my dear. Only a little way to Farley Wood, to that particular clearing in it where, as a boy, he had so often filled his little wagon with firewood and dragged it home in a race with the failing winter light.

They reached the clearing by midday, crawling through a gap in the hazel fencing. They kept, too, a good lookout for mantraps and for keepers or labourers at work. Once in the clearing, they lay back against a great oak-bole and the woman ate sparingly of potatoes and drank obediently the water he brought her from the spring cupped in his hands, lined with dock-leaves. But that was not enough. Tired out as they were, now the real work must begin.

In this plan, wiser than most and with the shrewdness sometimes perceived in people during acute distress, they had taken the precaution to have the law for once on their side. The Shattucks — a couple browbeaten, homeless, hustled, famished, inured already to all the spites of Fortune, were not going to be prevented from achieving their aim now by any opposition from that Holy Trinity — Bromewell, Spens and Marsham. The law was on their side — if they could do it. If they *could* do it, not all the king's officers and men, or judges and juries, could ever say them nay. They set to work with a desperate will.

They proposed to be squatters, not cottagers; and this being so, they proposed to claim Squatter's Rights. To achieve these rights the man knew, and his wife knew, that they must have a shack built with a fire coming out of its chimney within twenty-four hours of arrival. Setting themselves this seemingly impossible task, they worked swiftly and ceaselessly, grateful for the still-long day and the fair starry night succeeding it, through which it was still possible to feel the work and so to do it.

Saplings were sawn through, their heads roped together with scraps torn from the woman's skirt. Their ends were planted wigwam fashion into the earth, so that the framework stood about seven feet long about six feet high. While the man laced the saplings together by weaving thinner branches in and out of them, the woman formed the hearth, half dragging, half carrying huge stones from the clearing's outskirts to do it and fitting them stone upon stone into the end of the wigwam, cementing them together with water and mud and the urgency of her hand's coaxing. Sweat coloured all their labours. The clearing stood about them, filtering down light and then half-light upon them, but they dared not pause in their work, continuing their fetching and carrying, balancing and mixing and weaving for hours on end with an unspeaking intensity more animal than human.

When the framework was completed, the man opened his bundle and took out his precious relics from the tanyard — four bullocks' skins, newly tanned. These he stretched over the framework, pinning them together with 'brooches' cunningly cut from the pliant willow. While he did this the woman carried armfuls of bracken into the shelter, laying it down for carpet and bedding. Her hearth was finished; above it the man had left a hole for the smoke to escape.

At three in the morning they were finished. Exhausted as they were, they were filled, too, with a silent delight. They had built their house in the clearing in less than a day; they had obeyed the law; nothing could now take it away from them. There remained only the fire — sign visible to the parish that a new house was built in it — if anyone cared to see.

While the woman lay in the bracken inside the shack, the man knelt before the new hearth-place and built up a little fire of dry twigs. He put his tinder to it, struck a spark, cupped his hands round it and blew, so that it began to smoke and sparkle exactly like a fire in the grandest house in the world. To crackle and smoke and then — after rolling about a trifle uncertainly as if a stranger in these parts — to stream steadily upwards, out of the chimney-hole in the roof, up above the oak trees and elms high into the midsummer sky. The man sat back on his heels and watched this fire he had built, his arms slack at his sides. The woman watched, too. It made the shack so hot that the heat became almost unbearable — but what matter? It was the law. They had obeyed the law down to the last particular and now could lie down and sleep in peace. Nobody could take their house from them or move them on, ever again!

They slept side by side, holding each other's smoke-blackened, work-roughened hands. The bracken beneath them did not stir with their weight, so utterly complete their exhaustion, so sunk were they in engrossing depths of sleep. High over their heads the thin blue-white smoke streamed upwards to dissipate itself into space as they into sleep. A stoat, weaving his way carefully though the clearing, sniffed at the tanned hides of the shack, pranced upwards to pat it a moment with tufted paws, and passed onwards into the shadows. Soon after dawn a robin chose the shack's roof for a perch and sang a resounding stave there before cleaning his bill defiantly on the ridge which was their roof. It was as if he accepted the building on behalf of the rest of the wood's community; but whether he accepted it or not was of no consequence to the sleepers below.

In the early morning the man woke coughing, and went outside to cough so as not to disturb his wife. Being up and about, he went, after that, down to the stream which threaded itself between elm-boles at the edge of the clearing, to fetch water for breakfast, and to seek for whatever other free provender the little wood could be persuaded to provide. It was while he was gone on this errand that his wife woke, fetched suddenly broad awake by the back-breaking pains which preceded, with surprising abruptness, the actual birth-pangs. By the time the man returned to the shack the labour was over and the baby lay at her feet in the steaming bracken.

'Oh, Nell!' he said, dropping on his knees.

She turned on him eyes that travelled so slowly they might have been shackled down by pain.

'The fire is dead,' she whispered; then, with an effort, 'Cut the cord.'

The man did what had to be done with anxious tenderness but with no feelings of novelty. He had done it twice before. Both children had died in infancy. Then he took off his coat, wrapped the new-born baby in it and handed it up to his wife. He had to crawl on all fours past them both to get to the dying fire.

It was not quite gone, but going. With the same anxious tenderness with which he had handled the child he now coaxed the fire, laying more twigs across it and blowing it into renewed being. The woman's teeth were chattering despite the normal September temperature, and she spoke, *staccato*, of being cold. It was true; her hands and feet, when he touched them, were as cold as the shaded running water he had just left.

'Soon be warm now,' he comforted. The fire leapt crackling in affirmation. The little shack was lit once more with its dancing flames, from ridge to bracken. Across the low roof they intertwined with long bronze tongues, above the shadowy bronze tongues of the bracken, so that the whole little shack became interwoven, tongue upon tongue, leaf upon leaf, flame upon flame.

The man went on doing his crouching chores. Then he made some tea in an old tin on the hearth and fed it to his wife in sips out of a bone spoon. He brought her in fresh bracken to lie on and swept out the old. He brought her some early blackberries, gleaming in a pile on a fern-leaf platter. He promised her eggs, later. There would be sure to be eggs from the late-laying pheasants which abounded (he knew) in adjacent coverts. She should have everything it was possible to procure, in due time.

'Are you glad that's a girl?' he queried. The others had been boy babies. Didn't everyone know boy babies were more difficult to rear — like young turkeys, just as tricky as young turkeys? But a girl would be more biddable altogether. Look at how little she had cried over the business of being born!

The woman hugged the bundle more closely to her. She felt supremely weak but supremely content. Outside in the now sunlit clearing, the grasshoppers had begun once more to saw away on their tiny fiddles, inside the shack the fire quivered and danced to the tune. It was *their* shack. They had built it and nobody could take it away from them! They would live in it, and as to what they would live on — God would provide; God, who sent the child, would send the food to feed the child, and to feed them. Meanwhile the blessed fact remained that to-day they could rest. To-day they need travel no farther, *to-day* they could sleep.

And the man took his bill-hook from his bundle and a snare from his pocket and went out to forage for fresh provender and fresh firewood.

CHAPTER VI

A SMOKING-OUT

That thee is sent, receive in buxomness;
The wrastling of this world asketh a fall;
Here is no home, here is but wilderness.
Forth, pilgrim, forth! forth, beast, out of thy stall!

CHAUCER

EXACTLY a year after the birth of the little miss at Redonda there came a funeral, and it was Mrs. Bromewell's. She had already been in a decline at the time of her daughter's birth, and she continued to slip down it afterwards, only more rapidly than before. The first time she came out of her bedroom since that important date, in fact, was the day she came out in her coffin.

The brothers Anderson were sober at the funeral; less out of respect for their late mistress ,than from a desire to see the coffin they had made her, well done by. It was of high-polished elm with brass handles. Captain Bromewell, with black crape round his hat and even round his riding-crop, and with extremely red eyes (he had been faithful to Cynara after his fashion), decreed that the affair was to be up to Redonda's highest standards — both home-made and well-made. Therefore the brothers Anderson had constructed the coffin from local elms, Redonda's smith had made the name-plate and massive handles, Redonda's gardener had supplied the wreath, and Redonda's oxen, groomed and tended by the yeoman-farmer so recently dispossessed of his property, and with black ribbons on their horns, had drawn the wagon to the graveyard.

Everything went off as it should, except that the little boys Clement and Clancy, appalled at the sandy hole in the ground into which their mother was slipping with such celerity, cried so loudly that they had to be removed before the end of the service. (Miss Harriet Bromewell did not cry, but slept serenely in her nurse's arms throughout.)

Although the baby was ready to be weaned, the wet-nurse showed herself in no hurry to be off and back into the bosom of her family, nor did Captain Bromewell desire that she should depart. He had long ago observed that she was a decent, deferential body of a woman who pressed her face almost into the wall if she ever chanced to meet him in the hall or on the staircase, and this immobile, almost unbreathing performance he accepted with complacence. The fowls ran from him if he went into the yard, hares crouched in their forms if he crossed a field, rooks rose in a body from the ploughed lands when he waved his crop — it was fitting also that Redonda's female servants should share this suitable timidity.

Mrs. Fitchet was buxom by nature, and a year of fattening up at Redonda's expense had rounded off her contours still more, so that occasionally when the Captain did meet her about the house and she turned her back so respectfully — but also so invitingly — upon him, he could not resist nipping her fat backside between thumb and forefinger *en passant* or tapping it smartly with his ubiquitous riding-crop — a procedure which resulted in small squeals satisfactory to both parties.

The Captain appreciated well-covered people. In an age which first began to take seriously the production of pedigree livestock, bigger and better than ever before, it was inevitable that a farmer should, with Caesar, like people round about him that were fat. So Mrs. Fitchet was, to him, a particularly good specimen of nursing mother, just as his cows, by judicious breeding, were becoming bigger and sleeker and richer in their milk-yield than any of his neighbours' cows.

Clement and Clancy took after their father — seeing so much more of him than they ever had of that invalid lady their mother. They were fair, fat, and florid, loving nothing better than to ride on the crupper behind Spens or the Captain on one of their over-seeing expeditions, or to supervise, with them, the April sowings, August harvestings, October pig-killings and Michaelmas goose-stabbings at Redonda. And seeing that he had no respect for Mrs. Fitchet, the boys had none either, although their mother's death had put them nominally under her charge.

'Mr. Clem! Mr. Clancy!' she would beg them, 'please to pick

up your toys, please to come with me to be washed for dinner, please to put the kitten down!' To which they would reply, as often as not: 'Damn your eyes, woman, mind your own business!' The baby Harriet, balanced in the crook of the poor woman's arm while she rocked to and fro addressing the little boys, would survey the scene with a calculating stare. Unless there was actual violence (she cried, for instance, if they kicked her nurse's shins) she was merely the interested spectator, absorbed and unsmiling. 'Lord bless us, how she takes it all in!' the other female servants would say.

She took in other scenes too, scufflings and squealings in her father's bedroom in the early morning after, according to command, her nurse had carried her in to be inspected. Laid down on the ottoman at the end of the room, the baby had a clear view of its activities — the horseplay between Captain Bromewell and the half-reluctant, half-fascinated wet-nurse, the excited aiding and abetting by the boys. Some mornings there were whippings ('Come *here*, Madam!' 'Oh, pray no, Cap'n!' 'Come *here*, I say! We'll make her, boys, won't we?'); some mornings there were murders, with a bucket brought by the boys (a slop-pail) to catch imaginary blood. Whichever it was, Harriet lay there watching it, the only silent person in the whole room. It would all end as rapidly as it began. 'There, that's enough,' the Captain would say, throwing them off — the tumbled wet-nurse, hysterically-excited little boys, and bedclothes all together, and rising from the bed half-naked, wholly magnificent: 'Get out with the lot of you; send Ivory!' Shuffling, scuffling he bundled them out. His patience used to evaporate with such abruptness. They amused him for a while, and then *pff*! — out they must get.

At such times the baby, snatched up from the ottoman and looking back over her retreating nurse's shoulder, still surveyed the scene with that quiet grave look; was still mistress of the situation — it would seem — as much as he was master of it. Indeed, she conveyed this fact so clearly to the Captain that sometimes that gentleman, standing afterwards in the middle of his room, one stocking off, one stocking on, would ejaculate, 'Now what the devil did she mean by *that*?'

In such an atmosphere the young Bromewells were destined to grow up. If they had been asked, later, to recollect their chief impressions of a childhood at Redonda, they would have been hard put to it to separate the noisy vitality of the place's inhabitants from the house's own innate dignity — the bare, echoing dining-hall, the gracious lines of hall and staircase; the magnificence of their father's own appurtenances — his silver-backed hairbrushes, delicate pomades, silver-gleaming pear-knife, silver-handled riding-crop — from the rough-and-ready manners of the man who owned and used all these things. The furniture, the silver, the glass, the leather all gleamed richly at Redonda, burnished as they were by plenty of elbow-grease. The man who owned them was as rough as they were sleek and shining, and his children grew to expect as part of the order of things that whenever he came into his ordered home it should be thrown into disarray. He was like a jovial earthquake, or a tidal river that acts without warning and leaves its pathway strewn with wreckage. So, the boys and their sister early grew to discover, they might track their father's progress through the house by dint of the open doorways, rugs askew, wet glasses, uncorked bottles and — in winter — the mud and leaves that inevitably accompanied his passage. Even if there were not these visible signs there was always his great voice echoing through the house, approaching or receding.

In summer-time he was outdoors all day long, and during those months Redonda had a sedate and chastened look. The curtains hung stilly in the tall windows; bees boomed in and out of the empty rooms unconcernedly and undisturbed. Whose was the housekeeping hand which thus did the place credit is not easy to say. Mrs. Fitchet had little more influence over the servants than over her charges. Nevertheless, by dint of her own ceaseless activities with brush and duster upstairs, and with the silent ministrations of Ivory downstairs, Redonda managed to do credit to itself as a great house, and as a gentleman's place, and as a farm of increasing renown.

When Clem and Clancy were six and seven respectively and their sister Harriet was eighteen months, Captain Bromewell brought home a tutor for the boys. Isaac Waters had started life as a warehouse clerk with one of the big East India firms. An attempt to juggle with moneys entrusted to him failed so disastrously that he had been sentenced to deportation, when the persuasive charms of Mr. Marsham had stepped in and obtained this Bargain for his client, adroitly deflecting the punishment from banishment to Botany Bay to banishment at Redonda. Mr. Marsham wrote to advise the Captain of this acquisition and where it might be picked up, setting forth, at the same time, some tender inquiries after the health of Redonda's pheasants and pigeons. The Captain had replied in his usual masterful fashion: 'Hold him, I'll come', had travelled to London by stage-coach, purchased a well-set-up Clydeside stallion from a backyard near the Angel at Islington, and brought tutor and stallion back to Redonda together, after a nightmare journey of some three days, to both.

The arrival of horse and man was unexpected, but Redonda was used to surprises from the Captain. The boys were immediately reft away from Mrs. Fitchet and put to share a strange bedroom with the tutor. At nights, while Spens as usual fell asleep after his fifth glass, Captain Bromewell found a new pleasure in goading young Waters, who was a fair youth and a prey to blushes at the least indecency. Since he would not take strong waters either, it may be believed that dinner with his employer was an interminable embarrassment, and the more he blushed the more the Captain relished the situation. For a time, indeed, this new victim absorbed most of his sadistic energies, and both Ivory and Mrs. Fitchet enjoyed a respite.

Poor Isaac Waters never protested against such teasing. He would far rather have eaten with the servants, but since this was not to be, he took it to be the will of God and a just punishment for past errors. He prayed a good deal and cried in his bedroom, to the children's great interest, and he found solace in the house-keeper Mrs. Fitchet, upon whose plump knees he would sometimes pour out his sorrows. He cried, poor youth, and was comforted by Mrs. Fitchet in a good and hearty way, and the baby Harriet, standing in her lap while the young man wept tears round about her ankles, looked down at the phenomenon first with her usual imperturbability and then crumpled her face up and cried in sympathy.

'Ah, *don't*, sir!' begged Mrs. Fitchet. 'See, you have set my lamb off now, indeed you have. She cannot bear a sad sight, her heart is so tender! The housemaid took up a mouse in a trap yes'day and she cried with all her heart. That's wunnerful in a young child, sir — '

'It's wonderful indeed *in this house*,' sniffed Mr. Waters. 'She must be a prodigy indeed! Those imps her brothers haven't a heart between 'em!'

'They're little gentlemen, sir,' explained their late nurse. 'They 'oudn't fare to be so tender-hearted as their sister — '

'They're little varmints!' amended their tutor.

Nevertheless time softens all impressions and, despite a mutual antipathy, the tutor succeeded ultimately in teaching his charges to read and write and to manage small sums of arithmetic. It was not easy going, but was perhaps rendered easier by an order from the Captain that he was to whop these subjects into them or be whopped himself for failing so to do. Nor did Waters doubt the Captain's word; he had seen the Bromewell crop used too effectively and ubiquitously for that already.

But we are concerned less with the details of the young Brome-wells' education than with the effect of this restless and yet somehow coherent household upon the youngest member of it. Harriet grew slowly but surely; her hair when it came was not fair but dark and sleek, curling in wisps about her neck and ears. She caused her devoted nurse no qualms, had no serious setbacks, and travelled on through the crawling to the walking stage with her usual steadiness of poise and purpose. She had, in the latter respect, far more character than either of her brothers, who were always easily deflected by another interest if one effort of theirs failed. Harriet, on the other hand, would set out to do a thing, whether to pick up an infinitesimal button between the floorboards, or the fringe of her shawl to bits, with unswerving tenacity. If interrupted by nurse or servants she would scream until set down again; it was almost the only time she used her voice. As long as she could get what she wanted without talking, she did not concern herself to talk.

So she grew, and her brothers; and young Waters settled down more, and blushed less, and occupied himself a great deal with praying, copying out sermons with good intentions and by a poor light, and following the itinerary of John Wesley as that evangelist covered the country. And Redonda continued to flourish and to expand its acreage, and to multiply its number of beasts and products of all kinds until there was hardly a place of similar prosperity within 40 miles, even in a time increasingly prosperous for farmers.

The years went by, and eventually it came to be time for Captain Bromewell to consider a companion for his seven-year-old daughter. The boys were too rough for her, and a scarcity of infant gentlefolk round about forced him to think over the possibility of a humbler stable-companion, as a pedigree racehorse may not disdain a donkey for company. Running his eye (from horseback) over the children on the estate, he let it roam further, until one day it rested upon Susan Shattuck, then aged four and living with her mother in the squatter's shack in the clearing in Farley Wood.

Susan was plump where the others had been starvelings. She did not run from the Captain as the others did, but stood her ground, a fact which at once piqued and pleased him. Both she and her mother had a way of looking at him which reminded him, a trifle uncomfortably, of some wild creature cornered but sure of itself as long as it could look its enemy in the face; a steady, secret, deep look which asked nothing and told nothing but noted all. . . . He meant to have the child to play with his daughter and would as usual not be gainsaid.

Mrs. Shattuck was appreciative of the honour but apprehensive. She clung to the shack which her husband had built for her, and where he had died while the child was still in arms. Strong in the conviction of her rights she spoke up to the Captain. He wanted her to move into one of his own cottages for convenience. She wanted to stay in the clearing: 'Squatter's Rights, Cap'n!' she quoted.

'Very well, my lass,' he said, 'I know all about Squatter's Rights! But I'll give you a kindly warning —'

'A warning?'

'There's talk amongst the womenfolk at Redonda. They say you've put a twist on this part of the wood; they've a notion you're a witch, Mrs. Shattuck, Ma-am, and they don't take kindly to witches!'

'If I was a witch,' Nell Shattuck said slowly, 'I reckon you'd not want my Sukey for your Miss Harriet.'

'Pooh, *I* don't believe such rubbish,' said the Captain, leaning forward reassuringly to clap his horse's neck. 'But you know how their tongues clatter. They say your husband vanished and that you spirited him away. They say you keep cats for your familiars — aye, the ones you let out of *my* traps at night!'

'They'd ought to show more sense — silly mawthers,' said Nell Shattuck, but she drew her child close to her nevertheless.

'Expect sense of women that believe in Pharisees and mermaids that'll crome them into the wells when they goo for water!' retorted the Captain, lapsing from cunning or carelessness into the broad East Anglian of his companion. 'What'll you want next, Nell Shattuck? Expect sense of those that hang hollow flints over their beds to drive away the nightmare or ask a man on a piebald for a cure for whooping-cough.'

'Roast mouse is better, fare to me,' said the woman.

'Mouse?'

'Yes, sir; or milk which a ferret has lapped, my grandmother used to say, was a fine cure — '

'And you believe *that* pack of nonsense!' marvelled the Captain.

'That ain't ne more nonsense, sir, than that a green sloe rubbed on a wart'll cure it — or curin' a little 'un that's old-fashioned by drawing that through a riven ash. I've cured *this* one, that way, toime that was ailin'.'

'She's as plump as a stuffed goose, she is, that,' agreed the Captain.

'I look after her well, Cap'n. She's my only one,' said the woman, quietly.

'Reckon you look after my rabbits and my pheasants' eggs, too,' rejoined the Captain. She did not answer, but he knew very well that if he were to go hunting for tell-tale eggshells or coney fur round her shack he would find them no more easily than his gamekeepers had, and *they* had been told often enough to keep their eyes skinned for such evidence. What did this couple live on,

then? Acorns, like the pigs? Nuts, like the mice and squirrels?
Berries, like the birds? True, the woman — he knew — did a small
trade in the summer with her osier-work, but was that enough to
keep body and soul together? Much more likely that she and the
brat went milking his cows at night, hedgehog fashion, and stealing
his eggs in their aprons.

As if she read his thoughts as he sat there, sulky as a child despoiled
of a promised treat, Nell Shattuck laid her hand on his horse's
bridle and spoke with great emphasis.

'I take nothin',' she said. 'On God's oath that's true, and you
know it, sir! As long as I've lived here with the child, aye—and
when my man was aloive too, we didn't take nothin' that was
yours. That's not for humble folk loike us to own things! I've not
foddered as much as a goose off your grass! All I have is this shack
which my poor man built and I've Squatter's Rights to that, isn't
that so, sir? Reckon you're a magistrate and know the law; isn't
that so?'

He would not answer at first. Furiously his mind was muttering
under its breath, *She got in by a trick with her brat and I'll have her
out by a trick. That's fair enough!* Aloud:

'Ay, it's the law,' he said — and his thoughts again, under their
breath: *Confound it, why don't she take her eyes off me; she looks at me
as if there was something she was bound to get to grips with!*

He was uneasy now, and impatient to be off. He had come to
make arrangements for the girl to tag about with his daughter —
a little maid for a little Miss — and this miserable creature was
refusing him; would not leave the shack. Confound it, a good
north-easter would do for the shack anyway — ramshackle hide-
and-wattle affair that it was!

But she would not leave it at that. Still with her hand on his
bridle-reins, she made one of the longest speeches she had ever
made in her life.

'Then if that's the Law,' she said, 'you're bound to aboide by that,
sir. You 'ouldn't want to hurt either on us, since we don't hurt
nothin' o' yours. That's four year now, that we've bin here, sir.
And before that my man and I were hunted from pillar to post.
We'd not done nothin' wrong, sir, but we were poor and the

parishes wouldn't fare to let us rest. My man was ill, he couldn't keep to his trade if he tried iver so; but if he *had* tried, that's the law agin, sir, isn't it, that a man mayn't work, not outside his own parish? And in his own parish his master turned him off, sir, owin' to the cough he got with the fumes from the hoides . . .'

She paused a little, and a little of the old pain she had felt at the sight of her husband's convulsed face and shaking shoulders, the memory of the cough that had eventually coughed him into his grave, made her contract her fingers even more on the reins.

'They reckoned to part us,' she went on, 'to take *me* to the work'us and leave him out to goo hedging and ditching and breaking stones when that was wet. But we couldn't face that, sir — bein' that the only thing we had in the world was each other. Reckon you cling to the oonly thing you have! But they went to force us. They'd the roight, that was the law. But when they saw how it was with me, they were willin' to let us goo, seein' the expense, like as not, that another pauper would cost the parish. So we come away, and my man remembered this wood bein' as how he lived in these parts when a boy, sir. And with the Lord's help we came here, sir, and made our house rightfully, by the law. And you ne yet anybody else can't take it from us, being as how we built it rightfully!'

Her eyes, brown as his dogs', blazed in her face with the earnestness of her speech — but her conviction, he knew, belied her words as much as his belied his. *You have no right but you mean to take it from me*, her eyes said to his; and his to hers, *Right or wrong I mean to have my own way and you know it!*

But the words went on, praying him, by virtue of their truth, to have pity:

'Reckon you know the rest, Cap'n. Sukey here was born soon as iver we made our house. And my man got a little work hedgin' and ditchin' when he had the strength, and I filled in, loike, with my osiers and the good Lord He didn't let us starve. And when my man died I buried him here in the clearin', sir, and dug his grave with his own spade, for they were bound to give him a pauper's grave, sir, and he wanted to stay here, with us.'

'It's a witch that makes away with the body of her husband

58

instead of letting it have decent Christian burial,' proclaimed Captain Bromewell.

At that Nell Shattuck had known it was useless. He was so clever — whatever she said he could turn into evidence against her. She would make a final effort, hoping the truth would speak for itself and for her, so she said quite plainly, not replying to his spoken words as much as his unspoken ones:

'He's buried here, sir. If you take me from here I shall die for sure.'

I shall die. A statement of fact, not a threat. But the Captain, accustomed to threatening, himself, interpreted it as such; as a challenge inferring *I shall give you the slip after all; you shall not be able to have your way with me!* *Very well, my girl,* was his only reaction. *Very well, we shall see. We shall see!*

The child had dropped on to her haunches, tired of all the grown-up palaver, and was arranging twigs on the ground in some crisscross game of her own. The sun flecked down into the clearing, and on to her strawberry-coloured woollen frock and her bare head. Her hair was drawn back and screwed in a wispy knob at the back of her head in ludicrous imitation of her mother's style. It was as pale as bean-honey.

As honey. . . . What had put that thought into his head? This woman was good with bees, too. On two or three occasions she had sent offerings to Redonda — great fans of gleaming honey-comb, abstracted by some witchery of her own out of the wild bees' store in Farley Wood. When he sent foresters for more, they had returned empty-handed. She had a special knack, they complained, in smoking the bees out.

Smoking them out. . . . Suddenly his raging impatience lapsed, even his fury at that detaining yet humble hand on his bridle rein. It was as simple as that.

'Well, well,' he said smiling. 'Think it over, my lass.' The brown eyes did not waver but fixed him as steadfastly as ever. He rattled at the reins, and her hand dropped from them like a stone, hanging straight down beside her ragged apron. The child looked up from its game. There was a disturbing dignity about the pair of them which made the Captain anxious to be off — something of the same dignity he had observed in dead pheasants. Alive, cleaving the air above one with panicky purpose, you had the better of 'em. Dead, with their necks limp and the glory of the cockbird's feathers suddenly dulled, so often the position seemed momentarily reversed. Ridiculous — but there was no doubt about it, *they* were after *you* then, not you after them! But not for long. By God, no! Not when they were basted and stuffed with chestnuts with plenty of gravy, and steaming vegetables by the side. No doubt whose was the advantage, *then!*

He chuckled, and that devil deep down inside him, which was for ever cooking roast pheasant over a fire made of other people's broken hopes, chuckled too at his master's reasoning. This, they may both have concluded, was how such heart-searchings usually ended, and the Captain could have laughed out loud at the thought of the way he got the better of sentiment every time, just as he got the better of everything else!

'I see you'll have your own way in spite of everything,' he said to the woman — apparently beaten, apparently lenient: 'Good-day to ye then, I must find another playmate for my daughter.' Wriggling short finger and thumb in his waistcoat pocket he fished out a small coin:

'Take that, Betsy, and mind ye don't swallow it,' he said.

The coin fell slantingly through the air and lay glinting amongst the litter at Sukey's feet. She looked first up at her mother and then down at the coin — not touching it yet but marking the place with her eyes.

Nell Shattuck's eyes never left the Captain's face.

'Good-bye to ye,' he repeated. His horse began to move in answer to his heels.

'Farewell, Cap'n.'

It was the traditional good-bye of the lower classes but to Captain Bromewell it seemed on this occasion to be overlaid with the same urgency the woman had used in all her utterances, including her threat of death. *And yet*, he reasoned, riding away through the bridlepaths of his own wood, *I'm damned if she knows how right she is, and how much of a farewell it is, for her! But not for me, never for me!*

A sense of triumphant well-being surged up in him at the thought, from the heel of his spurred boot, controlling the stirrup, to the crown of his admirably-wigged head. He was alive, active, cunning — getting his own way with his own property as he always did — managing his own estate as he chose, and no one should stop him! Redonda should continue to flourish under his care, and under the care of his sons and his sons' sons. The rest of the world could go to hell — indeed, looked like doing so, with the way the Government was mismanaging affairs in Ireland and in the Colonies. Business might be shot into small pieces, overseas trade might suffer even more than it had done already through blockade and sea-battles — especially now that those blackguards the French were assisting the American rebels. But farming would flourish, whatever else went to perdition, and a man standing foursquare on his own property, with his own gun in his hand, could look after himself!

It had been a dry summer and the leaves on his elms were already golden as he rode slowly home, past the quarry, and up Redonda's drive. Too often he missed this entrance, coming in by the back way and the dairy door like the farmer he was. Yet now as he rode homewards, and saw the great patient façade of the house staring out eastwards, it seemed to him to have the same dignity about it that he had met somewhere else that day — yes, confound it, in the clearing! But this was a more substantial dignity, *this* was something Clem and Clancy might inherit with satisfaction and keep up with pride!

A secret smile tucked up the corners of his mouth. Thinking of the boys and of Harriet brought inevitably recollections of the stable-companion. He would have the little Shattuck to tag along with his girl within a fortnight — and Nell Shattuck thankful for his charity, be damned if he wouldn't! Nothing he planned ever failed!

Nor did this plan. No sooner was he back than he began, by way of Mrs. Fitchet, to feed the fearful superstitions of Redonda's servants with brand-new rumours concerning the witch in the clearing. He expressed himself as sorry that a woman should be so maligned, nevertheless there *were* stories, etc., and it was not hard to gather that the Captain would bear with equanimity any consequences that might ensue. Rumour added itself to hearsay, and ignorance and fear doubled the total. *The Witch Shattuck must go!* became the universal cry! *Duck her in the horse-pond, burn her house down; the Witch must go!*

The Shattucks were consequently smoked out as thoroughly as any bees, and under the malicious enthusiasm of some fourteen-year-old hooligans the small shack collapsed inwards upon itself, emitting steam and sparks and a suffocating odour of burnt hide. Bracken in the clearing caught fire from the sparks and in the general excitement, Spens, the agent, rescued Nell Shattuck and the child from their prospective ducking and escorted them to the very same cottage on the Captain's estate that had been originally proposed.

'You'll be safe enough here, I reckon,' said Spens, as he locked them both in. He did not look Nell Shattuck in the face, fearing — not her reproach, which she *could* help — but the Evil Eye, which she could not.

'Leave her to simmer a bit,' said the Captain when told. 'She'll settle down well enough when she's hungry, and used to the place.' It was the identical procedure he adopted with new cattle or poultry brought to Redonda. He was well satisfied. The windows were too small to poke even a child through, the one door was locked and the key was in his pocket. Further, Spens and his men were there to patrol the lane and to punish any witchhunters who might choose to persist in their sport past the limits which suited the Captain. He had got the better of *her* now — just as once *she* had got the better of him!

All the same, he did not care to pass down that lane during the next forty-eight hours. He tried it once, to prove to the gaggle of frightened farm folk that the Witch had no influence here at least. But there was something about the absolute stillness in the locked cottage which worked unpleasantly upon him. So, in his childhood, had a cage looked, when the mouse, rabbit, or bird in it had chosen to vacate it by death. Yes — be damned to the bitch, it was not human, and he hurried past, saying to himself, with more emphasis than anyone would have supposed to be necessary: 'They're better off there than living in a tent like gypsies!' — and kicking Ivory with an odd sense of having to take something out of someone, when that long-suffering negro had been summoned to pull off his boots.

CHAPTER VII

GROWING PAINS AND GROWING PLEASURES

We would never have loved the earth so well if we had had no childhood in it.   GEORGE ELIOT

NELL SHATTUCK endured an autumn and winter in the cottage which was also her prison, and then she was as good — or, to Captain Bromewell's mind, as bad — as her word. She died. Not painfully or protestingly but exactly as animals die. She was there: suddenly she was there no more. There was a certain amount of smallpox about at the time and the smallpox therefore obligingly carried her off — or so the doctor said.

On the death of her mother, Captain Bromewell gave orders that the child Susan Shattuck was to be received in Redonda itself. As a plaything for the Little Miss she had been fairly convenient at the cottage, but mud and rain sometimes intervened with the full use of the plaything, whereas when both were together under one roof no obstacle remained. She was accordingly lodged in the attics with the goosefeather girls — two red-haired sisters whose lives moved largely to the rhythm of hatching, tending, plucking and stuffing geese. The feathers they plucked went to fill Redonda's many mattresses and, after that, to market; the geese also went to market and to Redonda's table. If the women had names, the Redonda children never bothered to learn them, for they were referred to universally as the goosefeather girls.

Captain Bromewell, in his few leisure moments, enjoyed watching his daughter Harriet playing with the younger girl. She managed Susan from the first with the same sort of authority with which he managed the farm affairs. The child was crammed into her doll's carriage and pushed about the house in it — rocked in the outgrown cradle, fed with a spoon by Harriet when she would rather have fed herself, bathed and soaped and dried by Harriet when Harriet decreed and put to sleep when Harriet thought it best.

The older girl's masterful solicitation for the young orphan touched Mrs. Fitchet's heart. She considered her a real Little Mother, just as her brothers, now grown to an age when rat-catching and birds'-nesting absorbed their attentions, were real Little Cap'ns. Everything was for the best in the end, in this world, for Mrs. Fitchet. Several of her own offspring had died since she came to live at Redonda, which bore out her theory. It was better so, poor lambs.

As for Susan, Mrs. Fitchet never ceased to admonish her on her great good fortune in being inside Redonda at all. 'You must love Miss Harriet,' she insisted, 'see how she cares for you!' and her eyes would soften as she watched her baby Miss Harriet kneeling beside the cradle into which Susan had been stuffed and rocking it relentlessly, her lips fixed, her eyes watching her charge for signs of naughtiness as craftily as a cat watches a mouse.

Such a relationship, some might claim, was as bad for the older girl as for the younger; baulked in no direction by her father and nurse, sheltered from her rough brothers, Harriet Bromewell had now been presented with a little creature almost completely her own, capable of being dominated as she had never yet been able to dominate anything else. If she had turned, as a consequence, into a tyrant long before she reached her 'teens it would hardly have been strange. But circumstances combined to prevent this—chief of which was that Susan Shattuck's own nature was so docile and uncomplaining that Harriet soon discovered there was less fun to be had out of forcing Susan to do her will than from the occasional, harder victories she achieved over her brothers.

Clement and Clancy were older than she, but she early discovered that their intelligence was inferior to her own. If she desired something from them she would not wheedle, but demand it — enlisting, as time went on, various supernatural powers in her support, with a *penchant* for pinching and pulling noses and legs and catching at legs on stairways. Her powers waned in the long, light summer evenings, when the boys could get away from her and when no shadows chased or daunted them. But in the winter Harriet and her allies achieved triumphant victories over the rebellious but credulous Clem and Clancy.

Their father could not fathom it in the least. The boys were not physical cowards; he did not understand how they could allow a small sister to dominate them. The supernatural allies she enlisted were no more to him than signs of Harriet's lively imagination and their own credulity. Besides, Harriet did not even raise her voice to shout at them; she seemed to drive them with the passion of her will, even to do things that they detested. It was beyond him. That she should dominate her live doll and little servant Sukey was understandable, since the girl was weaker and of inferior breeding; that she should get Clem and Clancy to do her bidding was, and remained, a mystery to him.

The mystery was deepened rather than lessened by an incident that took place one December evening, when the fire in the drawing-room had been lit and the curtains were still undrawn. A spasm of gout in his left foot had kept him cursing indoors all day, so that he was forced now to observe several things. How, for instance, the elms in Redonda park kept their distance in the daytime but as the light went out of the sky so their skeletal selves seemed to draw nearer to the house, closing in upon the warmth and light there, looking in at the windows. (He had had the children brought down for his amusement. The boys were busy with some game at his feet; Harriet, sitting opposite to him in a big chair, was threading a needle with grave purpose. She was then aged nine.)

'Clem, fetch my thimble,' she said, suddenly, 'it is upstairs in the basket on Fitchet's table.'

Her brother looked up and groaned. He was constructing a drawbridge for Clancy's castle, of books and rulers precariously balanced. Clancy, having finished his part, was merely looking on. Surely it was fairer that *he* should go!

Clement looked up at his father; sometimes it was possible to obtain sympathy from that quarter.

It was fairer, in the Captain's opinion, that the servants should run errands, not his sons.

'Sukey!' he roared.

The plain face of young Susan, comically topped by a mobcap several sizes too large, peeped round the door. She was never to be found far from Harriet.

'Sukey, fetch Miss Harriet's thimble,' said the Captain.

'No,' said Harriet, diverting her gaze from her needle to her father, but not bothering to look at Sukey at all. She did not want Sukey to go because she knew Sukey was willing to go. Sukey loved her and would do anything for her. She did not even want Clancy to go because (of the two brothers) Clancy was the less susceptible to her 'influences'. There was no pleasure in making people do things if they did them more or less willingly. Where lay the power in that?

Some of this she tried to convey to her father in the clear gaze of her steady grey eyes. *Do not interfere with me*, said the eyes; *I am your daughter, and I do things the way you do them and get pleasure from exercising my power in the same way that you do.* But she did not say any of this aloud, merely repeating:

'No, Clem must go. Sukey must stay here and pick up my threads.'

'I *won't* go!' shouted Clem. 'Father, *must* I go?'

Captain Bromewell tapped the arm of his chair with stubby fingers, irritated. It was not right that the family should be divided against itself even in little things like this; the family must be united, Redonda (if need be) against the world ... And yet, and yet ... The power within him which expressed itself just in Harriet's way held him back now, saying *Watch her and see how she does it! Damme if she isn't worth two of the boys, the little bitch!*

So sure of her power was Harriet that she did not compel Clem with her eyes — returning them again, from her father, to fix her gaze upon the thread as she drew it finally through the needle. (Susan was on her knees, picking up the dropped threads.)

'If you do not go, Clem,' she said, 'Martin will not come and tell stories under the table any more; he detests boys who will not obey their sisters.'

Martin was chief of the many invisible and powerful allies of

66

Miss Bromewell. He invented admirable stories and told them to her (so she said) in the night watches, for her to repeat afterwards for Clem and Clancy's delectation. The stories were consequently invested with a supernatural atmosphere however prosaic their contents might turn out to be, and in an age when there were no books for the juvenile reader worth mentioning, these tales compelled the fascinated attention of her brothers in a way that nothing else could do. God might have an all-seeing eye and be able to discern their inmost thoughts, as Mrs. Fitchet and Isaac Waters declared He had and could; nevertheless He did not make His pleasure or pain felt in them so awfully, promptly and directly as did Harriet — through the medium of the unseen Martin.

Clancy fixed his eyes accusingly on Clem. He knew it was hateful to go upstairs to get a thimble for silly Harriet, but since Martin approved this course and would tell no further stories if Clem refused, then clearly there was only one thing to do — obey. *Go*, said Clancy silently through his clenched teeth; *I hate her too, but go!*

Captain Bromewell tapped the arm of his chair even louder; Harriet's invisible and irresistible Power was spreading its way through the room in a way which, while admirable, threatened eventually to clash with his own. Besides, his essential masculinity had begun to side with his sons. He did not understand this Martin nonsense at all but he knew one thing — that it was for men to order and women to obey.

Susan was uncomfortable for another reason and a large tear dropped amongst the threads on the floor. She could not bear unhappiness in anyone, and now she felt Clem's unhappiness beating about the room like a trapped bird; a very small helpless bird with the great eagle of Harriet's Power after it. It was too much. She could do nothing, and she sobbed aloud.

'Yah, *Sniveller!*' shouted Clancy, relieved to find something on which to release his baffled temper. He threw a book, which had been part of the castle ramparts, at her head. Susan dodged him with an agility born of much practice (with her, meeting Harriet's brothers had come to mean the same thing as to dodge). Unfortunately in the action, what with her long apron and her overpowering cap, she slipped and fell across the Captain's gouty foot. 'Hell and ten thousand devils!' roared that gentleman. 'Get off! Get away with ye!' and he poked and whacked at her with his crop as he did at the dogs or at Ivory. The boys gazed in admiration. They loved their father's expostulations when these were directed against anybody but themselves.

Susan, bundled up ridiculously in her long gown, rolled over and away out of range; Clem and Clancy kicked out at her as she passed them. But the full fury of Harriet's wrath was not directed against them but suddenly (and inexplicably to him) against her father. Power met Power and finally clashed, like clouds clashing, making thunder of the result. She did not speak, but with blazing eyes and set lips she advanced upon him, digging her needle into his arm. Despite the second roar of rage that the astonished Captain let out at this, somehow everyone in the room could hear his daughter saying through it, in the same set, even tones in which she had requested Clem to fetch her thimble:

'How dare you! How dare you touch Susan! I will punish anyone that touches Susan!'

'And I will show *you*, my girl!' roared Captain Bromewell, grasping his wounded arm and struggling to rise from his chair. 'I'll show you who is master here and who you can assault with impunity! You bitch, I'll whip the wickedness out of you, that I will!' and he roared for Ivory to come and help him until the dogs in the hall barked and scratched at the door. The boys stood fascinated. This was better even than Martin's stories!

'If you touch me,' they heard their sister say, still firmly and quietly, 'I will leap out of the window upstairs and kill myself; and then *you* will have murdered me.'

'Oh! Oh! Hell and damnation! Fitchet! Ivory!' roared the Captain. 'Get me out of this chair. Let me get at her! *I'll* teach her!'

In a perfect pandemonium of barking and whining the door burst open, admitting the dogs, Waters, Ivory and Mrs. Fitchet all together. During the subsequent ministrations and expostulations Susan escaped by crawling through various legs and then making her exit.

By the time the Captain was on his feet and ready armed for the assault, Harriet too was out of the room, at the top of the staircase, standing and looking down at him. Somewhere in the back of the Captain's anger-clotted brain another picture of a girl at the top of a staircase tried to piece itself together; but too much time had passed and he made no real effort to remember who and where it was, and exactly why.

'I'll whip the life out of you, I tell you!' he shouted up at his daughter.

Harriet stood still in the shadows, hugging herself, her thin arms crossed in front of her, her hands holding her elbows. In this way she could persuade herself that Martin was behind her, his strong arms supporting her, comforting her, squeezing her elbows. (She squeezed her elbows.)

She did not waste breath on her father, only repeated: 'If you come up here after me, I shall jump out of my window,' and began to walk backwards, slowly, in the direction of her room. *Let* her, damn her! thought the Captain. It was not so high, and a broken limb might bring her to reason! But Mrs. Fitchet could not bear it another minute, laying a restraining hand on his arm and nearly toppling him over (*she* who had been called to support *him*!):

'Don't, don't, Cap'n, sir,' she said. 'She will do as she say! You know she will!' with mingled pride and pain in her voice.

'Let her do it and break her neck!' said Captain Bromewell, and made as if to follow her. But the gout in his foot restrained him even more than Mrs. Fitchet. With a curse and a groan he turned away, back towards his study, banging the door after him. Upstairs, in the Winter shadows of the landing, he knew that he left victory with his daughter.

It was a victory which made a profound impression on the rest of the household. Somebody had stood up to the Captain and won! For the boys, it merely convinced them beyond all doubt that Martin was a wizard at Harriet's beck and call, and it made Susan more devoted than ever to her protector. (Was it not on her account that the scene had taken place?)

Still more, it deposed Mrs. Fitchet, at a stroke, from the position of nurse to that of personal maid. Henceforth she took orders from Harriet instead of essaying any longer to give them, and what duties she did not do for her mistress Susan was delighted, under her tutelage, to discharge.

The relationship between the children remained, however, enigmatic. Susan was half-doll and half-servant to Harriet, and Harriet half-mother and half-mistress. They neither ate nor slept together, yet spent more time in the company of each other than in that of anyone else. They quarrelled hardly at all, since Susan was as glad to obey as Harriet to command; and there were — as with all children — long stretches of idyllic time in which neither obeyed and neither commanded but both played together with mutual pleasure.

The boys left them more alone as time passed. They outgrew the mysterious Martin's influence at about the same time as Mr. Waters departed, which was a year after the needle incident. He left as suddenly as he had come. The sight of his highly coloured but abstracted features gazing into a spiritual space had struck Captain Bromewell with more than the usual irritation one evening at dinner, and he had been packed off in the Woodbridge coach two days later, consigned Care Of Mr. Marsham with instructions to that gentleman to employ him, if possible, in some other of the Captain's concerns. Mr. Waters was accordingly appointed as ship's clerk on a Bristol merchantman in which the Captain was interested and, joining her under kindly compulsion about a week later, sailed miserably off towards the Canaries and out of this story. Mrs. Fitchet wept to see him leave Redonda — and Susan wept because she wept, but they were the only ones. The boys, released from his conscientious care, were sent away to board at a grammar school, and somehow lost all fears of and interest in Martin during the term there. They returned in the holidays taller and far less amenable to their sister, though, since they still respected her natural if not her supernatural authority, they kept a good deal out of her way.

Harriet, too, had learnt as much from Mr. Waters as he had been able to impart. (She had insisted at an early age on sharing her brothers' lessons.) He found her an apt pupil, though her passion for putting knowledge to use, for remembering only those things for which she could see a practical application and forgetting everything else immediately, somewhat intimidated him. He almost preferred the young gentlemen's ignorant respect for the subjects he tried so painfully (and it must be admitted, so indifferently) to instil into them, to their sister's contemptuous comprehension. She learnt to read and write with great facility. Such accomplishment meant Power. She took to the multiplication-table and subtraction and addition, even to fractions, with as much liking as her brothers had loathing—for knowing one's numbers was Power, too. History, literature, the little French that Mr. Waters could muster, interested her not at all. She left the room during those lessons and went her own way.

And her own way, in the summer, was out of doors, with Susan in attendance.

The Garden of Eden before the Fall must have seemed to Adam and Eve as perfect a place as Redonda and its environs to Harriet and Susan in those days. They knew no other home and desired no other. Familiar prospects stretched for ever before them, continually promising pleasures and continually fulfilling what they promised. A stable-boy, told off to accompany his young mistress, was frequently deceived and left on his own — and saw no reason for acquainting anyone with this obliging circumstance — so that Harriet from ten years upwards enjoyed a freedom of action exceedingly uncommon to other young ladies of her position, and a freedom which she continued to enjoy all her life. A white, barrel-bellied pony which had been loaned to Mr. Waters during his sojourn was commandeered by Harriet on his departure, and she began to ride round the estate sometimes with her father, silently appreciative of his easy grasp of every situation and of the speed and snap with which he set his little world going at the start of each day. Out on the dun-coloured February fields, viewing the ranks of wheat, still thin and small, springing up like green hairs on the back, thought Harriet, of some huge hand; or in the cold, sweet-smelling Great Barn where the grain flowed through one's fingers like water; or in the warm, filthy cow-byre, listening intently to details of siring and calving; or sitting on the bank in Spring, while the goosefeather girls called the ducks and geese 'Lil' boys! Lil' boys!' and the whole world was green and yellow, full of April's wavering light. It was all part and parcel of Redonda; of the habitation which was Harriet's whole ecstatic life.

How explain the difference between Harriet's feeling for her home and that of her brothers? They lived *on* the place, casually happy as young animals. She lived *in* it, loved it as a part of herself (and she loved herself dearly). The face of the house, looking for ever seawards, was to her a beautiful and a patient face. The wood-pigeons coo-rooing in the woods in summer sent thrills of inexplicable joy coursing through every vein. The delicate vine-leaf pattern that ran, in plaster, round her bedroom ceiling was something that every morning she smiled to recognize — and every night to trace with her fingers upon the coverlet in the dark. Not only Summer was lovely to her but every season. Spring first, for its largesse of young life bursting out all over Redonda as riotously as the cowslips and primroses in its meadows.

As for Summer, its riches were so abundant that the season never symbolized one specific pleasure; though looking back on it each Winter she seemed to see it as one endless and shining day, through which she and Susan, crowned with flowers, wove a way through a meadow of grasses as tall as themselves, with meadowsweet and cow parsley holding parasols of white spray above their happy heads. That was Summer — that and a birdsong which shimmered continually upwards into the blueness, making one together with the fragrance and the heat; Summer growing, ripening, swelling — bursting finally into showers of sheaves of golden wheat — into Harvest, a glorious five weeks during which her father ceased to be merely master but was king and emperor! How should she not love Summer best?

Because Autumn when it came, in its turn, was also best, season of brilliant star-spangled nights and misty mornings, gossamer and wood smoke, bryony berries, blackberries, mushrooms which, once seen by human eye and left unpicked, vanished to leave no trace; hoar-frost which magicked the muddy ruts of the farmyard into ridges of glittering iron, and froze the ducks solidly into the horse-pond; goose-killings, pig-killings, burnishing of plough and plough-harness; clean brown of furrowed fields waiting for the wheat-grain.

Winter was heralded by the water-smoke — those salt sea-vapours which came rolling inland unannounced, to bury Redonda's park fathoms deep in mist. Never did the coast seem so near to the farm as then, when it was most invisible. Under its nebulous influence the flat Suffolk landscape lay melancholy, unprotected, at the full mercy of Winter and its hardships. Even Redonda and its farm buildings, standing foursquare behind the stripped elms, had, in the grip of Winter, a helpless and a fragile look. They never seemed so small as in Winter, just as they never seemed so large as in Summer—a phenomenon which was to perplex Harriet as long as she lived.

There was other smoke in Winter more welcome than the water-smoke, and that was the smoke from the fires burning in the dining-hall and study. The brothers Anderson tended these fires as if they were altars, and the smell of the different woods burning — trophies from the 'enclosed' spinneys and from Farley Wood, was sweeter even than cowslip to Harriet's nostrils. To crouch over the fire, to warm cheek and chin, breast and knee before the blaze of the fire, to read by the leaping light of the fire and to hear its roaring crackle, was to draw Winter's whole essence deep, deep into herself, in a way that could never be equalled. 'Thank God,' her father used to cry at nights (as he struggled, with Ivory, to rid himself of his muddy boots) 'for a good fire and nobody in it!', repeating a local saying of whose history he knew nothing and cared less. (His ancestor, whose signature had made legal the burning at the stake of so many Suffolk rebels, could have perhaps explained.) Be that as it may, Redonda's fire was a noble and satisfying thing to the entire Bromewell family. Congregated about it, basking in it, doing honour to it, they bore each other perhaps less grudge than at any other season, and their eyes followed its sparks upwards with complete and appreciative accord.

In Winter the path by the Shearings—a favourite walk of Harriet's — became inundated, very often, by floods from the River Alde which ran alongside. The Shearings was a reedy stretch of ground, bounded on one side by the Alde, on the other by a neighbouring farmer's ground. Good for nothing agriculturally, it had long been abandoned to the reeds and moorhens which inhabited it, until it gave way, in the end, to merge into the sandy shingle of the beach at Aldeburgh. Harriet loved it, less because it led to the beach, and so to the sea, than because of its quality of wild mystery; the reeds in it out-topped her head as the meadowsweet in other places; the very water in it tasted brackish and bitter, since there the Alde joined forces with the daily influx from the sea. The place had not a good reputation, except for wildfowling — and Harriet had been forbidden to use it on the score of danger. The spice of danger being added to the spice of prohibition made it naturally irresistible, and she and Susan continued to use it, and to be punished when discovered so doing. The girls nevertheless persisted in walking by the forbidden Shearings, for — courageous both in their different ways — together they would have defied the world.

Harriet's high-water-mark of bravery, after the episode of defying her father, had occurred on a day which (Isaac Waters had prophesied) would be the last in the history of Redonda or indeed of anywhere else. The young man had, after a brief attachment to Wesleyanism, taken up with an extremist religion which specialized in eschatological phenomena — finally deciphering a date for the End of the World which coincided (conveniently enough) with that of a total eclipse of the sun. Isaac Waters, bearing this bad news to Redonda at a time when the eclipse had begun and when the master of the house was away on magisterial duties, successfully filled it with forebodings. Labour lagged, women wept, his young pupils locked themselves into their bedroom with their father's wine and tobacco, to make merry with these until the awful dream-like atmosphere of a day with its sun totally withdrawn induced them gropingly to join the company downstairs.

Isaac Waters had been moodily triumphant. With the servants congregated on the front steps watching the baleful light and waiting for the promised crack of doom, and with Clem and Clancy uneasy at his side — for once in a way he dominated the situation. Even the hysterics of the goosefeather girls, and the mutterings of Ivory and the brothers Anderson, were in their own poor way a tribute to him. He had said there would be an eclipse; there *was* an eclipse. He had said the End of the World would follow, and the End of the World assuredly would not be far behind. Mrs. Fitchet went so far as to stand on the top step beside him with her bag ready packed and a Bible in her hand. She was pale but resolute. She believed in him as she believed, invariably, all bearers of bad news, which was, nevertheless, 'for the best'.

One heretic alone had remained—Miss Harriet Bromewell. She would not even come outside for the End of the World, but sat at her bedroom window upstairs, looking down on them with contempt.

'Come down, Miss Harry, do!' begged Susan. Of the End of the World she could guess nothing except that, like an earthquake, it would bring the house about their ears.

'It is all nonsense, Sukey,' Harriet had said, her chin resting on her hands, her elbows on the windowsill. 'Mr. Waters would not dare to talk so if my father were home!'

'It is so dark!' Susan whispered.

Truly it was dark — dark and still, with all the Summer noises, the familiar comforting farmyard noises, silent in deference to coming dissolution.

'Lord, Lord, forgive us, we are miserable sinners!' intoned Isaac Waters.

'Amen!' chattered Ivory, 'Amen!' echoed the others.

'It is nonsense,' Harriet said again more loudly, 'you are a parcel of ignorant and foolish people! Eclipses cannot harm people! The Captain has told me of an eclipse when he was a young man, and *he* came to no harm!'

But hardly any of the servants turned their heads. It was part of the dream-like atmosphere, of course, that they should not. They dare not take their gaze off the blacked-out sun lest in so doing they might miss doing homage to the End of the World. *Prepare to meet thy God*, the Bible and Mr. Waters had told them — not prepare to obey Miss Harriet Bromewell. And it was so completely dark now that only God mattered any more.

'Go down, Susan!' commanded Harriet. She alone disbelieved in the End of the World. Susan was as stupid as the rest of them and should join them on the steps. 'Go down!' she repeated shrilly, without turning round. The scene before her was pitch-black now, with only the thinnest rim of light round the moon, and the figures below her mere shadows.

Susan whispered through dry lips: 'I dar'sn't leave you to die, Miss Harry — not up here be your lonesome!'

'I shall *not* die, it is all nonsense, I tell you! Go, go at once!'

Susan had obeyed then, going downstairs to squat at the foot of the staircase, her head buried in her petticoats (as she afterwards confessed) and her teeth chattering. She would die within reach of Harriet, come what may!

'All we like sheep have gone astray,' intoned Isaac Waters.

Amen, said Ivory, *Amen* said the servants, crowding their agreement on to the heels of his words to show how ready they were—how little they wished to be caught napping by catastrophe. The world waited, black, sardonic, the violently bright ring of light round the black moon trembling as if with suppressed laughter. Perhaps, thought Harriet, he is right after all, and this *is* the End of the World.

But how *could* it be the End of the World with her father away from home? Only unimportant events took place in his absence — unless one counted the time that Silversides the pedigree mare had dropped her foal and laid on it. Thirty guineas the siring of that foal had cost and nothing to show for it afterwards but a dead foal with a coat as silky-wrinkled as a kid glove. . . .

Staring straight at the ringed moon, Harriet defied the End of the World. With all her force she willed it not to happen, praying against the fools and the faint-hearted down below, hard, hard, like swimming against the tide.

'O Lord, lighten our darkness with Thy supernatural light!' said Isaac Waters. 'Take us to Abraham's Bosom forjesuschrisake amen!'

'Amen, amen, Lord forgive us!' prayed the congregation about him.

Sun come out come out come OUT, prayed Harriet, through clenched teeth, with clenched fists pressed against her cheeks, *O Sun come out and let my Father come home!*

She prayed so hard that her stomach felt like a band of iron round her and she could hear the blood ticking in her wrists — end-of-the-world, end-of-the-world. . . . For seconds that dragged into minutes and minutes into hours. . . .

And then, of course, the sun had come out again and the world had *not* come to an end and Harriet had retired from her window and been quietly and very thoroughly sick in her basin.

And that was that. Incidentally she had scored a second authoritarian victory in the eyes of Redonda, and her brothers less than ever liked to linger anywhere near such a know-all. She had stayed inside the house and defied the Eclipse from her window while they had gone below to join the souls waiting to be saved. From so ignominious a memory nothing in their youth could ever protect them.

That was Harriet's kind of bravery — a bravery against the Unknown, yet sudden noise could frighten her as it never disturbed the more stolid Susan. Once when they were returning through the park from some expedition both girls were overtaken by a summer storm — a 'tempest' in Redonda parlance. The sky had blackened then, though not so ominously as during the Eclipse, and thunder and lightning had roared their guns and flashed their swords from the sky. They began to run through a hail of bullets of pattering raindrops, Harriet keeping to the drive, Susan edging away towards the trees to get under cover.

Though frightened almost out of her senses, Harriet retained enough of them to remember that trees were dangerous companions in a storm.

'Keep to the drive!' she called, still running for dear life towards Redonda.

Susan had returned, and running obediently at Harriet's side, with wet yellow hair plastered down each side of her wet face, had panted:

'Oi was lookin' fer an elder-bush, Miss Harry. Th'owd Cross was made of elder-wood. Reckon we sh'd be safe under that —'

Harriet panted, in her turn: 'Do you believe that?'

'Ef I was to die for sayin' that, I believe it —'

Still running through the deafening downpour, Harriet said: '*I* don't believe it.'

Susan after all had believed in the End of the World when the Eclipse came. It didn't do to believe things — only to stand up against them and overcome them. *She* did not even believe that her prayers that day had triumphed over Mr. Waters'. The world would probably *never* end, that was all there was to it. So of course nothing had happened and her prayers, or rather her instructions to God, had been quite unnecessary.

Susan was a silly baby and a servant. Servants believed all sorts of nonsense, her father said so. Old wives' tales and parsons' stories. (Another roar from the gun — another sword!) She was terrified again, would like to believe the elder-bush theory, but daren't. 'Run! Run!' she gasped.

Pity them as you see them, two small drenched figures, battling their way against blinding wind and rain towards the house. Never had the drive seemed so long, the park so deserted . . . Another jagged streak of lightning, another deafening peal —

Harriet's nerve gave way. Drenched, frightened finally beyond words or will power, she suffered herself to be dragged off the drive on to the grass by her companion, to the advantage of the shelter proffered by a gaunt and dripping holly-bush — there to crouch down.

With teeth chattering so that she could hardly articulate, Harriet asked: 'Are we past the quarry yet?'

The quarry was a well-known landmark to them, exactly half-way between the road and the house.

'Reckon we're well past the quarry, Love.'

And when the fury of the storm grew with what it fed on, and a peal of deep thunder followed close on the lightning-flash, seeming to split the very sky wide open above their heads, Harriet was not ashamed to bury her face in Susan's neck, gripping Susan's shoulders with her nervous hands and feeling Susan's comforting arms about her, hugging her tightly, and Susan's ordinary voice saying: ''Tis nothing, Love. Don't be frightened, Love, reckon there's nothin' to that but a great old noise . . .' And noting inwardly without protesting (for so great was her distress just then) that 'Love' was what Susan called Mrs. Fitchet in moments of confidence — and the goosefeather girls, and kittens and ducklings — but never, *never* Miss Bromewell.

Apart from class distinctions, it was unfitting that a girl of eleven should be protectress to a great girl of fourteen. It was odd that neither of these considerations carried much weight at the time.

CHAPTER VIII

PREPARATIONS FOR A WEDDING

... But most of all would I flee
From the terrible madness of Love. ...

TENNYSON

HISTORIC events never weighed heavily upon the serene acres of Redonda and its neighbourhood. The grass blades made recumbent by the invading foot of Belgic tribes had sprung upwards again and withered in complete forgetfulness before ever the Roman sandal pressed downwards their descendants. They in their turn sprung upwards, blew for a season merrily in the salt wind and turned to rustling ghosts of themselves before the Saxons and the Danes succeeded to the occupation of that coastline and its towns and villages, rivers, burial-grounds, fortifications and farmlands. The years passed; the invaders themselves passed and through it all East Anglia itself remained unaffected. The grass continued to grow, the corn to shake in the wind, the trees to drop their leaves each autumn, the yellow paigles to sprinkle the meadows each spring—whatever the human beings passing so temporarily to and fro upon its surface might be doing; whatever Crown or Church they acknowledged. As for the Continent — well, the Continent and its continual alarums had been long ago (by an act of Divine Wisdom) separated from East Anglia by waters broad enough to keep it in its place. Invasion itself seemed a thing of the past, for only the tides invaded now, and their activities on blustery nights were better worth discussion than the activities of men, who were foreigners at that. Even an alarum as portentous as the French Revolution was hardly more than a nine days' wonder in East Anglia. The general feeling expressed in market places and in farmers' ordinaries was that foreigners were queer cattle in any case; a few more straws in the hair really counted for very little, one way or the other.

Harriet Bromewell remembered the year of the French Revolution chiefly as the year in which she first adopted a powdered coiffure. She was seventeen years old and, in honour of her elder brother's wedding, she had chosen the hair-style of Marie Antoinette, just as that unhappy queen was about to discard it for ever. The barber from Ipswich had been sent for and Harriet had been transformed, under his ministrations, into a vision of splendour. She sat now before her glass with her grave face confronting her in the mirror and Susan's hands hovering correctively over the swept-up horns of white hair. Which was more pleased with the result, it would be impossible to say.

As well as a new coiffure, Harriet had a new dress — a silk one. This event (which took place only once every five years or so) was occupying her mind quite as much as the coiffure. She had tossed her old cream-coloured corded silk to Susan and had chosen, for the wedding, a blue-purple of the colour of the bloom on a plum. The silk was Chinese silk, of a texture smooth as rain-water and on the inside of its capacious hem (ah, *this* it was which rejoiced her as she viewed herself in the mirror!) was a narrow border in a design of peacock's feathers — black, blue, green and gold — embroidered in minute and most exquisite stitchery, so perfect in its detail that it was easy to believe what Harriet had been told by the shopman — that the Chinese embroidresses of such dresses went blind after working upon three.

'Oh, Miss Harriet!' breathed Susan, fingering the hem of the new gown as it lay opulently displayed upon the bed: 'to do work like this and then to hide it upon the inside of the hem where nobody can't see it!'

'*I* see it!' replied Harriet.

'But nobody else, Miss!'

'Perhaps I prefer it that way. It makes it more my own,' said Harriet. As a rule she was not particularly interested in her wardrobe, but the staggering cost of this new dress, together with its secret embroidery of peacock-feathers, excited and charmed her as no garment had ever done before — and more than she would care to admit. The folds of silk had exuded a strange fragrance when first lifted from the box — delicate, subtle, a fragrance utterly foreign to Redonda. For the first time in her life it had suggested to Harriet that there might be other places outside Redonda — outside England even — worth seeing, worth loving; but only for a moment or two.

The Marie Antoinette coiffure was an uncomfortable one. It dragged the powdered hair up from her slender neck and piled it on top; it pulled the hair back from her brow over a padded shape so that — as she said to Susan — it looked as if she had a white turban upon her head instead of hair. Susan stared without speaking, as her mistress manipulated the hand-mirror — twisting this way and that, viewing the finished effect from all angles.

'D'you think it becomes me, Suke,' said she, 'to be white instead of black?'

The younger girl did not answer immediately. It was not that Harriet Bromewell was suddenly made beautiful by this grown-up coiffure, or that she minded Harriet Bromewell's beauty; it was because she was made so suddenly conscious, in contrast, of her own plainness. Beauty and the Beast. So it had seemed to her once long before, when the two little girls had been occupied, one day, in hopefully dropping horsehairs into a pool that they might be transformed into eels. When the troubled surface stilled for a moment the prettiness of the dark-haired child and the plainness of the fair-haired one had gazed up from the water beneath them, with the clarity of very truth. Susan had perceived the contrast and wept silently for a minute. Harriet had perceived neither the tears nor their cause, being intent upon the horsehairs and their to-be-expected transformation into elvers.

'Your eyes look darker, Miss Harry, and larger,' said Susan finally.

Harriet, sitting upright before her mirror, still twirling her hand-mirror this way and that, turned her top-heavy head so that the delicious smooth line of nape and shoulder, or brow and cheek, might peep out at her first from one side, then from the other. All she said was:

'It will need jewels.'

'Jewels, Miss Harry?'

'The dress,' said Harriet impatiently. 'And you must not call me

Miss Harry any more now, Sukey. I am seventeen and it is not becoming.'

'Reckon when Miss Hannah Bromewell come she'll see about jewels,' said Susan.

'Pah!' Harriet swept the suggestion from her, rising and prowling about the room in her long stays with the flounced lemon-coloured petticoat bursting out beneath them like a pale daffodil trumpet out of its sheath. She stole covert glances at herself in the mirror as she whisked to and fro. She wanted to see the effect of a smile bestowed upon and coming from this counterpart of herself but was far too proud to attempt it with a servant in the room.

Susan, kneeling, tidying up Harriet's discarded slippers and stockings, said no more. She was aware (as the whole household was) of the deep cleavage of opinion between father and daughter over the matter of Miss Hannah Bromewell's visit. Aunt Hannah, as Harriet had told her father with emphasis, had never stirred out of Westmorland to see him or his children in the whole of her seventeen years; yet now, because there was a wedding — because Clem, forsooth, was marrying from Redonda — and Redonda itself was to hold its first big house-party since the death of Mrs. Bromewell — Aunt Hannah could not resist it. She must come bouncing down from Westmorland to usurp Harriet's place as mistress of the house and — crowning insult! — to supervise her niece's behaviour.

Captain Bromewell had made matters worse by hinting at the gifts his sister would bring with her: fleeces from her own Westmorland flocks to be woven into blankets and shawls for the Happy Couple (coals to Newcastle, commented Harriet); cases of extra fine tobacco for the Captain and for Clancy; garments for Harriet. 'The girl will of course have nothing fit to wear,' she had written, 'since Sophy's jewels were lost on the way over, and the garnets —'

The letter continued at great length about the garnets. They were priceless it appeared; exquisitely set in silver; any young girl would go mad to possess them — count herself a queen to wear them.

'I hope she is not one of your insipid creatures,' wrote Aunt Hannah, 'for the garnets will look pale on a pale girl and lose all their fire. But if she is as I expect your daughter to be she will do honour to the necklace and bracelet.'

A fine way of putting it! Harriet to do honour to the garnets — not the garnets to Harriet! Even the Captain, under Harriet's withering scorn, could see the phrase had not been happily chosen. 'She means well, Harry,' he said. 'And you know it's right you should have some finery since your mother's is at the bottom of the Atlantic. I've never bought you any — a trinket-shop is no place for a farmer — but at a wedding it is right you should make their eyes wink and your aunt will know what suits a young girl best —'

Harriet had demanded to be told the colour of garnets.

'Why — a sort of blood colour — a deep red —'

Whereupon Harriet had ordered a blue silk dress the colour of plum bloom. Fashion's intricacies lay outside her scope but even a fool knew one could not wear red jewellery with a blue dress! So she defied her aunt, in advance.

And when the dress had come, and Harriet had tried it on again and marvelled at its silky softness and the delicious secret of the peacock's feather embroidery brushing her ankles, she had confessed, almost without knowing it, 'It needs jewels'.

But not the garnets! Never, never, *never* garnets! No, she would not wear garnets, though she died with refusing!

The wedding was to be solemnized at the chief church in Bury St. Edmunds. After it Clement and his bride were to join the wedding-feast at Redonda, stay one night there, and proceed thereafter to London, where Clem's doting father-in-law waited to hand them their tickets for Vienna, a substantial dowry and his blessing. Clem had certainly stepped into good fortune. Precisely how he had done it his family could not guess, but the dashing young man had certainly won the goodwill of Sir Joshua Lowndes together with the hand of Miss Sophy. 'Influence', wielded by Sir Joshua, had propelled Clem out of his studentship at the Inns of Court — procured for him by the ever-obliging Mr. Marsham — and into the Diplomatic Service instead. He was to take up a junior appointment in Vienna directly after the wedding.

Thus much the family knew. Of the bride herself, very little. The Captain, influenced by the fact that she bore his wife's name and brought Clem ten thousand pounds, waxed appreciative over the prospect of her in the evenings. Clancy, still tied to Redonda as a dog to its kennel, and chafing to share Clem's London life, envied his brother his marriage as he envied him everything else. Harriet, when shown an engraving of the young lady in question, scrutinized her dispassionately and told Clement she had popping eyes and too short a neck.

'You will breed children like frogs,' she said.

The Captain roared with laughter. 'Not like frogs!' he protested. 'Damn it, Harry — not like Frenchmen! Clem couldn't let the family down so low as to breed Frenchmen!'

Clement was not amused; such pleasantries offended him as a budding diplomat and as a *fiancé*. 'We are at peace with them now, sir,' he said. 'There's no call to abuse the French, *or* Sophy!'

'As to Miss Sophy, you'll be doing the abusing yourself before very long,' countered his parent. 'But Frenchmen! He belched, and hit his boot with his whip to cover it. 'Frenchmen are frogs and always will be! Long live Old England! Down with the frogs! — And don't come the fine diplomat over *me*, Clem, for I won't stand it!'

Clancy was better company for the young bridegroom-to-be. If he did not envy Clem the particular hand of Miss Lowndes, he envied him the dowry she brought, the Vienna appointment, all the freedom and fun of life in London which had led up to these *desiderata*. 'I am as sick of Redonda,' he confided to his brother, 'as I can well be. Game is shy, sport is poor, and it's my belief Father and the poachers have scraped the place bare between 'em.'

'Stock it afresh,' Clem advised.

'What — to have it stolen under our noses?' (He touched here on a topical grievance, temporarily sunk into the background during the wedding celebrations.) 'Half the able-bodied fellows have left, I tell you — slipped off overnight to the north to work on the looms there. They've heard there's more money there than in farm-work. But they leave their teeming families behind 'em, damn them — and the boys aren't above lifting our rabbits and pheasants. What's one keeper to twenty poachers?'

'You need a couple of those new man-traps,' said Clem, yawning more at the subject than at anything else. 'Set 'em right, and they'll break a man's neck as soon as look at him. Have you seen the teeth on them? Fearsome things!' And he clicked his own good teeth together after another yawn. With his fancies already disporting themselves upon the Continent he really could not spare enough interest from them to solve Clancy's problems.

'I doubt Father would spare the money for the traps,' gloomed Clancy. 'Bloodstock is all the cry these days!'

'If it pays him, he'll do it.'

'Ah, but how to persuade him it'll pay him? I tell you the stud-book is his Bible these days! He takes his sport where he can get it — doesn't lay out on it any more as a gentleman ought to! It's all Clydesdale stallions and Suffolk punches! He reckons to set the world on fire with Suffolk punches, the old — !'

The strangeness of this operation did not apparently amaze the listener; perhaps because his Viennese fancies still held the centre of the stage. Dimly through the halls and mirrors, the beauties waltz-ing, with Sophy's image approaching and receding through a revolving hail of discs marvellously like golden guineas, Clem could hear his brother's voice complaining on in a steady drizzle.

'Nothing for the guns . . . Nothing for the dogs. I want ye at home, he says, to learn the way of things. It'll be yours when I'm gone if Clem doesn't choose to farm it. But damn him he's so close with it, and so short when you ask him questions, and he bores me so when he stands out in the cold all those hours talking to Spens, that I could die of the whole thing!'

'He lets Harriet in on to it. She was doing the accounts with him last night,' said the heartless Clem. Clancy groaned agreement.

'That's another thing! Harriet slips in under his elbow and picks things up in that devilish quiet way of hers, you — looking at things as if she could eat 'em if that would help her to understand 'em any better — and I *can't*! Besides, she's brighter than I am, I know that . . . And *she'd* put her foot down on any more pheasant coverts! It's all poultry with her — and geese and ducklings! She wants the grain for *them*, and what's more she keeps the key of it!'

'To hell with her, anyway,' yawned Clem, echoing a favourite sentiment of their boyhood. But the mention of ducks reminded him. 'Let's go after the wildfowl,' he said. '*They*'ll still be there, at least!'

Clancy needed no second asking. Taking their guns and a couple of their father's dogs, they went down through the Shearings, following the streamlet of the Alde (by the way Harriet and Susan had travelled so often as children) until it grew wide and reedy, where pollard willows clustered in a group. A punt had been kept moored in this spot as long as they could remember. They took it now and loosed it, launching themselves, crouching, into the silent salty dusk which promised the sport they loved.

It was a Spring dusk, with the daylight withdrawing from the sky so reluctantly that the yellow paigles, or cowslips, still shone in the meadows each side of them, as if illumined from within. Here and there, between the meadows, more water gleamed up between the paigles — copper, bronze, leaden-coloured — according to the way the receding light still lay upon it, but all still as glass. It was a scene familiar to them from their youth, but to-night for the first time — perhaps because it was likely that it would be, for so long, the *last* time — it touched the hearts of the two boys not only with pleasure but with a momentary solemnity, much as it would have touched their sister's. They did not say anything. Clancy knelt in the bows, with his cold hands clasping the gun-barrel. Clem, behind him, paddled with the short oars, and the little craft sped on into the shadows. A whispering ripple behind them, repeating itself over and over, carried some message to the dark banks which caused the tall reeds there to bend their heads together and shake them for a moment of time.

A courting snipe, invisible in the distances of dusk, sent his tiny drumming reverberating down upon them and upon the meadows. Farther away, fainter still, a bittern boomed like a gong.

Clancy said, tossing his head in the direction of the sound but not turning it:

'That's a rise in the price o' wheat!'

Clem grunted affirmatively. A man-about-town, a diplomat-to-be, a bridegroom of the morrow — he could hardly concern himself with these local superstitions.

'Ah well,' Clancy went on. 'It'll please the Governor, anyway.

He went mad at the wheat prices this year; came back from Market black in the face with temper, swore he'd turn off half the land to pasture and beasts if things didn't improve. He will, too, at Michaelmas, I shouldn't wonder. Prices have been shocking since the peace.'

Clem rested on his paddles, head bowed over his knees, ears unhearing, eyes gazing unseeing into the bottom of the punt, intent only upon the future. The two dogs, smelling unaccountably of fish, leaned against his knees, shivering more with excitement than with cold. The future they are concerned with is less remote than his. Meanwhile the dusk, grey, tender, melancholy, passed its tenderness like a hand over all these finite creatures, these tiny *animalcules* with their hopes and fears, setting off so determinedly to be clasped into the night's nethermost and closest folds. Neither young man is perhaps very worthy. Clem is ambitious, selfish, greedy to possess all things, to 'see life'; to eat it up and spew out the parts of it he doesn't care for, as his father has done before him; Clancy is less ambitious, a trifle less selfish, but just as determined, in his slow-coach way, not to be downtrodden or outshone by his brother. Both are rather small, rather mean; of utter unimportance — if one examines them in large perspective — to their country or century. Nevertheless at this precise grey-green moment, when with their mutual youth and hopefulness they slip, slender as minnows, into the shadows together, one must pity them! The spring evening about them is so poignant, putting on its crepuscular perfections so gradually, with the perfume of cowslips and the fluting of blackbirds for accompaniment. But so many other equally lovely, equally cowslip-decked, bird-haunted springs have passed since then, and the river which bore their craft that night has flowed so far since then, and both brothers have been so long dead and forgotten, so very long dead, so completely forgotten! Nothing remains of them and that casual expedition, except perhaps an invisible essence of youth and hope and liveliness in the air, palpitating over the perennial reeds at the waterside, anchored there (if we could see it) as surely as the fragment of a woman's dress, caught on a twig and shaking with every breeze, its print faded from many summers' exposure.

With heavy head and aching neck, and wrapped in a voluminous

Paisley shawl, Miss Harriet Bromewell of Redonda sat in her sitting-room upstairs, awaiting the arrival of her Aunt Hannah. A padded cushion filled the hollow between head and shoulders and this was to be her only pillow during the night, since so complicated and magnificent a coiffure made any sort of reclining out of the question. Sitting there in the quiet of the falling dusk, with the discreet noise of servants preparing a meal drifting up from time to time from below, she, too, heard the booming of the far-off bittern and smiled at her image in the glass, at the idea of a rise in the price of wheat. The image, under its towering, glittering head-dress, smiled back. If wheat rose, her father would perhaps listen to her on the subject of horn and corn. She had warned him, some time back, that his passion for pedigree beasts could go too far. What were beasts without good well-dunged pasture to run them on — without hay and straw, without turnips and swedes for winter feeding? To concentrate entirely on cattle was, in Harriet's youthful opinion, to make a mock of Redonda's spacious acreage which, if adequately managed, could carry scores of heads of such beasts and still produce wheat better than any other in the district — *and* barley, rippling like Rapunzel's hair! Where else could you find barley like Redonda's? Where else did it grow to such perfection as in these low-lying coastal fields?

With eyes closed, scalp tight and tingling, head resting gingerly against the back of her chair, Harriet plunged her hands deep into the folds of her shawl, feeling again in imagination the grain sliding through her fingers as she plunged her hands, wrist deep, wriggling down and down, elbow-deep, into the cool musty-smelling sacks of barley-grain out in the Great Barn. To feel this plenitude running through her fingers had been to Harriet a keenly voluptuous pleasure for as long as she could remember. So, she had always known, must a miser feel, handling his money.

The barley-grain was cloven so neatly, two plump swelling sides with a dip between them like the dip between a woman's breasts. She raised her hands at the thought, cupped her breasts with them, pressing violently against the Paisley shawl until it hurt her. Something of this pain would be her sister-in-law Sophy's lot to-morrow night, for Clem would be clumsy, she was sure. She recalled Clem's face for a moment, flushed and swollen in a sudden access of sexual excitement — as when she had encountered him once down by the hedge in the Long Field, at harvest. There was a woman crying, where Harriet could not see her, behind the hedge. She had wanted to see her, it was aggravating to be kept in the dark about anything, but that was one time when she had not been able to prevail over her brother's intentions. But she remembered *him* with malicious exactitude — the beads of perspiration on his forehead and upper lip, the blurring of his features, his quick breathing, dishevelled clothing and the heat of his hands as he had seized her roughly by the shoulders (she shuddered her shoulders slightly now at the recollection) and pushed her away, before him, out of the field.

She shuddered more at the idea of sex than at this particular manifestation of it. If this was the way humans behaved when they coupled, she despised them! The symptoms were always despicable, whether evinced in her father — yes, even in him! — or in Clement or Clancy. That it took and shook all of them from time to time she knew, just as from time to time they took a passion for drinking themselves silly. Afterwards there were sulks and curses, and some woman on Redonda's estate would vanish, temporarily or permanently. One, a freckled creature called Jemima Roffey, wife of a cowman, had been found — after some such bout — drowned in the Alde. (Captain Bromewell, whose arrival at the magistracy coincided most conveniently with this affair, had guided the jury with efficient zest and a sure hand on the reins to a verdict of Accidental Death.) Whether her father or one of her brothers had been implicated in the Roffey affair Harriet never knew, but she suspected the Captain — despising the preliminaries of the whole thing and yet admiring the finish. 'Well, *that's* done with!' he had said. She understood that! It was like an animal, calm, unself-conscious, unregretful — feeding one minute, coupling the next, feeding again the next. The fever surged, subsided, left them free again. Her father could shake it off almost as easily as his prize bull. That at *least* was admirable!

Not so her brothers, or the various women about the place who were so foolish as, from time to time, to fall in love. They became sick, langorous, useless as broody hens; she detested the soft unseeing eyes, the slow movements that were symptomatic of such attacks. Heaven preserve *her* from such vapourings, declared Harriet silently (as every girl in her teens has, at some time or other, likewise declared). Her breasts might heave and swell under her hands as she held them now — as they did now — but *never* if she could help it with the stress of love; any other passion but that!

It was while she sat there, half-dreaming, half-dozing, that Miss Hannah Bromewell, accompanied by the Captain, fell upon Redonda like one of her own north-country rivers in full spate. She overflowed everybody and everything, bursting eventually even into the dreamland in which Harriet sat, as a tide might break through clenched lock-gates.

Forgetting her top-heavy head-dress for the moment, Harriet leapt to her feet, swaying a little to recover consciousness and balance. The candles were not yet lit, and in the dusky light her father roared out that she had a turban on and did she intend to go to the wedding as a Cannibal Queen? When he came closer —

'Don't touch me!' she said sharply. 'The hairdresser has been.'

Mrs. Fitchet glided in with the candles, placing them as advantageously as she could behind her baby, her darling, her adored mistress. The voluminousness of the Paisley shawl seemed to minimize Harriet despite Mrs. Fitchet's intentions, and Miss Hannah was not impressed by the small figure she saw before her. She advanced in full flood, shaking all her flounces and bringing an odour of orris-root with her. She tipped up Harriet's chin with a finger and thumb which might have been of iron, so firm and unrelaxing were they.

'The child looks peaked,' she said to her brother, for all the world as if Harriet were not there. 'What's the matter? Has she been ill? Why is she not dressed? What is all this tomfoolery on top of her?'

The Captain, in one of his gay and unreliable moods, tweaked Mrs. Fitchet's apron strings undone as she passed him — an old joke which never failed to amuse him. He had already drunk very bountifully and was pleased with everybody and everything, including his charming and ridiculous daughter in her turban or what-d'ye-may-call-em.

Harriet was, however, quite sober and therefore taken aback by such a beginning. She had intended — if only she had not dozed! — to slip into her second-best gown and be down to welcome the visitor on the door-step, making quite clear that she received her aunt as a hostess receives a guest. But all this had been frustrated by her falling asleep. Instead she had been greeted herself (in all the disadvantage of *déshabillé*) with 'The child looks peaked'.

Withdrawing her bare toes as well as she could under her petticoats, she replied for her father and herself:

'It's the latest Paris coiffure.'

'Very fine, now I see it in the light. Ve-ry fine,' declared Captain Bromewell, tipping backwards and forwards on his toes before Harriet's fireplace, warming his hindquarters before Harriet's fire.

'Birds and Bows!' remarked Miss Hannah Bromewell, exploding her b's with colossal scorn. She even went so far as to flip the tail of the bird-of-paradise (which topped the coiffure) with an irreverent forefinger. It quivered quite as much with Harriet's indignation as with this action.

'Upon my word, I don't know where this silliness is to stop!' went on her aunt. 'We spend our lives fighting the French and then ape all their fashions. If their laws are good for nothing how can the clothes they dress themselves up in be any the better? Folly could go no farther! . . . Come into the light where I can see you,' she added in a gentler tone.

Harriet, being examined by candlelight in her own room, without permission or compunction, stood as rigid as a rock.

'Don't bite your lips, child,' said her aunt, 'you'll spoil them and they're pretty, or would be if you left 'em alone. Not a bit like her mother,' she threw back over her shoulder at the Captain. Somehow the general impression was received, without any need for further explanation, that this un-likeness was all to the good. Harriet, still pinching her upper lip between her teeth, still stood rigid, while her aunt went on exploring the lines of her face and figure, with greedy affection. It seemed that the sight could not tire her, despite her long journey. A pretty girl, after all, is a restorative for more than one sex and age.

'Well,' said Miss Hannah finally, with a sigh of repletion, 'I suppose you'll do. At least they'll have something to look at besides the bride and that was what you wanted, eh, Tom?'

This sudden and unexpected addressing of her father by a name nobody else had called him for years made Harriet glance swiftly across at him as if expecting to see another person in his place — but it was still her father. He was whistling, 'Softly go down', to his boots and smiling to himself foolishly, as he had done time and again when he was in a good humour, as she knew he would always do.

'Have you a sweetheart, child?'

The question prodded her as sharply in the mind as her aunt's hand had prodded her back — feeling her, touching her with an odious and matter-of-fact intimacy as she never *had* been touched, stroking her down as if she were a nervous filly to be gentled into submission. She heard herself answering shrilly:

'I *detest* sweethearts!' hoping it sounded great lady-ish, fearing it sounded childish (as it did). The quivering plume of her birds-tail head-dress shook in a great dark shadow against the wall, emphasizing her detestation.

'Nonsense,' said her aunt briskly, sweeping away such a notion as easily as she swept to the best chair in the room — Harriet's own chair — and sat down in it amid a dying sigh of silks and flounces. 'Every girl of any capacity and sense has a sweetheart, isn't that so, Tom?'

'I don't *wish* one! I don't intend to marry!' shrilled Harriet again. The shockingness of the speed with which this oppressive woman worked quite appalled her. She had been in the house but five minutes, in Redonda five minutes, and already was criticizing and analysing and overpowering Harriet's whole life! Sheer nervousness — a vague dread that in some way her own position there, her very security, was threatened — made her counter-attack.

'*You* never married, Aunt,' she said.

'Not for want of being asked, Miss,' replied Miss Hannah Bromewell. 'I had my chances, didn't I, Tom, hey?'

'Softly go down, go down' continued its pleasant course, undisturbed and undisturbing.

'And then there was your Uncle Lucas to care for.'

'Lucas?'

'Yes. He was killed out hunting before you were ever born. Somebody had to manage him, and his farm after him, when he was gone —'

'A wonderful woman, your aunt,' the Captain announced, stopping 'Softly go down' just long enough to pay this surprising tribute and then resuming again. His hindquarters were warm from the fire, his stomach and head with brandy; he could afford to dispense verbal largesse. Harriet, sober and chilly by the window, had time to note to herself that, however wonderful her aunt might be, Captain Bromewell had never been roused before to pay her such a compliment. As for her Uncle Lucas, she had never even *heard* of him. . . .

'We must find her a good match, Tom,' announced Miss Bromewell from the chair. Harriet's head, already sufficiently burdened, began to sing. She stamped with her bare foot.

'I tell you I shan't ever marry!' she repeated. 'I help my father. Isn't that so, Father? I help him with Redonda.'

Her aunt snorted. Swiftly, almost piteously, Harriet rushed on. 'If you can do it, why can't I?'

'For three excellent reasons,' replied her aunt. 'Firstly, I was never a beauty, and you are, if you would learn to stand straight and not pull your mouth about in that grimacing manner. Secondly, a beauty always marries well, or should, else she shames her family. Thirdly, your father has Clement — or is it Clancy — to inherit Redonda and to look after it when he is gone.' Concluding, she placed her two hands together, one crossed upon the other in her capacious lap, with a finality that suggested the whole subject had been entered upon, thrashed out and settled once and for ever amen.

Suddenly her old eyes, searching restlessly through the open door into the bedroom, lit upon the dress spread over the bed.

'Is that the gown?' she asked. 'Bring it here.'

Mrs. Fitchet, who had been hovering in the outer shadows, made for the door obediently.

'Nobody is to touch it!' cried Harriet.

Mrs. Fitchet stopped in her tracks.

'Country manners, I see,' said her aunt. 'Tom, you have spoilt this young woman. She has no more sense of fitness, of *obligations*, than a baby. You should have had a governess to her, years ago.'

'Aye, I often considered a governess,' agreed the Captain. He was in an agreeing mood. His daughter's eyes flashed contempt at him. The governess-considering was, she knew, an occupation born of the sixth or seventh glass; it concerned pretty young women cornered in remote corridors by the Captain rather than sensible females capable of imparting information and manners to his daughter.

'*Why* may I not see the dress, Harriet?'

Because it has a secret sewn along the inner hem, was the only possible answer — and you may not see it, or *anyone*. But obviously one could not say *that*.

'It is still damp from the pressing-room,' grudged Harriet.

'And you think I would spoil it?' responded Miss Bromewell. 'You have a mighty fine opinion of your relations, I am sure!' She continued after a pause, 'Come, let me see it, like a good girl. How can my old eyes tell from here whether it will suit the garnets?'

Harriet's shoulders shrugged ever so slightly beneath the shawl. Mrs. Fitchet, who lived by such signs, much as a dog does, accepted this assent and took up the precious gown in both arms — bearing it across the room like a baby, to Miss Hannah Bromewell.

'I see you like contrast,' the old lady said, thumbing a corner of the delicate silk. 'A silly girl would have chosen cream delaine or else a watery pink — but *you* plumped for blue! I couldn't have chosen better for the garnets myself!'

Still unflattered, unflatterable, Harriet answered sullenly: 'I don't intend to wear the garnets.'

As this terrible statement took up its position in the room, Mrs. Fitchet's doggy eyes rolled beseechingly between the two women, with an occasional wary glance reserved for that uncertain element, the Captain, in the background. If she had had an ear large enough to cock, she would certainly have cocked it.

However, if Harriet hoped to provoke her antagonist to an open quarrel, she did not know her aunt. Flat denials neither sent her into a passion — as invariably they sent the Captain — nor produced that appalled acquiescence typical of the rest of Redonda; they merely rolled off her, an old expert in the art of Straight Dealing and Plain Speaking, like water off the backs of the ducks in her own farmyard.

'Nonsense,' she said. 'Give me a hand up, Tom.' Groaning, she rose to her feet again, among her sighing flounces. 'I'm tired, and I won't listen to a silly child who doesn't know her own mind or what's good for her. Where are my rooms? Where's Ellen?'

An old servant, still hooded from the journey, waddled forward in answer. 'I'll have my dinner sent up, I think,' went on Miss Bromewell, pausing in the doorway and addressing her brother, not her niece, 'or my old bones won't be fit for the wedding to-morrow.'

Without another word she followed Ellen and the candle out into the corridor with Mrs. Fitchet dodging along behind them, indicating the way.

Baffled, raging, Harriet began to pace the space of floor between her two long windows — back and forth, back and forth, continually casting her shadow across her father in front of the fireplace. She would not trust herself to speak without a cue and yet could barely keep silence.

'You should have been more civil to her, Harry, ye know.'

'*Civil!* She comes here without by-your-leave, bursts into my room without it — yes, and you too! — as if I were a child to be picked up and tossed down again! Tells me this and tells me that, says my coiffure is tomfoolery, that I look peaked, that she must find me a good match, if you please — and then begins about the garnets! D'you think I want that old woman's garnets? I would die rather than wear them!'

'Softly go down, go down' the Captain advised his boots *sotto voce*, still balancing himself, first on heels then on toes, quite at his ease, before the fireplace.

'And she takes me by the shoulders, *touches* me,' went on his daughter — much as to say POLLUTES me — 'and all but pokes her fingers into my mouth to see my age as if I were one of our mares! And *then* you say I should have been more *civil* to her!'

'She called you a beauty and by God, Harry, I believe you are one!'

95

This admiringly from the Captain, not to placate the implacable but merely as a statement of fact, observed somewhat late in the day.

'Bah!' said Harriet, who would at that moment have thrown Beauty out of the window with the whole world's supply of garnets if she could. A thought of real pain and fear was gnawing at her heart behind all this superficial anger — the thought of Redonda ... 'She is like all old women! She wants a hundred weddings — not one!' She was still pacing the floor, flogging her father with her shadow. *Swish, swish, swish*, went the lemon-coloured petticoats under the Paisley shawl, depreciating, with such susurrations, the lustful interfering ambitions of all old women.

'If you will not marry,' teased her father, head on one side as he watched her, 'What will you do?'

She stopped still, 'I will stay here and look after Clancy as *she* looked after my Uncle Lucas!'

Captain Bromewell put his head back at that and laughed, ho-ho-hoing it in his familiar way. Harriet stamped her bare foot through the noise of it.

'Oh you are *odious*, Father!' she said. 'My aunt hurts and insults me and all you do is to laugh!'

'Not at you, my dear; at the notion of you and Clancy living here together in loving-kindness when I am gone!' But he became suddenly serious: 'Don't delude yourself, Harry. The boy will marry as his brother is doing and will bring his wife here. *She'll* be mistress then!'

But, fond though he was of his daughter, the thought of her thus supplanted was so delectably amusing he could not help laughing again.

'Why, I believe the notion of *you* sitting down taking orders from *her* will shake me out of my grave with laughing!'

This deliberate (so it seemed to her) savaging of her nerves, this deliberate blindness, on her father's part, to the real depths of her affection and devotion to the place where she had been born and reared, filled Harriet momentarily with such a brimming-over of hatred that, had a knife been within her reach, there is no saying what she might not have done. But there was no knife and she was barefoot — and anyway behind all the moment's urgency, loomed the large piteous *façade* of the house she adored.

She swallowed with difficulty. 'Redonda — ' she began.

But the gong under Ivory's ministrations boomed out its message, drowning the words on her lips.

'Not dressed *yet*?' mocked the Captain, following up his advantage.

'What will your aunt think of you as a hostess, ho, ho, ho!'

Harriet hardly heard him as he chuckled his way along to his own room, for she slammed the door on him. In the bedroom she found her second-best gown laid out by Susan and — on the dressing-table — Susan's necklace of cornelians.

A gift gains full significance only when presented at a suitable time. Harriet's eyes no sooner lighted on the cornelians than she knew Susan's purpose in begging for time off that afternoon. It had been to go to the rectory, to bring back from the rector there (who for long had been guardian of Susan's few material possessions as well as of her spiritual ones) the dearest possession of all — this necklace of cornelians.

The stones symbolized a part of the two girls' childhood. Together they had hunted for them, stumbling together over the shingle on Aldeburgh and Dunwich beaches, squatting over the strips of graded pebbles left there at low tide. Of all the clean bare gifts of the seashore the cornelians had always ranked highest. Their transparency had about it the wan light of sunsets, their shining qualities singled them out amongst the plebeian pebbles, calling *Come and find me*!

In those days Harriet had always desired the stones more ardently than Susan, and had found them less easily. Her own collection, paltry and ill-assorted, lay long forgotten at the bottom of some small drawer or tidy-box. It had been a grievance to her that she, Miss Bromewell, should have been treated so cavalierly by Nature on such occasions, and that Susan should have been inexplicably rewarded with such bounty. So, since Harriet was impatient by nature, her part in the expeditions had gradually ceased and the more patient Susan had gone on alone, searching the wet shingle year after year, for the semi-precious stones, and gradually discarding, in the fullness of time, the ill-shaped for the well-shaped, the small and opaque for the large and purely transparent. Such perseverance had been rewarded, for the kind old rector, impressed by it, had himself paid for the collection to be set on a silver chain and had presented it to this humble parishioner with an injunction not to love the world of which (alas!) it formed a part.

The necklace was, Harriet knew, Susan's dearest possession, but alas for the ill-chosen moment of its presentation! She had flounced into her bedroom in a mood utterly unable to accept anything gracefully from anybody. Surprised for a second, she took up the stones in her hand, crunching their glowing coldness together and smiling darkly — not at Susan's kindness in giving it to her — this necklace so much finer than her own had ever been — but rather at Susan's stupidity in supposing that a sunset-coloured necklace could ever match with the new blue dress. That they had been submitted as an alternative to the garnets, she had no doubt. Harriet had said of the dress, 'It needs jewellery' — had despised the garnets in advance — and Susan out of her impossible, idiotic devotion, had given her the cornelians to take their place.

'I may be a country booby,' she told her image in the glass, but really addressing her Aunt Hannah, not herself — 'but you shan't catch me out wearing yellow beads with a blue gown! Even if I have to go bare-necked, you shan't do *that*!'

Soon after that she flung off her Paisley shawl to dress for the evening meal, and part of it had fallen across the cornelian necklace, putting it out of sight as well as out of mind.

And since she spent the rest of the night, as aforesaid, sitting up in a high-backed chair in the sitting-room, so as not to ruin her coiffure, the necklace never came into the picture again.

CHAPTER IX

THE DAY AND THE NIGHT

These violent delights have violent ends,
And in their triumph die, like fire and powder.

SHAKESPEARE

CAPTAIN BROMEWELL had had good reasons for selecting a particular day for the wedding in Bury. Once every month, in the week following the full moon, he had held an assignation with Everybody's Friend, otherwise Captain Twigg, at the tavern of the Blue Goose in that same town — for almost as long as he had lived at Redonda. This had proved to their mutual advantage. Captain Bromewell had regularly handed over to the kind care of Captain Twigg various consignments of Redonda's cheese, butter and bales of wool for transport to the Netherlands and had received, as regularly, payment in cash, or in wines, tobacco or a certain very fine linen from Normandy which made up into incomparable shirts and sheetings. Other persons might consider that these transactions came under the crude title of smuggling; Captain Bromewell and Captain Twigg never put a name to them but on occasion they could both be heard inveighing loudly against smuggling as a general practice; while Captain Bromewell had even gone so far as to sign a petition — in company with several other East Anglian farmers and landowners — beseeching the Chief Minister, Mr. Pitt, to look into the Ruinous Activities of the smugglers along their own particular stretch of coastline.

Captain Twigg — not being a landowner — had not been asked to sign such a petition. But he too could play a part. So he had volunteered, as Master of the fishing-smack *Speedwell*, and with the lads of the companion smacks *Sweetheart* and *Peggy Tovey*, to assist the Royal Navy in keeping what he described as a wholly tidy and valiant look-out for smugglers over that part of the sea roughly covered by his (legitimate) trade of herring-fishery.

The Admiralty had received the offer with gratification and had been pleased to award to Captain Twigg, otherwise Everybody's Friend, a badge with mermaids and His Majesty King George the Third inextricably entwined upon it, as a sign of his position as servant of the Government. Their Lordships had also been prompt to thank Captain Bromewell, J.P., for his kind and useful recommendation of Twigg in such a capacity. *He is as honest and trustworthy as I am*, Captain Bromewell had written. This was true enough — though perhaps not quite in the way that their Lordships understood it.

Naturally the transactions between both these parties had been, in the past, advantageous to both, otherwise they would not have continued so uninterruptedly. If Captain Bromewell could have wished for any improvement, it would have been that Captain Twigg's offices were less plaguey far from Redonda — but that was all. If Everybody's Friend could have wished for any improvement it would have been that Captain Bromewell had allowed him to use his ingenuity a little more — had desired him to procure merchandise rather rarer and more exciting than French wines, bolsters and baccy. For Captain Twigg had a romantic soul and liked to think of himself as a magic djinn, born to delight and amaze the dull country bumpkins who employed him.

But, although Captain Bromewell was his largest customer, he had never really allowed Captain Twigg to use any imagination. The suggestion of perfumes for his daughter had been impatiently brushed aside; likewise the Toledo blades for his sons, brought with persevering ingenuity over the Pyrenees and embellished with the choicest French workmanship upon hilt and scabbard. No — even though these were a bargain, Captain Bromewell had never been interested. He never was — in buying for buying's sake.

And now at last Captain Twigg had been allowed some licence! The wedding was the occasion of it and his instructions had been to procure a French fan of fine ivory for the bride, the Toledo sword for the bridegroom and new saddles for Clancy and for Harriet. But there was method in his generosity; Captain Bromewell never gave without getting something in exchange.

'It comes to this, Harry,' he had said at breakfast next morning (the wedding morning), finding her still adamant against the garnets. (He was still determined that she should wear them, and she was just as determined that she would not.) 'I want you to please your aunt on this occasion and, damn it, I want to dazzle the eyes of Sophy Lowndes' relations too! Would ye have them say that the mistress of Redonda was so poor she couldn't afford jewels? You say Sophy Lowndes has no neck — but that won't prevent her father from twining diamonds round what there is of it! And *my* daughter, who has a neck and bosom worth twenty of Sophy Lowndes's, chooses to go as bare as a plucked goose!'

It was a long speech for a farmer to make, or a J.P., or a military captain, or a plain bluff man of action — call him which you please.

'I won't wear the garnets,' was Harriet's sole rejoinder. She was tired — not only of being pestered about the garnets, but from having sat up all night in the high-backed chair.

'Then, God damn it, you shan't have the side-saddle!' roared the Captain.

Harriet, whose eyes had been fixed sullenly upon her plate, raised them anxiously, inquiringly to his red angry face at this. He was rubbing at his lips with the napkin as if he wanted to rub away all his previous pleadings and flatterings; nevertheless the power still lay in his hands for all that. Both he and she knew it.

A side-saddle had been Harriet's dearest ambition ever since she had reached her 'teens. To ride crupper behind her father or Spens when they went the rounds of Redonda was not good enough, and a man's saddle, sat woman-wise, was more trouble and danger than it was worth. Again and again she had demanded a side-saddle as her right — she would never ask him for anything else after that, she had said. But the side-saddle had been postponed, promised and postponed again until her heart had grown sick with hoping. And now here it was, on the brink of bestowal at last — and he was determined to humiliate her in payment for it!

He saw her bite her upper lip at this realization, saw her chin tremble, giving her whole face its old childishness back again under the absurd maturity of the powdered coiffure; and he pressed home his advantage.

'It's on order from an old friend in Bury,' he said, 'the same one that's bringing the gew-gaws for Sophy and Clem. When the man talked of the Spanish leather round the scabbard of Clem's sword I vowed you should have a saddle of Spanish leather, too! There won't be another like it in the whole country!'

He rose suddenly, throwing down the napkin and bawling for Ivory and his boots both together. Ivory came running through the general noise and began his ministrations.

'And now,' the Captain went on, 'now you spite me and your aunt and the whole family out of wicked obstinacy, nothing else at all! Pull, you black devil, pull!' he directed the kneeling negro, who, at his feet, was struggling as usual with the top-boots, and pulling desperately upwards. In another moment the impatient riding-crop would descend upon his shoulder, whacking the dust out of his coat, stirring in tiny motes in the imperturbable air. Harriet waited for the familiar action with as little emotion as she would have waited for the cuckoo to burst out of his clock at the appointed hour. All she thought was: How he loves to have people kneeling to him! He would like to have *me* kneeling to him, best of all!

And she could understand why. Because she was the hardest to subdue to his will, then her subjection would be the most gratifying of all. Ah yes, that was inevitable!

'So I warn you,' went on her father, stamping his feet finally into comfort in the boots, and kicking out at the negro to warn him to look lively, nothing more, 'I warn you, if you persist in this behaviour, Harry, you'll never sit your pernickety bottom on that side-saddle because I shall give it to your sister-in-law, and you shall have her French fan instead! Ho ho!'

The idea of Harriet sitting sedately using a fan amused him enormously. He stamped out of the room to visit his sister, still chuckling at it.

When he had got as far as the foot of the stairs, and his hand was resting on the carved wooden pineapple at the foot of the balustrade, Harriet surrendered.

She ran out after him.

'You know I *must* have the saddle, father! I will wear the —— ' Her throat contracted over the hateful word Garnets.

'Good girl!' he said, patting the pineapple approvingly, as if it

102

were her head. 'I knew ye'd come to your senses! I'll tell your aunt. It'll please her.' He went on upwards, whistling.

'You may tell her,' Harriet called after him, 'that I'll wear them because I have nothing else. *There!*'

But he did not hear her. He had won the battle and gone on without bothering to listen further. The servants downstairs were all that heard — and Susan, who was tidying her mistress's room with the door ajar, and who consequently gathered up the cornelians and slipped them into her pocket — but only when the turn came to dust the dressing-table, not before.

Everything, everybody at Redonda was *en fête* for the wedding. The family coach had been well scoured, oiled, aired and trimmed for the occasion, the coachman on the box and the footmen behind wore a livery as gay as the horses' harness and decorated equally with white silk favours. In the coach rode Harriet and her father and aunt. Clem and Clancy, dressed in their finest, had preferred to gallop ahead like outriders.

So, rocking along the roads somewhat like a great galleon caught in a stiff breeze, the Bromewell coach went to the wedding at Bury. Each inside it was occupied with personal thoughts: Miss Hannah Bromewell with affairs at home in Westmorland and with (at the same time) a critical observation of the farmlands lying either side of the roadway; also with affectionate pride in the fact that her garnets were, after all, at that moment round the neck and arm of her niece; Captain Bromewell was occupied with mental calculations of the alteration to his income that the new Trade agreement with France foreshadowed, alternating oddly with other, less checkable calculations concerning the bride's behaviour in the marriage-bed; Harriet was preoccupied with the mental bruises sustained in the breakfast-room tussle and, surprisingly enough, with a certain well-concealed excitement concerning the adventures of the day before her.

The sensations she had were not those of the Harriet she knew, at all. Everything about her, from the feel of the satin lining of her elegant new slipper against her instep to the top-heavy magnificence of her coiffure; not to mention the cold weight, round neck and arm, of the garnets (no longer quite opprobrious, since they at least achieved her a side-saddle) — everything conspired to produce this dream-like sensation of being a Harriet quite other from the one she had always known. When she breathed deeply the new stays, laced by Sukey in the candlelight, creaked slightly, constraining her body strangely where it had known liberty before; when she moved her feet, her new petticoats rustled and whispered and the peacocks' embroidery on the inside hem of her superb plum-bloom gown laid (so she guessed) tiny glossy cheek to cheek. The odour of musk, rising up from the gown so faintly yet so disturbingly, seemed to sweep in eddies upwards like swirls of scented mist enwreathing the whole interior of the coach. The garnets, blazing from neck and wrist, were lovely. She had covered them with her cloak on entering the coach, the less to gratify her triumphant relations, but now that their attention was elsewhere, by shifting her wrist ever so slightly, by turning it from left to right, she could see her arm lying there in the darkness of her cloak like a serpent in a cavern . . . a white serpent with a crown of scarlet garnets to lighten his cold and endless prison. . . .

That was nonsense, of course. But pretty nonsense! It recalled Isaac Waters' readings from the Book of Revelation when he had wanted to frighten her brothers into obedience. They did not always work. Harriet smiled and frowned at the remembrance, edging her slender shoulders back, ever so little, between the plump contours of her father and aunt. If *she* had read from Revelation, it would have worked! But Isaac Waters was so stupid. He could not even make phrases about dragons with crowns of twelve stars sound remarkable. . . . Did the garnets blaze? She stole another covert glance at them, and was more gratified than she cared to admit. Long, long ago she had heard that pearls looked pale and sick on a sick person and creamy and glowing on a well one. These fiery drops, too, could pale and deaden on a pale girl—her aunt had said so. She was *glad* she was not what her aunt called Insipid! She was glad she had been wrong in supposing that her blue gown would 'kill' such jewellery. Perhaps, after all, she would stagger the congregation as her father desired!

'Ned Marsham is to meet us at Stowmarket,' the Captain informed his sister across Harriet's head. Miss Bromewell grunted but did not open her eyes. She had slept badly. Nothing daunted, however, Captain Bromewell began a panegyric concerning Mr. Marsham which it would have greatly diverted that gentleman to have heard.

Harriet, profiting from her aunt's example, closed her eyes too. She was dimly aware that her father intended to impress her as well as her aunt by the recital. She was much less dimly aware that that old friend of the family, Mr. Marsham, considered her to be marriageable in the personal as well as the legal sense. The notion faintly amused without disturbing her. It had never occurred to her — at least, not until her aunt's advent — that anyone could seriously consider that she should ever marry; for that would mean going to live in some place that was not Redonda. With the unthinking certainty of youth she had been absolutely *sure* of that. She would stay the same, and Clem and Clancy would stay the same. True, Clem was marrying to-day but that was somehow just a part of his sameness — it enlarged without altering his character. But Clancy, like her, would not marry! She had never pictured the stolid Clancy as a marrying man — still less considered the actual possibility of a wife of his who might one day be mistress, over her head, of Redonda. The thought, now, pricked her through her present pleasures. That was what her father had promised last night, quite casually, as if it implied nothing unusual at all! He had presented her with a side-saddle with one hand and taken away her birthright with the other.

And now she could see that he was stealing the same kind of sidelong glances at her that she had been stealing at the bracelet of garnets. He meant to do more business that day than to get Clem married; he meant, she could see, to try to arrive at some 'understanding' between herself and Old Friend Ned Marsham. Probably her aunt was an accomplice, too—otherwise why had she been so sedate at the mention of Marsham? Why, indeed—unless the whole plan had been gone into and agreed upon between them the previous evening? Ned Marsham will meet us at Stowmarket . . . and her aunt had grunted as though to say, Indeed, so Harriet's husband-to-be is to meet us at Stowmarket.

Harriet leant back further, stretching herself from the tips of her toes in the satiny slippers to the crown of her head. Two could play at that game! Her father's eyes were still slyly upon her. Her aunt, waking for an instant as the coach lurched round a bend in the road, opened her eyes, too, upon Harriet and smiled involuntarily at the sight. They were both in high good humour, as befitted two elders taking a beauty to a public ceremony. Harriet, dropping her lashes, looking again, under them, for the crowned serpent in the shadow of her cloak, could afford to smile too. They might triumph in an affair like the garnets, but come what might they would *never* succeed in marrying her and removing her from home!

The glass in the coach windows had been polished until it shone. Catching sight of herself in it, Harriet saw suddenly why her relations were so unusually gentle and manageable. She was beautiful to-day! A sense of elation possessed her. Beauty meant power — and pursing her lips she began to whistle lightly her father's tune of last night, 'Softly go down'. It was a habit picked up from the goose-feather-girls and detested, as she well knew, by Captain Bromewell. Would he shout at her? At his daughter, his strange grown-up daughter in her plum-bloom dress and the garnets, in all her dazzling display? She whistled louder, still with downcast, seemingly demure eyes. The most she could get from him was an irritated fidgeting in response. This was triumph indeed!

The wedding went off, subsequently, in the splendid, rather showy fashion which best suited anything concerning Mr. Clement Bromewell. The many-windowed church showered down its many-coloured lights upon the scene, adding to the splendour — except in the bride's case where, like everyone else, it had to admit bafflement. That lady, already little-enough known to Clem's relations, was concealed on her wedding day in a veil of double Valenciennes so thick that it might have been pledged to eternal secrecy; but her plump little hand, tucked through Clem's arm towards the end of the ceremony, trembled perpetually, much to Harriet's contempt. She nudged her father with an elbow still sharp through the plum-bloom flounces.

'A robin has died in her hand!' she whispered.

Captain Bromewell replied to this superstition by frowning so deeply that his grizzled wig moved forward quite half an inch on his

forehead. Robins, he would like to have informed his country bump-
kin of a daughter, did not frequent the smart places where Miss
Lowndes had been brought up; besides, dead robins were unlucky
things, even to mention in joke. The church was chilly, he wished
the whole business was over. The couple were wed legally by now,
only the palaver of the parson-fellow was holding them up. Lady
Lowndes, in a front pew, was weeping as if it were Sophy's
funeral instead of her wedding. He despised her and all her elegant
sycophantic relations who had come in droves to see Sophy married.
It seemed to him that they looked about the church—and, damn it,
what town could produce a better! — as if it were an outlandish sort
of place for a London girl to be married in. To hell with them all!
Particularly with the young booby at the end of the row who
was sucking the agate top of his cane as if it were a lollipop.

Much the cane-sucker cared for Captain Bromewell's opinion.
His eyes were upon Harriet, bulging with admiration of the lady in
blue. So were Mr. Marsham's eyes, from the convenient seclusion
of the pew just behind her. They could not see her face but they
took, Harriet was uncomfortably aware, an appraising inventory of
her coiffure, the nape of her neck, the set of her shoulders and the
smallness of her waist — also of the garnets. Once at a pause in
the ceremony he had leant forward, so that his warm snuff-scented
breath came over her bare shoulder, saying in his soft London
voice:

'Next time I suppose we shall be here for you, Miss Harriet?'

She did not answer directly. The cane-sucker, she could see, was
furiously envious of Mr. Marsham's proximity, furiously desirous
that she should snub Mr. Marsham. Waiting for her to answer —
even though from that distance he could not possibly have heard
her words — he popped his cane-head out of his mouth the better
to listen. She wanted to laugh, he looked so exactly like a day-old
calf when the teat has slipped from its mouth — pouting and puzzled,
unable to help itself.

Wanting to laugh, she began to laugh, her prayer-book against
her lips, her shoulders shaking silently. Father and aunt, either side
of her, were unnaturally uninterested, unnaturally determined to
leave the way clear to Mr. Marsham for this *tête-à-tête*.

Taking her silent risibility for encouragement, the lawyer leant forward again.

'Who is to be the lucky man, hey?' he whispered.

But he did not look into her face. His eyes, wrinkled at the corners from too much tobacco and snuff, too much burning of other people's candles, at other people's expense, at both ends, were fixed studiously, almost anxiously, upon her breast as he spoke and upon the garnets winking and flashing there. If he had been instructed to learn their precise shape, size and number upon pain of death he could hardly have looked more steadily or more long.

Harriet could bear it no longer. Her breast heaved, tossing the garnets into a more restless brilliance.

'There will *be* none!' she answered from behind her prayer-book. Still without changing the direction of his gaze, Mr. Marsham pursed his lips, shocked. This was not the way the game should be played and even this lovely hoyden was aware of as much. But badinage from behind prayer-books cramped the style. He would be bolder, taking advantage of the studied indifference of Miss Bromewell's chaperones.

A curl on Harriet's neck, stiff with pomade and powder, curled temptingly upwards like the tip of a particularly young and innocent feather. Her neck below it was very white — for a country girl, that is. Her shoulder, rising so touchingly naked out of the blue gown, was more than mortal man could resist.

Harriet, waiting for the reply to *her* reply, was staggered at this point to feel Mr. Marsham's mouth pressing her shoulder in a damp and devoted kiss. *This is the way we deal with rude young ladies in London*, seemed to be the message of it — but she did not wait to hear more. Swinging her left hand back over the affronted shoulder she caught Mr. Marsham smartly on the cheek with her prayer-book. *And this is the way we deal with impudent friends of the family*, was the too easily interpreted reply.

If all action had been left to these two perhaps few in the building would have been any the wiser but the young cane-sucker, so quickly had both incidents passed; but it was not to be. The Captain and Miss Hannah Bromewell came to life at the second incident with astonishing simultaneousness. Things happened quickly thereafter.

Captain Bromewell slapped his daughter's face, Harriet stamped on his gouty foot and Miss Bromewell dropped her fan and gloves all together, so that the commotion in the pew reserved for the bride-groom's relations was great indeed. Nor did Clancy, who had observed most of the dumb-show from Mr. Marsham's side, im-prove matters at this point by guffawing so loudly that the noise of it could be heard even through the organ's peals, and several Lowndes relations turned their heads to see what it was all about.

There was so much furious anger in the pew just then that it seemed as if so much spontaneous combustion must set the very wood ablaze. At a moment when devout echoings of Mr. Addison's hymn should have filled the nave, crude interpolations of 'Damn ye, that's the end of the side-saddle then!', and, still worse, 'Devil take the side-saddle!' might be heard. The congregation, temporarily distracted from the singing, turned their heads, uncertain whether to be more amazed at this piece of undignified byplay or by the astonishing sight of Mr. Marsham's cheeks, one scarlet, one white as snow. The cane-head of the booby in the Lowndes pew was popping in and out of his mouth continuously in his delighted ex-citement. Clem himself (resplendent in a claret-coloured cut-away coat, with a tremendous cravat choking him to the chin, and top-boots whose glossiness shamed even that of his father's) turned a look upon his family of supreme dislike as he marched down the aisle with his bride, and on into the vestry. She remained, however, anonymous and trembling until the end.

The many-coloured lights continued to shower indifferently down from the windows but the peal of the organ died away, as if shocked into silence. '——!' said the Captain with an oath as rough as his temper, 'I'm getting out of this and so are you, my girl!'

Grasping his daughter's arm in a grip showing no mercy, he hauled her outside. Miss Bromewell followed, scolding all the while.

'A *fine* scene to make at a wedding! A *fine* scene indeed!'

She went on scolding Harriet long after the Captain had swung away and been swallowed up by the Lowndes party. Harriet was rigidly unrepentant.

'He did not kiss *your* shoulder with his nasty wet mouth,' was all her reply. She had triumphed. Her prayer-book had had the last word — and yet, with the saddle receding once more into unattainability a certain tremulousness possessed her, the imponderable weight of elders and betters who can bend youth to take the shape they desire, no matter what injustice is perpetrated.

Mr. Marsham was tact itself on the church steps. He bowed to Harriet as if it were the first time he had seen her that day and remained close with the male section of the party — Sir Joshua Lowndes, Clem, Clancy and the Captain. He was helping, she knew, in the legal part of the proceedings. His cheek was still pinkish from the clout she had given him and he kept his head turned so that his cravat helped to conceal his discomfiture.

But when the cane-sucking youth, under the protective shadow of the Lowndes relations, achieved an introduction to the brilliant young beauty in the blue dress, Harriet saw that Mr. Marsham's eyes could not remain on the legal documents but continued to look up and follow her movements with an interest that was almost pitiable. If Harriet had ever felt a gleam of sympathy for him, she felt it now, although she knew that this softness of hers towards Mr. Marsham was doomed to fade as swiftly as the flush upon his cheek. She could still feel, in fancy, the nauseous touch of his lips on her shoulder and rubbed at the place angrily under her cloak.

Miss Hannah Bromewell was the most implacable. She was so indignant that she could not bring herself to show Harriet off as she had looked forward to doing. More meetings might, for all she knew, mean more brawls with more sacred books. So they stood together on the steps waiting for the coach — a cross, upright old woman with an old-fashioned grey hood over her grey hair, and a cross and equally upright young one with brows bent together in a truly Bromewellian scowl, and with an upper lip pinched between her teeth in a way which was, as Miss Hannah Bromewell did not hesitate to inform her, undignified as well as unbecoming.

'What will they think of you!' she said.

'They are not thinking of *me* at all,' burst out Harriet. 'It is Clem and Sophy's wedding, not mine! You are so mad to have me married — you and Father — that you can't even wait till Clem is married!'

Here she was constrained, her eyes brilliant with mutinous tears, to stand silent and listen while her aunt exchanged pleasantries with some more of the Lowndes. Her heart ached suddenly to be away from Bury and back at her home again; again and again her eyes sought the Bromewell coach, over the heads and through the clustered groups of the still loitering congregation.

The bridal pair, source of all the delay, appeared finally, Clem descending the steps with all his customary happy bravado, the bride still clinging to him, a bundle of mystery. Together they crept into the coach that was to carry them to Redonda, the door clicked to, and the slender thing swung away, amidst the subdued cheers of the bystanders, carrying them home. Clancy preceded them, still acting as outrider, waving his whip trimmed with a white satin favour. But away ahead of both her brothers, faster than any horse could travel, ran Harriet Bromewell's heart, making for its home and its haven, jealous — as always — to be first.

But Captain Bromewell had to interview that other Captain before he returned home with the women. At the Blue Goose tavern, he kept the said women waiting over an hour in the coach while, safe inside the private quarters of Everybody's Friend, he drank with that gentleman to the health of the Happy Couple and the speedy dissolution of Mr. Pitt's ill-advised Trade Treaty with the French, which took money out of honest hard-working sailors' pockets and was in any case a snare and a delusion, since everyone knew the French could no more keep to their bounden word than they could — well, something else.

But the best of friends must part, and finally Captain Bromewell made his reappearance, together with a man and a boy, who under his somewhat indistinct instructions strapped the precious goods he had come for, to the roof of the coach. Harriet could hear them bumping over her head at intervals all the long journey home. In amongst the goods was the saddle, the longed-for saddle, tantalizing in its proximity. Alas — perhaps she would never be closer to it than that!

Whether it was Captain Twigg's cognac, or the unusually festal atmosphere of the proceedings at Redonda that evening — the effect of the musicians from Orford, the applauding guests, or merely a sudden access of good-nature which after all sometimes attends the meanest man — however it was, Captain Bromewell did not carry out his threat about the saddle. He forgave Harriet, even if he didn't forget. (And he certainly never forgot, for he said he would never go into a church with her again in his life, and he didn't.) But when the neighbours had all gone home and all the retainers returned at long last to their humbler lodgings, the Captain made a speech to the assembled family and presented his gifts. The bride was glad of the fan to cover her blushes — or pretended to be. Clem was delighted with his sword, trying the blade forthwith on the satin ribbon of Sophy's bouquet. Clancy, too, was pleased with his gift and with his father's kindly references. Harriet when her turn came was given no speech; a toss of her father's head indicated where the saddle lay. When Ivory went to bring it to her she would have none of it, but left the table quickly, picking it up herself in all its ungainliness and stumbling straightway from the room with it, also without a word. No one's eyes but hers should be allowed the first glimpse of this most beautiful, most desired of all acquisitions.

It would have been a courtesy, on Harriet's part, to have left the saddle till later; to have accompanied the bride upstairs after dinner, to help her to prepare for the night. But the thought never occurred to her, and Miss Hannah Bromewell, deciding that if you want a thing done properly you must do it yourself, undertook this task; more, it must be admitted, from curiosity than courtesy, to see what precisely her nephew had married, and why.

The new Mrs. Bromewell, however, turned out to be as unrevealing as an onion; the more that was peeled off her, the more there was to peel. Miss Bromewell, after half an hour's tussling with small buttons and endless garments, had the feeling that even if she were finally to peel the whole epidermis off Sophy, a fresh lot would instantly appear below it and the mystery would begin all over again. Thus baffled she left the bride sitting up in bed, pale but self-possessed, and retired with relief to her own apartments. The men would follow later.

So they did, in due course. The Captain, dead to the world, went upstairs on Ivory's back and was undressed by the faithful Fitchet, and left to snore his way back to sobriety. The bride, hearing this procession and familiar with similar ones at home, fancied, poor girl, that her husband would not be long thereafter and merely hoped his own feet might suffice to bring him to her. But, a long wait succeeding the first ascent, she grew impatient and, muffled to the chin in her wraps, tiptoed out into the chilly passage to see what she could see.

Through one door she could hear her father-in-law, breathing — as she inelegantly expressed it — 'fit to bust'; she tiptoed further down the passage and through another half-open door she could see her sister-in-law, lying fast asleep in a shaft of moonlight in the middle of her bedroom floor, with her cheek resting — of all things — on a saddle for pillow. Tipsy little chit, she said to herself. But still Clem did not come, and eventually the disconsolate bride was forced to return to a lonely bed where after a while she fell asleep, like Harriet, from pure fatigue.

It was as well she did so, for Clem and his brother were a long while celebrating, ending the triumphant evening — after an orgy of glass-smashing — with a baiting of Ivory which ranked high in their memories ever after, and in the memories of certain others of Redonda's inhabitants.

One only does such things once in a lifetime, of course, and a thing worth doing at all — as his aunt would have said — was worth doing well. Ivory was used to being plagued by the young masters and it was, he knew, more than his life was worth to have argued with either of them on this occasion. They had been very fond of him — oh, very fond! They had nothing personally against him at all, the young masters, and when he had ventured to protest just a little, he knew that his rolling eyes and imploring gestures only added extra fuel to the flame of their mischievous intent. Still, one has to protest, just a little — even if it is quite ineffective.

They had taken Ivory to his own buttery and there gently, almost affectionately, stripped that unhappy black man of his clothes and forced him naked into a great tub of Jamaica treacle until he was submerged to the chin. The more he struggled to rise out of it, to address them gently and persuasively, the more they had shoved him down again, shrieking with laughter, until only his curly grizzled head with its loose-lipped mouth and rolling eyes remained above water, as it were. 'Mas'r Clem, Mas'r Clancy!' he kept saying, magicking with their names as if that would help him. He had had the longest day of any and the hardest work — had worked, indeed, like a horse — so that to end the day with this horse-play was indeed the last straw. But of course they took no notice. They were kindly disposed to him but excessively intoxicated, and they had never enjoyed themselves (or so it would seem) so much in their lives. It was a wonderful scheme; silly old Ivory to want to spoil the fun!

Clem thought of the treacle; Clancy thought of the feathers. Like tarring and feathering, they said together, loving each other for this rare synchronization of inspiration. The subsequent journey upstairs, Clem pricking the incredibly glutinous negro up to the attics with his new sword, Clancy stumbling behind, almost helpless with laughter, was unadventurous enough.

'Mas'r Clem, Mas'r Clancy,' Ivory tried again. A last attempt — but they had no mercy for a spoilsport, and might have reminded him with Shakespeare (if they had ever read any Shakespeare) that Ripeness is all.

The goosefeather girls, as has been said before, occupied one of the attics. To reach this particular attic they passed through the plucking-room, where the feathers of hundreds of Redonda's dead poultry and geese were collected to serve their turn in pillows, coverlets and feather overlays. A swift walk through this passage-way produced always a miniature snowstorm amongst the mound of feathers heaped in the corner — they rose and stirred themselves and subsided as the visitor came and went. But Clem and Clancy gave the feathers no time for this little whirling dance of theirs; instead, arrived in the attic, they pushed the unbelievably sticky and shining Ivory deep, deep into the mound, burying him in them as if in a bath of feathers, gasping protestations and all.

The ripe moment was reached when Ivory, resurrected from the feathers in a most astonishing condition, was locked into the furthest attic of all by the two young Gentlemen — together with the newly-awakened kicking, biting and scratching goosefeather girls. Only when this crescendo of hysterical hilarity was reached did the bridegroom cease his exhausted laughing and wipe the tears of fun from his eyes, remembering a consummation somewhat overdue.

He descended to it two, and sometimes three, jaunty steps at a time, and it may have been pleasurable or it may not, but the fact remains that the night was remembered thereafter by Redonda less as a wedding night than as the date of the frolic of Ivory and the goose-feather girls.

It was just as well that Mr. Marsham had refused the Captain's pressing invitation to make a night of it with his family. The night was not one of a kind he would have much enjoyed.

CHAPTER X

AN ESCAPE

'We have no lack of system or device to measure and parcel out these poor days of ours; wherein it should be our pleasure that they be not . . . suffered to pass away in vain, and without meed of honour, leaving no records of ourselves in the minds of men. . . .'

Leonardo da Vinci

JAN VANDERVOORD had not been a prisoner in Peterborough for more than a few months when he began casting about in his mind for a way of escape. The place was too dull to hold him. Better, he thought, a risk of quick extinction following capture outside, than a repetition of the slow decay which had been eating him up all the previous frustrated year in Portsmouth and on Dartmoor.

That he was imprisoned at all was a ridiculous blunder. It had also been a blunder in Portsmouth and on Dartmoor, and all the time this very fact grew harder to bear, not easier. True, his repeated representations to the various authorities that he was a Netherlander and not a Frenchman had removed him, at last, out of the company of the French sailors at Portsmouth into the officers' quarters in the prison camp at Peterborough — but they were French officers, nevertheless. He was still treated as an enemy alien — whatever he might do or say — and the fact that he was now amongst gentlemen instead of riffraff, with better food (even that was not saying much) and a mattress instead of a heap of straw to lie on, was still no cause for gratitude. It would not do, in short, any longer for Mynheer Vandervoord.

Had he ever asked to come to England in the first place? He had not. He had been a *bona fide* citizen of the Netherlands, returning from Batavia to Utrecht, his birthplace, on urgent family business. He had had the misfortune to be travelling on a French vessel — a merchantman, which had fallen prey to a Bristol privateer. He had been, shall we say, not altogether wise during that hour of violence wherein the vessel had changed hands. Since then incarceration in one prison or another had been his lot. He had explained the injustice of it until he was tired. All it had resulted in was an amelioration, in some sort, but not a cancellation, of his circumstances — and this was not enough.

Explanations having proved useless, action without explanation remained. Vandervoord still had his clasp-knife and the few toys carved out of the bones retrieved from the bottom of those unspeakable stews served up on Dartmoor. From these he had evolved several slender bone whistles, a bone crucifix of great artistry, a bone brooch formed of a circlet of ivy-leaves, and a bone windmill, three inches high, with sails carved after the fashion of filigree which revolved furiously when one merely sighed upon them. This last had taken three months to achieve; it was his *chef d'œuvre.*

It was fortunate, Vandervoord reflected, that when he *did* leave he would have no luggage other than these small articles to cumber him. These — and a very excellent sketch of Portsmouth Harbour and its environs which he was invariably at such pains to conceal that he wore it flat against his naked breast under his shirt, and under the now somewhat shabby brown-and-yellow striped nankeen waistcoat and the brown nankeen jacket and breeches in which he had been first captured aboard the *Agréable.*

The map of Portsmouth Harbour was, needless to say, an exceedingly dangerous thing for an escaped prisoner to carry about his person — indeed to be caught with, whether escaped or not; but something of Vandervoord's perverse passion for living on the brink of danger — of seeing just how far he could go without actually toppling into it beyond recovery — had inspired him to cherish and preserve this. It was the work of a French naval Lieutenant, one Lanfranc, who had completed it (also in imminent danger of discovery the whole time) whilst immured in one of the hulks for French prisoners-of-war moored in Portsmouth Harbour. This hulk had been, also, Vandervoord's first place of detention. Lanfranc had died of a fever induced by the insufficient food and the rats'-cage conditions of the hulk, and his sardonic bequest to Vandervoord of this map had been the last joke he enjoyed. (In civil life he had been a most excellent draughtsman.) 'Take it, my friend,' he told Vandervoord. 'There are three reasons why you will never wish to part with it. One, it is the bequest of a dying man and therefore sacred — oh yes! undeniably sacred! The second is that the English authorities would give their clumsy big boots for it. The third is that it is done with as much artistry as accuracy — and I am privileged to say that, you must admit, because I am dying. How long did you say you fiddled over that miserable mutton-bone windmill of yours? Three months? I have spent six months on this map, working below-decks all the time. And if you ever succeed in returning to the Continent you must make your way to France and see that it is placed in the right hands. Long live the Revolution!'

Lanfranc had died that night and been buried at once in the lime-pits reserved for dead prisoners of war. This was the first hygienic treatment he received in England, as it was the last. The tame French priest had been drunk in a Portsmouth tavern at the time and so the ceremony was service-less — a fact which would certainly not have distressed the dead Lanfranc.

But he had spoken truly of his map. It was indeed a marvellous and meticulously executed piece of work, as well as an exact presentation of Portsmouth's batteries and naval dispositions as perceived through the portholes of the hulk. If it was a death-sentence to Vandervoord should it ever be found upon him, it was almost equally a passport to life and honour should he succeed in escaping with it to France. (The accurate delineation of each other's fortifications was always a saleable commodity in France or England.)

Vandervoord never mentioned the map's existence to any of his companions at Peterborough, though it would have given them a new topic to discuss for at least a week or so.

Chief amongst all subjects which came up for discussion was, naturally enough, the subject of how to escape. The smugglers of that coast who imported French wines and silks were also known, on occasion, to arrange for the export of live goods — just as the Sussex smugglers did. But one still had to run these gentlemen to earth. The sergeant on night duty, on being bribed, admitted that such an introduction might be possible. By hints and winks he conveyed that if the money were forthcoming he might, just possibly *might*, but he wasn't sure, mind ye, be able to put one of the more persistent French prisoners in touch with his brother-in-law, otherwise Everybody's Friend, who — it was understood — worked in with a gang who did the monthly 'run' from Aldeburgh to Bury. More he would not say, unless more cash were forthcoming.

'The man is a scoundrel!' bewailed the young Lieutenant who had first raised the subject. 'He leads us on and on and then *says* nothing!'

'Why do we not hear from M. Otto?' asked another.

'Yes, why do we hear nothing? There is *sabotage* at the post-office, depend upon it,' said another.

M. Otto was the *chargé d'affaires* in London deputed to look after the interests of French prisoners of war, but for one reason or another inquiries directed to him from Peterborough very seldom elicited any sort of reply, or any easing of the hardships still endured by the prisoners.

'It is three months since I sent inquiries through M. Otto to my bankers at Marseilles!' said a third prisoner.

'We should never be allowed to bring the money into this country in any case,' gloomed a fourth.

All the same, writing to M. Otto, pleading with M. Otto as a man and a brother, abusing M. Otto as a traitor and renegade, and just plain writing to M. Otto remained the prime hobby of all the French prisoners. If they did not hear from that much-abused man they could at least go *on* abusing him, making him chief scapegoat of all their misfortunes. M. Vandervoord's correspondence with the Netherlands *chargé d'affaires* was a failure for another reason, for that gentleman *did* reply, and failed to give any consolation or indeed to recognize the fact at all that Vandervoord was what he claimed to be — a Netherlander and a civilian.

What reason? Who shall guess what reason? Bonapartist sympathies perhaps — bought or genuine; malice, plain stupidity, red tape muddles, there was no way of ascertaining the origin of all the misunderstandings. Nevertheless what had started as a plain duty with Vandervoord — a simple desire to set right this blunder concerning his identity in the quickest possible way — degenerated presently into a sort of joke, so persistently satirical was Vandervoord in all his side of the correspondence, so woodenheadedly stubborn and stand-offish was M. Elesius on his; and later still, as week ebbed into week, month guttered into month, so the whole affair became almost sinister.

For free men it is perhaps difficult to conceive of such a misunderstanding being anything more than tiresome — a wrong that required to be set right, perhaps compensated, no more and no less. But to men with little else to brood upon — particularly to a man of Vandervoord's lively impatience, it soon became more. It was typical of him that he never disclosed this to his companions, even at times when they, unusually downcast by M. Otto's inexplicable silences, were ready to deplore treason, malice and injustice on every hand. 'Devil take my countryman!' Vandervoord would exclaim laughingly, exhibiting yet one more crumpled package addressed, as always, *To the French Prisoner M. Vinvaud*. 'See how he twists my name to make me one of you! Devil take him, he will make me out to be an Indian next, I shouldn't wonder!' And, not to be outdone, he would write back to *Citizen* Elesius, ending his letter with *Long live the Republic* and thereby damning any chance he might have had of serious consideration. On another occasion he would desert Gallic levity for Netherlands thoroughness, would set out with mathematical precision a list of his proofs of identity, demanding an investigation with all the dignity of a man wrongfully detained, and citing the full names of his grandparents on both sides together with a note addressed to the burgomaster of Utrecht, addressed familiarly to a Christian name and signed Jan v. de V. After all, he had plenty of time to prepare such documents. But whatever his tactics, they were doomed to fail. They served to amuse his fellow-sufferers who, when the letters were read aloud to them, suggested alterations or emendations with unusual disinterestedness. But there their function ended. After a while M. Elesius ceased even to acknowledge the letters and the Prison Commandant, when appealed to forthrightly by this too-authoritative prisoner, succeeded only in making matters worse.

'In the last analysis,' Vandervoord observed to the Commandant, 'we shall confirm my identity and nationality by denials if we can't do it by assents. Ask the *other* embassies and legations if they have ever heard of me! Ask the French gentleman, M. Otto — since everyone is so determined that I am a Frenchman! I defy him to produce a Vandervoord!'

But as ill-luck would have it, on this occasion M. Otto *did* reply. Through mistaken zeal and entirely out of a desire to please the English prison authorities, he succeeded in unearthing — from Heaven knows what archives — a certain Jean Vinvaud, and sent off particulars (but not dates) to Peterborough with cries of delight at being able to assist, etc., etc. The particulars agreed in no single detail with those of Jan Vandervoord — which was not surprising, since later it transpired that M. Jean-Baptiste Vinvaud had been a French doctor in attendance on the queen of King Charles the First . . . Vandervoord became, after this, more of a French prisoner than ever.

All this to-do could be taken in two ways. One could be morose and suicidal about such muddles, like the Frenchmen, or cheerfully contemptuous, like Vandervoord himself. It was bad enough to be captured on a French ship, he used to say — but to be considered French *because* of that circumstance was really the last straw. But lying awake at night, long legs crossed at the ankles, long arms tucked cross-wise behind his head, and staring up into the darkness, it was permissible to begin to wonder a little whether some evilly-intentioned Fate were not, after all, taking a hand in his misfortunes, and delighting in pushing him back into them whenever he tried to clamber out; much as (in his boyhood) he had seen the town boys down by the canal tormenting a cat—pushing the streaming creature back into the water with brooms, loosening its agonized clawing at the bank, time after time, until it drowned.

Such thoughts do not belong to daylight hours — at any rate not to people like Vandervoord; but in the silence of night it was not strange that identity should sometimes recede with consciousness — growing ever more questionable. As long as one wasn't delirious, of course, one didn't begin to wonder whether there really *was* a Jan Vandervoord; whether Vinvaud, after all, by some idiotic turning-inside-out of truth, might not be right . . . Of course, such a time, such a doubt, might one day come. It was not a pleasant possibility.

The French officers, absorbed as they were in their own troubles, could be excused for overlooking their companion's. The eternal grievance of not being allowed to live in the town on parole (it had been too often broken) occupied their minds, together with all the other grievances. Vandervoord's trouble was tiresome, no doubt, but the question of their allowances from M. Otto, of repairs to clothes (supposed to be authorized by M. Otto), of complaints about conditions, or inquiries concerning their families, were all far more important. And always, above all, there remained the familiar but ever-fascinating topic of escape.

Vandervoord took little part in these discussions, except to gibe good-naturedly at them. They were always talking about the cost of such an escape. If he got out himself, it would be by the use of his wits, not of money.

'My God, if we are here another year,' said one shabby Colonel, 'we shall starve where we stand!'

It was true the food was very bad, but then it was not exactly plentiful anywhere just then.

'I think,' said another, very much older Colonel, very slowly, 'that they feed us on the principle of the farmer with the horse. First day a handful of oats, second day half a handful, third day a quarter . . . sixth day a single grain. It was to educate the horse, gentlemen, to learn to live on a grain a day — by gradual means. But they have forgotten that the horse died.'

'If you would not talk of food so much I should be less hungry!' protested a sick Cornet. Poor boy, he lay in his corner all day, reading his single volume on the Gallic campaigns of Caesar over and over again. He was suffering from an intestinal disease and was so thin and gaunt that his own mother would not have recognized him. But his mother was dead — perhaps fortunately — in the Republic's 'clean-up' of a certain town in the Alpes Maritimes, though the Cornet was ignorant of this.

The most passionate and voluble of all was also the most blue-blooded, a certain Captain of Horse who spent his time, not in trying to escape, but in trying to persuade the English to accept him as an ally. (In this he was unsuccessful.) The execution of his King and Queen, the reign of Robespierre, had spelt for him the end of France. 'I shall never go back!' he used to declare passionately, 'Even if they released me and gave me a safe-conduct, I would not pollute myself by standing on French soil together with such *canaille*! *A bas la Republique! A bas le Directoire!*'

In the depths of the night he could be heard sobbing quietly because he would never know what had become of his wife and his two gifted children.

'You are not a patriot,' said the old Colonel with the shaking head. 'True, our country has passed through great tribulations, but it is only in times of tribulation that great men arise! The hour produces the man!'

(The man was, of course, General Bonaparte.)

'A Corporal!' exploded the Captain of Horse, incorporating all the quivering scorn he could muster into the word.

'Well, sir,' said the thin boy from the palliasse, 'no sane man has any objections, surely, to corporals; too many of us have been corporals! It is because he was a Corsican before he was a corporal that I — that I — ' He could think of no way to finish the sentiment, merely falling back on his pillow and muttering, 'We should have a *French* leader! France for the French, I say!'

'The hour produces the man,' repeated the old Colonel, 'and I will not have disloyalty talked here, gentlemen! Besides — France for the French, what defeatist sort of talk is that? The *world* for the French, I say! And if it is a Corsican commander who leads France to her high destiny as this one is doing — why, then, I say that he is inspired to that task by Providence!'

After this, to discuss the whole topic seriously — oh, that delight and solace of all true Frenchmen, 'seriously' — was the second pleasure of the interned men. How, when and where to escape remained the first.

Both subjects, working on half-empty stomachs and systems debilitated by fever, they allowed to absorb them in a way that would have been impossible had they been free. France was their peculiar pride and grief. Even if they could not be sure that, after these constantly resumed and as constantly broken off series of military engagements, France was to prevail as the Liberator of Europe, they could be sure that England — her principal rival — was breaking up. The word Decadent was constantly on their lips. The successful defection of the American colonies — that huge lump that had torn itself so successfully away from British pride and power — was too recent in memory to be forgotten. India would follow — as the Warren Hastings affair very clearly showed. Only the French were fit to govern the Indian Empire, that was very certain! Then there was the recovery of Toulon — under the very nose of the British fleet, mark you! There was Ireland, fermenting with revolution — ready to be a second America. Wherever, in fact, British rule abounded, there pillage and oppression and every kind of misrule abounded — history showed it. The beneficent rule of the New France, on the other hand, spread itself like the sun, further and further over all the lands of Europe. The plutocrats, the oppressors in England, resisted it, naturally. It was to their scheming advantage to pretend that the Directory spread disorder and starvation instead of bringing order and plenty. . . . But there would be a New Order in the Continent before Bonaparte had finished with it (of that the Colonel was perfectly sure), and all the small countries, swallowed up in it, would live to bless the day.

'I shall *never* live to bless the day!' declared the Captain of Horse.

'Nor shall I,' agreed Vandervoord, 'I should know for I am a

Netherlander, and your pernicious compatriots are over-running my country!'

Being a partner in the Frenchmen's distresses, it may be observed, made him no partner to their patriotism. On occasions like this he would go on to ridicule the *Contrat Social*, to make mock of the Revolution, to address his companions — final insult! — as Citizens. But, being Jan Vandervoord, he was permitted these liberties; after all they owed him that much, since he had been captured originally on a French vessel.

There was no doubt about it, they were extremely fond of Vandervoord. This tall, long-faced Netherlander with his un-European tan was the least representative member of his country that they had ever known. Were not Netherlanders boors? This man was as cultured as a Tourainer. Were they not stolid fellows, slow in the uptake? This one was quicker on the draw with his wit than any of them. The sight of him pacing endlessly with that long, prancing gait peculiar to him — as if he had more energy locked up within himself than he knew what to do with — up and down, up and down, with his hands clasped behind his back and his chin thrust upwards so that the queue of his peruke stuck out most comically behind, was a sight both irritating to them and yet re-assuring. And always, as he walked, he teased them, tearing down the tricolour in so many words, gibing at history, at all man's efforts to make the world by the arts of war a better or a nobler place.

The old Colonel used to try to convert him, in his gentle old trembling voice. 'M. Vandervoord,' he would say, 'there is a tide in the affairs of men. An irresistible moment comes, and a great man takes it. George Washington is a great man. He has freed America from the tyranny of this country — with *our* help, mark you! *We* have a great man, too; give him time, and he will free Europe from English tyranny in the same way. Then what a relief! An end to the endless *braggadocio*, the insupportable blockades! Your own country, M. Vandervoord, the Danes, the Swedes, the Russians — you will all be thankful when we have swept the English from the seas and ended these insupportable blockades!'

'Can you promise us, then, that there will be no French blockade?'

asked Vandervoord, pausing in his stride and still prancing, just a little, on his toes where he stood.

'There will in all probability be a little judicious supervision —' began the Colonel.

'Aha!' said Vandervoord, 'under the English it is a blockade; under the French it will be judicious supervision! So you promise us judicious supervision. To hell with the lot of you!' and he resumed his striding to and fro, chin stuck out again, eyes turned upwards, laughing to himself as if he saw something irresistibly funny in the too-familiar ceiling.

'You are not a soldier, M. Vandervoord,' the old Colonel replied with dignity; 'you cannot appreciate the full significance of the situation.'

Jan Vandervoord used a Dutch word whose full significance at least was instantaneously perceived by the rest of the company; they had a French one which served the same purpose of conveying complete disbelief. He used it and then he said, 'No, I am not a soldier, I am an engineer! The kind of power I am interested in is not personal or political power, it is that vested in pistons, in steam, in steel! *I* am not interested in the age of Liberty, Equality and Fraternity — I am interested in the age of Machinery! You do not understand machinery. You have none of you any conception of the miraculous discoveries which await us, if we work to find them! But you go on bawling about France, about Liberty, Equality and Fraternity, and the more you do this the more you hinder the progress of machinery!'

'Ah, he is off again on his hobby-horse!' said the Lieutenant who had first spoken, looking up from his game of cards.

'It is a horse which will one day be steam-driven!' replied Vandervoord.

'The Balance of Power —' began the old Colonel.

'Power!' echoed Vandervoord, 'there is more power in an engine driven by steam, a hammer driven by steam, than in all the frenzied dreams and schemes of military commanders! At least, there *could* be, if one were free to work on them!'

'He thinks his steam-engines will produce another Revolution,' said the Captain of Horse, with the kind of pity appropriate to a good rider.

'Machinery is composed of revolutions — how then should it be content with a mere paltry *one*?' said Vandervoord, ' — but what is the good of talking to any of you? You are all soldiers, you have long forgotten what little mathematics you ever learnt!'

'At least we are patriots!' they said; 'you are not even a patriot!'

'I am an engineer!' he answered, as always — just as they had expected him to.

To him, too, the mere reiteration of the declaration was some measure of relief. Shut close in these foetid quarters with these hungry and stupid and eternally bored men — sickened finally of his efforts to prove his identity to the authorities, his mind ached at times like this to be free of his body, to rove in the pure air of mathematics where neither France nor England was right or wrong, or half-right or half-wrong, but where two and two most gloriously made four, whatever language they were counted in. Yes, he was an engineer. This was his testament of faith, his sacred conviction from which nothing could shake him, as all the company knew. Whenever he had to supply the information necessary for certain prison files and documents it was in the same manner that he would answer. Name, Vandervoord; Religion, Engineer; Nationality, Engineer; Profession, Engineer; Rank, Engineer. It was beyond a joke, they said. Yes, he parried, it was beyond a joke with him, too. It was *serieuse*. He alone was sane in a crazy world.

But with all his teasing and effrontery, he could be kind, too. The Cornet's disease was by now so far-gone that the nauseousness of it infected all the air about him, yet Vandervoord went closer to him than any of them, and sat on his bed by the hour together, amusing and comforting him. He would, too, try to console the boy, as he sat there, with the sort of quiet reasoning by which he would not have troubled to justify himself to any of the rest of them. 'You see,' he would explain, 'I have no sympathies in this war on either side. I am a Netherlander and all I want is to be free to return to my work. You are soldiers. To you, after all, there is nothing fundamentally crazy about this situation we find ourselves in, locked up here like a crowd of baboons. It is just the fortune of war. But to *me*, who didn't ask for such a situation or train for it, it is not just unfortunate, it is crazy! While I am here, how can I work? How can I learn?'

At another time, sitting in the same place, he said, but to the whole room: 'Men should be free! Not just us, gentlemen — but *everyone*, Englishmen, Irishmen, Swedes, Negroes — all of them! How can a man work or learn unless he is free?'

At another time he said, pausing as he whittled away at one of his eternal bone trinkets at the boy's bedside: 'If I were not cooped up here, what a lot I should like to see in this country! The looms, the spinning-mules, the water-mills, the steam-engines — above all, the men who have produced such things. They are harnessing power in this country to an unbelievable extent!'

And again he said (this time when he was a little drunk one evening): 'Gentlemen, the earth is as full of power as it is of coal and iron and tin — but it is an invisible element! It has to be lured out to give up its vast secrets, and the vastness of those secrets we in this century shall never know!'

When the Cornet became convalescent again, Vandervoord was kindness itself, played on the bone flute to him, sang, with his excellent voice, the old Provençal melodies which made him weep his fever away. He had another accomplishment, too. When the others needed cheering, it was he who breathed upon the window-pane and drew with his forefinger the most delectable, thought-provoking female shapes.

'If they would only give us bread instead of these eternal potatoes,' he said, 'I could present you with a small Venus de Milo, each of you!' They believed him. They tried breathing upon the glass themselves and drawing female shapes — but the Vandervoord touch was needed. Nevertheless, as long as he was there, it was he who cheered them, teased them into a less neurotic, more pro-portioned attitude of mind, entranced them finally with imitations of the prison authorities, of the night sergeant, of the Captain of the privateer who had boarded the *Agréable* and fallen over his own sword on the quarter-deck.

Yes, it was difficult not to be fond of such a man. They should have been jealous of him (for he was the warders' favourite as well as the prisoners'); they should have resented his sacrilegious comments on French institutions, personalities, ambitions; they should have taken umbrage at his skill on the flute, his luck at cards and dominoes, his popularity with everybody, from the Commandant down to the women who came to empty the slops. It was not fair, but it was somehow inevitable that the very mouse they were attempting to tame and to bribe with cheese-crumbs each night after supper should go to Jan Vandervoord's hand before it went on to any other man's, and sit cleaning its whiskers there, in superb confidence that it had taken the right course.

In only one thing was the Netherlander not their peer. When it came to sharing confidences — and men long confined in close association with each other must occasionally disclose the deepest secrets of the heart or burst — then Jan Vandervoord shut up like a mussel. Of his past life, his family, his private hopes and griefs they knew nothing. Of where he hoped to go and what he would do with himself (apart from his beloved engineering), once he was free again, they knew just as little. Love? Had he indeed any other love but his precious mathematics? While they schemed and plotted ways of escape, envisaging scenes of passionate reunion with friends or parents, wives or mistresses, in a weak never-ceasing frenzy which yet had a quality of permanent hopelessness about it, Vandervoord sat doing his happy hieroglyphics, reassuring himself with the sublime certainties of a perfectly worked out mathematical analysis, yet sparing, even from this, sufficient attention to overhear and to ridicule their plans at the same time.

'What is the use of escaping?' he would inquire of the Captain of Horse; 'if you succeeded in getting back to Paris they would only cut your head off. Bonaparte's police have had five years to collect your *dossier*. You may be sure they have not been idle!'

To the Cornet: 'My dear boy, your commander-in-chief says that the French army is to march henceforth on its stomach. YOUR stomach is certainly not strong enough for any such promenade. I advise you to take up something quieter, like astronomy or religion — but, of course, if you take up religion you cannot return to the land of liberty; man is only free to be an atheist, there!'

To the Colonel: 'My dear sir, you are as well off here as anywhere else. True, the food is disgusting and there is too little of it, but at

128

your age the appetite is insignificant, one might say unimportant, and it is extremely doubtful whether, under a sentence of court-martial at home, it would be any greater.'

This all with the most disarming and heartless grin, while his fingers were still busy racing over·the paper in the service of an Euclidian problem which had no *ifs* and *buts* about it but only the divine Greek-browed dispensation of *therefore* and *thus*.

Nobody, therefore, according to Jan Vandervoord's reckoning, had any sort of reason for attempting to break out of confinement. Everybody was better off where he was. Nevertheless it was Mynheer Vandervoord who was missing at the roll-call one fine morning, and nobody else.

The exasperated Commandant held an inquisition on the elopement of his favourite prisoner.

'I expected better of him, sir, I did indeed,' said the sergeant on night duty. True, he had expected *much* better of him—the customary Fifty Guineas in fact, which was the fee exacted by the sergeant for helping a prisoner to escape and to join the smugglers on the day of the 'run'. Instead of which, he had been lured away into his own quarters to discuss this very question of fifty guineas, and had there been knocked insensible with the butt of his own rifle, deprived of his own clothes and left gagged and bound with his own shirtsleeves, exactly as if M. Vandervoord were one of the dirty French cut-throats and not a Dutch gentleman after all!

The fact that Vandervoord had been content with such rusty old methods of escape, was added insult to the authorities, great and humble. He had been, finally, as contemptuous of them as he had been of everything else during his incarceration.

Well, if Vandervoord had so offensively under-estimated the wits and powers of the prison authorities, they did not so intend to under-estimate *him*! The usual bill was printed, advertising an escaped French Prisoner at such and such a time on such and such a day, wearing such and such; the usual crude personal descriptions—height, six feet four inches, face long, brown-coloured, eyes blue, wig grizzled, *with a prancing kind of walk* and a good command of English, was circulated and pasted up in all the appropriate places. The final sentence: 'This Person may attempt to pass himself off as Dutch' might have amused Vandervoord had he chanced to come across the description. At least, he could argue, the authorities were consistent to the bitter end!

CHAPTER XI

A RECAPTURE

... And I beheld, and lo a black horse, and he that sat on him had a pair of balances in his hand. And I heard a voice in the midst of the four beasts say; A measure of wheat for a penny, and three measures of barley for a penny, and see thou hurt not the oil and the wine. — REVELATION

THE erection of a lighthouse at Orford Ness in the year 1792 served a double purpose; to warn honest mariners of the dangerous tide to be expected there (which moves at seven and a half knots and takes all the shingle bottom along with it), and to warn smugglers that an eternal eye of unprecedented candle-power would, in future, keep watch and ward of all their movements.

Captain Bromewell, as a local landowner, was naturally concerned in and by its erection and with his brother landowners he had attended the opening ceremony. Afterwards he had talked on the shingle for some time with Captain Twigg, whose *Speedwell* happened just then to be unloading a blameless catch of mackerel at the Haven, discussing the affair from all possible points of view.

From most points of view the lighthouse was a mixed blessing. True to their prognostications, Mr. Pitt's treaty with the French had not been worth the paper it was written on and — with a renewed prospect of the opening of hostilities between both countries — smuggling was again almost as prosperous a trade as it had been before the treaty, and would have gone on being so but for this lighthouse, with its much too curious staff of look-out men. And yet, as a patriot and a local bigwig, Captain Bromewell was bound to approve of the whole scheme, though Captain Twigg was under no such obligations.

So they stood together one day on the shingle, looking down on the new lighthouse. In Captain Twigg's opinion, which he was never tired of expressing, 'Reckon that wunt nawthen fer to guide th' mariners by, that's agin the Frenchies!'

Captain Bromewell, surveying the lighthouse through his telescope, could not agree. He said so, repeating for the hundredth time that we were ostensibly at peace with those so-and-sos.

Captain Twigg shut one eye and spat into the shingle. An odour of mackerel came from him — more of it than Captain Bromewell (who had a sensitive nose) would have tolerated in anyone but an accomplice. But one cannot accuse an actor of playing his part.

'Ah, that don't niver do to trust the Frenchies, Cap'n,' went on the ancient mariner. 'Look how they treat their king and queen! Look what they did to the King of Prussia, ay and Hungary and the Dook of Austria! Mark my words, Cap'n, we ain't finished with the Frenchies yit and the gemmen up in London fare to know it! That's why we got that!' He spat once more towards the lighthouse. 'They'll be tidyin' up the little owd Castle nixt, see if they don't!'

Though his companion was still unresponsive, this did not deter Everybody's Friend; how else should a title of universal friendliness have ever been won? He went on, laying a hairy hand, still silver with mackerel scales, on Captain Bromewell's arm and spitting expertly, this time inland, in the direction of Orford Castle:

'When I wore a little owd chap that high,' he said, 'they towd me of th' Monster in that; that had no legs, they reckoned, only a little owd tail like a mermaid and great ears like a bat, and that hadn't skin, only scales like the mackerel, so they useter say. I reckon *he* were a Frenchie too, come to spy out th' land.'

Captain Bromewell's only response was to shift his weight restlessly from one foot to another; the shingle shifted with him. He still applied the telescope to his eye but this time wrong way round, as if by minimizing the building optically he could in some way reduce its activities also to minute proportions. He did not bother to remind Captain Twigg that the nationality of Orford's time-honoured 'Monster' changed through the centuries with the local feeling of the district. When we had been at war with the Dutch, the Monster was rumoured to be a spy from Rotterdam; when East Anglia had fought against the Crown in the Civil War, the Monster had been a man from the Shires — an inept clumsy brute, an Englishman inside out as it were. And for some time now, needless to say, the Monster had had a French record, though the record was all of him that remained.

Nevertheless, both Captains could agree on one point absolutely, which was that it never paid to trust the French. If the lighthouse were really 'agin the Frenchies', then both men could endure its erection with a good grace. For they both lived in a flat land with an open and vulnerable coastline which, in times gone past but never forgotten, many invaders had broached. The Celts had been some of the first. Romans followed Celts, landing their legions where later the Vikings would tread, building great walled cities and splendid roads across from the East of England to the West. Children with buttercup-coloured heads scattered over the fen country proclaimed their Viking ancestry. William the Conqueror in choosing the shorter sea-route was merely the exception which had proved the rule. After the Normans there had been the Dutch and the Spaniards to prepare against and now, from all accounts, it was the French. The French were up to no good, one didn't need to look through any telescope to see *that*, nor yet to turn the beam of a lighthouse upon them to disclose their evil intents. They were all too apparent by land or by sea.

It was a couple of months after this conversation that France, boldly ignoring the lighthouse and all it stood for, declared war upon England and Holland, simultaneously boiling over her own frontiers in all directions, carrying all before her. This same year had seen the capture of Vandervoord and his companions and a year after that, to the month, Vandervoord made his escape.

Having escaped he turned his face, as instinctively as all other escaped prisoners, towards the coast, rejoicing to journey into the morning sun as soon as it was up and to feel it setting behind his back in the evening. Such exhilaration filled him at his recovered liberty that on passing a sand-quarry on his first day he paused to fill his shoes with sand, lest his springing gait, even more springing in the joy of liberty, should betray him. It was a shrewd move.

Luck went with him on the whole. Ripe cherries in wayside orchards helped to stay the pangs of hunger though not to abate them, but they were fruits of Paradise, since he had tasted no fruit in the prison camp. Best of all, when he was half-way to Stowmarket (and was not Stowmarket itself half-way to the coast?) he had come upon a gypsy bathing in a pond. Vandervoord took the sweaty clothes at the side of the horsepond as a Gift of Providence, leaving the gypsy to wonder and blaspheme over the sergeant's outfit.

Disguise as a regular gypsy would not have been wise, for gypsies were unpopular folk, but we have said that luck was with Vandervoord, and the gypsy had lately benefited from the wardrobe of a clergyman. The dingy black coat, green at the cuffs and worn at the buttonholes, with six steel buttons to clasp it to the figure concealing all beneath, fitted Vandervoord like somebody else's glove. He chuckled as he wriggled into it, twisting his old cravat about till nothing of it showed above the coat but a thin white band. There was no hat — a drawback certainly — but Providence was still not neglectful; two miles further on he was able to take one from a scarecrow in a barley-field — undeniably the worse for wear but still with crown and brim. It protected his head from the sun thereafter and hid his features from too curious eyes; what more could he ask of any hat? It was also reasonably plain and clerical.

Despite the sand-ballast in his shoes the French Prisoner could not help prancing along the dusty wayside tracks in a distinctly unclerical way, filling his lungs almost to bursting with the pure air which grew (or so he fancied) ever more salty as he journeyed on. The miles vanished under his feet as if they had been mere paces. The first breath of freedom, doubly precious because it had been reft from him in the first place without cause or warning, had an alchemy in it which defied all fatigue. A man so happy *could* not be tired. But he had to have a Bible, of that he was convinced, for what Minister ever travelled without a Bible? Other luggage he might happily dispense with in that disguise, but a Bible was a veritable necessity.

Well, he was Fortune's darling that particular day for in Bury, which he reached towards evening, he stumbled almost directly across a second-hand bookshop with Bibles and other devotional volumes displayed casually in a box on the pavement outside the shop. Luck could go no further. The shopkeeper was engaged, he could hear, in an argument about the morality of Revolutions with another gentleman, who was standing listening with his eyes shut as if to prevent any possibility of his seeing the bookseller's point of view. Under cover of their joint absorption, Jan Vandervoord smuggled a Bible under his arm, dropping the silver buckle from his shoe into the box by way of exchange.

The Bible he kept tucked closely but not, he hoped, inconspicuously under his right arm; the chart of Portsmouth harbour crackled against his breast under his shirt; in the clergyman's capacious pockets rested his bone toys, the little windmill, the set of chessmen, the brooches, flute and other trifles.

It would have been folly of course to have considered disposing of the bone toys while still so far inland; they were recognizable, easily enough, as prison products in that part of England as much as on Dartmoor where, as Vandervoord knew, every peasant with an egg or loaf to spare on market-day could exchange it for toys such as his at the prison-gates, and did. Hungry as he was, he put the idea from his mind, lunching at midday off the rest of the cherries. A drink from a convenient stream and a handful of watercress to end with, sent him further on his way, a little less tired, a trifle less hungry, into the sun.

There is not room to describe in detail the ingenious shifts by which Vandervoord made the journey and eventually reached the longed-for coast, coming down to it, in the end, not far from the very spot on which Captain Bromewell and Everybody's Friend had stood, discussing the lighthouse. His flute had procured him the money for one meal; his hat (used as a collecting-box) during the discourse of a genuine Wesleyan preacher, procured him the money for another; a friendly farmer, jogging homewards towards Saxmundham, had given the courteous stranger a lift to take him to the bedside of his dying friend — what man could refuse such a request? At Saxmundham, or just outside it, there had been a shady and convenient dell with a cow in it docile enough to be milked.

The dell with the cow in it gave him the milk; the hill succeeding it gave him the view of Orford Castle with beyond it, unbelievably beautiful beyond it, a glimmering line of grey-blue waters which could only signify the sea.

Had Vandervoord indeed been of the persuasion which his clothes suggested he might at this point have knelt down like Columbus's men and, in gratitude to Providence, have kissed the ground which showed him his heart's desire. But all he did was to kick the sand out of his shoes as an impediment no longer needed and run, with strides almost as long as his evening shadow, down the hill slope and across the intervening meadows towards Orford and its Haven. The toys thumped in his pockets as he ran, the Bible bumped under his arm. It would not do. 'You've served your purpose, *Camarado*,' he told it, stopping long enough to cram the book into the open bole on a much-polled oak (where for several years after it greatly puzzled and incommoded the squirrel which commonly used this spot as winter larder).

Free of this burden, and ever more confident in the safety of the now rapidly-descending dusk, the French Prisoner ran onwards, drawn irresistibly despite his footsoreness towards his journey's end on this side of the water. The sight of the lighthouse, which opened its wary yellow eye suddenly ahead of him made him stop dead in his tracks—but only for a moment. If there were a light-house, that meant there were boats about — and a boat was his ambition. Enough of barns and ditches and haystacks, he would sleep in a boat to-night — and push off for freedom and the Dutch coast in the morning!

The cleverest of us sometimes blunder. Perhaps Providence had been just a little too kind to the French Prisoner up to that moment; perhaps after the long strain of travelling his quick wits were too tired to weigh the wisdom of his actions any longer. At any rate, no sooner had he thought of sleeping in a boat than it seemed to him that absolutely nothing else would do. An hour or so's careful skirting took him past the dangerous precincts of the little town and on to the dark marshy land of the foreshore. He was safe enough, here. The military would still be searching for him round about the smug-glers hide-out, the Blue Goose at Bury (he had seen to it that his final words to the trussed-up and half-conscious sergeant had contained a passing reference to Bury). He would seek out a dinghy or some other small craft, sleep for an hour or so in it to recover his strength and then, as soon as the nibbling tug at her rope betrayed the tide ebb, he would set off on the bosom of the receding waters towards the dawn — and home!

Stopping on the last slippery tuft of grass which fringed the shingle of the seashore, Vandervoord wet his forefinger and held it up. A palpable breeze from the West convinced him even more in his purpose. Aboard for freedom and the Netherlands!

Perhaps we shall never know more of this man than is shown by this decision; all his wit and ingenuity, the genuine ability of his enterprise ruined finally by a piece of bravado as gallant as it was foolish. He found his dinghy bobbing sleepily amongst its sisters and the seaweed, made fast to an ancient groin; he tested, by touch alone, its ropes, rudder, rowlocks, persuaded himself that the reefed canvas about the mast was as seaworthy as the rest of the equipment. He was in luck again. From the prepared state of the dinghy it was evident that a small family crew had intended — as he now intended — to slip out with her on the next ebb. Only the oars were lacking — but the breeze from the West rendered oars unnecessary. All he had to do was to wake in good time — while the real owners were still rubbing the sleep out of their eyes — and slip out, letting the breath of Heaven blow him home! With this intention he entered the dinghy, baled out the inevitable dregs of water (more as a gesture, as one offers a wisp of oats to a still unbridled horse) and, ever gently, ever silently, ever gingerly, lowered himself into the space he had contrived between ropes and nets and, curling round once or twice as a dog does to make itself comfortable, lay back to sleep, utterly tired out yet preposterously at ease, and winking back at the winking eye of the lighthouse once or twice before he drifted off into unconsciousness, as if to say 'Aha, we know a thing or two, you and I! We can beat the world together!'

This is all we know — for what else can we know? We see the man sleeping there, so gloriously, so uncomfortably, with his peruke slipping back off his head on to the rope-coil and his thin, clever face resting enigmatic in slumber upon his arm; his hand lying thrown over the rowlock in something which would seem abandon in anyone else but which still, even in sleep, has about it (since it is his hand) a sort of awareness, as if it were ready even then to be up and doing any one of the hundred tasks its master had taught it. Why should he be here at all, at this moment, abandoned to dreams, upon the restless yet subdued rocking of the waves? Why escape now? To what purpose? What, if he makes his escape and gets overseas, does he purpose to do?

He was taken, of course, next morning by the first batch of fishermen coming down to their boats on the foreshore. Although he could still have gone on sleeping for a week, he woke at a touch as he had always done — instantly awake, instantly good-natured, instantly aware — as he showed by a comic grimace, a half-Gallic shrug — that the game was up. Nevertheless, true to the last to his identity, he ran up as always his own flag; 'From there,' he said, pointing across the North Sea to his invisible country, 'I'm a Netherlander, gentlemen'.

It was no use. They had been on the look out for him, they assured him, helping him solicitously once more on to *terra firma*. Yes, they'd been told to look out sharp for an escaped French prisoner.

They were quite kind to him. After all, he represented prize-money. He was helped so tenderly up the shingle indeed, by these good sailormen, brushed down so gingerly, handed his ridiculous borrowed hat so reverently that it almost seemed as if they feared that — without these civil attentions — he might expire untimely amongst them and so do them out of their honest reward. He could have laughed at the thought if he had not been, under his surface awakeness, still so confoundedly and overwhelmingly tired.

For want of a better place he was taken to Orford Castle where, as the sergeant conducting him there genially informed him, the superstructure might not be in the best repair but the dungeons were as good as ever. 'We'll have the rest of it in as good trim soon,' said the man. '*We'll* show you Frenchies!'

There was a small gang of men working even then on the castle ramparts, repairing, in a leisurely fashion, the damage of centuries. A man-of-war stood out to sea beyond the vigilant lighthouse and two small but powerful-looking cannon with their attendants, Vandervoord saw, kept watch with their snouts directed over the Haven. In the innocent light of early morning it all looked like a flat panorama, some detail from an Italian primitive, charming but unconvincing. Still, the guns must receive their due, so Vandervoord-Vinvaud said to his gaoler as they passed them 'Pourquoi ces armaments?' in the best Bonapartist accents, and his gaoler replied appreciatively that that was the lingo, damn him if it wasn't, and don't talk it to him but step out smart and look lively my lad or you'll know the reason why.

Coincidence takes as much delight sometimes in a near miss as in a bull's-eye. Vandervoord could not know it but one of the groups of gaping fishermen which looked up as he passed them was the crew of Speedwell, the gallant men of Captain Twigg. Captain Twigg himself, peering out of the bar parlour of the Bull as the smart-stepping sergeant and his capture went by, could not know that there, but for the grace of God, went a cargo which might have been worth Fifty Guineas to him (on the other side). Nobody knew except Coincidence, and she must have been laughing up her sleeve.

From the prisoner in Orford Castle, we turn to the prisoner of Miss Hannah Bromewell.

Dear Father, wrote Harriet from the fastnesses of Westmorland, If you do not let me come home for haysel I shall run away from Here and you'll not see me again, I have done London as I promised and now I have been Shut Up here for I dont know how long while you and Clancy have all the Fun. Let me come home and even if you dont let me I shall come! If you think my Manners improved by this stay I shall be surprized, my temper gets worse each day and no wonder. Dont believe my aunt if she says I Help her, I dont, she has no need of help and well you both know it. I want to be at Redonda again!

Dear Harry, wrote Clancy on his father's orders, Father says I am to thank you for your letter and say you have no gratitude but you may come home for Harvest if you are so set on it, you are too late for Haysel, anyway the rain spoilt the last rakings. Clem and Sophy have a daughter, they have gone to Lausanne. Horney Macallister is studying at the Temple, I am to come for you on Tuesday, which will be more fun at least than sticking here in this hole. Meet me at York at the Mitre.

Dear Tom, wrote Miss Hannah Bromewell, It's no use, the girl pines for her home and will never do here, though she has had every kindness shown her. She's a true Bromewell, consequently when her heart's set on a thing she won't do till she gets it. It was the same in London. I flatter myself her manners are less brusque than they were and that meeting with company as she has done lately has a little rubbed off the uncouthness of which I complained to you. But you gave her to me too late by six years, I should have preferred a filly foal to a two-year-old. She's so handsome too when she flares up that I scold her — as I expect you do — partly for the fun of seeing her stamp and sparkle. But as to marriage, I can't get her near enough to a man here without fear of a scene of some sort like that in the church! I had great hopes as I told you of Sir Roland's eldest but all *he* has said after two sets of words with my fine lady, was that I should have tied a red ribbon where her tail should be to show she was a kicker! I am very much afraid he is right and that Harriet in genteel society will never do. Our one chance would have been to dazzle her quickly and marry her off before she had time to catch her breath. But how can you dazzle a hoyden with no eye for a uniform? The whole Garrison at York never made her so much as wink an eyelid, it is all Redonda, how we do this at Redonda and what will be doing now at Redonda all day long. If you can tell me how to cure this unnatural homesickness I will tell you Mason's drench for stopping a cow breaking service and that would be the best tit for tat I could make you. How is it with you there? According to Harriet it is all Up Horn and Down Corn with you and you are ploughing in your pasture land because of the wheat price. Thank God I'm not tempted to do likewise but will live and die with my sheep, war or no war. P.S. She goes like a demon possessed on that sidesaddle!

In default of there being an army tribunal within reach the French Prisoner was brought before the local magistracy to be charged with his offence. These gentry, not having had so unusual a culprit brought before them for some time, could not bear afterwards to part with him, and sent messages to Peterborough asking their permission to incarcerate him at Orford Castle 'pending further investigations'. Peterborough proved only too willing to shift the responsibility for M. Vandervoord on to other shoulders, further investigations and all, and consequently Vandervoord spent some weeks in the castle dungeons, the most interesting prisoner there since the Monster of ancient fame. His quiet civil manners reassured the population, which had begun by expecting flames to issue from his nostrils and fire from his mouth. As Orpheus with his lute tamed trees, so Vandervoord with his flute tamed the burly sergeant, the nervous troopers, the local seamen and peasants all. He had a sweet plaintive way with it and made music which used to dissipate itself through the prison bars of a summer evening – notes which frolicked and then lost themselves in the air over the village green amongst the last swooping swallows and the first bats. Indeed, the green outside the castle became quite thronged whilst this music was on, and groups of local worthies might be observed sitting there, evening after evening, puffing contentedly at their pipes or knitting their mittens and stockings, to the piping airs of the French Prisoner.

Nevertheless, despite the balmy summer weather, the small but absorbing occupations and interests of the country people in East Anglia, war was slowly but surely beginning to play its usual part in reducing everything to a slower tempo and a drabber tone. Across the Channel and the North Sea, too far for English eyes to descry but still too near for comfort, loomed the hitherto invincible armies of the new France. Behind these, again, palpitated the heart of the Revolution, smoky, hardly yet satiated with civil blood. Paris and the word Terror became a species of unholy sisters, and the plains of Europe, spreading far and wide around them, deteriorated slowly but surely into places for military occupation instead of for life and labour. Even the mountains of Europe were not immune. A shepherd or farmer looking down from those pure heights might still see, on every side, evidences of war and conquest and plunder with the flag of the Tricolour flying above them. Brigades, platoons, regiments, divisions parcelled out all Europe between them – groups of tired but wary men, far from home, resting with their muskets ready between their hands. Anxious populations from the North to the South of the whole trembling Continent asked themselves, *Where will Bonaparte strike next? Who will fall next?* and hoped that it might be towards the West — towards England.

Inevitably in this pause between one invasion and another, the trade of Europe dwindled and all but died. The English fleet — the strongest hope and stoutest protection of the English people — block-aded the French and Dutch ports in the hopes at least of inconveni-encing the enemy. Neutral countries, equally inconvenienced by an affair they considered none of theirs, were not slow to protest, sometimes even to show their admiration for the active French and their scorn for the passive English who, nevertheless, proved so unpleasantly unpassive when it came to stopping merchant ships upon their lawful occasions and searching — even confiscating — cargoes.

But all this, the irritable reactions of neutrals, the forebodings of all Europe, the future machinations of the enemy, concerned the English people less than any other people as always, and affected their lives and thinking least. There was a war on; yes, but so often there was a war on. There was a War with France; well — so often there was a war with France too. Who were they to get excited about it? It was tiresome; so is a summer of wet weather — and nothing is to be done about either except to bear with it and get through it somehow and emerge again — as one always did — into peace and sunny weather.

But the price of living has a way of rising in wartime, however little — or much — one thinks about it, and so it did now, slowly, inexorably, month by month. Least of all, so far, it affected the country places. Bread — at the moment — there was a-plenty and when Harriet Bromewell returned to Redonda it was through a countryside as rich in rippling acres as only predominantly agri-cultural land can be. And wheat was Lord of the Harvest — at the unprecedented price of one hundred and fifty shillings the quarter.

Wheat at a hundred and fifty shillings a quarter; a farm labourer at seven shillings a week. Put the two together and observe that a labourer may, out of that sum, buy three loaves of bread and a pound and a half of beef — if he can get it — for a week's supply for himself and his family. But meat was growing scarcer every day. The farmers, as Miss Hannah Bromewell had pointed out, had upped corn and downed horn with a vengeance, and now beasts were becoming as rare as the pastures which once ran them. *Grow Corn!* was the national cry, the patriotic duty, and the farmers, praying Heaven to preserve Mr. Pitt and keep the war a-going, rejoiced in profits so heartening that they were ready just then to turn even the seashore and the rough moors and marshes into ploughland and to harness the draught-oxen to an improvised plough.

Captain Bromewell was not slower to take advantage of this situation than the rest. He had some acres of marshy land bordering on to the Shearings — lush enough fields to take beasts in the summer months but waterlogged and useless through the rest of the year. These too, he reckoned, should be brought into service-able condition and grow the inevitable, the only crop. As to drain-ing it off, well that feller at Orford Castle was a Dutchman, or so he claimed, and Dutchmen sucked in knowledge about drainage, pumps and dykes with their mothers' milk. With such a brain to be picked for the asking, Captain Bromewell was the man to do the picking.

It was thus that, one evening in early autumn, Harriet Bromewell first set eyes on the French Prisoner. He was standing before the desk in her father's morning-room at Redonda, his battered hat between his hands, the picture of submissive attention. Her father was deep in explanations — a trifle too loud and aggressive but meant well for all that. Harriet intended to put down the accounts for her part of the farm (the fowls and geese), and depart with the usual impatient flouncing of her skirt as if it, like its mistress, was eager to be off and about some further urgent business.

This was her intention. But as she put the accounts down she could not resist running her glance quickly over the face and figure of the Orford Monster of whom she had heard so much. She knew at once that it was the Orford Monster for, though he still wore the dusty black jacket and breeches in which he had been captured, they had sewn a flaunting yellow circle between his shoulder-blades as a target for the sentry's Brown Bess in the event of another attempted escape. This circle had caught her eye on entering. So now she let her eyes take their fill, scornfully, of what she could see of the man's face and bearing.

He did not appear to notice her, perhaps because she was partly behind him, perhaps because he desired to give his full attention to her father. With brown hands clasping his hat in front of him at thigh-level, brown eyes fixed steadily upon her father, he was to all appearances absorbed in the task of being a man on probation — a prisoner whose co-operation might earn him some bettering of strict circumstance. Captain Bromewell's voice roared on and on; *my* land, *my* fields, *my* ditches, *my* ploughs, *my* horses, *my* corn. It was a theme dear to both father and daughter, but the responses from the stranger were not, to Harriet's mind, quite as quick as they should have been.

It was odd. He said very little, in a deep grave voice, and that little was respectful and to the point — yet Harriet, lingering in the doorway, had the strong impression that this man was making a fool of her father. Her fine black eyebrows flew together at the thought, her nostrils quivered and her grip tightened on the door-handle as if she would crush it; but still she did not turn it and go out of the room.

If he would look at her, she would know better whether her suspicion was correct. It became a monstrous impertinence that he had *not* looked at her. Anyone else but a Monster would have leapt to open the door to the mistress of the house! But no. The French Prisoner — or the Dutchman or whatever he was — stood only as if stuck to the spot by the desk, his lowered gaze never wavering from Captain Bromewell's face, his hands never stirring from their submissive clasping of the hat.

Furiously angry by now, with her grip of the brass door-handle imprinting the full impression of Diana Hunting upon her palm, Harriet willed the French Prisoner to look at her. To be ignored by her father (when he was deep in farm affairs and unless he wanted her advice upon them) was one thing; to be ignored by any other single human being was shame unendurable.

Unendurable too the suspicion, ever deepening, that he knew she was there and would not look at her out of pure contrariness;

that he knew she desired him to look at her; and that deep down inside him, beneath those deplorable garments with the sign of shame between the shoulder-blades, he was shaking with silent laughter at them both.

CHAPTER XII

THE INEVITABLE OCCURS

I did not choose thee, dearest, it was Love
That made the choice — not I . . .
WILFRED SCAWEN BLUNT

BECAUSE it was the last thing that Harriet desired, her father 'took to' the French Prisoner. The man was intelligent, respectful, anxious to be useful, and though he had had no actual experience of land-drainage he claimed to be an engineer, and pumps, like pistons, interested him. It was worth taking him on trial, at any rate. So, the word of a J.P. proving sufficient magic, the French Prisoner was released from Orford Castle and lent to Captain Bromewell by the military authorities, on extended parole.

This was particularly annoying to Harriet. Wherever she went upon her lawful occasions it seemed she must inevitably come up against the French Prisoner with that odious yellow circle on his back. It shone out like a horn-poppy when he was pacing the fields with Captain Bromewell; it affronted her to catch up with it and its solitary owner on the drive. If it was a muddy day she did her best, on such occasions, to spatter him with the mud from her pony's hoofs; and when the winter had passed and the March winds had dried the roads to dustiness again, she delighted to shower him with dust in the same manner — switching her pony suddenly and clattering away, with a great show of heels, from her misdemeanour.

There was an occasion when — if he had been a man — he would have opened a gate for her. But he did not. Instead, he merely leant back against it, positively resting on it and rubbing his shoulders (with that shameful sign between them) against the topmost bars. The March sunlight wrinkled his face into numberless lines and she set her pony at the gate just to *teach* him, the heels swooping past less than a foot from his shoulder (a performance which frightened the pony, it must be admitted, more than the other two).

He had not stirred from his position at the gate-side, though he had had the grace to cast his glance backwards over his shoulder to watch her progress. She wheeled round and came dancing back, letting the pony toss its head and fling bubbles of saliva about so that some of them landed — as she had desired — upon his dusty shoulders.

'It would have served you right if I had killed you!' she panted, remembering only after she had spoken that these were the first words she had ever addressed to him. They had the air of being the tail-words of an ancient quarrel rather than the introduction to a new one.

He was busy brushing the saliva-bubbles from his coat, carefully, with his clean handkerchief. (To see such a clean handkerchief come out of such a dirty old coat was like seeing the silky-thin petals of a white peony burst from its battered green case.) He brushed and brushed — just as though the old thing was in danger of spoiling!

'You would have been mortified beyond words, Mademoiselle,' he said at last, 'if I had done what you wished.'

'What do you mean? How do you know I wished anything?'

'I mean, you wanted me to see your horsemanship and that if I had opened the gate for you, you would not have had that pleasure.'

'*I* would not have had — !' began Harriet.

'Ah yes, it was a pleasure to me, too. It was *unique*.' He pronounced the last word in a foreign way, screwing up his eyes into slits in the brittle Spring sunshine and looking at her as if she were a distant, somewhat difficult view.

The pony danced to and fro, curvetting, anxious to be off. Harriet would not let her. There was a savage sort of satisfaction in having exchanged words with the Monster at last; in finding that he, as she, was capable of dealing blows.

It tormented her not to know what he meant by unique. But

nothing would induce her to ask. No, wild horses themselves should not drag the question from her!

'What do you mean, M. Vandervoord, by unique?'

He paused, reaching his long arm negligently over her side of the gate — not to touch her but to pull a cluster of hawthorn leaves off a twig on that side. He slipped them into his mouth and began to chew them up, thoughtfully. Finally:

'It was the first time that I have seen you at ease with another being,' he said. 'While you were jumping the gate, you were not fighting. You were one with your mount. All the other times I have seen you, you have been fighting.'

'What a farrago of nonsense!' Harriet burst out, not knowing what farrago meant but using one of her aunt's phrases to express contempt. Yet it delighted her, in a way she simply could not understand, that all the times before when he had seemed not to notice her existence, he had been, all the same, as acutely aware of it as she of his. Didn't his last remark show it?

The pony had given up the effort to make off, and was by now snatching at the grass at its forefeet in the greedily caressing way of small horses. Its loud cropping was the only sound.

Vandervoord was looking at her now with his arms folded along the top of the gate and his head resting on his arms. His eyes were still screwed-up against the sun.

'Yes, you are very handsome,' he said at last. 'That is what you wanted me to say, isn't it? And you are very young. You wish to deny that you desired me to compliment you. You want to fight me, to spatter me with contradictions as you have spattered my coat, in the past, with your dust and mud. But you see, I don't *want* to fight —'

Harriet snorted: 'And you a soldier!'

He shrugged a little, without moving his arms from the gate or his gaze from her face.

'All prisoners of war are not soldiers. I am an engineer —'

'Yes, you told my father that! It was a trick, I daresay, to prevail upon him to give you your parole!'

'It was *his* desire that I should come here to work for him — not mine.'

Mutinously, disconnectedly, Harriet said after a minute, glancing down and picking at the thong of her whip.

'You are quite wrong. I don't know what you mean when you say I want to fight!'

'Yet you understand very well what I mean when I admire your beauty.'

She looked up at him at that, with a lively and yet humble joy (after all, compliments did not often come her way) and was staggered to hear him continue, on an indrawn breath:

'Do not come near me!' — but as if he had not intended her to hear.

A wave of rage mounted to her cheeks, flushing them to rose-colour, making her handsomer than ever.

'You are quite safe, my cowardly little *engineer*,' she said. 'There is the gate between us. I won't eat you!'

He had a way, as she was soon to learn, of making the wrong response — the unexpected, disturbing response. So he said now, correcting her:

'You would not *intend* to. Haven't you a proverb that you cannot eat your cake and have it too?'

'I see! So you are a cake now! One minute you are an *engineer*' (she said the word with ineffable scorn), 'and the next you are a cake. A fine state of affairs, I must say! Even if you *were* a cake — which I deny,' she went on, still divinely rosy with rage, 'I should want to eat something more appetizing!' And her nose wrinkled contemptuously as she looked him up and down.

Strangely enough even this insult did not dismay him. He did not wink an eyelid but still looked at her with his head laid along his folded arms and said, in the same sort of private, indrawn breath he had used before:

'No. You would like to swallow me at one gulp.'

There were many more encounters between them after this, of a similarly rewarding and yet unsatisfactory sort for Harriet. Her deep-lying suspicion remained that, under his quietly correct exterior, Vandervoord was making game of the whole Bromewell family. The odd thing was that her father appeared not to notice this at all. He enjoyed himself with the French Prisoner; he enjoyed straddling his bulk across the table the French Prisoner was working at, watching this invaluable piece of flotsam from the war wrestling with Redonda's drainage problems and — what was more — solving them. A crude kind of *gaminerie* grew up between them — Vandervoord had lewd tales as well as a quick brain and skilful fingers with which to delight his keeper; and some odd part of him, sensing the greedy gusto with which his companion ate up every word, idea, argument, linked itself to a sympathy for Bromewell. He could not have explained it to himself logically; when he tried to do so, he found himself saying that, *au fond*, it was simply because Bromewell accepted him for what he was — a Netherlander. It was heart-warming, a little. A little of one's manhood returned.

But not enough manhood to satisfy the Captain. The longer he and Vandervoord worked together, the less he felt inclined to leave Vandervoord out of his sight. The French Prisoner must do everything with him, go everywhere with him. But there were limits — a-whoring Vandervoord simply would not go. As long as the Captain was sober this idiosyncrasy was merely irritating, but after the second bottle affairs, alas, appeared in a different light and what had been merely an idiosyncrasy became an Insult to English Womanhood. And if the man could so insult the whores then be damned to know what he would do to the good women!

Being baffled in this way was bad for Captain Bromewell's blood-pressure. He began to blame the French Prisoner for shoddy work, for idling, for playing hookey when his back was turned. He threatened him with a return to prison at Orford or Peterborough. But the fish would not bite. There were too many scenes like it to please the Captain — the Captain angry, whacking out his argument with his riding-crop on the table or the back of the chair or against his boots — anywhere handy, and Vandervoord silently standing before him, head bowed, manner acquiescent, but maddeningly remote, for all that.

One could never get *hold* of the man, that was the damnable part. There was always this invisible barrier when you went past a certain point with him — thus far, and no farther — and Captain Bromewell was not accustomed to meeting barriers in his way through life. They had short shrift with him — were made to be flung down. But how to fling down something that you cannot, in the first place, lay hands upon?

There were moments, nevertheless, when the barrier seemed almost to withdraw; when they sat together in Spens' dusty little office, working on the drainage scheme for the fields by the Shearings; when Vandervoord was explaining the working of the model of his proposed pump; when the model was set in motion by those clever, brooding hands and demonstrated all the ingenuity which had gone to its making; when the phrases he used, the mathematical calculations he wrote down were seized upon with delighted avidity by the other man — appreciated, praised, acknowledged to the full. If the discussion of the invention could have remained in the realm of discussion, as an idea, pure and simple, man could have met man and have been friends. But Captain Bromewell had little use for the invention as an Idea he wanted it for practical application, for good honest reasons of prestige and profits.

The hands hovering so deftly above the model, as it went through its evolutions with such uncanny regularity and efficiency, would fall then to Vandervoord's sides. The intimate moment would pass. If the Captain persisted in reducing the whole subject to gross enough terms, Vandervoord would even begin to belittle the invention.

'It won't be all gain, Captain. You can't drain here, and *here*' (brown finger stabbing the chart of the fields) 'without remembering the landfall *there*.'

'To the devil with the landfall there!'

'It *will* be to the devil, sir. There' (with another stab), 'allowing for the gradient, will put you twelve foot under water at high tide.'

The twelve feet under water, however, was outside Captain Bromewell's boundaries.

'Is that any concern of mine? Damnation, Vandervoord, d'you think I'm spending money on this thing (and it'll cost me a deal of money before it's finished—more than *you've* ever had the handling of) to benefit myself or my neighbours?'

Still the monitory finger, stabbing. 'Mr. King's field, isn't it? A nice south fall, you see. A good field for his ewes — Spens says he puts ewes there.'

'To hell with Mr. King's ewes! Are you working for him or for me?'

At that the finger is removed and the chart, uncontrolled, rolls itself up *snap* like a hedgehog, hiding its secrets.

'He can go to law if you ruin his land, I suppose, sir?'

'Suppose what you like! I know that I'm a Justice of the Peace and the largest landowner in the district and that Humphrey King is a Roman Catholic and a newcomer. You needn't exhibit such a precious concern for my interests, I can take care of 'em *myself*, sir! You needn't have sleepless nights on *that* account!'

'As you please, Captain,' and the rolled-up chart is balanced, one end against the other, between the French Prisoner's finger-tips. His eyes are downcast but the crow's-feet at the corners of them are beginning to deepen suspiciously. Captain Bromewell can see perfectly well that M. Vandervoord does not really give a damn about Mr. King's interests, nor yet about his. The subject has only been raised because it amuses M. Vandervoord to upset him before dinner.

'Rot you sir, with your insinuations! I've a good mind to report you for impertinence and have you shut up again!'

'As you please, Captain.'

Knowing, of course, that it does *not* please the Captain and never would — not at this delicate state of affairs. If it is unwise to kill the goose that lays the golden eggs, what consummate folly would it be to wring its neck while it was still in gestation of the very first egg! Ach — it was humiliating, neither to be able to knock the stuffing out of the fellow, as out of Ivory, and bring him to heel just as smartly — nor yet to be able to cajole him to do his tricks, as one wheedled the parrot with sugar.

What was particularly humiliating was that, months after the Captain had given it out to all and sundry that the fellow was a eunuch, it turned out that he had a couple of favourites at Slaughden Quay — in the poorest quarters of Aldeburgh — and visited them whenever the fancy took him. This was not often (if it had been often, it would have been discovered sooner) but still often enough for the late discovery of it to annoy the Captain.

And yet — no longer in embryo in Spens' office but in the

splendid isolation of a barn especially cleared for it — there stood the beginnings of the Vandervoord drainage system. Wreck the master and you wreck the machine, warned Captain Bromewell's shrewd brain. He has mocked you by refusing your help and by choosing his own amusements — but bear with it. There's nothing to be done as yet but overlook it.

If such things were hard for an impatient man to bear, it was also hard to bear with the fellow's popularity. All the servants at Redonda adored him — and had from the first. Wherever he might be about Captain Bromewell's business, whether it was taking mysterious measurements in a damp meadow or jotting down calculations in the barn or the office, there too was a knot of followers. As wasps find out plums so they found out Vandervoord; and the laughter and idleness grew and buzzed, and there was Life.

To a farmer and landowner not unpopular himself until Vandervoord came, this was of all things the most galling.

What irked the father irked the daughter none the less. Together the pair of them burned the months through in their resentment. whilst Clancy went over unashamedly to the enemy's side. To see the House follow the Farm in this manner was unpardonable; it was on account of it — so strange are the workings of Providence — that Clancy was finally awarded his dearest desire — permission to follow in Clem's footsteps and go up to London to study there.

'Let him go!' Harriet had urged. 'He does no work here! He moons about after the French Prisoner all day just to hear his stories — you know that he does! He doesn't care for Redonda at all!'

'He can go, now!' savaged her father. 'But he'll have to settle down here sooner or later if it's the last thing I make him do! I don't fatten up this place for you, Harry — it's for the boys and their children. You must get a place of your own!'

'How shall I get a place of my own, Father? — Listen! Listen!'

Running after him as he marches forward with the dog-like Spens ('Yes Captain, that's so Captain. It would be so Captain, I wouldn't doubt . . .') clutching at the thick coat, striving to make impression, through it, on the solid unyielding flesh of the arm beneath, 'Father, don't be so tormenting! How shall I get a place of my own, and where?'

Beautiful Redonda behind them both, bending forward like a queen. Give her to me. She is my child. She will look after me when I am old.

'Oh, don't fuss so, Harry! How should you get a place? Why, to be sure as other women do, by marrying one — how else?'

Scenes like this were played out regardless of watchers. The French Prisoner himself counted no more than the trees or the furniture — or so at least they made shift to have him believe. He had a tripod which he used for outdoor calculations and one day the sight of him using this, balancing its splayed legs with the utmost calmness and deliberation over the very ground upon which she had just stamped during another battle with her father, was not to be borne. Harriet was old enough to know better — much better — but she darted at the tripod and kicked it over.

It lay with one leg comically in the air, a great daddy-long-legs *in extremis.*

Captain Bromewell, seeing his assistant's work set back by the action, swore at her with passion. The French Prisoner said nothing, but he bent down and rescued the tripod, restoring it patiently to its previous position, and feeling for fractures as a groom might feel the legs of a valuable race-horse.

'If you do that again, my girl,' quoth the Captain, 'I'll have the hide off your back!'

Harriet bit her lip so hard that the bitter taste of blood stung her palate. She could for once say nothing.

Months later she remembered, quite clearly, how the French Prisoner had said to her (but without looking at her, still looking at his tripod) as soon as her father was out of earshot:

'Don't upset yourself too much over a place, Miss Harriet. It isn't worth it.'

And remembered the bitter taste of blood and the red stain on the ball of her thumb after she had sucked it.

She had glanced at him quickly, her eyes full of tears so that she saw only a blurred figure bending over a blurred tripod; and had said with real anguish breathing through her words, and swelling against her stays:

'I think my heart will break!'

'Ah no,' he had said, shaking his head slowly and speaking very quietly (but still to the tripod, not to her), '*People* break hearts, not places!'

And after that they had not spoken for weeks together. Their ways and occupations had lain apart. For him the perfecting of his invention, the pumping-machinery that was to rescue the drowned acres of Redonda; for her the awful beauty of her surroundings — no less awful because familiar — smiting her in each successive season with ever-growing intensity.

In this sensitiveness to her surroundings Harriet was at least unusual. It was not an age or a time for women to let their surroundings impinge upon them — except for such rare spirits as the sisters of poets. For most of them, Outdoors was a space to be traversed between one house and the next. But to Harriet the very ground beneath her feet was sacred, and she had a passion for lying full-length in the meadows, with her cheek pressed against the springing grasses, which was as out-of-season as out of sex.

Her father did not like it, it was unfitting before the servants and senseless sort of behaviour in any case; Susan did not like it, she feared for Harriet's health. She was for ever carrying out shawls and hats and veils, which were flung impatiently away upon reception. Harriet wished Susan to follow the offending garments; to see the girl's feet standing there beside her so patiently, to feel the girl's shadow across her, was enough to madden anyone.

'Go *away*, Sukey!' she said crossly, and — if the feet delayed in moving quickly enough out of her line of vision — 'What thick ankles you have. They get worse and worse!'

After Susan had withdrawn, discomfited until the next time, the grasses she had trodden down would jerk stiffly upright again, one after the other, throwing off remembrance of her weight. Harriet could not dismiss the affair so easily. For a long time after Susan had returned to the house her unwelcome solicitousness stayed behind her, seeming to smother her mistress in its kindly blanket-like persistence. Susan fussed over her, her father roared at her; there was only one person who treated her like a human being, quietly and honestly, and that was the French Prisoner.

The knowledge that she had fallen in love with Vandervoord

came upon Harriet so suddenly one day as she lay out in her favourite spot, that her clenched teeth bit sharply through the grass held between them and her outstretched hand, grasping as much as it could of Redonda's growing greenness, pulled it up by the roots. Her eyes, already closed against the too-ardent sun of May, let a tear trickle slowly downwards as if in premonition of some deadly event and her heart, after bounding within her, felt sucked empty, full of a huge ache and all the accumulated misery of all the world and all the beings that had ever inhabited it, and lived, and loved. It was a different sort of ache from the kind that the thought of losing Redonda sometimes induced in her — a living spasm, not a dead weight of grief. The dazzling dragonfly, agonizing out of its old carcase into newness of life, suffers the same passion of transmutation that Harriet suffered — when she discovered first that what she had conceived as hatred, was love instead.

That day for the first time for weeks she went out of her way to avoid Vandervoord. She who had lain in wait to waylay and wound and taunt him fled now instead in the opposite direction, terrified not of him but of her own behaviour on seeing him. And since there was no place in the whole estate where she might be certain of not encountering him, she kept to the house.

She kept to the house for a week, pleading indisposition to her father. In the evenings, when the French Prisoner had returned to his lodgings in Aldeburgh, she crept out to his workshop (what he called his Toyshop) in a corner of the farm buildings, to feed her eyes upon his possessions — the pencil he had held, the paper his hand had lain across, caressing the hook behind the door where his old hat had hung, kissing the scribbled numerals on the squared paper, and laying her soft, egg-shell brown cheek against the neat ruled specifications of the Vandervoord pumping system. Nobody, needless to say, saw her at these oblations or suspected them; and he himself, resuming his work each day where he had left off on the previous one, knew nothing of the ministering tendernesses which had come between.

If he *had* known, he might indeed have been tempted to escape once more — never to return.

CHAPTER XII

A DREAM—AND A DISCUSSION

> O for the wings of a dove, that I might fly away and be
> at rest! — PSALMS

WHEN girls who have been out in all weathers suddenly keep to
the house and refuse proper nourishment, one may suspect sickness
or love. Love being (from Captain Bromewell's point of view) out
of the question for Harriet, since no proper object of affection was
in sight, and the doctor concurring with the Captain's viewpoint,
Harriet found herself abruptly packed off to her brother Clement's
establishment, which was the top floor of a modest hotel in Lausanne.

Midsummer, if Captain Bromewell had known it, was not the ideal
season for a young invalid in Lausanne; the continent of Europe
itself was not perhaps a restful place for recuperation, since a great
part of it was once more involved in spasmodic war. Nevertheless,
with the areas so vast and communications so slow and with the
Swiss cantons still carefully neutral, it was possible both to reach
Lausanne — despite Bonaparte — and to disport oneself there in
normal fashion, if so desired.

Not that Harriet did so desire. She had been dragged from home,
made violently seasick, jolted across atrocious roads, cheated in
atrocious inns and finally dumped at Lausanne by Clancy 'like a
parcel', as she was not slow to complain. She had not seen Clem
or his wife for eight years and might as well, she felt, have been
visiting strangers. Clancy had immediately left her high and dry
there, to go off pursuing more manly pleasures with his fellow-
spirits from the Temple. He promised to write to Harriet from his
different stopping-places but did not. Nor yet did her father, and
this second omission was much the harder to bear.

There was the further thought, to add to her disquiet, that her
father intended really to dispose of her, this time. She was getting
on; she was twenty-four. No doubt he hoped that under Sophy's

chaperonage some suitable partner might be found prepared to overlook this great age in favour of her undeniable good looks and the dowry. Perhaps he hoped she might discover a passion for some rich *émigré*, and settle down permanently in this land of violent contrasts, lakes and mountains, light and shade, sombre pine forests, joyful bells, and never come home again ... and never *mind* not coming home again. How was one to know *what* he thought, since he did not write? But one had precisely such fears and forebodings, especially round about midnight, lying on a feather bed, not one's own, that goodness knows who had slept on.

Why she had ever allowed herself to be posted from one place to another 'like a parcel', she could not explain. Except that it was not possible to stay at home, with *him* there — and not possible to tear oneself away — and of the two impossibilities one had been achieved for her by other people. But the achievement of it did not make her any more satisfied with her situation. She found Clement changed — much less smart, youthful, ambitious; she found her sister-in-law Sophy as uncongenial as she had always suspected she would be — though not in the way she had suspected; she found her eight-year-old niece Sabrina as reserved and unforthcoming as herself — a plump child with sloe-black eyes and a preoccupation with food and dolls which seemed unhealthy to Harriet, though entirely suitable to Sophy and the servants.

Taking these various circumstances into consideration, it was hardly strange that the mountain air did not benefit Harriet as her elders had intended it should. She felt a prisoner, stifled if she stayed on the Bromewell balcony, looking down at the too-beautiful lake of Geneva with the little boats like painted toys upon it, yet soon exhausted if she ventured forth beneath Sophy's solicitously-balanced parasol, into the shimmering dry heat of out-of-doors.

What exhausted her, invigorated Sophy. The once-secretive bride might have had the sun for paramour, so delightedly she prepared for him with lotions and unguents, so voluptuously rendered herself up, later, to his full gaze. Modest to the point of obliteration in England eight years earlier, in Lausanne Sophy emerged as positively brazen. While the wise natives rested in the heat of the day, while the mutinous Harriet stayed in the shuttered rooms both in the heat and the cool of the day, tapping her foot with impatience to be upon the Harwich boat once more — Sophy Bromewell kept her solar appointments. She would patter indefatigably after her purple shadow in search of equally intrepid society and amusements, her pale face never a whit browner however much she uplifted it to let the sun kiss it, her hand (when she returned after a full two hours' exercise and laid it compassionately across Harriet's damp forehead) still triumphantly dry, like scented paper.

The action, repeated day after day, finally exasperated Harriet. 'Don't touch me, Sophy!' she snapped (and close upon the words, like a loving cheek laid swiftly against another cheek in the darkness, rose up the echo, 'Do not touch me! Do not come near me!' so vigorously, yet so unasked, that angry tears coursed down again from her closed eyes).

'Clem says you have a consumption,' replied Sophy, without pity, but equally without malice; 'I think you have a fever myself, or else you must be in love. Tell me, Harry.' She was odiously close again, sitting down with a smacking contentment, a swirl of flounces — so close to Harriet that the scent of lavender-water in which she was perpetually bathed rushed over her sister-in-law in a warm surge of breath. 'Is it a secret, or have you met Someone?'

'What rubbish you talk, Sophy! I don't intend ever to Do That Thing (she *would* not utter the silly phrase Fall in Love) nor to marry!'

'Aha!' teased Sophy, 'but I *know* Someone . . . !'

That, Harriet grew to learn, was the most intolerable part of Sophy. Every day she *knew* Someone; she drew other people's confidences, hopes, ambitions and small passions to and about herself, whilst she was out with the flies in the noon sun, and buzzing busily — in a way which would have astounded her parents. She could flirt these days, too. Above suspicion like Caesar's wife, as the wife of an English attaché must be — she took liberties and permitted them with a freedom which would have surprised Clem, too, could he have seen them.

And Harriet was a convenience to Sophy — no doubt of that. She was a topic of conversation to be tossed like a ball in the bright sunshine — to be caught again deftly — and to wind her own conversational self round. She was a sure draw for the curious eyes of promenaders, and therefore an asset. Various gentlemen, led on by the topic of Miss Bromewell's visit, piqued by a glimpse of Miss Bromewell's looks, interested — in spite of themselves almost — in the so-difficult-to-see Miss Bromewell, by Sophy's suggestive hints and slight dispraises (calculated, ah so artfully! to arouse male chivalry), made various advances to the young lady. A box of Swiss lace, a volume of Goethe, a bouquet of syringa (too large, too fulsome, too shining to be Redonda syringa and so angrily discarded), tickets for the opera, for the *fête* upon the lake, for the drive up into the mountains . . . all these to be laid at Miss Bromewell's still impatiently-tapping feet — and not to induce any cessation of impatience. And all the time Sophy hovering, half irritated, half amused, wholly unashamed, with the sun pouring his tiger-stripes upon her through the shutters as she stood in Harriet's room, slyly persuading her gloves upon her fingers, preparatory to another rendezvous with the sun. Small wonder that Harriet felt like screaming!

'You should come out, my dear, if you have a headache. You stay in far too much. The breeze will drive it away.'

'The breeze! There never is a breeze, here!'

'Excuse me, Harriet, there is a regular wind off the lake at this hour of the day. A warm wind, too. Colonel Chivers is dying to meet you.'

'He must die then! Tell him I will order better flowers for his funeral than that vulgar syringa he sent me!'

'Harriet!'

'Don't look so shocked, Sophy, it *is* such a pose! Nothing ever shocks you, really. Clem is more easily shocked than you are . . .'

Sophy, pulling and patting at her gloves in tiny movements, eyes downcast, lips smirking a little as if echoing, 'How right you are!', the sun blazing down upon her bare shoulders, turning them to satin (lavender-scented):

'What strange things you say, Harry! It is because you are too idle; you should occupy yourself with something if you won't come out and be civil.'

'You mean be vulgar — let them touch and paw me — ugh! I can't bear it!'

158

Sophy shrugged her shoulders in mock despair. 'I won't dispute with you — you turn round everything I say! But it is a shame to get no benefit from your stay here. Learn French at least!'

'Why should I?'

'It will teach you *les manières engageantes*,' said Sophy, popping her glove-buttons *snip-snap* with a charming finality. Then she tilted her large hat slightly before the glass, held instant, ardent communication with her mirrored self as she always did on such occasions, and sidled downstairs and so out into the sunshine.

'Good-bye, Mamma!' cried Sabrina, emerging for an instant out of her play with the baby-carriage on the balcony and waving down. Mamma's shoulders shrugged again, Mamma pouted, blew a gloved kiss to her precious, descended the iron steps, encountered the waiting cavalier and was immediately caught up with him, in that delicious secret confidence that was her way of talking ... Sophy ordering soap over the counter, Harriet told Clem with spirit after one such demonstration, could make soap sound like the Forbidden Fruit.

Clem laughed, a trifle wryly. There was not much to laugh at, these days. An internal ulcer, unguessed at, gave him the irritability but not the privileges of an invalid. Eight years of dissipation had taken their toll. He had not risen in his profession but rather sunk, being now a kind of *liaison* officer between the commercial and diplomatic interests — no more. He was not happy in his marriage and deceived himself that Harriet did not know it. By mocking at his wife with her, he deluded himself further that in some way he was balancing the score.

'Where have We been to-day?' he would ask.

Harriet would enumerate the streets where We had promenaded, what We had bought, heard said, pronounced Ourselves, and how We looked. She repeated, too, the incident of Our dry hand, dropping the elaborate mockery to blurt out:

'Is she dry like that in bed? All over? I'd as soon sleep with a lizard!'

'Damn it, Harriet, you mustn't bring that vulgar country way of talking with you, out here!'

But it made him writhe; likewise his sister's wriggling imitation of Sophy's shoulder-shrug; the voluptuous casting of the eyelashes upwards, the demure puckering of the mouth as if saying 'I could tell you such things if I would!' The vivacity the 'idle' Harriet put into these mockeries of her sister-in-law showed at least that she was in no consumption. The fire that blazed in her eyes was of scorn, not of fever.

But who is consistent in all his actions? Harriet, whose one pleasure had been to baulk all Sophy's suggestions hitherto, accepted with surprising meekness the suggestion that she should learn French. Sophy—surprised but gratified—intimated that she would share the lessons. There were so many royalist refugees to pick from—it really cost hardly anything at all, and one felt as if one were conferring a favour, which was charming.

'Besides, it is more suitable, Harriet. You must be chaperoned. It will do my accent good even though I have the language already.'

You took French lessons because you were jealous of *her*, Vander-voord was to tease Harriet later. You wanted to show her how quick you could be when you were on your mettle!

No, Harriet's answer was to be. I could endure *her*. Her accent was atrocious, she had no ear and never will have. What I could not endure was having things translated into English for me by Sabrina (for Sabrina was as bilingual as most children brought up on the Continent).

But that was not the true reason either. The true reason was hidden so deep in her own heart that she did not know it herself, until she learnt something of it in a dream.

She dreamed one night that she was a swan, sailing in a grey veiled light upon a lake enclosed by willows and weeping elms. One elm had fallen and its rough trunk lay, a living bridge, across the lake from bank to bank. Upon the half of the lake where the swan that was Harriet sailed, all was grey and sad and quiet — but the other side of the elm-bridge, on the other half of the lake, there were no trees enclosing the water and it shone in the light like a shattered mirror.

The swan that was Harriet was oppressed and sad on her own side of the lake. She struggled to reach the other side, impelled by dream motives, urgent but undisclosed. But her feet were tangled in duck-weed, and leaf-fronds trailed greenly across her white shoulders, restraining her from the attempt. There was poison in the lake — she knew it. She said to herself, with the lucid madness of a dreamer: *It cannot hurt me if I do not drink from it; it can only make me ache with this intolerable sadness, which must, however, be borne.*

Suddenly the air was filled with a whistling sound — an ever louder whistling that broke up into the beating of great wings. The grey sky was darkened still further by these wings, and Harriet cowered under her crowding tree-branches. Another swan, a black one, cast his shadow over the sky, over the lake — followed his shadow, swallowed it up into himself and settled upon the waters of the lake without a sound, so that the surface stirred no more than treacle: then, he lowered his handsome frowning head with the most grace-ful searching gesture, to drink of the deathly water.

The swan that was Harriet cried out in soundless agony at this, *Stop*! But it *was* soundless; her beak was bound about with clinging weeds, her wings and feet were fast in the same weeds, he was doomed to drink and die — the dream decreed it.

He drank, was poisoned almost to death. His black head with-drew itself, sank back upon his black shoulders, a prince dethroned. His eyes were shut, his beak piteously gaping with black poison dripping from it in little sidling drops. The same spasm of lucid madness stirred the swan that was Harriet to a renewed frenzy. *The other side of the elm-bridge*, said her dreaming mind, *the water is pure. A drop of that water will cure him. For he comes from that water, not from this.*

What struggles then, what heaving agonies, what wild flailing of feet and wings to strike clear of the cumbering dream-weeds, to creep forward, up to and under the elm-bridge, pressing hard, hard against the thorns there (sudden inexplicable thorns) so that her swan's breast bled and the dancing, shining water upon the other side became, when she emerged there, specked with crimson! To fill one's beak with one drop of that sweet life-saving water, to face the thorns under the bridge again, to prick one's breast again against them and to stain the water again with blood; to flail and beat and struggle back against the sullen obstacles in the grey sad water, and to bestow that precious drop, that bead of life, into the beak of the dying black swan. . . .

Before she could do it she woke, sweating with terror and endeavour, and guessed, for the brief second before all was sucked back into Unconsciousness, something of the meaning of her dream.

In the mornings, during the next three months, Harriet took French lessons in Lausanne, with Sophy approvingly beside her. In the afternoons she rested, thinking of Redonda and of what would be doing there; and reading the month-old English newspapers with passion, looking always and unsuccessfully for news of that unimportant part of the world that was her home. In the evenings, as often as not, Sophy would be out again at some card party or *musicale* the like of which Harriet would not — after a sampling — join, and which Clem could not, because the crowds and the over-heated rooms made him feel iller than ever.

Yet they proved to be better company to each other — these stay-at-homes — at that time than ever before. A not divine but too human discontent in both generated a sympathy of feeling that was soothing at least in its novelty. Harriet would rail to Clem against her father's sending her out of England for nothing, and at her father's not writing to her; at Clancy's not writing to her — at half a hundred things; while Clement, more quietly but more bitterly, would rail at the international situation, at Bonaparte, at Sophy's unpunctuality and insincerity, at her frivolity and fashion in hats; at his own lack of advancement and the way he was put upon, in the office; at his father's stinginess in not helping him more financially; at Sabrina's lack of affection for him — at everybody's lack of affection for him; finally at the incivility of the old servant responsible for sweeping the offices where he worked, in not uncovering in the mornings when Clem passed him. It was all too apparent, from these accusations, that the whole world was against the once so happy, so confident, so healthy young man, and the knowledge that nobody really cared about such a state of affairs except himself added both to his disease and to his discontent.

Harriet listened and half-listened. Over the whole series of confidences (though unacknowledged) flew the great, torn, black banner of disappointed love. Under its gloom Harriet too found shelter;

and the fact that Clem listened no more intently than she did, feeding inwardly upon his own grievances to the tune of the airing of hers, encouraged her to talk finally of the subject that was in her mind and heart day and night — simply because she could not contain it any more. .

She approached the topic by way of Redonda farm and her father's ambitious new drainage-scheme. Clem was uninterested. When she pronounced the syllables Vandervoord he was still uninterested; when she dared not attempt them again, fearing that her voice caressed the loved syllables too audibly, and when she said instead The French Prisoner, he sat up — or, at least, rolled his head sideways in her direction and looked at her directly for the first time. His father employing a *Frenchman*! A damned rascally Bonapartist! —

Harriet explained that anomaly, too.

'Ah well,' responded Clem gloomily. 'As long as the fellow isn't French . . .' He sat slumped in his *chaise-longue*, not desiring to hear any more but too dispirited to stop her.

Precisely because he did not want to hear — did not properly attend to her — Harriet talked. She exclaimed, as her habit was, against the French Prisoner, how conceited he was, how self-confident, how full of showing-off. She described his pumping-apparatus, nevertheless, with a faithful and accurate enumeration of detail that would have astounded and flattered its inventor could he have heard her. As if it would ever *work*! she ended scornfully.

'I hope at least that he won't persuade the old man to drain those marshes off the Shearings,' commented Clem, out of the depths of his gloom and his cravat. For one moment, in all its tremulous crystalline beauty, he was again mentally in the punt with Clancy, going duck-shooting the night before his wedding, so long, so very long ago. . . . Then the moment vanished into the dark waters. Hail and farewell. He gave a great shuddering sigh, ushering in the words: 'It's a fine place in autumn' upon the last half of it.

'What is, Clem?'

'Redonda.'

Harriet turned swimming eyes upon him at that, smiling most

divinely but unperceived. Her whole beauty, now at its zenith, had always lain in her colouring when illumined by that sudden, rare smile. If Vandervoord had seen her then, he could not have resisted her. Clem could have, but he did not even raise his eyes at the glad movement she made.

Desiring to prolong it, to profit from this underlying sympathy between them, Harriet dropped from her chair to sit on the floor beside him, tucking her feet under her skirts, leaning her head back against his chair.

'Clem?'

'Well?'

'Hear me my French.'

'Oh, the *devil*!' he groaned, half smiling, half with feigned despair; 'go to Sabrina and let her hear it for you; it makes my head ache.'

Harriet stiffened slightly against the chair.

'Thank you, I've no wish to be corrected by a child.'

'You don't like Sabrina.' He didn't accuse, he merely stated a fact.

'She's spoilt,' said Harriet, 'and she's too babyish.'

'Susan makes her more so.'

'Nothing in the world,' said Harriet with bitterness, 'will stop Sukey from making a fuss of people. She would fuss over me if Sabrina weren't here. I am grateful to her for *that*, at any rate!'

There was a pause. The windows before them were open upon a twilight giving way to a summer night. From the invisibilities of the other side of the lake came the fiddles and flutes of Sophy's *musicale*, twinkling across the twinkling water. The great mountains loomed beyond both, encircling the whole scene.

Clem said suddenly:

'You don't like being loved; I don't like *not* being loved.'

It was too true, he seemed to indicate, to need answering, but Harriet answered remotely out of the dusk:

'I *do* like being loved ... At least I *should* like it — but not by servants!'

The sharp regret she felt at having uttered this sentence— once rashly out of her mouth — was wasted, for her brother gave no indication of having heard it. The silence between them continued, the lights continued to prick the blackness over the darkening lake, the fiddles and flutes continued to twinkle with the lights. At last Clem said with another quiet sigh:

'It's odd one can't ever tell how things will turn out. Me now, I'm — what? Nearly thirty, and devil a bit happier than when I left you all at Redonda. You're — what? Twenty-four. Getting on, Harry — getting on! And no more contented than I am, I swear! Yet you never wanted the same sort of things that I wanted, did you? And you were a fiend for getting what you *did* want. Us out of the way, for instance. And now you have even got Clancy out of the way!'

'For a while,' Harriet admitted.

'For a while,' conceded Clem. Even in repeating each other's words there was soothingness — a strange, sad kind of sympathy.

There was another silence, long enough for an angel to fly over Lausanne perhaps, and to stir that great black banner that Clem had set up, with his unheeding wings.

Moved by some such invisible, intangible impulse Harriet cried out then:

'Oh, Clem, what do you suppose is to become of us?'

'What do you mean?'

'Of us *all*, Clem! Why are we here at all! Why should *you* be here, now, in Lausanne? Why should *I* be here — '

And why, continued the unspoken end of the sentence in her mind and her heart, why (most important of all) should the French Prisoner have ever come to Redonda, and have driven me out like this?

Clement answered the spoken half of her question:

'My dear girl, too easy! I am here because my duties compel me (he laughed sneeringly as he said it, as he always laughed these days at personal references, seeking thus to forestall Fate, or perhaps Sophy) and *you* are here because Father sent you to us for your health; or to keep you out of mischief perhaps. Perhaps,' he went on, feeling suddenly better — more confident and well than he had felt for weeks — 'perhaps there's some young fellow at home making advances to you — '

'There is *not*!'

'Or some foolish fancy of my sister's — how's that, eh? that the old man hopes that time and absence will cure.'

'He thinks nothing of the sort!' flashed Harriet. 'Who should there be of that sort at Redonda?'

Clem was abruptly tired again — too tired to tease further. 'Oh — I don't know, it's so long since I saw the place or knew the neighbours there. *You* usen't to be the fine lady you are now. . . . Seriously, Harriet, what is to become of you?'

Without remembering it, he echoed her earlier words, so bringing her chief fear home to roost. Her heart thumped:

'If Father sent me here so that you and Sophy might find a suitable *parti* for me — !'

'That no doubt occurred to him. It does, you know, to parents.'

'O-o-oh!' she said on a long, low note, disturbing in its very quietness, 'he doesn't want me back!'

Clem stirred restlessly, thrusting his hands deeper into his breeches pockets.

'Fiddlesticks. He wants you married and settled — that's all there is to it. You are old enough, and more. He gets no younger. He wants to see you settled before he dies.'

'There is only one place I will *ever* settle — and that is Redonda!'

'In Clancy's house?' asked Clem, 'with Clancy's wife?'

The old gibe again. She met it with the old rejoinder.

'He may not marry.'

'Fiddlesticks again. Of course he will marry — after a bit of a fling. He'll marry and make a bigger fool of himself, no doubt, than he has already. (Perhaps even a bigger fool than I have made of myself.) And you are not the one to sit away from the head of the table, are you, Harry? Will you be happy, then?'

She had rolled her handkerchief into a tight little ball to clench her fingers on it the better, to vent her sorrow and rage the better.

'It is an iniquitous arrangement!'

'What are you raging at now?'

'This arrangement that takes the house and the property from the one it belongs to, that loves it best and knows best how to care for it! All on account of sex! Is it *my* fault I was born a woman?'

'No, my dear, but some day it may be some man's misfortune.'

'That is stupid talk — Lausanne kind of talk,' she said. 'Sophy might have said it ... But it is no use appealing to you or to anybody. It's the way things always have been done and I am supposed to endure it meekly. Mr. Mogus assures me that meekness is the Christian virtue I should cultivate!'

'Old Mogus, the parson? We none of us ever cared for parsons, did we?' said Clem. 'And *you* always thought you were worth a pack of 'em! Remember the End of the World? I believe you thought you stopped it from happening, on that famous occasion, by sheer force of will!'

'How do you know it wasn't so?'

'My dear Harry! ... Why — by *reason*, of course! Only a madman or a child would believe in such rubbish!'

'All the same, you can't *prove* it wasn't so,' she persisted.

He gave up the argument. 'Then if it was so, upon my word I could almost wish your will power hadn't been quite so strong,' he said (with the same quiet bitterness with which she had cried out earlier 'He doesn't want me back!'). 'But what is the use of talking to you? You still think life a fine thing — or capable of being made into a fine thing. I don't. You still think you can get what you want. I don't. You still want your own way in it, and would, I believe, commit murder to get it!'

She didn't deny it. It was now completely dark in the little room.

'Though,' went on Clem thoughtfully, 'you would have to be thwarted first and put out of temper, I grant you that.'

'Thank you,' said Harry, 'for such a testimonial.' She rose silently, reaching her arms up, up into the darkness in a slow youthful luxury of stretching that her brother could sense but not see. She yawned, patting her mouth, breaking the sound into staccato — a broken, humdrum sigh.

'Shall we ring for the lights? How late Sophy is!'

'She is never too late for me,' said Clem. It was not a remark that invited reply. 'Never marry, Harriet! It's a disease one can't get well of. Ah, yes — I know your fierce vows, but one of these days you will be caught in some tender gushing moment. Your French accent will charm some yokel to such devotion when you go home — or else Father's dowry —'

'You may save your breath,' said Harriet, going out on to the balcony, 'I shall never marry — nor fall in love either!'

The fringe of her little shawl rose up in the warm night breeze, patting silkily at her mouth and cheeks. She had spoken the last words to the night and the stars — not to Clem. She would not fall in love, she would fall *out* of it — break herself free of it, whatever it cost her. Why else had she ever consented to leave the place she loved best on earth?

When she sent below stairs, shortly after, for her maid to come and undress her and brush her hair, Susan came up with swollen eyes. The 'tender gushing moment' had all too apparently swept over her, and Harriet, without wishing to know it in the least, guessed that the young footman of Lord X —, who had shown her maid such attentions during their stay in Lausanne, had now departed with his lordship and left no comfort behind him. She would not even have known this much had it not been for Sophy's handing-on of gossip. Nothing escaped Sophy on any floor of the hotel.

'You are pulling!' said Harriet, wincing genuinely under the brush.

'I'm sorry, Miss.'

'And you have the most atrocious cold, Susan. Give me the brush and go to bed. I can finish by myself — '

Susan sniffed. 'That's not a cold, Miss Harry, that's — '

'Go *away*, I said! I don't want to hear! Why should I have to listen if I don't want to hear?' cried Harriet in a passion. The girl did not give her the brush but laid it, with the tenderness she used towards all Harriet's possessions, down on the toilet table; then she finished laying-out her mistress's night garments, swiftly, noiselessly, without even sniffing again — so that Harriet had no grounds for complaint however much she might long to have. But all the time her foot was tapping wrathfully, waiting to be left alone.

With the door finally shut behind Susan, she heaved a sigh of relief. It was hard to be sharp with the girl but further confidences she could not bear — certainly not just then. Not that this was the first tender gushing moment Susan had undergone. Even to eyes as indifferent as Harriet's there had been occasions before — oh, for quite a long while now — and if Susan did not plague her about them, what she did when she was not in attendance upon Harriet did not concern Harriet. Lying straight out upon her bed with only the thinnest linen sheet between her and the summer night, Harriet reflected that just now, no, she *really* could not endure any more. She had her own overwhelming problem of how to forget the French Prisoner; how to be able to collect herself enough, to purge herself of this utterly unreasonable preoccupation enough to be able to return to Redonda, all passion spent; with no more than a reserved polite interest in anything a certain privileged employee of her father might say or do. Ah, she cried silently to the night in the pure frenzy of twenty-four (as powerful a torrent and as ceaseless as any Swiss waterfall could show): If it could be like that again — as it once was! If I could pass him on the drive, in the fields — yes, and just *pass* him! If I could see his old coat hanging on the nail in his office and not want to stroke it — and not want to kiss the marks his pencil makes on the paper — no, never again, never any more!

She tried to pray *Our Father which art in Heaven, let me come home soon, and let him be gone!* But she had an idea that if an Almighty God existed, He was not likely to listen suddenly to petitions from one who had ignored Him most of her life until now; nor could she blame Him for so reasonable a reaction. Besides, when one is accustomed to demanding and not merely asking, one cannot ask with any good grace. Prayer is saying Please. When had Harriet ever said please?

In the morning, spreading butter with that secret confidential manner so typical of her, upon the thinnest possible piece of toast, Sophy said to Harriet:

'That girl of yours is *enceinte*, I can tell by her eyes — '

'Fiddlesticks,' said Harriet.

Sophy nibbled at the toast, inviting it, as it were, to enter into a conspiracy with her to be eaten.

'Very well, my dear, take the consequences if you care to! I should get rid of her, myself.'

'Harriet will do whatever she wants to do,' said Clem surprisingly out of the centre of his newspaper. He went on without a pause —

so that Sophy should not have time to profit from it — 'They have killed Robespierre. *That's* something, at least!'

'Now perhaps we shall hear a little less about French politics and a little more about the French language from M. Hendaye,' said Harriet. Sophy looked at her over the toast with reproach. She had chosen the tutor so carefully, with such regard to good looks and gentility — it was ungrateful of Harriet. She resolved to protect the tutor, shutting her eyes to say:

'If you, my dear Harry, had been through one-tenth the miseries and injustices that M. Hendaye endured in that horrible Revolution —'

'Well, she didn't, and she won't,' said Clem, again unexpectedly, 'because, thank God, she's English, and such outrages don't happen over there.'

Sophy did not open her eyes: 'It may surprise you to know, *Clément*,' she said, pronouncing his name in the French way by way of additional reproach, 'that M. Hendaye has an uncle whose school-friend is on the staff of the First Consul. He has heard from that source — under the rose — that England is certainly on the list for conquest. After Bonaparte has finished with the Netherlands — and M. Hendaye says his uncle's school-friend is really surprised at the rate Bonaparte has advanced in the Netherlands (he had known the army and organization were good but not as good as all that) — he intends to recuperate for a short period and then to attack England. Naturally M. Hendaye himself does not approve of this,' she added hastily, for the gratification of the glum Bromewells: 'He wants us to win. He wants Bonaparte to be beaten, there is no chance for a Free France until that man is beaten! Nevertheless, that is the plan.'

One hand of hers still held a wafer of toast; the other, with what she conceived to be a gracious gesture of explanation of all this, she lay down, face upwards, upon the breakfast-table. Clement leant forward and gravely trickled a handful of centime-pieces into it.

'Thank you Madame Nallidaspus,' he said, 'for the prophecy. Will you now tell us when the End of the World is to take place?'

Harriet succumbed to one of her rare fits of laughter. It was just the sort of thing her father might have done. She laughed until she was quite out of breath and had to put down her coffee-cup. Sophy was furious.

'You are a couple of country bumpkins!' she said, rising and dashing the centime-pieces down on to the table. 'M. Hendaye is quite right when he says the English never understand anything until it is too late! He says he weeps for us, he prays for us!'

Clem rose, too, wiping his mouth: 'Very considerate of him,' he said. '*I* shall do a little prophesying now. I prophesy that M. Hendaye has some interesting papers, oh — extraordinarily interesting papers, obtained from his uncle's school-friend and available for the perusal of not-too-particular ladies if they care to call to see them. Remember to bring a paper away with you, my dear — husbands are fools but they like a little evidence, for all that — '

He was as angry as she, by now. Between them the newspaper slithered unnoticed to the floor. Harriet picked it up.

'The news of the war is not good, is it, Clem?'

'He's getting on,' Clement admitted.

'And *we* are driven back [studying the map]. Why — we are much farther back than we were a month ago! And Father said the war would be over before I came home!'

Sophy struck in again: '*Just* what M. Hendaye said! The indescribable futility and illogicality of English reasoning! Always they say, The war will be over, or not over, or long, or short, but *never* The war will be lost. It never occurs to them that it might be lost!'

'The poor soldiers . . .' said Harriet. For a split second she was vouchsafed a glimpse of what this remorseless advance in the Netherlands meant in terms of human life and death. A bright clear picture — horribly bright and clear — of a wounded man, perhaps from Ipswich or Norwich — left behind, crushed to pulp under the wheels of Bonaparte's ever-advancing cannon,. with the blood running out of his nostrils and mouth. Dying there, most horribly. Never going home any more. . . .

'*They're* all right,' said Clement. 'They'll fight with their backs to the wall, if need be' (an apter phrase than he was ever to guess). But the returned quietness in his voice quietened Harriet too.

'Tell me just one thing, *Clément*,' said Sophy, edging up to her husband and taking his elbow for one moment in her insinuating little hand: 'How was it you knew that M. Hendaye has those interesting papers in his possession? It is a *dead* secret, he only told me himself yesterday!'

CHAPTER XIV

A HOMECOMING

We are called in the present age to witness the political and moral phenomenon of a mighty and civilized people, formed into a horde of banditti, throwing off all the restraints which have influenced men in social life, displaying a savage valour directed by a sanguinary spirit, forming rapine and destruction into a system, and perverting to their detestable purposes all the talents and ingenuity which they derived from their advanced stage of civilization, all the refinements of art and the discoveries of science. We behold them uniting the utmost savageness and ferocity of design with consummate contrivance and skill in execution, and seemingly engaged in no less than a conspiracy to exterminate from the earth all honour, humanity, justice, and religion. —WILLIAM PITT, 1794

CLANCY and Harriet Bromewell returned in early autumn to an auburn England instead of a green one; to a countryside richer in grain-harvests than ever before in its whole history. Even the unfertile moors of Dartmoor had yielded to the plough, and grown some sort of crop; even the seashore fringes had, in places, been cunningly coaxed into some sort of tilth for some sort of a harvest. The plough reigned supreme in agriculture from Lands End to John o'Groats. It was Up Corn and Down Horn with a vengeance. *Grow Bread*, cried Pitt. *Feed the people despite the French Blockade!* And the farmers ploughed up their best pasture land and slaughtered their cattle and their milking cows and sowed oats, wheat, barley, rye! And oats, wheat, barley, rye sprang up in likely and unlikely places in plenteous wealth, unfolding in wave after wave over the landscape, filling the people's eyes though they could not, and did not, quite suffice to fill the people's stomachs.

In the Eastern counties the new agricultural drive was particularly in evidence, for East Anglia had been until then predominantly cattle country, famed for its dairy products in London and abroad. Now the cattle that yielded the milk which made the butter and cheese were seriously depleted. The pastures on which they had been fed were reduced to a third of what they once were and there was consequently no longer milk to spare for young bull-calves, or for pigs. No milk at all except for human beings — and even then an insufficient allowance at a fabulous price. *Up Corn*, cried Pitt to the big farmers. *Up Corn*, echoed the big farmers, ploughing, harrowing, sowing, weeding, harvesting with a will. And the corn thrust upwards everywhere, in hills and valleys, moors and mountainsides — green, yellow, gold and white — beautiful, ubiquitous, insufficient, ripening to the wicked tune of a penny for a handful of wheat-ears.

With so much profit mingled with so much patriotism, small wonder that the big landowners tore up their acres of pasture without wincing and made more and better ploughs to tackle the job next year. Even the small farmer, the cunning peasant of two acres and a cow and calf, who had contrived in the past to avoid Enclosure — even the peasant-farmer, going out at sunset and viewing this God's Plenty rippling in his neighbour's fields — went out and sold his cow and calf and begged, borrowed or stole a plough, and harnessed himself and a horse to it and turned his grass under and sowed the precious seed at Michaelmas.

He did not sow it as well as the big farmers; he had not the tools or the knowledge to do this. He grew it that he might feel, between his work-roughened finger and thumb, the precious weight of a penny for a handful of wheat-ears, while Captain Bromewell and his fellows became professional corn-growers.

Such men as these were the innovators, the men who discovered that by growing clover and trefoil with the grain crop they could both cleanse the soil and get hay for the remaining cattle; that a new and lighter plough would do the same old work with fewer horses and in half the time; that a special breed of horse, the

Suffolk Punch, worked better on heavy soil than the big Shire horses; that mud from ditches and ponds, seaweed and forest sweepings, as well as farm manure, could all be fed back into the soil to replace what went out of it and up into the grain; that such an implement as a seed-drill might be manufactured and used, to replace the old wasteful way of sowing by hand; that such a thing as a pump-mill might be come by, for draining useless old marshes and bringing them under cultivation; that such a law as that which did away with the old 'gleaning rights' of the villagers might further eliminate waste, and so profit the farmer and the farm.

Side by side with these knowledgeable fellows — the innovators, the ruthless and daring discoverers — and side by side with their ever-extending acres of perfect grain, was the peasant farmer's contribution; the corner, here and there, of hand-sown, hand-weeded and hand-harvested wheat — tended with sweat and blood and tears but destined to be swallowed up inevitably, one day, into the larger farmer's farm.

But both flourished meanwhile. However much both grew, in whatever way, there could never be quite enough for a hungry nation at war, even in a year of bountiful harvest. It came to this ironic state; that the ground itself was better fed than the people it was nourished to provide for, in the year that Harriet Bromewell returned to Redonda from Lausanne.

Clancy did not accompany her all the way. After putting his sister and her maid into the Norwich coach he conceived his duty done, sending his regards to his father and staying in London with his fellow-students, though the new term, strictly speaking, had not yet started. Captain Bromewell had sent a letter to them at the Suffolk House in London; from it they learnt that their father 'couldn't rightly complain' of the harvest. From this expression (which represented the peak of enthusiasm in the Captain) Harriet divined that the harvest had been exceptional. This she was soon able to see for herself from the coach windows, when the London houses ended and the countryside began. Truly it had been a bountiful harvest! *March dry, good rye*. (It had been a dry March — Bonaparte had not been able to prevent that, at least!) *April wet, good wheat*. (And April had been wet, obligingly laying the dust of

March and feeding moisture into the seedlings.) A scorching May and June had coaxed on the wheat — the king of the crops — in a way it rejoiced one to see; a dry August, betokening a full drouth, did not hurt it when it stood in heavy soil, while ingenious irrigations, undertaken by the farmers when the young crops were already lemon-green, ran soothing wet fingers through the thirsty earth, lifting up the hearts of the oats and strengthening the feeble knees of the barley, even as one looked.

There had been nobody, indeed, after all this, whose heart had failed to swell with pride at the sight of the harvest — unless, it might be, some labourer's wife whose child had gone too short of milk to think it worth going on living, or whose husband — unable (as the Bible had warned him) to live by bread alone, or tea and potatoes alone (a more usual diet) — had gone out one night and cut his throat by the light of the full moon for want of the meat no longer procurable, at any price, for him or his family.

Harriet, viewing the plenitude either side of her as the coach rolled on north-eastwards, could not know of these details; nor yet could Susan, marvelling likewise at the harvest from her vantage point on the roof of the coach, amongst the luggage. There had been no talk in Lausanne of the seriousness of the English food situation — and misery like poverty was always with us. The war might of course enlarge both but it did not engender them. *Up Corn — Up Famine!* Out with your scythes and sickles, farmers and men! Death walks with *his* scythe too, between the stooks and in the rickyards, and sleeps in your new-built granaries and haunts those grassy tracks between your cornfields where once the Romans trekked, and sleeps in the little woods and coppices that still survive between the ever-encroaching yellow waves of corn. *Up Corn!*

But the corn is, nevertheless, a beautiful sight as it stands, ripe for the scythe: to Harriet's experienced eye it is the nicest, healthiest lot she has seen in all her remembrance; to Susan's less experienced eye on the roof it is a promise of plenty; to the farmers it is gold sovereigns glinting richly upon one another in the wind.

Only Mr. Pitt and his advisers in London, able in some abstruse fashion to balance production against consumption, and price against ability to pay the price, and an ever-increasing price against an ever-sinking standard of living, and the number of deaths from starvation and malnutrition against the number of farmers applying for the right to become fine gentlemen with coats of arms and seats in Parliament; and taxation against the cost of the war, and manufacturing demands against agricultural demands, and labour for both against capital for both; and the ability of the ordinary people to hold out against the continually-victorious French when he (in his turn) has nothing yet in the way of hope or comfort that he can hold out to *them* except the advice to tighten the belt a little and endure — only the Prime Minister and his kind are not held in the spell of this harvest when they see it; only he hears Death whetting his bigger scythe through the noise of the sharpening of the scythes of innumerable human harvesters in August 1794.

In the neighbourhood of Redonda, harvest was normally a process of five weeks or so. Because of the miraculous weather, this period had shrunk into three — consequently every possible sort of labour had been pressed into its service. Cattle and horses, grandfathers and toddling children, the halt, the blind and the feebleminded if they could glean or pitch were all coralled together by the farmers for the great gathering-in. A fever of enthusiasm spread inevitably over the countryside. No bees, plying ceaselessly through all the daylight hours to fill their hives with honey, could show a more patient frenzy, a more ceaseless energy than these country people during that harvest season. It was as if their hungry bodies knew, even though their minds had not yet discovered, that every grain of this new corn was a pearl beyond price.

It was Spens who met them that evening with the gig at Woodbridge. Harriet normally did not like the man; he was foxy-looking and she had always had suspicions that he cheated her father at market-days in some faint-hearted untraceable way. But because he belonged to the farm, belonged to Redonda, she could on this occasion almost have kissed him.

'The Cap'n couldn't come,' he explained. 'He's frit of the night air for his eyes.'

'His *eyes*, Spens?'

'That's roight, Miss Harriet. He's got the same as a catarack, so the doctor reckons. He have to be careful.'

176

The gig bowled onwards.

'Did you loike that old Switzerland, Miss Harriet?'

'Not as much as home,' Harriet admitted, still marvelling at the scene around her: 'What a harvest, Spens!'

'Yis. If we'd had a splash of rain at the end o' July reckon th' barley'd have been the better for it.'

Bouncing a little, inevitably, holding on her large hat with one hand, and the side of the gig with the other, Harriet asked, half-dreading the answer:

'Is ours all in?'

'All but the foive-acre, that's to be started to-morrow. That's the end. The Cap'n will be glad you are back, Miss Harriet. Did you bring the gloves?'

He meant the harvest-gloves, the perquisite of every harvester from time immemorial.

'Yes. They weren't cheap, Spens. I had to give sevenpence a pair.'

'That's this wicked ole war, but the Cap'n won't grudge it. Harvest should pye for that, I reckon!' His shoulders shook in soundless laughter at his own joke.

'Who is Lord of the Harvest?'

The odd archaic phrase fell oddly from her lips, she hoped, because the words themselves were so strange and not the question. Surely anybody could ask a question like that!

Spens took his gaze off the horse's back for one minute to turn a sardonic eye upon her, which told her everything.

'The French chap,' he said.

Harriet sighed. She should have known it. She *had* known it. Primly from beneath the brim of her huge hat but speaking loudly to be heard above the sound of the wheels she said:

'Well, I hope they won't spoil him!'

'Eh?'

'I said that I hoped they won't spoil him! He gives himself enough airs already!'

Whatever Spens answered to this she did not hear it, and was much too proud to ask him to repeat it. Obviously it had been brief and to the point and not — she guessed — complimentary to

Vandervoord. But then Spens had no reason to love him — why should he have? *She* had no reason to love him either. She had let herself be packed off to Lausanne so that she might recover her reason and with it her wholeheartedness. I am going to see him very soon, she told herself, and I am not going to mind at all. It will mean no more to me than seeing Spens. She looked sideways at Spens, from under her hat-brim. He is really no better-looking than Spens, she told herself, except that he is not so foxy. He is not *really* much younger than Spens and he is vain and shows off, and he thinks he can make anyone love him, even Father! I am not going to stay in the house any more to avoid him. Why should I be a prisoner in my own house because of him? From this moment he is going to mean no more to me than those sheaves of corn stacked in the fields we are passing. . . .

The trouble was, that since the wheat-sheaves were Redonda's, they filled her with pride and joy and love to overflowing; and pain too, that they should have come out of *her* ground, in *her* absence, and grown to fruition without her constant attendance. But the pain was less than the joy. Nothing can ever take me from here again, she said from the very depths of her heart. Nothing, nothing, *nothing*. And I love nothing and nobody in the world as much as my own home!

As luck would have it, there was to be no test of her new state of mind that evening. The daylight still lingered, the harvesters were all busy beyond Farley Wood; the farmyard itself was unusually quiet and empty of men. Her father greeted her explosively:

'Damn it, come close and let me see if I can see you, Harry!' Holding her at arm's length, peering into her face, he looked hard for those features he knew but could no longer clearly distinguish. Next to his sons and perhaps his prize bull, he loved his daughter. Harriet was shocked by the change in him. His eyelids were crusted red, the once bold blue eyes were bloodshot:

'What is it, Father? Your poor eyes!'

'It's a damned cataract, that's what it is!' He embraced her roughly. 'No good, I can't see you, but I can feel it's my girl.' And he ran his big, still beautifully-kept hand down her face, under her chin: 'How does it all look, eh?'

He did not need to explain further.

'Never better!'

She did not need to explain further, either. He beamed blindly at her, then groaned:

'The best harvest Redonda's ever had and I can't see it! What d'you think of that for luck? These cursed eyes of mine!'

'You said nothing in your letter — '

He went on to explain that it hadn't happened then, but that now he must be careful, must have his eyes bathed night and day, must not venture out after dewfall or on a windy day, must cut down his wine and tobacco —

'But how did it happen, Father?'

And on that he was curiously uncommunicative. Didn't know, couldn't say. All right one day, half-blind the next, damn everybody, particularly doctors who couldn't or wouldn't produce remedies overnight.

'Where's Ivory? *Ivory!*'

He roared the name as of old, making the windows rattle. Harriet smiled faintly, it was all so familiar. But not so familiar the sight of him striking out with his cane against the chair, the table — anything — from a real need now, instead of mere temper.

'Where's Spens? Spens! Get Spens!'

Still striking out with his cane, angrily clearing his way through his own house as if it were some encumbered jungle, Captain Bromewell turned his burly back on his daughter, following Ivory by hooking his cane, finally, into the negro's coat-collar, in search of Spens:

'The accounts, Spens. Bring me the accounts from Woodbridge!'

Upstairs in her bedroom — her lovely, *lovely* bedroom! — helped to prepare for bed by Susan, Harriet said:

'What do they say about my father's eyes?'

The servants' hall, she knew, would have the story, some story at least, from which she could finally unravel such fragments of veracity as it contained.

There was surprisingly little to tell. Captain Bromewell had come back like that from Bury, after his usual visit there three weeks ago. He had gone there his usual healthy self; he had come

back groping and roaring, and had conducted the farm's affairs
thereafter principally from his office. The only people he had seen
— apart from Spens and certain farm people — were the doctor and
— surprisingly — Mr. Mogus, the parson.

Harriet could hardly believe her ears:

'The *parson*?'

It was the first time that any parson had actually set foot in
Redonda within her memory.

Yes. Nobody knew what they talked about because the door was,
alas, shut. There had been a lot of roaring, some even said a
bellowing noise like (*a*) crying, (*b*) a cow that has lost its calf, and
(*c*) a Lost Soul looking for salvation. And then a disturbing silence
which made the dogs whine, and then Mr. Mogus's voice talking
very low and then a thump, which might have been the Captain
hitting Mr. Mogus or the Captain going on to his knees to pray.
The betting was even.

But the roaring had been really tremendous, and was, it appeared,
a recurring feature of the case. 'They say that's worst when Dr.
Wilson come,' declared Susan: 'For then the Cap'n have to have
Ivory to hold on to, and the more the doctor hurt *him* (and he can't
in the natur' of things help hurtin' him, can he, Miss Harry?) then
the more the Cap'n grips and pinches Ivory until *he* hollers out too.
Reckon Ivory don't like the doctor's visits ne more than the Cap'n
do!'

Harriet could well believe it.

'Do they say he will get well again?'

That Susan couldn't say; didn't know. All sorts of opinions had
been aired, some kindly, some so uncharitable that they were not
to be passed on.

'Very well,' said Harriet. 'You may go to bed now.'

She would not have the curtains drawn in her bedroom. Instead,
she had ordered the bed to be pushed close to the window, as in her
childhood, so that lying in bed, even with her head upon her
pillow, she could still look out upon the dear familiar landscape
and rejoice to the full in reunion with it. The night was very still,
the air very fragrant, with that feeling of tired happiness overhang-
ing all which is the essence of Harvest. From the Great Barn, where

the Harvest Dinner would take place to-morrow night, after the last load had been brought home in triumph with the Lord of the Harvest atop of it, there was a distant sound of a flute and of laughing voices, muted by the house that came between. Harriet knew whose was the flute and whose fingers and lips coaxed the sweet notes from it. I haven't seen him, she told herself, but it would have been all the same if I had, I should be just as calm and self-possessed. I should belong to myself, just the same. And I shall be able to hand out the gloves and to pour out the cider and to lead off the dance with the Lord of the Harvest to-morrow night — and one action will mean absolutely no more to me than any other. On that thought, and hope, she slept.

Captain Bromewell lay awake, going over in his mind the unfortunate occurrences at Bury which had culminated in his present disability. Whatever the servants were saying about it — not that he cared or gave that side of the matter an instant's thought — nothing could be as sombre as the truth.

He and Captain Twigg had been drinking as usual, and whoring as usual, with Moll and Bet. After that they had set to drinking again, and on coming out of the inn, preparatory to going home, they had encountered a preacher sort of fellow with a text plastered across his chest in white and red flannel, reading:

IF THE BLIND LEAD THE BLIND BOTH SHALL FALL INTO THE DITCH

Seeing that he was past the amorous and at the truculent stage, Captain Bromewell had instantly taken exception to this. When sober he was a tolerant man and could ignore religious maniacs and feeble little namby-pamby Wesleyanites full of texts about burning in hell. But on this occasion, feeling this man standing so rudely (or so it had seemed) in his path, and with this warning thrust so unwarrantably upon them, he had taken real offence. He and Captain Twigg—still Everybody's Friend in a crisis — had set about the preacher forthwith, knocking his hat off and wrenching his buttons off and tearing up his placard with the red flannel letters on it, and had finally pushed *him* into a ditch, full of nettles. 'Who is blind *now*, eh?' they had shouted. 'Who is in the ditch *now*?' And that had disposed of *that*!

But not quite, it would seem. For, on being driven out of the town afterwards to be dropped at some convenient spot by Captain Bromewell, Captain Twigg had never ceased to talk about blindness and what a terrible affliction it was; how sad it was for a sailor to be blind — or a soldier, yes let's be generous, *or* a soldier — what a lot of sadness there was to be found in the world in any case . . . Consider, Bor, he had said to his companion, if *you* were blind, and had — from the best of intentions — covered Captain Bromewell's eyes (which were already doing wonders considering that they had to subtract half of everything they saw) with an encircling movement of his hands.

And Captain Bromewell, blaspheming *fortissimo*, had swerved violently off the road by pulling the reins tight in his annoyance, and the gig had tilted, throwing them both out into the ditch.

As if that were not bad enough — for it was a foully dirty ditch — Captain Bromewell had woken up next morning with a stinging sensation in his eyelids, and had perceived things only mistily; and the doctor, summoned, had pronounced a cataract — double — and had prescribed the treatment which was proving so painful and ineffective. Since then Captain Bromewell, try how he might, could see hardly at all.

And, as if this were not bad enough, what was worse was what Captain Bromewell *could* see. Just as now, when he lay in bed with his eyes closed, and the stinging a little abated, so the great text with its red flannel letters filled his vision:

IF THE BLIND LEAD THE BLIND BOTH SHALL FALL INTO THE DITCH

And for the first time in his life, Captain Bromewell was afraid. Not only for himself — but if this sort of thing could happen to him, it could happen equally to Redonda, to the prize bull — if to Redonda then to Harry or the boys; if to them, then to the countryside, to London — to the whole of England. Catastrophe (administered through the implacable hand of a Deity with whom previously Captain Bromewell had never made any endeavour to come to grips) might be nationally as well as personally distributed — at any moment — yes, at any moment! It was an awful thought, but an abiding one in the watches of the night, for Deity and not

Chance had surely been responsible for the warning and the cataracts — and Chance was there to be conquered and overcome but not, Captain Bromewell quite clearly saw — not Deity.

So, while his daughter slept he lay waking. Fearing the warning for what it might portend of worse to come; true, the harvest had been spared — was a royal one — and prices were unsurpassed. But the war was responsible for the demand and for the prices — and the war, like Deity, might have evils as well as blessings to bestow.

For the first time behind his closed eyes, Captain Bromewell saw ranks of men as well as of grain. The grain had sprouted through the ground where he had sown it and was good to eat; but dragon's teeth had sprouted in the fields of Europe and Look, they are already white to harvest with an unspeakable crop! Who has been blind? asked the Captain soundlessly, who has been blind? And how big is the ditch into which we still have to fall? And is it for me, or for my children — or the whole country? God help us all!

Such thoughts brought out beads of sweat upon his forehead, as much as if the most strenuous physical labour had produced them.

CHAPTER XV

THE FISHERMAN'S CABIN

'See how I come, unchanged, unworn!'
BROWNING

JUST above the line of shingle to the south of Aldeburgh, and just below the fields known as the Shearings, lay Redonda's frontier-line, which extended to the mark of spume left on the wet sands each day by the tide. There, in a no-man's-land of its own, a small two-roomed cabin had stood as long as anyone could remember, braving time and tide with rough-cast stubbornness. Its roof, once red-tiled, was now lichened over with a coarse grey-green growth, of much the same colour as the tufts of grass on the sand-dunes in the surrounding landscape. It stood empty now, but not long ago a fisherman and his wife had inhabited it and had left a mark of life upon the small square of garden-plot, by fashioning a path there, edged with cockle-shells, and by planting a tamarisk hedge on which to dry the washing. Nothing else remained of their labours but these.

The couple had vacated the place for reasons unknown. Perhaps the behaviour of the river Alde in the Shearings had something to do with it. A fisherman likes to know where he is with the rise and fall of waters but the land behind the cabin had degenerated (since the pump-mills had started) into something now land and now water — now a mud-flat with iridescent islands of land still visible and again, five minutes later, mysteriously and totally submerged.

The cabin beyond the Shearings was a landmark well-known to Harriet since her youth. In the days when they had gone hunting cornelians on Aldeburgh beach, she and Susan had been often glad of its low flint walls as a shelter, when — after fighting sun and wind on the beaches all the morning — they would struggle up the shingle to these walls and sink down against them, leaning back against the knobbled surface with their bare toes curling in the sun — the sun warm and salt in the world of clean-washed pebbles all about them, and the air suddenly hushed and silent about them though the wind still roared above the level of the walls. The cabin had been inhabited in those days, and a cow the same colour as the red tiles had grazed in that rushy pasture of the Shearings which was now swallowed up and spewed out again, swallowed up and spewed out, at such indeterminate and puzzling times by the river Alde.

In those days the fisherman's wife had brought Harriet gooseberries and cream more than once — handing them down to her over the flint wall in a wooden bowl as bone-clean and smooth as was everything to do with that place. The gooseberries had a peculiar bitterness of their own which Harriet attributed to their growing so near the salt water. The whole flavour of childhood seemed to be encompassed in the recollection of that tart, globular mouthful — a pebble of a gooseberry or a gooseberry of a pebble — warm from a salt, tremendous sun.

Recalling these circumstances, Harriet approached the cabin now in leisurely fashion, skirting the edge of the Shearings and coming up to the little place gradually by the old way, the way of the foreshore. She had been home three days, she had thanked God passionately for two nights that she had not yet encountered the French Prisoner (an unaccountable travel-sickness, delayed, had laid her low and prevented her appearance, after all, at the Harvest revellings) — and that now she did not care if she never saw him again. And on the third day, consumed with a longing to see him which she could contain and disguise from herself no longer, she had pocketed her pride and her ambitions and demanded his whereabouts from Spens; only to be told that he was usually to be found, these days, in the disused cabin, 'Makin' observations from that there contraption o' his'.

The day was as hot as remembered days of childhood — with saltness whitely quivering in the air over the shingle now, as then. The tide was out, far out, roaring away to itself, deeply pre-occupied with its own ceaseless convolutions. As she walked, the shingle slipped away continually under the thin soles of her shoes, in the way familiar from childhood, and she helped herself over the bank of larger shingle when she came to it just as she had done in the old days, by leaning forward and balancing her body against the slithering pebbles beneath her, and gripping anything large enough to help her in her ascent in the way of old spars of wrecks, sea-lavender or tufts of grass.

Here and there amongst the sandy approaches to the cabin, and amongst the shingle itself, the yellow horn-poppy was in full and blazing bloom. Even to the very lip of the pebbles that were covered and uncovered each day by the tides, this shining scentless flower raised its head, stirring ceaselessly in the breeze blowing off the sea — the only living, moving thing upon all that expanse of clean, bare stillness. On the horizon above the horn-poppies were the wild white tree-lupins, clumps of them growing in the very first patch of ground which was not pure sand and thickening, as a crowd of spectators will, the nearer they grew to that symbol of human life, the cabin.

As the warm shingle beneath her feet gave way in its turn to warm sand, so Harriet's approach became abruptly soundless. The moment gathered itself together in importance, the whole place seemed suddenly to hold its breath to watch her. The air became poignantly sweet with the scent of the tree-lupins. She put her hand upon the worn wooden gate between the tamarisk hedges, observing — even at such a time of portent — the cracks in it, wide and smooth as healed wounds, and the glittering crystals of sand reposing between them, graded perfectly as glass peas in a pod. She lifted it gently and opened it, then, stepping over the path and over what had once been a garden-bed of sorts, she made her way not to the door but to the window.

The first room she looked into did not hold what she wanted ever more hungrily as the moments went by. She passed on from its dim clutter of old paraphernalia to the next. In this, furnished barely with a truckle bed, a deal table and a chair, the man she looked for was sitting at work.

Her heart gave a great leap at the sight, so that she laid one hand involuntarily upon it to still it, lest in its savage exultation it should jump altogether out of her breast. Vandervoord had not heard her approach. The model of his work was on the table before him and he was sitting facing it, head supported between two propped elbows, brooding over it, touching it occasionally with his fore-finger, inviting it, it would seem, to yield up more secrets.

The window frame, innocent of glass, was just wide enough for Harriet to insert head and shoulders. Here, too, the wood had been sucked clean through years of purifying wind and sea-foam, blanched and bleached by salt and sun, until it felt (to her acutely sensitized touch of that moment) to be composed of slippery bone rather than of wood; some very ancient, enduring, hard-working little bone which was part of the other bone that made up the structure of the whole dwelling, such as it was.

She watched, loving deeply, hardly daring to breathe. 'What he does down there,' Spens had said disgustedly, 'I can't say! The Cap'n, of course, won't hear a word agin' him, no more will the sergeant, who he's wholly bewitched! He *say* he c'n work easier there, owin' to folk leavin' him on his own. But suppose he were a spy after all, Miss Harriet? Suppose he was after signalling from there to Boney? Reckon none of *us* aren't to know! He's taken a bed down there, too; say he want to see the toide workin' on the Shearings. Reckon he think if he's on the spot he can catch that at it, and tot that down in his ready reckoner! Not that the Cap'n moind the Flood!'

'It's Mr. King's land, isn't it?' Harriet had asked.

'Ay, that *was*.'

'*Was?*'

'He was riddy enough to sell that to the Cap'n once that went below water, Miss Harriet. At foive and twenty shillin' an acre!'

Harriet's frugal mind was appalled. 'Isn't there — wasn't there Compensation?'

Out of Captain Bromewell's disputatious past, his daughter remembered and fished up the word. Not that she cared, from Mr. King's point of view, but it was like her to want to *know*, to get the hang of things now that she had returned.

'Not fer him there worn't! He's one of them priestly chaps, Miss Harriet. Best thing *he* could fare to do was take the cash and kip quiet, I reckon!'

So that was it; just as Vandervoord had prophesied before ever she had gone abroad, Mr. King's land — his field for his ewes — had been drowned because the activities of her father's pump-mill decreed it.

She could not feel sorry for Mr. King, it was no use pretending. Since the pump-mill worked for Redonda, enriched Redonda, she was proud of it — was passionately proud of Vandervoord for having designed it.

And now, looking silently in at the window at the man still absorbed in his model and recalling all these things, she knew that all her prayers had been useless.

Is it possible not to stir, almost not to breathe, almost to stop the heart beating with the intensity of absorption — and yet for so full a force of love to flood out of one (as dumbly upon the air as the wings of an owl at dusk) so that these unseen waves of loving strike against the consciousness of the beloved as the feathers of an owl's wing might be laid against the cheek? As if this might be so, Vandervoord — without appearing to have sensed either sight or sound from the window, suddenly turned his head (cheekbones red with the pressure of his doubled fists upon them) towards the window, and saw Harriet there.

Everything was so still in the bone-clean room, so quiet in the quivering haze of sunlight rebounding off the shingle outside (except for the far-off, preoccupied roar of the tide), that his quick intake of breath at the sight sounded almost like a breath drawn in pain.

'Miss Bromewell!'

He stood up quickly, bending his head instinctively as he did so, to avoid striking it against the low whitewashed rafters of the cabin.

'I did not know you were home again!'

He was still in the same clothes in which she had envisaged him all these long months — the grey-green coat with the tell-tale patch on its back, the black breeches; the buckle, even, was still missing from his left shoe.

As he stood there with inclined shoulders and bent head, staring at her and at the dancing light in her brilliant eyes, the thing happened. Vandervoord discovered in one moment all that she felt for him and stepped involuntarily backwards, knocking against his chair.

'Ah — you are going to say again *Do not touch me, do not come near me!*' cried Harriet, loving him with an ache that would not be contained, that must, she felt, be so enormous and overwhelming that — breaking out of her and unfolding like some huge flower, fuller of sun even than the silky horn-poppy petals ever were, and sweeter of breath than the tree-lupins — it must push against and break down even the stout walls of the cabin in its intensity and ardent joy.

Her eyes were dancing as she said it, her mouth smiling, her very sweet mouth curved into that bow of laughter and love that came so seldom to it; he had never seen her face so lit up before. It was irresistible.

'No,' he said, 'that would be rude, Mademoiselle.'

'Nevertheless it is what you are thinking!' she teased him. 'You are afraid of me, M. Vandervoord! ... Well,' (as he would not answer this charge) 'won't you shake hands with me and say you are glad to see me back safely, or are you still thinking only of your old pump?'

She thrust her hand in at the window, holding it out towards him, palm upwards.

There are gestures so ingratiating that there is almost no refusing them. The whole of Harriet went into the holding-out of her hand towards him. Her slight, straight body was leaning forwards towards him, framed in the aperture of the window, her laughing face was held upwards as her hand was, looking into his.

It was a challenge as well as a gesture of friendship. He took a step forward out of the darkness into such sunlight as she allowed to fall upon him — bent down, took her hand in his and kissed it swiftly, without, however, releasing it afterwards.

'Don't go away,' he said quietly, looking down at her hand. 'I still cannot believe you are more than a mirage. Wait.'

He dropped on to his knees, as close inside the window as she was close outside. They were now almost on a level with each other.

'That is better.' He still held her hand, which had begun to tremble a little.

'Why, it is you who are afraid of me, now!'

'I didn't mean — ' she began.

'Not that form of salutation? But in Lausanne — '

'Oh, don't speak of Lausanne, I am *home* now!' she cried. Then: 'Let go my hand, please.'

He still looked down at it, gripped gently between his two.

'No,' he answered, 'you asked for a handshake. You come, a vision to my window, so lovely, ah, you can't *know* how lovely, framed in the window — and you ask for a handshake like some old soldier or *camarado* back from the wars!'

Almost as if he were talking to himself, as if she were not there, he bent his head again, brushing his lips and then his cheek against her hand, closing his eyes and going on to say very quietly:

'But you were wrong. Yet — if you had given me time to collect myself, there would have been a handshake. I am not a prisoner for nothing, I do what I'm told! But conceive for yourself what it is like, to have been working here in solitude, oh — quite enjoyably, I admit that — but to have that solitary *intent* employment interrupted in such a way — and not even knowing you were back!'

She pulled slightly at her still-held hand, so that he opened his eyes again, after his solemn speech, to look at her. The corners of her mouth still curved upwards in the divinely childish way he had perceived during that first moment at the window. He could not take his eyes from her face, though every so often, without looking at it, he raised her hand and held it against his cheek.

In a voice trembling a little at the circumstances — the novel circumstances (to her) of love-talk and love-play, which yet had a kind of homecoming about them — Harriet protested faintly:

'Anyone could have told you that I was back. You cannot have cared very much! —'

Ah — the inevitable challenge of love to love, the inevitable response! So intimacy between the two of them leapt forward upon this astounding day, this heaven-sent day, at such a rate and in such seven-leagued boots. Between one whispered sentence and another, one tender gesture and another, one glance and another, it had made such progress that it was off the earth, and on the moon — off the moon and amongst the stars, sprinkling itself ecstatically upon them as well as upon space and eternity . . .

His hands about hers were very warm. His shoulders, as he knelt at the window, were on a level with hers; his face, looking so ardently and seriously into hers as if learning all its lineaments by heart, was so near that his breath fanned her cheek as the kiss of the south wind. Events, it seemed to Harriet, had taken charge of them both with a compassionate inevitability the like of which she had never suspected in her whole life until this day. There was surely no withdrawal possible, of either passion or person.

And to Harriet then, as to so many million million lovers, came the sensation: *This has not happened before and yet it is not new and strange to me. Whatever it is, however lovely, however terrible, however pregnant of sorrow, I may no more throw it off and be the girl I once was than the horn-poppy, bruising its thin cheek against the shingle outside, may tell the wind to stand still or the pebbles to withdraw from about its base. It is decreed to bloom and shrivel and perish as I am decreed to — this present moment and all that it comprehends.*

Then — 'Come in,' said Vandervoord. He had released her hand almost before she knew it and was standing up again, still with bent head because of the rafters, 'it is absurd to stay like this. Come in and see how you like my workshop.'

Harriet stepped over the low windowsill and into the dim little room.

'There.' He took her by the shoulders. 'Yes, you are real. It is really you, home again,' and his eyes brooded tenderly over her, still taking in her face hungrily, and her hair and the sweet smiling mouth. He was not smiling himself, but solemn.

'Are you afraid still that I shall eat you?' asked Harriet, in so small a voice, and so tender, that the question should have made him smile surely. But he remained serious.

'What is the use? I am already swallowed up. I cannot be afraid any more.'

His hands still rested upon her shoulders. They stood closely together as lovers in the low little room.

In spite of herself Harriet felt her arms rising, as if they knew what to do and where to go without the instruction of her will or her imagination. *They ache,* she said to herself wonderingly, *to be locked together behind his neck.* Strange, strange arms!

Suddenly Vandervoord gave a half-groan and caught her to him, almost lifting her off her feet.

'My darling, you should never have come here!' he said into her hair. 'It was my workshop but it was also my refuge! What was the use of my absenting myself so righteously — yes (let me confess it now) even when Spens tells me you are nearly home — when everyone tells me you are nearly home? And what is the use of my hiding away here, my loveliest, my dearest dear — if you seek me out so mercilessly and make it too hard for a man to bear?'

He was not teasing now, Harriet knew. He was not smiling. There was a real anguish in him, hand-in-hand with delight, its inseparable twin. *Shall it always be thus,* asked her wise mind, striving to impose itself upon her rushing senses; and the Unseen answered implacably — just as she had feared, at that moment, or for ever, even from long before she had known of his existence — *Yes, yes; always thus. You must bear it.*

His arms tightly clasped about her waist, and her arms about his neck; where they had ached with not being; where they had longed to be.

'Ah,' she breathed, 'at last. This is *right*; this is where they have wanted to be ever since you first came to Redonda! My arms have ached till now to rest here. Now they are where they should be. They are at rest and at home!'

He arched his head back to rub it against her gripped hands, as if fearful to lose any sensation, any single aspect of this tenderness, so amazingly and unexpectedly bestowed. He bent his head forward again to brush his lips and his cheeks against her face.

'Nevertheless you should not have come,' he repeated gently.

'Aren't you glad?'

'That has nothing to do with it. One can be too glad, and no good comes of that . . .'

'Do you want me to go then, Van?'

The foolish pet-name slipped out as naturally as her arms had sidled their way about his neck. It was the secret name she had called him to herself for the last three months; the pass-word to a dream.

He answered: 'I shall die if you go. You know it, Harry.'

Pet-name to pet-name, as hand to hand and cheek to cheek.

She laughed at that, shut her eyes and laid her head with a sigh of pure happiness against his breast.

'You *are* difficult to please!'

'Listen —' he began with great urgency, then — 'No, don't listen. People talk too much — and what is the use? What will be will be, we can't prevent it. Isn't this the proof?'

'How loud your heart beats,' was her answer. 'Like a clock. I am sure mine is not as loud as that!'

'Let me tell you,' he said.

Such old sweet tricks, such endearing movements performed so repeatedly, so unfailingly by so many million millions, through such aeons of time; as the bird seeks the twig when Spring returns, even the young bird, and takes the twig and lays it across another with unthinking dexterity, to build a nest, though none has taught it the way or even told it why.

'Do you believe in omens, Van?'

'Yes. Why?'

'I think they are silly, and you must not believe in them if you love me.' (Ah, the old imperiousness, the old wielding of power, and doubly precious power over the beloved!) 'If *I* believed in omens,' she continued, 'do you know who I should have for my husband? *Spens!*'

'You would be married to Spens?'

It was really very slow of him — to be almost spelling the words out like a real foreigner; as if they were about some entirely different subject instead of — as she saw so clearly, as who could fail to see — the one that they had been discussing all the time:

'Yes, Spens! The maids have a silly superstition here, for husband-choosing, and last Summer Susan teased me to try it. We were shelling peas. You take the ninth pea in a pod — and, of course, it is only the really *good* pods, you know, that have nine peas in them — and you lay it above the centre of the kitchen door and the first man to come in under it is to be the husband of the one who places the pea. Of course,' explained Harriet, 'I could not use the *kitchen* door, but I put my pea on the ledge over the morning-room door — and it was Spens who came in first.'

She waited for him to laugh at this ridiculous anti-climax. He did not.

'Well,' she said, tilting her head to look up at him, 'would you not *mind* if I were married to Spens?'

She wanted an outburst, a protest — more than anything. Instead:

'My dear,' he said, 'I do not see how it would affect matters whether I minded or not. I should be *desolé*, of course —'

She drew a little away from him. 'But you would not *mind*!'

'I have just told you, how would it affect matters whether I minded or did not mind? After all, the opinion of a prisoner of war is worth mighty little!'

'Now you are pretending to be modest!' she flashed. 'And you are not in the *least* modest, underneath, I know very well! You have an excellent opinion of yourself!'

'Why should I not have?' he returned. 'Nobody else has!'

He was laughing a little now — not with happiness but in faint ridicule of both of them — or perhaps of this lovers' tiff, blown up as suddenly as a squall upon the lake of Geneva.

He had let go of her shoulders and returned to his table, sitting on it and swinging one leg as he tinkered gently with his model pump-mill.

'Yes,' he went on, looking down at the pump, not at her, 'you are quite right, my darling girl. I have an excellent opinion of myself. I cling to it through thick and thin! I am one of the finest engineers in the world!' *Pff!* He gave a deft turn, at that, with finger and thumb and the little model began to perform its revolutions, whirring busily round as if confirming all his statements.

'If I were a free man,' he went on, 'I could make a fortune with this toy of mine. You know that? However — ' and he shrugged ever so slightly in a way she knew well: 'I am not a free man; I am not even allowed to be an engineer. I am a prisoner on parole, handy with his fingers. I am not even a Netherlander,' he added, 'they take even that from me! I am a French Prisoner because I was captured on a French ship; I was classified as a French Prisoner, I escaped as a French Prisoner, I was recaptured as a French Prisoner and nothing can *un*make me one unless I can die like Jesus Christ and be born again!'

Harriet shivered a little. 'I see no reason for blasphemy — '

'You little hypocrite!' He took her by the shoulders again, and she could not tell whether he were laughing at her or not. 'A fig you care for religion! Like father, like daughter! You drive the servants to church, you wear out *their* knees on your damp stone floors to pray for the right weather for your crops, you frighten *them* with tales of hell-fire to keep them in good behaviour — but the Bromewells themselves do not participate! Why — you have not stepped inside Mr. Mogus's church as long as I have been here! And yet you expect to be suitably received, no doubt, when you come to be buried there. You have reserved your *grave* in holy soil, at least!'

'Van!' she said, really shocked this time.

He caught her to him again, crushing all protest out of her.

'Now you see how foolish it was to come and seek me out here! It can only make you unhappy, my darling! Nevertheless,' kissing her eyes, her lips, her soft, tanned cheek, 'I am glad you came. Do you love me?'

Such bewildering changes of temper made her more breathless even than his bear's hug.

'Do you think I would have sought you out — as you call it — unless —'

'Then I give you fair warning, my dear, *dear* Harry. Do not love me! People who love me always become unhappy —'

Half fearfully, half ironically, she heard herself asking:

'Are there — have there been so many, then?'

He shrugged a little, again:

'Well, you know, one has relatives, comrades —'

She did not respond, still fearing she knew not what. Again a swift change of mood assailed him and he besought her anxiously —

'You won't desert me, will you? Not after *this*?' making a gesture embracing the room, time, circumstances. 'Promise you will not disappear again! It is as if you had made me alive again, after I had been dead for years . . .'

Memory of her dream swam back into her mind as he spoke — the dying black swan, the poignant drooping of the head, the grey unassuageable sadness over all the waste of poisoned water. She longed to assure him: *Never! Never! I will never desert you! It was my breast that bled against the bridge of thorns: coming and going: it was I who brought you the water of life in my beak: the precious drops to save you!* But it would have been childish to speak so and he would not have understood, so aloud she said simply:

'I love you, Van. How could it be possible for me to desert you? As long as you want me — and you *do* want me, Van?'

'Most desperately!'

'You have thought of me, sometimes, while I have been away?'

'I have envied those who were with you, every waking hour.'

'Oh — and I too, I *too*, Van! I have envied the very labourers here, I have envied Spens because he was seeing you daily — and my father as well! I have been madly jealous of your pump-mill because I knew your hands touched it and your mind and brain were absorbed in it!'

'But my dreams,' he said, 'were of you . . .'

Sweet assurances, doubly-sweet counter-assurances, chiming like bells answering each other across the mountain-tops.

'Do you sleep here?' asked Harriet, wondering *How does he look when he is asleep? Is it possible to pierce to the heart of his secret then? Shall I ever see him then?*

'Sometimes I am allowed to, when I have permission from your father and the Lord Lieutenant's man. The Lord Lieutenant has suggested that I may sleep here if a guard remains with me —'

'A guard? What nonsense — when you are working for this country!'

He lifted his shoulders slightly again. 'I admire the suggestion at any rate. It shows some sort of vigilance. But naturally I send the guard home to sleep.'

She said, half-pleased, half-nettled: 'And he obeys you? But of course! The men about here trust you, they would do anything for *you*, Van!'

''M . . . You think it wise of them?'

'Wise?'

'Yes, my darling. For what, after all, do they know of me? What do *you* know of me? This —,' indicating the model, 'may be a feint. I may be, after all, in the pay of the French —'

'I am *sure* you are not!'

'Thank you.' He bent and kissed her eyes. 'You have been walking by the sea, haven't you? I can taste the salt on your eyelids. Oh, my lovely, my incomparable Harry, to think that anyone as profoundly *bourgeois* as your father could have produced such a beauty! Or perhaps your mother deceived him with a merman out of the sea? *That* is why you taste salt!'

Harriet wriggled slightly. 'I *hate* the sea — and you, too, when you talk of my father like that! If you love me you should at least respect *him*! He has shown his trust in you, at least!'

He grimaced. 'I am not flattered by that. So he *should* trust me! . . . As much, that is,' he continued quizzically, 'as anyone should trust me, and that is precisely as far as they can see me. Why should they do more, when I do not trust myself? Do *you* trust *yourself*?'

She was puzzled again. 'Naturally!'

'Yes, naturally. It comes, I suppose,' he went on 'of having so perfect a profile.' And — his mercurial mood changing again, now he *was* teasing her, even while she was still two, or was it three, moods behind him, angrily panting to catch up with him. He drew one forefinger lightly down her forehead, nose, upper lip, chin, continuing:

'Yes, if I saw as pleasant a sight as this in my mirror every morning when I shaved, I should consider myself the most trustworthy fellow on earth! I should give myself a *parole* to go everywhere and do everything!'

But this was a stage of ridiculousness that Harriet would not endure; it mocked all that had gone before. She turned as if to go, but he was in front of her:

'Must you go, *ma Mie*?'

'Yes, there are things to do at home —'

'To be sure. But do not forget me!'

'Forget you!' Here was the real blasphemy — worse than that other one; to believe such a thing possible! He went on, apparently in all seriousness:

'You have a proverb, haven't you, Forgive and Forget. I would never ask that of you, Harry. Forgive me — yes, a thousand times — but not forget! Never forget!'

He said the words with such emphasis — it was odd, to-day he seemed to be emphasizing all the wrong words and touching too lightly, too mockingly, on all the right ones ... Or was it that her own state of mind (in her delirious happiness) misconstrued his common sense? She was more puzzled than ever.

'Perhaps you can't conceive of such a thing,' went on this strange, baffling lover of hers, 'but the most terrible thing in life is to be forgotten; no trace of one to be found in the archives. We regret, my dear sir, that we are unable to confirm ... Have you a notion of what I am talking about?'

'I might have, if you did not jump so abruptly from one subject to another!'

He laughed at that, throwing back his head. He had taken off his shabby cravat to be cool to work and the firm brown column of his bare throat, extended as it was, was irresistible to Harriet. Vexed though she was with him, and bruised by passages of arms not to be refused but not understood, her hand stretched upwards again to caress him.

He seized upon it as it touched him, pressing it fiercely against his flesh, as if he too felt the justice and necessity of the act. And — as she was to discover so often later — her physical touch brought him back, temporarily, out of his wild nonsensical theorizings to the immediate and understandable.

'My dear, how I love you!'

It was not enough in English. He repeated it in French, and in his native tongue, adding, three times repeated: '*Je te veux! Je te veux! Je te veux!*' Then:

'What was it you called me?'

'Van?'

'"Van" — yes, that is good. Call me that! Nobody has ever called me that before!'

'Are there — have there been so many?' she teased again (but still anxiously).

He said, 'There is only you. Yes — go, but do not forget me! If you do, how shall I know for certain that this afternoon has ever existed? That I have not dreamed it?'

Action once more precipitated itself upon Harriet. She wriggled a small signet ring off her finger — the only piece of jewellery she wore.

'By this,' she said, dropping it from her hand into his with the sweetest and most confiding gesture.

He stood stock still, looking down at it, his long face inexpressive.

Baffled again, Harriet asked: 'Aren't you pleased? Shall I take it back?'

(This insufferable coquetry, which yet must play out its part with the rest of the actions!)

At last: 'I have nothing to give you,' he replied, 'in exchange.' He still stood looking down at the ring. He was not overjoyed as she had fancied he might be, by this tangible proof of affection — but somehow, she fancied, embarrassed.

'Very well,' said Harriet, nettled once more on this extra-ordinary afternoon for the thousandth time, and very near to tears, 'if it is such a burden to you, give it me back!' and she snatched it up again, pressing it angrily back upon her little finger, mortified beyond words. Still he did not protest, or move to restrain her as she had hoped he would — only repeating:

'You see, my darling, I should have nothing to give in return — '

The tears were standing in her eyes, so brightly, that Vandervoord could see the square of light through the window frame reflected in them.

'You have yourself!' she said, 'nobody can take *that* from you!'

'Ah, if you could assure me of *that*,' he said, blocking the door to her exit by standing in it — and by now she was anxious to go — madly longing to go, so that she might conserve what joy had happened before it disintegrated between the weight of these after-woes. But she had, without knowing it, touched on something which stirred him deeply. 'Yes,' he said, 'if you could assure me of *that*, really finally, I should love you twice as dearly as I do already — which is absurd, as Euclid tells us.'

'*Who* says we are absurd?'

'No, no, my little ignoramus! Listen; perhaps after all it is possible — '

'But Van — I have not the *least* idea what you are talking of!'

'Of your powers,' he said surprisingly. 'I know you have great powers. I sensed them the first moment I saw you. You said just now that nobody could take the Self from one. Yet you cannot conceive how often I have been tempted to believe — yes — really severely tempted — that they can deprive one of oneself as well — '

'They? Who are they?'

'The Authorities. The Gods. Fate, Fortune, what you will! It is not an uncommon feeling, I assure you, in prisoners — '

'But you are not a prisoner any more, Van. You are on extended parole!'

'That does not break the bars down,' he answered. Then quickly: 'Do not misunderstand me, my dearest. When I say you have great powers, *unseen* powers, do not think that, because of what has passed between us, I am going to ask you to use your influence to achieve more favours and ameliorations of my situation than I enjoy already. That would be nothing. No, I mean that *here*, sometimes' (and at this he pressed his hand hard against his breast), 'there is the most terrible chasm. Do you believe the soul inhabits the body, *really* inhabits it? Or have you never thought about such a subject? Well, it is just as if, sometimes, the soul had vacated this body of mine; as if only the frame of this man that is me was left. It is a sensation not to be endured without the acutest—horror.' He went on gently beating his still clenched fist against his breast. 'When I say that you have powers, I mean that I believe — as solemnly as if I were on my knees in church — that you may be able to exorcise this evil spirit which takes hold of me —'

He had been speaking, looking out of the window as if afraid to look directly at her, but now he glanced down. Burdened with this fresh disclosure, Harriet looked more distraught than he had yet seen her. He smiled: 'My poor darling! You see — the first present I make to you is the secret of my unhappiness! I told you that those who love me are doomed to unhappiness! But don't be afraid — I shan't speak of it again, you may be sure of that. I talk like this about once every ten years and then always repent it.'

Harriet shook her head: 'I don't know what you mean by my Powers, but I will not allow this "emptiness", as you call it, to trouble you. Be sure of that! If I love you, how is it *possible* I should let you suffer from such moods?'

It was so plain, so crystal-clear to her. He could not help smiling again, but whether at her simple wisdom or his tortuous foolishness perhaps he could not have said.

'Yes,' he said, holding her hands, 'you will be my good angel, my Haven of Peace, I know that.' All the same, she felt that he did not quite believe her, not to the uttermost. So they stood, holding hands in the small doorway and looking into each other's eyes searchingly. They did not kiss when she left.

All the way home, with every gesture, every word that had occurred whirling fierily in her imagination — some sweet, some sad, some with veiled faces, all unspeakably dear in recollection — Harriet felt the last caress of his hand on hers. She clasped one hand over the other to conserve the remembrance of this pressure, and let the sweetest words of all repeat themselves: 'I have envied those that were with you, every waking hour! . . .' 'But my dreams were of you!' She repeated them over and over, cherishing them as something precious because understood and reciprocated to the fullest possible extent. So—proud yet chagrined, happy yet oddly defiant, shivering a little at what misfortunes might lie ahead for her and her lover, but determined with all the aid of her 'powers' to overcome them—Harriet Bromewell returned to Redonda.

CHAPTER XVI

WHEN THIEVES FALL OUT

... My spirit's bark is driven
Far from the shore ... — SHELLEY

PRECISELY how Harriet expected her father to take any announcement of her feelings towards Vandervoord it is difficult to say. Open and frank in all her dealings as it was her nature to be, she desired nothing better than to disclose to him what had passed, and to ask for his consent to some 'understanding' between them, even if he could not, during hostilities, bestow his blessing.

But it did not take her long to perceive that he was not the same man that she had left behind when she went to Lausanne. It was not only that the trouble with his eyes did not clear up; his character too was affected. Confined to a darkened room with bandaged eyes, unable to pursue his ordinary activities, first he chafed and stormed at the circumstances, then this irritability gave way to a more disturbing quietude. The household at Redonda became gradually conscious of a sense of constrained silence emanating from the morning-room, more sinister than any of the previous commotions. Maids going to and from their different businesses stole shocked glances through the window at the Captain as he sat, hugely immobile in his chair—his wine and riding-crop both well within reach, everything else remote from him. He became accustomed to sit so, hour after hour without moving, staring into the black of his bandages, seeing something nobody else could see ...

He did not want Harriet's company. He did not want Spens, complaining that the agent's account of the day's activities only gave him a headache — which was true in a way, since it had always been essential for Captain Bromewell to have things tangibly and visibly before him. Life moved for him only if he could handle it — through the medium or thought of another man, not at all.

Redonda could have endured this inactivity without undue dismay. The times were so rich and auspicious for the big farmers, the land itself was by now in such good heart and his affairs in such perfect order that — for the time at least — the absence of Captain Bromewell himself from the head of affairs bore no ill results.

But upon the inside staff of servants and upon Harriet the strain of this continued silence — this sense of an internally active volcano not yet erupting but likely to do so at any moment — was an increasing one. It could not last, they told one another — yet it did last. It was not to be endured and yet it had to be endured: whilst the unexpectedness of the invalid's other reactions was an additional mystery.

Firstly, Captain Bromewell loathed the doctor, pretending to hold him responsible for most of his troubles and enduring his visits and ministrations without any attempts at self-control. Ivory being called in on such occasions to hold bowls and towels had passed on to him, with interest, the pain that the doctor was inevitably inflicting upon his master. The doctor protested:

'You treat that fellow worse than you do your dogs, Captain!'

'Why shouldn't I? The dogs are less clumsy by far!'

'Still, he's a human being, sir, even if he *is* black'. (The doctor was not for nothing related to that Liberal group known as the English Athenians, in Norwich.) 'Besides — he might run off and leave you —'

'Let him try it, that's all. I'll stripe his hide for life if he does, and what's more I'll have the law of you for inciting him! *Ouch! Ow! Grr!*'

The doctor was a well-intentioned man but no fool, and after this he held his peace. He guessed that it would be as useless to advise the negro to leave Redonda as to plead with his employer for better treatment. True, slavery had been abolished in England but Ivory, born a slave, was a slave in his mind and no legal statutes could eradicate a state of mind sucked in with his mother's milk and — worst of all — utterly unresented. Ivory blamed *him*, he knew, as the author of his discomforts, and not his poor tortured master — and unfortunately he could not insist on turning Ivory out of the room as he insisted on turning the snarling dogs, who were convinced of exactly the same thing.

Further, the visits of his crony, Everybody's Friend, did not have the restorative effect upon her father that Harriet had hoped for. Twigg, quite recovered from the effects of *his* drinking bout, sought to enliven the Captain with news of all that was going forward in Bury. Such and such a cargo had come in safely despite the French privateers and the English naval patrols, and such and such would be the rake-off for the collaboration of a Justice of the Peace on the night of the run. He had better news still. It appeared that the Gov'ment, forced by circumstances and the increasingly serious turn of the war to make use of all materials, was now out to enlist the Twiggs of the East Coast as additional secret agents — employment in which their smuggling experience (it naturally went without saying) would stand them in good stead.

It was over this news that the two Captains first fell out. Captain Twigg had, it appeared, a chance to become both patriotic and rich, if he could acquire another member of the crew who could 'talk the lingo'. He wanted Vandervoord, and the Gov'ment in London, he hinted, would see that he *got* Vandervoord if such was his desire.

But Captain Bromewell had no intention of releasing Vandervoord to earn good money for someone else. They were in loud dispute over this very point one afternoon when the French Prisoner, entering the morning-room without formality, as by now he was privileged to do, broke in upon the pair of them fighting over his body, as it were, and threatening each other with a thousand dire penalties for non-compliance.

'There!' said Twigg, confident in the fact that he had his eyesight at least — not to mention Influence at Westminster. 'Talk of the Devil. Here he is, Cap'n! Now then, Van-what's-yer-name, are you prepared to shift agin, and come wi' me? 'Tis the chance of a lifetime!'

'Confound you, Twigg! It's of no concern *what* he's prepared to do! He's bound to me by the strictest indentures and be damned if I'm going to break 'em for anyone!'

'There now,' said Twigg, with mock resignation, 'It's the interests of the country, Cap'n' (and here through a confusion of Captains he addressed Vandervoord by this title too). 'And he 'on't let ye goo! Here we are at war with the French agin, want all the help we can git, and when I reckon to give ye a chanst, Cap'n, to jine us, *on good authority*, he 'on't hear of it!'

Vandervoord stood silently before them both. From his expression it was not to be guessed what he was thinking, but his eyes, with their gaze fixed out of one of the windows over the coast-line, showed the direction his thoughts were taking.

Captain Twigg made the most of his chance. Unsure of his ground, he wheedled, ignoring Captain Bromewell's furious expostulations. He put his hand out and laid it flat upon the desk, the picture of honesty and friendship.

'It's like this, Cap'n,' he said, 'we need someone to speak the lingo. That's dangerous work, but well-pide, and that's all for the sake of Old England! Not as how you can be expected,' he went on, his chest swelling at the thought of his own broadmindedness, 'to feel like us about Old England. But reckon you want to rescue your own country from that bastard the same as that General Doomoroo who came over here, *he's* a Frenchy, too!'

'Except that I am not French, sir,' said Vandervoord.

'But you're a French *Prisoner*, Cap'n!'

'No, sir, that's a common misapprehension. I'm not even a Captain. I have never been in any army. I'm an engineer from the Netherlands —'

If he had said he was a unicorn from the Antipodes, Captain Twigg could not have looked more dumbfounded.

'Well . . .' For once he could find no words, then: 'They towd me in London you were a French Prisoner,' he explained lamely. 'Reckon that's why they thought you'd fare to speak the lingo —'

'——! . . . ——! . . . ——!' roared Captain Bromewell. 'Will anybody do me the favour to listen to *me* in my own house?

204

He's not going to get the chance to speak *any* lingo! He's going to stay *here*, sir, under parole to *me*, sir, and do work at Redonda!'

Captain Twigg took up his hat with a sidling movement, rather as if he expected it, fishlike, to dart from his clasp and elude him.

'Very well, Cap'n. We'll see what they say in London . . . You *are* Mr. Vandervoord, I suppose?' he added, turning to the French Prisoner.

Vandervoord bent his head in acknowledgment: 'That is my name.'

'Can't understand it,' said Twigg, waddling towards the door without even a backward glance of sympathy towards the invalid. 'That don't fare to fit together at all, nohow! They towd me you were a French Prisoner!'

'Nothing, sir, will persuade them that I am anything else,' said Vandervoord. 'I ought to know. I have been trying to convince them myself for two years!'

'And you *can* speak the lingo?'

'He can talk the lingo of the man in the moon for all I care, or for all the benefit *you'll* ever get out of him!' shouted Bromewell, drowning the response of Vandervoord, if he made any.

'Cap'n, Cap'n, what a way to treat an old friend! I was trying for to do ye a favour — '

'You were trying to put money in your pocket, you scoundrel, at my expense!'

'It's not patriotic,' was all that Captain Twigg would reply. He slipped his shiny black straw hat, the garb of all honourable seamen, upon his head with that brief sleight-of-hand action peculiarly his own, and a waft of stale mackerel followed the gesture into the air.

'Get out of my house, sir, before I have you thrown out. You stink!' responded his host. 'Where's Ivory, where's that bone-lazy black?' and he began to thump the ground with the butt of his riding-crop, and to strike out with it against the legs of the desk, the chairs — anything — so that his companions withdrew hastily out of its reach.

Long after Everybody's Friend had gone his way, and the echoes of contention aroused by his proposal had died down, a certain soreness remained, and Captain Bromewell was more than usually silent. He was so still, so contemplative, so suggestive of an unspeakable rage consuming him from within and rendering him speechless, that the maids stole past the window fearfully, hardly daring even to peep inside.

As for Vandervoord, the incident left him angry, not amused. 'To hear them haggling over my services,' he told Harriet, 'as if I were Ivory or one of the cattle! To have no say in the matter myself — to be impotent, *impotent!*'

Harriet said: 'If my father would have released you — after all, he *could* do so if he wished, he can pull more strings than Twigg can for all his boastings — would you have gone?'

It was a solemn, strained moment:

'Who knows? I don't say so — but one likes to be consulted for all that. To be a man, not a piece of personal property!'

'But what would you have said if you *had* been consulted?' Foolish girl — expecting a simple answer to a simple question! Instead, Vandervoord shrugged again, repeating:

'Who knows? Naturally one occasionally has a desire to see one's own land. If I went with Twigg that — opportunity — might arise. Even in peacetime there are spies plying almost as regularly as the fishing-fleets, between Rotterdam and Harwich.'

He would commit himself no further than that. Nevertheless, she found him looking seawards rather more than usual, for about a week after the visitor had gone.

Such reticence was — as Harriet was sooner or later bitterly to learn — characteristic of him. When she begged him to tell her something of his childhood in Holland, he would say nothing; made excuses of a poor memory, or that there was nothing of interest; turned the conversation always into other channels. When pressed: 'But I don't *remember*, I tell you!' he said. 'Can *you* remember things that happened when you were a child?'

'Of course I can, Van! As clearly as if they were yesterday! I remember running home up the avenue with Susan, during the most dreadful storm; I remember willing the end of the world not to happen, when the boys' stupid tutor said it would; I remember the hot elderberry wine we drunk in front of the fire on Christmas Eve; I remember Father saying "Thank God for a good fire and nobody in it", which he always did the first day we had a fire in autumn . . .; I remember being given my first pony and how I cried because it took such short paces beside Father's mare; I remember Redonda in autumn and leaning out of window in my shift to count the shooting stars — and trying to catch one in my hand —'

'Marvellous child!' he smiled; but she felt that by smiling he mocked such recollections and ambitions. He was not happy during those days. If Captain Twigg had kept away from Redonda it might have been easier — but he was not the man to give up after one attempt. He made it his business to find out as much as could be known about Vandervoord — both locally and in London, so as to be able to meet Captain Bromewell upon equal ground. And the more he learnt, the more he set his heart upon acquiring him, for tales of the French Prisoner's prowess were to be had for the asking far beyond the confines of Redonda. Besides, he saw the pump-mills — two of them, now — whirringly hard at work in some (to him) magical way, draining Bromewell's land for him, and pouring gold into his pockets as surely as they poured the water, by means of ingenious pipes and sluices, back into the river that led to the sea.

He came to pay a second visit to the invalid, entering the room without announcement and finding Captain Bromewell and the French Prisoner — as luck would have it — once more together. Vandervoord had constructed a new toy — a clay model of Redonda's farmland, laid out within the boundaries of a large wooden tray, and his hands were guiding the blindfolded Captain's ones over its miniature environs — the hedges, barns, ponds, dykes, ploughed fields (scratched rough by a needle), even the two pump-mills. Field by field, hedge by hedge, acre by acre, the clever creative hands guided the possessive and destructive ones. For the first time since his sight had so treacherously deserted him, Captain Bromewell felt that he had the situation and the property — *his* property — under effective observation and control.

A casual onlooker might have supposed the two men to be playing some game together — so intent they were, with their heads so close together — but Everybody's Friend (despite his sidling movements) was never casual. He took in the new model at a glance, and could hardly restrain an ejaculation of wonder at the perfection of its proportions, the exact reproduction, in miniature, of Bromewell's whole estate.

Captain Twigg's second visit was not welcomed by Captain Bromewell, and their interview was both briefer and stormier than before. Ejected, still unsuccessful, Captain Twigg happened to meet Harriet descending the staircase. He disguised his real feelings under an affected solicitude for her father.

'You want to watch him, Miss Harriet. He's a master hand at doing himself wrong. You want to watch that French Prisoner too. Don't — and you'll regret it!'

'What do you mean, Captain Twigg?'

'I mean,' said Twigg, confidingly wrapping his great hand about the wooden pineapple at the foot of the balustrade (and leaving fish-scales inevitably upon it), 'You can't be sure o' foreigners. And now the poor Cap'n's bloind — well, as good as bloind — that wouldn't be hard for the young feller to start tricking him some way. He's clever as a cageful o' monkeys — '

Uncertain of her ground, and wary of this change of tone in Everybody's Friend, Harriet merely responded that at Redonda they were well able to look after their own interests. Twigg replied he was happy to hear it — had never doubted it for one instant. All the same, if ever Harriet needed his help — if ever anything queer or 'old-fashioned' looked like going forward, and she needed advice — all she had to do was to send for him, Twigg — and he would see her and his old friend and Old England put to rights. As for Vandervoord —

'He shouldn't oughter occupy that owd plice on the foreshore berights,' he concluded.

'He has to watch the floods there, Captain. We have permission for that from the Military.'

'Ah! You take care he don't goo watchin' for suthin' else besoide that owd flood,' said the Captain.

And he went his way again, playing the game as he had played it as long as he could remember; if you can't board the enemy's ship and take her in tow and get prize money for her and her cargo — why there's such a thing as ramming her and sending her to the bottom — and stopping anybody *else* getting her — that's good seamanship too!

If Harriet could have had the leisure to think things over afterwards, something in the manner of Everybody's Friend might have made her fear, not only for her father but also for Vandervoord. But she was young and — acting proxy for her father and brother — fully occupied with supervision of work in the house and on the estate. Also, she was violently in love for the first time in her life. So she sang as she walked, happy in all her tasks, happy to meet Vandervoord half a dozen times a day in the course of both their business, happiest of all in the thought of what the future held in store. Already, to her mind, he moved about Redonda as its master — Lord not only of the harvest but of the manor as well. Clement and his family were still in Lausanne, almost beleaguered there now by Bonaparte's encircling and ceaselessly victorious armies — but secure by reason of diplomatic immunity. Clancy was still in London at the Inns of Court. Soon the war would end, her father would retire from the actual management of Redonda and she and Van, triumphantly co-operative, would wrest the inheritance and Redonda from her brothers — come what might! She desired this to happen, and so, by all the power of her willing, she would see that it came to pass.

Meanwhile, Vandervoord was as good — or as bad — as his word. Since that first meeting in the cabin, he had never again spoken at length to her, and certainly not about his own feelings. He had been gentle and lover-like, and teasing in the old pre-lover manner, and always entertaining and amusing beyond all words. But he did not encourage her to come out again to their old meeting-place.

'People will talk,' he said.

'Let them!' flashed Harriet.

'No, my darling. You are as free as the air, I know, and can snap your fingers at them with impunity. But it is not fair to your father, and it is not fair to me.'

'To *you*?'

'Certainly. Do you think that, because I am circumstanced as I am, that I have no feelings at all?'

She giggled at that and kissed him violently upon the mouth.

'Ah — you are afraid I will compromise you!'

'No,' he answered slowly, 'I have no status worth the compromising. I am much more afraid that you will put too great a strain on me as a man whose passions are, after all, as violent as your own.'

Harriet was outraged. *Passions?* She?

But certainly, he said again, had she not the most violent and passionate desires for many of the best things of life? And — being a woman, did she not desire him? Certainly her kisses said as much. And that being so (for even frowning silence is consent), would it not be wiser to keep away from a place where the very fact that they would be completely undisturbed lent impetus to mutual passion? 'You may be able to answer for yourself,' he concluded. 'Calm, self-assured little Harry! You are always sure of yourself! But I cannot be sure of *myself*.'

This tacit admission of her power in a field of which, until recently, she had been more or less unconscious, delighted Harriet. Here perhaps was the battle-ground *par excellence*, the Field of the Cloth of Gold where the richest trophies of all waited to be won! Nevertheless, it was maidenly to concur, for the moment at least. Perhaps, at any rate, until she had spoken to her father.

But Captain Bromewell, if anything, grew harder to communicate with, instead of easier. He had forbidden Captain Twigg the house and, being desperate for entertainment, or perhaps for something more solid, had commanded Mr. Mogus the parson to continue to come up and instruct him in certain matters whereof he would have knowledge.

It has been said that this was the first time a parson had set a welcome foot in Redonda since Mr. Mogus's predecessor had paid a visit of condolence on the death of Harriet's mother. He had been a nervous man, but Mogus was a bold one — going boldly in and closing the door of the morning-room behind him with the brisk sacrificial inspiration of Daniel locking himself into the lions' den. But no roaring, on this occasion, came from within. The listening servants (as before), and Harriet, could hear the drone of Mr. Mogus's voice and occasional interjections from his parishioner and then (as on that previous visit) a thump betokening kneeling, followed by a silence as shattering as that of Captain Bromewell wrapped in the solitude of his own company.

When the first two or three weeks of this new *regime* lapsed into two months, then three, the visits of the doctor grew fewer and those of the parson increased. The blind had led the blind and one of them at least had fallen into a ditch so deep and dark that there was to be no clambering out of it. In other words, Captain Bromewell's ever-increasing blindness proved to be incurable, and, since there was no salvation to be had of the doctor, he was seeing what the parson could do for him instead.

Although the state of his eyesight never varied, his moods changed with the temperature of every day. Sometimes he was almost tender with Harriet — would have lectured her, if he knew how, on the inadvisability of short-sighted companions and the proximity of unsuspected ditches; of the power of prayer, the task of redemption, man's duty to God and to his neighbours. Again, sometimes in the watches of the night Harriet would hear him groaning, lamenting and arguing with his Maker, imploring divine co-operation. But in the daytime he grew increasingly taciturn (except where the farm was concerned); lost in a world of his own behind the band-ages, his lips moving frequently in expostulation or confession.

These were the first-fruits of Mr. Mogus; other results followed inexorably, particularly the raising of the moral tone of a house previously content (as far as Mr. Mogus could see) with the standards of morality of its own farmyard, no more and no less. A little legitimacy about the place — especially with a young lady in charge — would in Mr. Mogus's opinion be no bad thing. Briskly, bluffly, bravely — taking the danger as he took the stiffest hedges in the hunting-field, Mr. Mogus advised the fallen Samson to put his house in order; and thereby made his first false step with Harriet, irrevocably, right in up to the neck.

Susan came running in to her mistress one morning before break-fast, sobbing and crying: 'Oh, Miss Harry, wake up! Wake up, do! They fare to send me away!'

Harriet, startled, half-awake, grabbed the sobbing creature by the shoulder.

'Don't talk nonsense. No one can send you away!'

'Ah, but Miss Harry, they *say* so! The Cap'n *say* so! Mr. Spens was told by the Cap'n to tell me so! Mr. Mogus told the Cap'n about this!'

With a gesture she indicated her now undoubted pregnancy. Harriet rubbed her eyes.

'And the Cap'n call me up, he did Miss Harry, just now — and he told me what Mr. Mogus said — and he felt me with his hands — '

She sobbed louder and louder. Yes, thought Harriet, that was just like him. A Bromewell even in blindness, he must know for *himself*.

'And he said I was a bad wicked woman and that I couldn't stay with you ne more, Miss Harry, and I'm to goo, roight away, or else be married to Tom Anderson, oh, oh, oh!' and still weeping and sobbing the poor creature flung herself down on the ground by Harriet's bed, too miserable for further explanation.

Breakfast that morning between the Bromewells was, in consequence, almost as lively as in the old days.

'How dare Mr. Mogus come interfering at Redonda and dictate to me about Sukey!' cried Harriet.

'How dare you keep on a servant lost to all sense of shame is more like it,' said her father. 'Hand me the toast!' (His appetite at least had not failed since his blindness. He now ate twice as much, inactive, as he had done in the days when he was in the saddle often until sunset.)

'Sukey is not a servant. Why — I've had her so long she is almost part of the family,' Harriet replied. '*You* chose her for me, if it comes to that, Father! The blame must rest with you!'

'Are you accusing your own father of siring that harlot's brat?'

'She is *not* a harlot!'

'Don't argue with me, Harriet, it brings on my headaches. Mind your own business and honour your father as the Bible tells you — '

'It *is* my business and if the Bible tells you that my Susan is a harlot then the Bible is wrong!' said Harriet. 'She's a poor silly wretch that doesn't know any better, that's all. Show me a servant that doesn't have a lovechild, then you will show me a curiosity! Why, to my certain knowledge there have been such children born in this house — yes, *and* on the farm — one every few months or so, as long as I can recall. You used to *like* it, Father! You used to say it gave you birdscarers and geese-minders for nothing. I remember a talk between you and Spens, when Spens wanted to pull down that old barn in the clover field, and *you* said No, leave it, that's where I get my birdscarers — I remember perfectly well!'

'A man may change, I suppose,' said the Captain, remote from behind his bandages. 'He can be saved —'

'Not at the expense of Sukey, Father!'

The candidate for salvation made a retrogressive step. Even the bandages could not disguise the old familiar manner.

'Take your choice then. She gets out by to-night, is married to Anderson as soon as may be, or by God, Harry, you leave here to-night yourself!'

There was a long pause while Harriet digested this ultimatum, staring at his hands gripping the chair-arms, trembling with familiar fury.

'You mean that?'

'Every word, my girl!'

'You know I can't leave Redonda.' Her voice was shaking as much as his hands. 'It is a wicked alternative to offer me —'

'You offer it to yourself, my dear Harriet, by shielding the sinner. I will have NO immorality here! He thumped his fist upon the chair-arm. 'And don't pretend there's any cruelty in it. Anderson will give her a good home, he was always fond of her as a youngster —'

'He's at *least* twenty years older than she is!'

'In years possibly — not in sauciness and wicked worldly behaviour,' said her father. The strange churchy phrases, issuing from his mouth, were as unnatural-sounding as foreign words. Mr. Mogus, thought Harriet bitterly as she stamped off to arrange for Susan's departure, has had an easy victory so far. It will not be so easy from now on!

Discovering the inevitability of the Captain's decree, Susan became quickly calm. She had the true countrywoman's reaction to acts of God such as lightning, thunder, pelting rain to spoil the crops or a killing drouth — and the Captain's behaviour partook of the nature of such violent, unexpected yet not-to-be-questioned acts. Yes, she would marry Anderson if he would have her, and would go to live with him in the old cabin next to the blacksmith's forge. She would oblige the Captain. With her eyes swollen with crying, her nose red with blowing, her body big with the child sired by the homesick footman in far-off Lausanne — it was apparent, thought Harriet, that all the obligation was likely to be on Anderson's side, for a long time to come. Something made her ask, as they were packing the pitiful baggage between them:

'Did you love that man in Switzerland, Susan?'

Susan sobbed again: 'I dunno, Miss! I was wholly sorry for him. He was homesick like me, Miss, and he — he had to goo on to that owd Italy. I was s-sorry for him, that was how it happened!'

'And will you love Tom Anderson when you are married to him?'

'I — I expect so, Miss—and he must love my little owd baby! We must all love each other, or that will be too hard to bear . . .'

Soon after that the baggage was packed on to Anderson's donkey-cart and taken down to the cabin next the smithy, whence the sound of hammer on anvil and the smell of scorched horn rose together into the air all the livelong day — and were both to be a part of Susan's life from then on. In her place Harriet took on one of the kitchen-maids — a shy creature of fourteen or so with no experience but with a quiet steady manner and a light touch with the iron.

What would be too hard to bear? The war? Truly, the war was two years old now and bearing down heavily upon the lower classes; but Susan, safe and snug with Redonda's rich reserves of food all round her had not as yet suffered. Anyway, the war could not last for ever. Boney would be beaten by us somehow, some-where — perhaps sooner than we dared to think . . . Until he *was* beaten, talk of marriage between Harriet and Vandervoord was, of course, out of the question.

And, with the change in her father, Harriet was no longer sure quite how he would take the news. At one time — before his eye-sight was affected — she could almost have sworn that he had grown to love Van as much as a third son, or at any rate as much as Don his dog. Cupboard love, no doubt; for what Van could *do* more than for what he was; but was not the doing of things the very essence of being Jan Vandervoord? And anyhow, was not that kind of reason for affection the most understandable, and likely to be the most enduring? Yet it had not endured or — if it had — there was no way of being sure of this.

There were days when he behaved to the French Prisoner as of old, telling him everything, asking him everything; there was a time when their hands met over the mimic hedges of the clay model and Captain Bromewell had gripped Van's hand then and said: 'You won't desert me, at least!' There were other days when he listened to Vandervoord only because — so he made it plain — he had to; when he snarled or snorted instead of answering and found fault with all the labour of the day.

There were other days, again, when he greedily accepted all that the French Prisoner had achieved for him and Redonda — thanking him by supposing that he was planning to make a get-away, hey? and join that smuggler Twigg? And escape back to France or wherever it was he came from? And there were days on end when he abruptly withdrew permission to Vandervoord to use the cabin on the foreshore; when consequently work on the land drainage scheme was inevitably held up. There was even a period when he insisted on the indignity of an armed guard — this ostensibly because Vandervoord happened to be working near some new coastal fortifications which were going forward. And then again there were days when Vandervoord was *persona grata* everywhere — must dine with Captain Bromewell and wine with him and sleep in the best bedroom but one (after listening half the night to his stories) and help him up to bed instead of Ivory.

So his moods veered like the winds — and none was judged as favourable by Harriet for the launching of the frail craft bearing her hopes and desires.

Meanwhile, since the primary objective could not be obtained there were plenty of smaller objectives to be tackled. Firstly, there was the question of revenging herself upon the Mogus family for their behaviour towards Susan. There was the Right of Way!

The Right of Way was a narrow track across a certain field of Redonda, which constituted, since time immemorial, a short cut between the village and the church. The Mogus family, living in a parsonage cheek by jowl with the church, naturally took advantage of it more than most other people. Harriet therefore — immediately after the expulsion of her maid — saw the Right of Way as an intolerable and impudent trespass by Mary Mogus. The sight of Miss Mogus's shawled figure, tripping possessively along the track across the field towards the village, brought Harriet's wrath to boiling-point. She had long detested Mary Mogus with that strong foundationless hatred of one girl for another of her own age — especially when their parents have desired that they shall be friends. Moreover, Mary Mogus was fair and blue-eyed and Harriet was dark and grey-eyed — was *petite* and neat about her person whilst Harriet was of the usual height and had not the time or patience to be neat. Moreover, Miss Mogus busied herself for ever with errands of mercy, possets for the sick, Bibles for the aged, whilst Harriet was busy with selfish secular work. Harriet's chief interest, on the rare occasions when she occupied the family pew in Snape church, was in staring Mary Mogus out of countenance and silently and unsuccessfully daring her to be rude back.

And now, after *l'affaire Susan*, she saw in Mr. Mogus's influence the thin end of the Rectory wedge. He's persuaded Father to turn Susan out in order to get Mary *in*, she told herself. He has told Father that Mary would be an ideal *genteel* companion for me — and Mary wants to come and bore me to tears with her silly chatter and her tales of her sailor lover. I won't have it! Instead of encroaching upon Redonda they shall be made to retreat!

In the farm office that morning Harriet told Spens to get the stile removed at the Right of Way; to fill the gap left with furze branches and to fence it with sharp palings. Spens was puzzled and unwilling, wanting to know why. Harriet chafed:

'Because I say so, isn't that enough?'

'What about the Cap'n, Miss Harriet?'

There was the rub — for, though Spens was too stupid to guess at whom the new arrangement was aimed, the Captain if told would seize on it at once as a provocation to the Moguses. Harriet temporized.

'I can't worry Father with these details. He leaves me to look after the details — you know that.'

'I'm so busy with the threshing, Miss Harriet, and the stacking, I haven't the labour, that's the truth! We lost six men to the press in

Ipswich last Tuesday and one or two others have run off to earn better money — '

'Very well, if you haven't the labour, it must wait. But you can turn the bull into that field, Spens — and directly.'

Spens was still puzzled. 'That 'on't be safe if anybody fare to use the path'y. He's got a rare wicked temper be now, after being shut up all summer — '

'The more reason for the poor beast to work it off. Put him into the field directly; it'll do his coat good and harden him up for the winter.'

This was not to be gainsaid — and from the north window of her bedroom Harriet that afternoon had the extreme pleasure of seeing Miss Mogus first advance along the Right of Way and then beat a hasty retreat over the stile, dropping her basket in the process.

'Now write and tell your sailor about *that*!' said Harriet, breathing her scorn upon the glass pane between them.

Vandervoord brought some chestnuts to roast in the evening, and sitting together over the fire after dinner, whilst her father snored in the morning-room, she recounted to him her story of the bull and Miss Mogus — biting into the roasted nuts with her sharp white little teeth with zest as she told the story and spitting out the skins afterwards into the fire.

Vandervoord said: 'I am sure Miss Mogus does not eat chestnuts like that; she is much too genteel.'

'Do you think she's pretty?'

'For those that like the type,' he answered, 'well — so-so! Why are you so cruel to the poor creature?'

'Because I *detest* her and her father and their interfering hypocritical ways, and because they are trying to get Father under their thumbs and gain a foothold in Redonda. Pah!' and she spat out the skin of another chestnut and ground it under her heel as if it too were a Mogus.

'Nevertheless,' said Vandervoord, 'I expect they are praying for your soul with the same pertinacity with which you do all you can to vex theirs . . .'

Harriet's eyes twinkled at him in the firelight.

'I believe you think it is for the good of *my* soul to stand up for all

the people I find most tiresome! It's no *use*, Van! I am incurable —
like Father! The best thing about me is loving Redonda — and
you.' And she laid her hand upon his arm. As she did so the firelight blazed, reflected, in the ring on her little finger — reminding her.

'Van, you wouldn't take it — all that time ago. Will you take
it now?'

For answer he bent and kissed the finger that wore the ring.

'*That's* no answer!'

He shook his head then, shaping the word *No* with his lips but
uttering it silently to the fire instead of aloud to her. The flames
leaped and crackled, sending great jagged lines of brightness across
walls and ceiling, so that the whole structure of the room appeared
to be moving, dancing with the flames. Ah, thought Harriet, her
eyes fixed upon Vandervoord as he sat beside her, hands clasped
round knees (clever, obedient hands, for once at rest!), head back,
leaning against his chair (clever, handsome head, for once at rest!) —
if this evening might last for ever; if I might have him so for ever,
sitting beside me in our own home, *safe* . . .

All the same, a vague discomfort possessed her at this obstinacy
of his in continuing to refuse her gift. The reason, she knew, was
the same one he had given often; people would recognize it, would
talk, they would be compromised, he might be sent away — or she
might. Thinking of such things, of the continued pain aroused in
her by his continued refusals, it suddenly dawned upon Harriet
that — though she had given him more things than she could
remember as tokens of her love for him (small, silly joking things —
a blown bird's egg, fragile as glass, left one morning in his engineering scales; a spray of pale sea-lavender tucked into the lapel of his
great-coat; a shirt of fine tucked linen — smuggled property and too
small now for her father; a mossy nest, brimming over with
blackberries she had picked for him; a gingerbread cake, baked by
Susan in the shape of his beloved pump-mills; yes — though she
had delighted to give him all these, to show that she remembered
him daily, that she loved him (as she had often told him) with
every breath she drew, he had never yet given her anything in return.

She knew that he would reply, if challenged, that he *had* nothing,
as yet, and so could give nothing. (Under the terms of his

peculiar 'agreement' with Captain Bromewell there was no payment for his services.) But was a nest of blackberries, a sprig of sea-
lavender, a yellow horn-poppy nothing? Could he not have thought
of her enough to return the compliment in the shape of some such
sweet — and cheap — absurdity? He had given her father the clay
model of Redonda, the pump-mills, all the work of his brain and
hands. Could he not spare for her even one of the small wooden
toys he could carve in five minutes — and which half the children
in Redonda had wheedled out of him by now?

Of course there *were* the chestnuts he had brought for them both,
that evening. But why did he still refuse the ring? 'You could wear
it,' she said, continuing her thoughts out loud, 'round your neck,
on a chain. Nobody would see it then, or suspect anything — and it
would be so romantic, Van!'

'Yes, darling,' he said, nodding wisely, almost as if in agreement.
'On a chain, round my neck, over my heart!'

'Oh yes, Van — over your heart!' she cried, enchanted at the
thought, and reaching out her hand, she placed it over his heart
where the ring at last should rest. There was a crackling sound —
not, for once, from the fire.

'Van — there is something there already!'

'Certainly. My chest protector. I always wear that.'

'What is it?'

'Aha, wouldn't you like to know? If you are not good, I shall
go and tell Miss Mogus all about it —'

But Harriet was already kneeling beside him, pulling at his shirt
to disclose the secret.

The map that had been given to him by Lanfranc unfolded stiffly
between her hands. Uncomprehending, she looked up from its
contours into Vandervoord's face.

He was still smiling down at her — at his little snatching villain
as he called her. He put out his hand in a gesture of protective
tenderness rare with him, and stroked her bent head.

'Do you know what you have there?'

'Ye-es, a map of some sort.'

'You are holding my Life, Harry.'

Then he told her, as entertainingly as he knew how, all about his experiences on the hulk, of the death of Lanfranc, the bequeathing of the map. He recommended the workmanship of it. 'He put his whole life into that map,' he told her. 'As it ebbed out of him — he knew he was dying — he guided it through his pencil on to this map. He wouldn't let it spend itself upon thin air like so many other men. He told me it was the finest piece of work he had ever done. I believe it. He wanted me to treasure it for him, to escape with it, if I could, to France, to hand it to Bonaparte's High Command for their special information. He warned me that if ever it was found on me, it would mean my death.'

Harriet folded it up with great deliberation.

'So you carry it everywhere,' she said. 'Van, you are the strangest mixture! You never had any intention of escaping with it to the French, did you?'

He shook his head.

'Therefore it would be safer, for your sake, if you destroyed it. Yes, it is very finely done, I can see that — but it is your life! It is worse than a charge of gunpowder to carry about. Why do you do it?'

'I suppose — because it amuses me.'

'*Amuses* you! What would Spens say, if he knew you had such a thing concealed about you? What would the Lord Lieutenant say?'

'Ah yes — and what, I wonder, would Miss Mogus say?' said Vandervoord.

It was always thus that they clashed; when she was most in earnest he was most flippant and light-hearted; when she was playful and teasing in her turn, he would be in one of his odd withdrawn moods when he said things as he had said just now of the map; 'You are holding my Life.' And then, by the time her mood had overtaken his — when she too talked of his life and how he risked it by such crazy behaviour, he must bring Miss Mogus into it and tease her with *that*! Was it always to be so, however long they lived, however long they loved each other?

'I almost have the heart,' she said, still looking down at the map, 'to burn it up in the fire!'

He put out his hand then and took it back from her, bestowing it carefully back where it belonged.

'I should feel quite lost without it by now,' he said in excuse; 'I have had it so long. It has been through so many vicissitudes with me. I like to walk in Orford or Aldeburgh among the throng of people there and know that they do not suspect its existence and how they would buzz if they did!'

'They would indeed!' Harriet agreed bitterly.

'Not as much, of course,' went on Vandervoord, 'as if they were Portsmouth folk. It would be more piquant to walk up Portsmouth High Street wearing it, or to drop it at the feet of some fat old gentleman and have it returned with a punctilious bow. Ah well — perhaps one day I shall have that pleasure, who knows?'

'You are not to talk of Portsmouth! You are not to talk of leaving Redonda!'

'But my darling — some day — '

'No, no, NO! Do not talk of some day, talk of now, of loving me!'

Vandervoord took her into his arms at that, kissing her hair, staring over her bowed head into the flames. The servants had brought in fresh logs that evening and upon the great half-trunk that lay blazing there, numerous small creatures — woodlice, wood-spiders, other tiny inhabitants of the crevices in bark and wood — were now running to and fro upon it, trying in vain to escape from the heat. The warmer their foothold grew the faster they ran; even the slow cumbrous woodlice finally were skipping like kids, running into and over each other — anything to avoid the heat and choking smoke. But there is no escape, Vandervoord told them silently. None whatever. I have tried it and I know. Far better cease your vain rushing to and fro — drop off the log into the red-hot cinders and have done with it.

'Van?'

''M?'

'You know that your secret is safe with me, don't you? I will never, never tell a *soul* of that map — I swear —'

But he put his hand over her protesting lips at that.

'My darling, don't promise anything. The Fates are listening! It inspires them to do their worst!'

'You don't trust me!'

'No,' he said, smiling ruefully, 'I don't trust the Fates, and they have more power than you, *ma Mie*!'

'Nobody has *any* power to make me do anything I do not want to do!'

'But how can you be sure that you will always not want to do it?' Before she could reply he went on: 'But come, don't let us talk of such dreary things. Let me tell you something much more cheerful. Do you know the name of the ship that captured my ship? — the one I was going home in, that is? She was the *Harriet*.'

'Ah — then she should have belonged to *me*!'

'But don't you see the coincidence? The omen? Captured by a Harriet, twice over!'

'Tell me again, Van, how you came to be taken!'

The little maddened creatures have all fallen off the log by now, are no more than shrivelled white skeletons in the glowing ashes below. The log itself is greatly shrunken — no more than a black horny-coated carcass with a glowing, palpitating heart of fire. The walls and ceiling of the room have ceased to dance in the firelight, but it is still warm on Harriet's face and neck and bosom and bare arms. Rose-coloured marble, thinks Vandervoord, of that kind they quarry at — what the deuce is the name of that Italian seaboard town? I shall be forgetting my own name next.

No — by God! For if *that* should go then indeed I might — as so many of them do, I am told — begin to doubt the reality of my own existence.

CHAPTER XVII

'JEALOUSY IS CRUEL AS THE GRAVE'

The coals thereof are coals of fire, which hath a most
vehement flame . . . — SONG OF SONGS

SUSAN SHATTUCK's forced marriage to Tom Anderson was not the act that precipitated the break-up of the original household of three brothers. William Anderson had been caught and pressed to sea, on the night when the cry 'Hawks abroad!' rang through the narrow lanes of Ipswich, warning all within earshot. Now his small ship was standing off and on the coast of Spain with the rest of the Fleet — worm-eaten, full of leaks and with canvas that you could, as he expressed it, count the stars through. On making port once, he had come back to Redonda, richer than ever in his life before from his share of prize-money, and with a withered arm — the result of a cut received in boarding the enemy. His tales of adventure and derring-do had held the village spellbound. Life was hard, he admitted, conditions were squalid and crowded, the discipline brutal. Nevertheless the thrill of frequent action against the enemy and the possibilities of yet more prize-money had made a sailor of him for life. To such a man, after such experiences, there could be no thought of settling down ashore again. The great house of Redonda itself, reigning over its thousand acres, seemed to him now no more than a Spanish galleon gone ashore, heavy with priceless cargo, on some shoals — a total (though magnificent) loss. He had seen one or two such — and had profited from their misfortunes as British sailors were bound to do (though not, of course, on the scale of British Admirals). But merely to confront the place now, to remember its influence over him and his family and their circumscribed occupations there, made him so restless that he could not stay within doors whilst on leave but was always walking up and down, up and down outside the cabin, followed by a knot of barefooted boys, gaunt, eager and inspired, like him, with a thirst for evermore for salt water and the uncountable riches which were for ever tacking to and fro upon it, waiting to be taken.

The sense of unrest spread to more than the boys. Jacob Anderson (the steadiest and eldest of the three brothers) was the next to go — choosing the darkest and stormiest night and the best riding-horse out of Redonda's stables to help him. There was no news at all of him after his getaway — both horse and man seemed to have been swallowed up in the gusty night — despite the hue and cry set up by the Captain and the other elder brethren of the parish for an escaped parishioner whose labours were of use to them. But Tom, the remaining brother, did not worry. No news to him was good news and he guessed that Jacob had reached the North, as he had intended to do, and settled down there to earn three times as good money in a mill as ever he had earned as a farm labourer.

In vain the authorities made the punishment of runaways more stringent; in vain they attempted to fence in such restive live stock. The times were against them, and the agricultural labourers — here and there, two or three of them at a time, or a single man with his savings sown into a leather pocket close to his thumping heart — again and again took the darkest night and the fastest horse and rode away from the certain death which was their penalty, if taken, to a life promising more, they believed, than they thought ever to be able to count.

East Anglian farmers, raising threatening fists to the skies on such occasions, turned to shake those same fists at the North, cursing the district that had so denuded them. And up in the North the great mills and manufactories arose, one after the other, sending up chimneys into the skies higher than the farmers' fists could reach, and belching out smoke blacker than their curses. And the wheels turned, and the pistons moved, and steam co-operating with human sweat began to turn out most marvellous precise articles — all identical, all perfect, all smelling of oil in the first stage as much as any new-born lamb. And the articles travelled to the great exchanges in York, Manchester, Birmingham, London — were thumbed, turned over — tried out, approved of — ordered by the dozen, and then the hundred dozen and the thousand dozen as the tale of their merit and cheapness spread.

And the ports received the articles and the dockers loaded them on to the waiting frigates and barges and coasting smacks; and the sails of the frigates filled as the wind of Commerce blew, carrying the ships with their wings spread like white butterflies, carrying their cargoes to new and eager destinations the other side of the world. Sometimes they were intercepted — the single vessels sailing without convoy. Sometimes they got the worst of it in the ensuing clash. Then the butterfly wings would droop, shot away from the mainmast, and the ship would stand still in her tracks while the articles aboard were transferred into French or Spanish holds or else to the bottom of the ocean; where some mermaid, perhaps, unrolling a bale of superfine linen or of gay cotton print for the African market, rejoiced in her acquisitions, trailing them behind her like many-coloured seaweeds in that deep-sea light that is no light at all.

But more, many more of those cargoes crossed the seas safely than were captured or destroyed, and the much-needed money came back again in the hold instead of ballast, and there was rejoicing of a quite undemonstrative kind in the North at increasing prosperity, and rejoicing (even more cautious) in the Government at Westminster at the gold coming in to replace the gold going out (the ever-increasing drain of outward gold to pay for a most expensive war), and at new sources of income from taxation of new industries.

It was not strange that, with his two brothers away and improving themselves, as the saying is, Tom Anderson too became infected with the general restlessness. Work at Redonda grew heavier and heavier as the war progressed, and as less and less hands were there to do it. And wages did not increase as the work did. The farmers put back into the land — under the new system of agriculture — much that they had drawn out of it in goodness and growing-power each year; horses doing heavy ploughing were given extra oats for it; heifers in calf got extra hay. But the agricultural labourer, up with the sun and down with him all day and every day except fairdays, got less, on an average, to fill his belly than his co-workers the cow and the horse. Worse still, the 'extras' in the way of gleaners' rights, commons-rights and free forage for cattle in the woods and on the commons, which had made the same sort of situation just bearable for his father and grandfather, had been taken from him by Enclosure. There *were* no extras to be had, any longer, without breaking the law — and in winter these days the average farm labourer very often had to choose between breaking the law or seeing his children starve.

Susan's first child was born two months after her marriage to Anderson — and was simple-minded. That much was apparent from the first to the Reverend Charles Mogus, who christened it with an expression that told he considered the sprinkling to be a waste of holy water. It was a quiet enough baby. Too quiet, too smiling, and curiously heavy in the arms. Susan, perceiving the obvious, offered to release Vandervoord from his promise to be godfather — a favour she had timidly requested earlier on and that he had good-naturedly agreed to. 'My good girl,' said he, 'not at all;

H

it will need godparents all the more for being simple.' And he carved it, out of holly-wood, the best rattle ever seen in Redonda, with funny faces all over it and wooden eyes that rolled and a wooden tongue that lolled out unexpectedly and wagged in the drollest fashion imaginable.

Susan's husband was the other godfather. 'Since I'm not father,' he had said, 'I'll be the next best thing,' and he wove the simple baby a cradle of Norfolk osiers, both strong and light, a creation as beautiful, in its way, as any of the French Prisoner's more elaborate efforts. The baby lay in the cradle all day, sleeping or smiling to itself, no trouble at all, but a weight as heavy and still as lead — almost as lifeless.

Its mother loved it, as she loved all helpless creatures. Out of the wealth of her unconsumable affection she could afford to smile at Miss Mogus on her errands of mercy, as that lady pointedly tripped past the Anderson door without even an inquiry after the child's health. Though she missed her old life with Harriet sadly, she had little time for regrets, what with the child to be cared for and the tumbledown old cabin in which she had borne it to be cleaned and made weather-proof as far as possible. It had no windowpanes, and the oiled paper which served instead had torn in half a dozen places. There was this to be mended, as well as rat-holes to be stopped, the old brick floor to be kept scrubbed and sanded, the chimney to be repaired and the sparrows driven out of the holes they had made in the thatch.

All this Tom Anderson might have done had he had the time. But the farm-work claimed him all the daylight hours so that it was his wife who, taking his yawning instructions to heart last thing at night, set about the tasks to the best of her ability.

Meanwhile the general food situation steadily deteriorated as the war progressed. For the labouring classes to fill their stomachs at all became a task that employed the whole of their resourcefulness — and they were never particularly resourceful. Since corn was insufficient even for human beings there was none over for the fowls, and consequently there were fewer and fewer eggs. Since the pasture-lands had been ploughed up, they had dwindled to a fifth of what they once were, and there were fewer and fewer beasts left to run on them, and consequently less and less meat and milk at an ever higher and more impossible price for the poor to pay. Most of the farm-workers at Redonda had not tasted meat (other than poached game) since the outbreak of war. (There remained potatoes and tea — the cheerful warming tea, still able to cross the ocean despite the French blockade.)

In such dire circumstances there were those who, like Susan, dug and cooked potatoes daily; who did not disdain nettles for the sake of variety, or sorrel for the soup; who went begging to the great house at Redonda and returned not entirely empty-handed; who followed the farm-wagons and tumbrils as they jolted along the lanes for the sake of five wisps of dropped barley-corn to put into a watery gruel, or for a muddied turnip. And there were those like Tom her husband, who, earning each day enough precisely for a loaf of bread and fourpence over, began to go to the taverns at nights instead of home and spent the pitifully small total in gin.

It was not Anderson's fault. He came of a hard-drinking family, and since escape from hardship was denied to him perpetually, he drank his way temporarily out of his worries — and out of Susan's and the child's as well. Nor was that all. He went out with six other desperate men with net traps and ferrets, hunting the rabbits which were — though they did not know it — one and all the personal property of Captain Bromewell. And (as it turned out) it was Anderson who was caught in one of the Captain's new mantraps, with teeth larger and crueller than ferrets' teeth. His companions were loyal — prized the trap open by moonlight and bore the badly-mauled man home across the very sacks they had hoped to fill with rabbit-meat. The doctor being, as aforesaid, a kindly creature and, though impotent to help in a large way, extremely angry and impatient at the shocking neglect of human life going on all round him, dressed Anderson's wounds, and gave out that he had blood-poisoning from a cut on the hand received in the course of work. Susan nursed him devotedly during his period of helplessness and — because he was helpless, because she belonged to that queer breed in which compassion and love go ever hand-in-hand and spring up together when they are most needed — so she grew to be fond of the big, shambling, foolish, desperate man. 'Don't do

227

it agin!' she begged. 'I'd rather go hungrier than I do now than have you run such risks!'

But he could no more help doing it again than a bird, trapped in a room, can help beating its life out in futile effort against the closed window. As soon as he could limp about again he was off with his fellow-poachers, and for a few weeks the mouth-watering smell of roasting meat — plump partridge, juicy hare — met him at nights as he bent to come in at his doorway. For Susan had no more respect for the law than he; her scruples were all for his safety, not his conscience.

It was not to last. Whether some other man, less skilful than Anderson had been, gave him away, or whether ill-luck dogged him, is not to be known, but he was caught red-handed not long after by an armed gamekeeper who would not have hesitated to use his gun. He was brought before Spens, and his case came ultimately before the Captain, sitting still blindfolded like Justice, in his morning-room.

It was a puzzle to know what to do. As a Justice of the Peace he had the powers to consign the thief to the hangman at the next Assizes; as a farmer, he hated the thought of losing a good worker in such difficult times. Fortunately the affair coincided with one of Mr. Marsham's business visits — still elegant, still casual, but grey at the temples under his bobwig for all that.

'What can I do?' complained the Captain. 'If I pardon him, as that softy Spens wants me to do, I keep a good woodman but my game will be stolen faster than ever — just because I don't make an example of the fellow. If I have him hanged, then there's the woman and child on the parish, and *that* comes out of our pockets, too!'

'There *is* a middle way,' hazarded Mr. Marsham.

The Captain's eyebrows went up in inquiry above his bandages.

'The men have been deserting from the Derbyshire coalpits to go into the manufactories. Better wages, less danger to their hides — the old story! My friend Lord Slope can get better prices for his coal than ever before (from these same manufactories, if you please!), but damn it if he knows where to turn for his labour! If you give me Anderson, we'll lend him, shall we say, to Slope's manager, and then justice and patriotism will both be served. If he's such a good worker they'll be charmed to have him and no doubt part of his wages can be paid to his wife and child . . . I don't think,' continued Mr. Marsham, leaning back in his chair and putting the tips of his long, snuff-stained fingers together, 'that you ought to hang him, considering the shortage of labour. Temper justice with mercy and lend him to Slope; you needn't specify a time-limit.'

The Captain shifted uneasily in his chair, then he sighed. 'Yes, I suppose so,' he said. 'We can't have these ruffians running loose over the countryside taking the law into their own hands. The game-keepers are overworked as it is. Take him with you when you go.' Then he gave a snort of laughter: 'And I hope,' he added, 'that he travels better than that other present I made you over twenty years ago, Marsham!'

As soon as the decision became known, Susan was down on her knees once more before Harriet, begging for mercy! 'If he goo,' she said, 'I'll never see him agin, never!'

This passion of misery over a husband for whom in the first place she had had no affection and who had, in effect, been as much coerced into marrying her as now he was being coerced into the coalmines, disturbed Harriet. She could not understand it.

'Oh Miss, if you'd had him lying helpless as your own babe afore you — having to heave his head off the pillow — that was so heavy — and having to be fed with a cup and a spoon!'

'I should regard it as a necessary nuisance,' Harriet answered. 'Come, Susan,' bending to lift the crying woman up, 'don't do yourself harm over this affair. He has done wrong and deserves his punishment, you know that. Father *could* have sent him to the gallows. You will still have the child — and after the war — '

'I shan't niver see him agin' was all that Susan would say. She had stopped crying and said the words (though she did not know it) with the conviction that was partly clairvoyance — the same way in which her mother had said, twenty years back, standing in that sun-dappled glade: 'If you take me from here, I shall die.'

In the same way now, nothing that Harriet could say — and to do her justice she wished very much to comfort Sukey, so long as she could do so without endangering any of Redonda's sacred rights — could alter Susan's conviction that if they took her husband from her now, she would never see him again. She knew that if Harriet had wished to, she could have prevailed, in this instance, over Mr. Marsham and her father. With Spens already on the side of clemency, and her father loath to lose a valuable worker, Harriet could have tipped the balance against the lawyer. But she quite honestly did not wish to do so, because to do so would be to encourage indiscipline at Redonda — to lessen the power of the great house over its labourers, to impoverish its game-coverts and rabbit-warrens. Susan knew this, yet she bore Harriet no ill-will for her attitude; it was impossible for her to bear malice towards anybody, and had she not known Harriet's character longer almost than anyone else — since they had, in fact, been children together?

At the end of the interview, Harriet took Susan Shattuck into the dairy and gave her a jug of cream and five nut-brown eggs from her own favourite pullet. It did not occur to her, nor yet to Susan, who took them gratefully into her apron, that they were pricing Anderson's life at a jug of cream and five brown eggs. Perhaps it was as well.

'And you may come *next* week,' said Harriet, 'and I shall see what I can find for you. You know, he will be paid quite well at the mines and you are to have some of the money. You shan't starve, Sukey!'

Susan's brown eyes looked into Harriet's grey ones, out of a face that had already lost all its youthful roundness. 'As long as I've enough milk for the baby — ' was all she said.

After Anderson's departure for Derbyshire she continued to live in the cabin by the smithy, doing odd mending and washing jobs for Harriet and continuing to live insufficiently, as before, on potatoes and milk.

Harriet was glad, as always, to see Mr. Marsham depart. Like everyone else he had been attracted by Vandervoord and had sat talking and drinking with him the whole of one evening, while the old Captain slept. She suspected that Marsham, like Twigg, was concerned only to reft the French Prisoner away from Redonda — to deprive her of his love and the farm of his services — and she hardly knew which deprivation she feared most.

So that Vandervoord might feel about the lawyer as she did, she

described to him, with great bitterness, the incident in the church at Bury and how she had once slapped him with the prayer-book.

Vandervoord was more amused than indignant, which annoyed Harriet still more. It was extraordinary that she never seemed able, however long she knew him, to gauge his reactions to any given situation. A fine show of manly jealousy would, in her opinion, have been appropriate. (She was still so much a child, despite her twenty-six years.)

'I didn't tell you while he was here,' she said, 'I was afraid you might challenge him.'

Vandervoord laughed out loud at this. 'What — without a weapon? Without my freedom? About an affair as long ago as *that* was? You have the strangest notions, Harry!'

'But *aren't* you angry with him for behaving so?'

'Why should I be? You have a very pretty shoulder; I have often kissed it myself —'

'Oh Van, Van, don't be such a *boor*! How do you suppose I should feel if I heard of you kissing —'

'Miss Mogus, for instance?'

'Very well then, *yes*!'

'I suppose *I* should be saluted with a prayer-book, too . . .' Harriet made a noise of disgust, exactly in her father's manner. He went on: 'But then you see, my love, *you* are free to do as you please. You are not a prisoner.'

'How you harp on that! Aren't you free to do as you please, here? Is there anything to stop you? Does Spens himself have more liberty than We give you?'

The royal 'We', used so, amused him, too. He put his hand upon her angry head in the beloved familiar gesture, and stroked her hair, as if he were gentling a restive filly back to stillness.

'It's no use,' he said. 'We can't understand each other about this, and never shall. Let it go, dear Harry. And do not, for God's sake, expect me to be jealous over a casual caress given ten years ago. I might have behaved so, once. I am not a boy any longer.'

And he would discuss the affair no further. Harriet, still unconsoled, still raw from her fears of some *entente* between him and Marsham, pelted him with questions:

'But what did you talk *about?*' she said.

'Politics — the War — naturally.'

'I can guess,' she said, 'Bonaparte, Bonaparte, Bonaparte. Nothing but Bonaparte. Oh — how *sick* I am of the sound of that man's name!'

'Marsham thinks he is a genius,' said Vandervoord (he pronounced the name in the French way, as if it had a P at the end). 'He thinks this country should come to terms with France as soon as possible; that there is no fundamental dispute between your two countries that can't be settled round a table. He says that pressure is being put upon your Prime Minister to that effect — '

'And what do *you* think?'

Vandervoord shrugged. 'How should I know? I don't see the people who get the real news. Marsham is a man of the world, he hears what is going about in London — '

'They do nothing but talk in London!' declared Harriet, repeating one of her father's sayings with the confidence that comes of quoting Holy Writ: 'Talk, talk, talk — and all the time about Bonaparte!'

'If you had conquered half Europe — more than half Europe — you, too, might be talked of, *Ma Mie.*'

But she disputed this out of pure pique; disputed everything he said that afternoon, fearing Marsham's influence and determined to show her thorough displeasure.

In a way she was rewarded, for the very next day she received what she considered to be her first present from Vandervoord. He had come up from the Shearings where the farm labourers, under his direction, had been finishing the dyke that was to circumvent the flooding trouble. His eyes were shining and there was a smear of yellow mud — real Aldeburgh sea-ooze — beside his nose. 'Come and see,' he said, 'what I have brought you. Shut your eyes and come outside; it is in a wheelbarrow.'

And there it was; a little leaden statue of a naked boy, with snake-like curls writhing about his skull all over his downcast head and with some musical instrument between his hands. He, too, was yellowish — not yet having been washed clean of the mud in which he had been buried for so long.

Harriet wrinkled her nose. 'What is it?'

Vandervoord put his head on one side, the better to consider. 'At a guess, I should say he was a god of some sort, brought over here in one of those Roman transports which was probably wrecked on its way up the coast. See, there are figures here – and half a word of Latin.' He bent and peered at the base, muttering to himself: 'No, I can't make it out. Nevertheless, he's a fine chap. Don't you like him? I thought you would like him for your rose-garden. Of course his legs are gone, but the smith and I between us could fix him up with some sort of stand, I am sure – '

Harriet's heart warmed towards the cold statue. Van had brought it all this way from the coast, in a wheelbarrow, as a present for her! A real love-offering! She slipped her hand into his, her eyes, too, shining.

'Dear Van,' she breathed, 'it was like you to think of it. I shall love to have him in my rose-garden, when he is washed and mended – '

'Good.' Vandervoord bent and lifted the leaden boy out of the wheelbarrow, propping him gently to the left of the steps, where he stayed, still apparently preoccupied with his instrument. 'Stay there, P'tit-P'tit'.

'*What* do you call him?'

'Oh, a silly name – it just came into my head, lifting him out. You may call him anything you please – '

'I shall call him what *you* call him,' said Harriet stoutly.

'I will give him a new pair of legs or a stand of some sort as soon as I have time,' Vandervoord said, and went back straight away to his dyke-work. The trouble was, these days, that he never *did* have time. Harriet had hoped that, once the pump-mills were installed and working, he might slack off a bit, as a gentleman should. But the Captain had other schemes for him to try his hand at. The old way of sowing seed by hand was slow and intolerably wasteful; furthermore, there was not the skilled labour available for sowing the still increasing acreage which, this Michaelmas, was to go under the plough. And seed-drills were hard to come by and very expensive when found. Couldn't the French Prisoner devise some sort of home-made seed-drill to meet the situation?

Of such and such dimensions, by such and such a date? So *P'tit-P'tit* stood there, propped against Redonda's stone steps, with his curly head bent absorbed over his obscure musical instrument, until he became a regular feature of the place, and never got as far as the rose-garden after all. 'When the war is over . . .' said Harriet to herself — as so often, of so many circumstances. And so did thousands of others like her.

Hopes of peace did not finally die that year until the Prime Minister, true to Mr. Marsham's prophecies, made the first overtures of peace towards the French Directory. Spain's entry into the war as an ally of the French had complicated the English position most dangerously. Was there anything to be gained by continuing a warfare which must perforce be conducted on our part mainly by sea; and which, however hardly waged, did not appear to upset Bonaparte's time-table for conquering the rest of Europe in the very least? He had overcome the Austrians and the Sardinians with, as the saying is, one hand behind his back. Now his eyes were fixed on the South, across the Mediterranean — upon Egypt. 'I will lead you,' he had told his armies, 'into the most fertile places in the world, and there you will find glory and riches!' And nothing that Great Britain had done or could do, so far as Pitt could see, would alter this grandiose scheme one whit.

The offer of peace was, however, rejected with the scorn which might have been expected. It is not for the victors to accept the terms of the unvictorious at any stage of history. It further became apparent that the most fertile places in the world might be interpreted as including England as well as Egypt. So London, at any rate, read between the lines of the contemptuous refusal to negotiate — though repercussions through the rest of the country (because they could not understand the full implications of such a situation) were slower in following.

All that the news meant to Harriet was, that a settlement of her own particular problems must once more be deferred. Peace was *not* in the offing. Vandervoord was *not* about to become a free man as other men, and her father was *not* likely to listen to any story of an engagement or understanding between them while hostilities persisted — that much was clear. Clearer still was the fact that marriage, owing to all these circumstances, was an utter impossibility. And every day she grew older! Twenty-six was a shocking age! Practically decrepit, Old Maids were always twenty-six — or over — and this state of frustration might go on for years.

She had considered the idea of a secret marriage, but the thought of secrecy in such an important matter was utterly repugnant to her, and oddly enough she did not dare mention the word marriage itself to her lover, fearing she knew not what. On a subject so vital to her peace of mind — the finger upon the lips. Upon all else, as much chatter and contradiction and conversation as usual.

Yet she could not altogether possess her soul in patience to know the best or worst. There were other ways — country ways — of divining the future if the prosaic way was to be forgone. She had recounted to Vandervoord the superstition, or 'omen' as she preferred to call it, of the ninth pea over the doorway. There remained a second 'omen', a more solemn one, which required the co-operation of the beloved.

'The trouble is,' she admitted, outlining her scheme to him, 'that I must have the church key for it!'

'Aha, that has foxed you, you little heathen! Don't you wish now you were on better terms with Miss Mogus?'

She was too proud to answer that, merely saying: 'I know where the clerk keeps it. It hangs on a nail just inside his porch. You must borrow it for me, Van.'

'*I* must? But I thought it was *you* who was going to initiate *me* into these mysteries — '

Harriet stamped slightly: 'I shall provide the Bible. You will collect the key — that is only fair! Don't be difficult, Van. If you will not help me — who knows? — we may not get any results at all.'

'And does this Black Magic of yours disclose to us how many dozen children we are to be blessed with?'

Harriet's heart warmed towards him for his impudence. One does not after all talk of children to a Bromewell unless one intends marriage. But of *course* he had intended marriage from the first — why should she ever have suspected or feared anything else? Thinking it over afterwards as she lay in bed with her arms crossed behind her head, she realized that in all their acquaintance and conversation this last was the nearest that Vandervoord had ever drawn to a 'declaration'. It was a most hopeful sign.

Nevertheless, he was still diffident about the church key, foreseeing, from Harriet's point of view, all sorts of nonsensical difficulties.

'You may take it at night,' she said, 'and replace it in the early morning. No one will see you. It *must* be at night or we shall get no results —'

'And if my leg is bitten off by the clerk's dog, will you buy me a new one?'

'The dog shall be poisoned rather than give you any trouble. I can get Spens to say it was poaching. Do you think I am mistress of Redonda for nothing?'

'No, no!' said Vandervoord, 'let him have one bite. He is entitled to one bite. But you may give me a piece of meat to placate him.'

'Oh — you shall have a whole ham if you are as frightened as that!' Harriet answered with scorn.

All these preliminaries had been difficult enough, but to get him to agree to the affair taking place in the Cabin on the foreshore was three times as hard. She had not visited it since their first meeting there after her return from abroad. It was natural to her, and essential, that the place which had seen the first blossoming of their love should also enshrine so solemn a ceremony concerning it.

They argued about it most passionately, he on this occasion as angry as she. In vain she pleaded her position, how that she was a woman and, being a woman, needed some such silly superstition to comfort her through these trying times. He need only do it to please her, he need not believe in it at all. To which he answered strangely and obliquely:

'You ask too much, Harriet! You want me to make life tolerable for you. I *can't* make it tolerable for you!'

'Van, *please*! It is such a little thing — such a *little* thing, Van! I will never ask it of you again, it is only once, just for my foolish sake — and then it is over!'

'It's no use, Harry! It's using the Cabin that I'm thinking of, not of this hocus-pocus of yours. I am not considering myself, God knows — but *you*, in refusing you.'

'But if you are thinking of *me*, Van, how *can* you refuse me, when I keep telling you that it is the only thing in the whole world that I want?'

And so on, and so forth. In the end she got her way. On the night of the full moon, he agreed, they should meet secretly in the Cabin down by the Shearings, and she should play with her omens and ask them to give the answer to what lay ahead.

Surer of her direction, more ardent in her desire, she was there on the appointed night long before Vandervoord. The full moon flooded the low little room with so cold and clear a glow that it was not even necessary to light the candle she had remembered to bring with her.

When he came he was pale and constrained. His breath clouded the waiting atmosphere, wreathing in it like the water-smoke from off the sea.

'Well — were you bitten?'

'No, but I'm damned if I'll go through this tomfoolery again for anyone, Harry!'

'My darling!' she was upon him at that, her arms round his neck, pulling him to her, kissing him fully and passionately. The key which was dangling from his hand between them, pressed unyielding against her stays.

'See, here is the Bible! Yes, I know it is all very silly, Van, and that you despise me for it — but all the girls do it in these parts and really it works surprisingly! The eighth chapter of the Song of Solomon,' she had turned to the table and was shifting over the big pages briskly, 'the sixth and seventh verses. Here we are! Give me the key.'

They took their appointed seats in the blue and luminous gloom, one each side of the small table. He handed her the key, huge and cumbersome, with wards almost as long as Harriet's little finger.

'You have to hold it *with* me over the verses, Van. See, we sit facing each other, with our elbows on the table so, to steady our hands. Then we have to say the words aloud slowly, holding the key like this.' (She had slipped a ribbon through the handle of the key and now invited him to hold it, lightly between finger and thumb with her, so that the key hung quivering over the open pages of the book below.) 'If, when we have finished speaking, the wards of the key turn *that* way, towards the verses, that means the course of true love will run smooth. If not — well, we needn't concern ourselves with that.'

He said something softly, in the blue-white glow of the moon, and the smoke from his words went wreathing about his bent head.

'You look deathly in this light, Van! What did you say?'

'I said How like you, *ma Mie*. To say we needn't concern ourselves with that — What, then, is the purpose of our coming here?'

'Why — to see the wards of the key follow the words of the book, of course, Van!' She was so impatient to begin, she could not waste time in futile discussion.

Now he was bending forward, wrinkling his forehead over the Bible verses:

'I can't see them in this light — '

'*I* will say them then, and you repeat them after me. I daresay it will do as well.'

Odd, she thought, that only with the tip of his forefinger and thumb touching mine on this ribbon he should be able to set me on fire so! Is *this* what he was afraid of? That the fire in him should light the fire in me and that both should commingle?' And she loved him the more for looking so worried, for fearing this strange power, above all for the trembling in his hand holding the ribbon with hers.

She began to read, almost intoning the words — solemn, strong, vastly powerful in themselves as was the not-to-be-resisted flooding downward of icy light from the moon:

'Set me as a seal upon thine heart,'

'Upon thine heart,' he echoed quietly.

'And a seal upon thine arm . . .'

'Upon thine arm.'

'For Love is strong as death.'

'Strong — as — death.'

'Jealousy is cruel as the Grave.'

'As — the Grave.'

'The coals thereof are coals of fire which hath a most vehement flame —'

Both their hands were trembling now. The key below them was never still, turning uneasily from this side to that, glinting silver in the pale glare over the silver pages of the book.

'Many waters cannot quench love —'

'Cannot quench love —'

'Neither can the floods drown it —'

'Floods drown it . . .'

'If a man should give all his substance for love, it would utterly be contemned.'

'Be utterly condemned.'

The last words were spoken in a whisper. The effect upon both of these lovers, of verse and response, had been profoundly uneasy. They had come lightly enough for omens and walked, it would seem, uninvited into the Holy of Holies. As children might search for paired pink seashells, 'butterflies', along the shore, and find instead some sunset-coloured shell, enormous, marvellous, containing the largest and purest pearl in all the world.

'Watch the wards!'

Harriet's lips formed the words but did not do more than breathe them upon the waiting air. The key had ceased its uneasy turning to and fro, that way and this; had paused, as if on the verge of moment-ous decision.

This way. *This* way. Make it come *this* way! prayed Harriet, willing the motion with all her might.

The answer was strange. A deep thudding roar shook the whole cabin at that moment, rattling the door and empty window-frames and shaking the key out of their hands down upon the book.

Vandervoord rose abruptly to his feet — remembering just in time to duck his head to avoid the rafters. The huge roar sounded again. Again door and windows rattled.

'The batteries at Landguard Fort!' said Vandervoord, going to the window, forgetting everything else but that intrusion of huge sound, 'Practising a welcome to Bonaparte!'

He did not at first feel Harriet's hands, pressing down on his shoulders from behind him. Then the flame began to warm him through.

CHAPTER XVIII

EXTRACTS FROM LETTERS AND OTHER MATTERS

'. . . This coast lyeth open and ready for foreign invasion, there bee so many havens, harbours, creekes and other places of ready descente. . . .'

Breviary of Suffolk, 1618

Miss Mogus to Surgeon-Lieut. Fiske, R.N. of H.M.S. Thunderbolt

. . . Which, you can guess, adds an extra two miles on to the journey. If I went purely on my own account I shd not trouble to mention this as I know it will make you angry with the Bromewells. But as you know, Father and I are attempting in our own little way to *do real good* to the lower classes. Though it is remarkable how they appear to resent it. As you know they prefer to take *no* thought for the morrow, even in wartime, and to leave the full responsibility for the carelessness and recklessness of their behaviour upon *us*. As an example of the sort of stubbornness we have to prevail over, I will now relate what I should hesitate to mention to a *fiancé*, but *seeing you are a medical man* and have been good enough to say you find all this tittle-tattle of mine of interest, I think you will like to know.

Father and I have been greatly concerned over the way Nature takes its course in family increases. The feebleminded poor (of whom we have far too many, alas) and the great drunken brutal fellows who soak themselves in gin are the fathers of the largest families. Whereas the self-respecting poor are not blessed with more than two or three little ones. As a student of Malthus, Father has been concerned *for some time* about this problem, for if Nature is allowed to take her course he considers that in less than a century we shall have nothing but rascals and rapscallions amongst the poor, and the useful industrious ones will have practically died out.

As you can guess, we have tried hard to interest Captain Brome-well in this problem. But the Captain is interested only in the breeding of fine *cattle* and *horses*, he says and prefers to leave — but I cannot translate his coarseness on to paper! We have therefore been thrown back on *our own resources* and have worked out a scheme which, if the poor would co-operate, would benefit posterity exceedingly.

You know they say that rice prevents an increase in the popula-tion, I suppose? But being a medical man, you must know it. Furthermore, it is well established in these parts — one may almost say proved by experience — that *rocking an empty cradle* will rock a new baby into it. My father and I therefore have been busy lately making up small parcels of rice and distributing these *gratis* to the undesirable poor (who *of course* have *no notion* of the sterile proper-ties in the grain) and I have taken upon myself the task of rocking the empty cradle in the cottages where large families are to be encouraged.

I hope you approve but my problem, dear Tom, is this: I have no difficulty in distributing the rice-packets — they are hungry these days and so uneconomic in their cooking that they will take it gladly; but in *a great many cases* the empty cradle has been removed out of the front room it usually occupies into some (I suspect) *attic* upstairs. This has been the case so often that I cannot help thinking it is done on purpose to thwart me. On other occasions, too, I have been disturbed in the very act of reaching out to rock it — though you may be sure I do this with as smiling and *encouraging* a manner as anyone could. If therefore the population decreases rather more rapidly than increases in our village, we shall know why! I wish you would tell me whether you dismiss our scheme as pure super-stition or whether — as a fellow-Malthusian — you approve. . . .

From the Lord-Lieutenant of the County to Captain Bromewell

. . . presents his compliments, and informs Captain Bromewell that as Sir John Moore will shortly be paying a visit of inspection to the Eastern Counties, with a view to assessing the possibilities of National Defence in the event of Invasion, he requires Captain Bromewell and/or his agent to render Sir John and his staff all facilities for free access across his farm-lands, particularly such as abut on to the coast. . . .

From Jan Vandervoord, Engineer, to M. Elesius, representing the Netherlands Government in London

It is now six months since I wrote to you, stating the whole of my case once more and asking you to investigate it personally, thus assuring yourself beyond any doubt of the solid ground I have for requesting such an investigation. I have now been wrongfully detained as a prisoner of war ever since I had the misfortune to be captured on board the brig *l'Agréable* – a vessel on which I had taken passage to Rotterdam from Batavia in March 1793. (But if you have had the courtesy to look up my previous correspondence, you will know all this by heart.)

Since the vessel on which I travelled was French, I was classified as French along with the crew – save for such as were Javanese and so, being yellow, were able to prove the country of their nativity better than I have since been able to do.

I see now that I was over-optimistic at the outset, for, discovering the Captain of the *Harriet* to be an ignorant man, all courage but no brain, it did not disturb me to be put into irons and thrown, together with the crew of the French ship, into the cramped hold of the *Harriet*; this was particularly so since, unwilling to be a looker-on at the *fraças* after we were boarded, I got in one or two good blows with a borrowed cutlass on British seamen's heads. As the Captain was therefore in no mood for argument, and much more interested – as his kind are apt to be – in our considerable cargo than in his prisoners, I decided – as I have explained on many previous occasions – to wait to put my case until we made port.

However I was given no opportunity – as I had expected – to straighten out my affairs, but was flung, on arrival, into a hulk kept *specifically for French prisoners* in Portsmouth Harbour. Here I lost sight of my original companions in misfortune, only to be confronted with others of the same nationality and equally unhappy! I decided to wait for inspection – but this never came. (Just as the food provided for the prisoners never got beyond the ward-room. They fed us with swill, like pigs.) Such money as I had on me when captured I used in bribing a man to take a note ashore, addressed to you or your representative in London; but whether it ever reached you or whether the fellow merely drank the money and pitched the note into the harbour I have no idea.

I will not weary you again with another detailed account of my different incarcerations after that time, merely reiterating that they were at Portsmouth, Dartmoor, Peterborough in Huntingdon and Orford in Suffolk — and finally on this present estate near Aldeborough where I am allowed to remain *en parole* to Captain Bromewell, its owner. Once more I must emphasize that the papers relative to me in every case (and despite all my representations) state that I am of French nationality and as such an enemy alien and liable to military law; although as I have often enough told you I am a civilian, an engineer by profession and of as good Dutch blood as yourself, having been born at Utrecht thirty-six years ago in the family of the late Mynheer Silden Vandervoord, Customs Official on the Crown Quay at Rotterdam.

As our country is now completely occupied by the French and as I have had no news of my mother and sisters for over five years, I beg of you to expedite the clearing-up of my case as soon as you can and particularly to use all your efforts to establish some sort of communication with my relations — the only people who can corroborate my story in every single particular.

From Clancy Bromewell to Harriet Bromewell

... and another brace of partridge or hare each week wouldn't come amiss either. The price in London now would shock you. Respects to Father and I am sorry his eyes still trouble him. Marsham tells me he thought you looked pale and tired last time he was down — don't overdo it! He took a great fancy to that French Prisoner of yours, considers him no end of a clever fellow and worth a dozen Spens to Redonda. And the beauty of it is, I hear he costs nothing for his keep!

O by the way I met Fiske at Whites the other day, that fellow Mary Mogus is to marry. He all but cut me on the staircase. But for the fact that we barristers don't have any truck with the Navy I'd have tripped him up and sent his dignity flying!

If you shd hear of any claret coming in by way of Everybody's Friend, you know who I mean, you can send that along too. . . .

Miss Hannah Bromewell to Captain Bromewell

I suppose with yr eyes still so bad Harriet must read this to you and I hope she will take it to heart though knowing her of old I rather despair of it. I am truly sorry for yr trouble, Tom but just as sorry, if you must know it, that you don't get Harriet's future settled. How much longer are you keeping her at Redonda, she gets no younger as the saying is and it can't be lack of a sufficient *dot* if yr corn crops did as well with you last harvest as ours did up here. I have sold all my sheep and bought two new ploughs — *there's* a conversion to own up to! Well, we must make hay while the sun shines — *and* grain too. I wish that Harriet wd learn that *her* hay is a husband and a home of her own!

Don't sacrifice her to yr own interests. No doubt you can't well spare her, feeling as ill as you do and with the head that she has for farming matters. But the longer the war lasts the more the likelier young men will be drawn away to it — and for all you know you may be left high and dry with the girl on yr hands at the end. Wd you care for her to come to me again for a while? There's a *very* nice company stationed at York this time but I hope she has lost some of her rudeness for *that* won't get her anywhere. . . .

Captain Twigg to Captain Bromewell

Presents his respects and wants to know is the Captain still of the same mind concerning the French Prisoner as the opportunity is a fine one and won't occur again.

Is sorry he overlooked the Captain in the matter of the last consignment to hand but begs to remind the Captain that Urgent National Duty must come first.

Is sorry he can't locate the six butter-casks the Captain says was loaned him some years ago, will do his best to locate same when time off from Urgent National Duty permits. . . .

Miss Harriet Bromewell to Miss Mary Mogus

Miss Bromewell's respects to Miss Mogus but she noted yesterday that the Rectory geese were feeding on the church green and wishes to know was this through their straying or does Miss Mogus wish to rent the Green which she must know belongs to Redonda and for which the rental is Thirty Shillings per year.

Miss Bromewell further states, on behalf of her late servant Susan Shattuck, now Anderson, will Miss Mogus not visit down there any more as it frightens the baby. . . .

Harriet Bromewell to Jan Vandervoord

I waited here in the Cabin all afternoon yesterday and you did not come. I told Father I was with Spens seeing about repairs to the threshing-barn, I know you said you *might* be busy with the dykes again but you did not think of *me* sitting here in the cold! You never do!

Dear Van I am sorry to be so cross but I have waited all this afternoon too and now it is over and you haven't come again and my fingers are so cold I can scarcely hold the pencil. I will be back after dinner, so come to me *quickly*! Every day this deception grows harder to bear, I love you. I *love* you.

H.

P.S. — This is the tenth note at *least* that I have written to you — not counting the chalk one on the wall. You have *never* written to me. You can *draw* very well, can you not write?

From the last of which it may be gathered that the Church Key had perhaps been wise, on that famous occasion, in refusing to predict how the course of true love between Harriet and Vandervoord was to run. It may also be seen that Harriet had not kept her promise about the Cabin. The occasion of the Bible ceremony had been only the first of many such clandestine appointments, since it had ended, as Vandervoord had foreseen only too well that it would, in their inevitable mating.

This physical satisfaction of her desire to have and to hold her lover certainly made Harriet happier, more contented and less irritable to those about her all day on the farm and in the house; but it in no way diminished the importunate demands she still made on him. She might have said of her love, with Orsino:

But mine is all as hungry as the sea
And can digest as much ...

And the sound of the sea, roaring faintly in their ears as they lay on his truckle bed in the Cabin, spent with passion, like two drowned bodies flung up upon the strand, was their perpetual accompaniment.

Harriet loved to hear it. Of all sounds she had most missed that sound at Lausanne. She loved it best in its stormy mood, with foul north-easters abroad pounding on the shingle — not as now stifled, satiated, holding itself in leash, as it were, until its appetite should grow again and it should pounce again upon this coast where its gnawing lips had made already such catastrophic inundations. Had it not swallowed up already, in the course of one single night at Dunwich, seven churches and half the town? Half the town, too, of old Aldeburgh was buried, by now, beneath tons of shingle and the tides lapped daily at what had been the old market square in the centre of the town, not at its edge.

As hungry as the sea.

Lying exhausted, contented, after their physical hunger for each other had been once more satisfied, she said to him, lifting up one white forearm and balancing it lazily in the darkness above her:

'Listen, do you hear the bells?'

'Bells?'

'Yes, at Dunwich. They say that on rough nights like these you can hear the bells of the buried churches ringing under the water.'

He roused himself on his elbow, looking down at her interestedly (how well she·knew his exact expression!) although they could not see each other in the darkness.

'But, my darling, that would hardly be possible. The pressure of the water would prevent —'

'Ah, now you are off on one of your old mathematical calculations again! I only meant you to *listen*! I swear I heard a sound like ringing, very faintly from the direction of Dunwich — and it isn't a chime hour —'

'An interesting idea,' he replied, dropping his head back heavily upon her arm, 'but an absurd one. How could one possibly hear such bells? They must be fathoms deep at Dunwich, the shingle shelves down there so steeply —'

'Yes,' she said, 'yet in my grandfather's time, you know, it was a thriving port. So were Wadgate Haven and Walton Castle! And now the sea has swallowed them all up. That's why they call this the "dead" coast. . . Do *you* think it is dead?'

'As to that, it reminds me very much of the Flemish coast, its counterpart on the other side.'

'Only the Flemish coast? I hoped it reminded you of home, Van! They always say that the Dutch prisoners, who were quartered at Southwold a hundred years ago, used to say it reminded them of Holland!'

'Do they?' he answered, indifferently, then — changing the subject: 'Which way did you come to-night?'

'The old way, of course — the footpath through the Shearings.'

'Harriet! I have told you again and again not to use that way — '

'But Van, I have used it ever since I could walk and it cuts two miles off the road!'

'That's of no account.' He was stern now: 'The behaviour of the water behind here is still uncertain. It doesn't obey any rules at all, as far as I can see. *You* think you are safe because you have always lived by the Alde. You can't believe, because of your superb self-confidence, that any water on your own ground could play you false. But I tell you again that it's *dangerous*! Especially at this time of year with the watersmoke, as you call it, rolling inland all the time and hanging over the Shearings — '

'What a fuss to make all about Mr. King's field!'

'Mr. King's field, my girl, is now a quicksand.'

She was interested despite herself. 'No, is it really?'

'Certainly. Last week some poor beast got bogged down there and was dragged down to drown. There's suction in that mud bottom, as I always suspected . . . For God's sake, can't you be reasonable, Harriet, and do as I say?'

It was delicious to her to hear the sharp note of anxiety in a voice which, too often, was merely gentle or mocking.

She answered without answering directly (almost as if she had caught the trick from him): 'It's quite true what you say. I suppose I *do* believe that, since the quicksand is on our ground now, it cannot harm me, it must know I am its mistress! But then *you* should not fear it either, for you are its master! You created it, didn't you? If it hadn't been for your pump-mills it would never have come into being!'

'I don't fear it for myself, I fear for *you* when you persist in walking by that way!' and under his breath, whispering into her hair so that she could not hear it, he said: 'I have your life on my hands — to have your death would be too much!'

The sea roared in the darkness, flinging great ropes of foam along the whole expanse of shingled shore, a bare twenty yards below their Cabin. Then, drawing the ropes once more back into itself, it drew back thousands of tons of shingle with them, sucking it all in with a huge grey-green sigh, very deliberate, very prolonged; and then, as if the suspense were simply not to be borne a moment longer (as if it repented of any shattering grandiose plan it may have conceived at that moment, for the very first time since creation), the huge sigh was released and the ropes of foam were flung forward again, all the tumbling, gleaming shingle with them, and the whole reverberative process was renewed, times without number, world without end, *amen*.

Harriet said quietly: 'You know once when I was about thirteen or so, and was walking along the shore here with Susan, looking for cornelians, as I have told you we used to do, I came on a drowned man! He must have been washed up on the night before. He was very bruised from the shingle and there was a piece of seaweed across his mouth, and sand all over his clothes and — in his eyes. I thought at first it was a Chinaman — a Mandarin, you know, with long moustaches. The seaweed made me think it.'

Afraid that this might sound a trifle heartless, she added:

'It was a great shock. To come upon a drowned man like that, I mean, when I was walking alone —'

'But you said Susan was with you —'

'Oh, if you count *Sukey*!'

'Certainly I count Sukey. If you read your Bible instead of slapping people's faces with it —'

'That was my prayer-book — not my Bible!'

'The principle remains the same. If you read it you would know that we are all equal in the sight of the Lord.'

She snuggled up to him, throwing one arm across his chest. 'Now you are teasing again!'

'I assure you I am not. It is an odd thing, but whenever I am most serious you think I am joking!'

Harriet said sleepily: 'There was a Wesleyan preacher who came and talked like that once, on the Green. Mr. Mogus said it was a perversion of Scripture and, I must say, I agreed with him for once. Putting ideas into the heads of the poor —'

'But Harry, isn't that what heads are for? To have ideas put into them? You talk like one of the French aristocrats that brought about the Revolution —'

'Oh *no*, Van! You are all wrong there, I assure you! It was the wicked *sansculottes* who brought about the Revolution, not the landowners!'

Vandervoord began to shake silently, hopelessly with laughter, turning his head from side to side on the pillow as if trying to shake the laughter off. When he could speak he said weakly:

'I suppose the Reverend Mogus said a short prayer and then fired off his Brown Bess at that Wesleyan!'

'N-o,' said Harriet. 'But one or two of the rougher men set about him when he was leaving, with dead cats, you know, and fir cones, and Mr. Mogus paid their fines next day —'

'Fines!' said Vandervoord. 'They ought to have been flogged. So ought Mogus —'

'Ah — who is talking like a French aristocrat *now*?'

Leaning over him again with her eyes gleaming, her dark hair falling forward over her bare neck and breast as he loved and feared to see it, her whole face dancing with mischievous triumph. Harriet taunted him. He reached up his hand to stroke her head, from the smooth candid brow above the fine black eyebrows down to the nape of her neck. She turned her head swiftly at the touch, seizing his hand between her teeth.

'Do you love me, Van?'

'What do you think?'

'That's no answer!' Yet he could never be made to answer with the one word she longed for. Always the equivocal, the oblique, 'What do you think?' or 'Isn't it apparent?' or 'How could

I help it?' Deeds, she told herself, counted more than words —
and there were loving ways of hers — graceful gestures, forefinger
caresses, small sighs, an upward glance — which he could not resist.
So now, when his stubborn lips refused to answer hers as she
desired, she laid her forefinger upon them in the darkness, tracing
their sensitive shape — until he shook himself free of it, turned
towards her, caught her to him and swallowed her up as the sea
swallowed the coast and the music of their own thudding blood
and of the sea mingled in their ears together.

Shortly before Christmas, Clancy came home for the shooting,
with a party of friends. His father was unusually glad to see him, or
rather, to lay hands on him and to feel that his son was there. Mr.
Mogus, calling for his bi-weekly exhortation, was shown the door
again by Ivory.

Mr. Mogus had never treacled and feathered the aged negro, and
yet Ivory grinned at his discomfiture, and rejoiced to hear, from
the morning-room, the short barking laugh of Clancy who *had*
treacled and feathered him, and on whose behalf Mr. Mogus had
now been shown the door. Ivory loved Clancy as a God to be
both feared and propitiated. Of the two Gods he had always
preferred Clancy, as being more prone to propitiation than his
brother; but he was devoted to them both, though neither had
ever cared a fig for him, and this seemed to him entirely suitable.

He partly loved Clancy now because, with a young male Bromewell home again, the sinister quiet which had settled down over
Redonda no more disturbed the indoor servants. (Harriet herself,
being out and about farm business most of the day, had been less
affected by this than most.) Even when he was off the premises
there was always an air of life about the place — a coat or whip
flung down, a door ajar, a pair of muddy boots discarded, a pair of
dogs, panting, waiting, flopped down in the hall with their eyes on
the staircase. It was all like old times to Ivory.

Harriet catered for Clancy and the guests and servants he brought
with him with surprising dignity and restraint. She had always
been an admirable housekeeper but on this occasion she did not
wear a face 'as long as a wet week' as her brother had predicted —
nor did she feed his guests on bread and turnips as more than one of

them — knowing something of her severe reputation — had feared. Redonda, in fact, did them proud, because she was increasingly proud of Redonda.

Except at mealtimes she did not see much of them. She was up hours earlier than they were, chasing the maids about their business; and she went to bed after a hard day while they were still drinking and talking over the day's shoot. On more than one occasion she had to go to bed simmering with indignation because they had invited the French Prisoner to join them and were making him sing for his supper by playing his famous flute.

The next day she accosted him: 'How dare you do it!' she said. 'You know I had said I would meet you at the Cabin!'

'My darling, I am *desolé*, but —'

'You are not *desolé*! You are laughing inside because I am angry! You are *glad* because you have proved once again that nobody can resist you!'

'Nobody objects to being popular,' he admitted. 'I have always thought I was a fine witty fellow, myself. It is pleasant occasionally to have one's opinion confirmed.'

'It makes you look so cheap!' she blazed. 'As if you were to be had at anybody's beck and call! We can't afford that! We have to think of the future —'

'We?'

He was obviously puzzled. Her heart seemed to turn over with a spasm of actual physical pain.

But one has to have the courage of one's convictions.

'Certainly,' she answered quietly, hoping that her voice did not tremble. 'One day the War *must* end and then this — this ambiguous situation between us can be cleared up. What will people think if they remember such scenes as last night? Why — at the end you were dancing on the table, Van — amongst the wine-glasses! I was standing on the landing upstairs, I saw through the doorway!'

'And I did not knock over a single one,' he confirmed, 'thereby winning Five Guineas from your brother Clancy!'

She was impotent to force him to answer otherwise than in this way, obliquely — just as she was impotent to prevent a repetition of the occurrence. Still, there is no harm in trying.

'I forbid you to do it again, Van,' she said.

His laughing face suddenly became serious — had that set absorbed look about it that it had when he was engaged on some work of his own in his 'toyshop'.

'*You* forbid? My darling,' he said quietly, 'I am bound to your father, not to you. And if your brother invites me to join him, why then I am afraid he too has a say in the matter — at least as much as you have. You really must not be unreasonable —'

There was nothing for it but the old way, the only way left:

'If you loved me,' she said, 'you would not do such things if I did not want you to do them. . . .'

He kissed her, then begged her not to talk nonsense — and that night the strains of the flute again ascended the stairs to cries of *Vive le Roi, Bravo Monsieur Van Vandervoord!*' (For nothing would convince Clancy's guests that he was not some distinguished French *émigré* who had escaped to England during the Revolution.)

Old Bromewell, lying upstairs in his great fourposter bed, could hear the flute too; very faintly, and could see figures dancing two-and-two on the bandage across his sightless eyes. *Man and maid, dancing on the green, As pretty and hearty as can be seen, Tra la la, Here and There, Moll and Betty going to the Fair.* It put another tune in his head — one he had whistled and made very much his own — long, long ago, called 'Softly go down'.

He began to whistle it now.

It would be fine if Harriet could be induced to interest herself in one of Clancy's friends — particularly the one who was an Honourable. The Honourable Something would be rich one day — and in Parliament. She and he could often visit Redonda, when Clement came home for good or — failing Clement — when Clancy had returned to the fold once more.

The fold. *All we like sheep have gone astray.* Out of the fold, well out of the fold. It was very wrong, Mogus said, to be stiff-necked. Well — if *he* was stiff-necked, so was Harriet. Covetous too. Outlining something of Harriet's feeling for Redonda (and nobody understood it if her father didn't) — just to show Mr. Mogus that the girl stayed at home not because she couldn't get married but because she wouldn't — Captain Bromewell had learned with indignation and surprise from Mr. Mogus that his daughter Harriet was covetous.

Thou shalt not covet thy neighbour's house.

Nor thy father's, nor thy brother's house.

It was a great mistake to encourage it, Mogus had said — and had prayed forthwith with what seemed to the Captain quite unnecessary emphasis for Thy Daughter Harriet. He had also announced with unnecessary satisfaction that Surgeon-Lieut. Fiske would be marrying Mary Mogus early in the New Year. They were going to live at a Little Place near Ventnor . . . Well — if Harriet would only take trouble over the Honourable Something she could live in a Big Place near London and be damned to Mary Mogus for evermore.

He resolved to mention the matter to Harriet. It would be very self-denying of him. God knew that without her at Redonda the place would be twice as hard to run. But it was a sacrifice demanded of him; some amends for his early years; and the Honourable Something would not be the loser by it — by God, no he wouldn't!

He resolved further to discover from Clancy precisely how 'warm' the Honourable Something was, and whether the amount of extra heat that he himself could supply as Harriet's dowry would be adequate. Though he did not really doubt it — thanks to Mr. Pitt and the Price of Corn . . . Harriet shall be raised on sheaves of corn, he told himself — as our old churches here were built on foundations of wool. It was a pretty fancy — and for some time after he saw Harriet quite distinctly on the inside of his bandages, sitting demurely just as she had done for the family portrait years ago — but this time on a golden throne of wheat — strong and straight in the stalk, heavy in the spike, golden-brown over all, as toast done to a turn.

Meanwhile, amends must be made to Mogus for his fruitless visit of the week before. Groaning, he called for his money-bags to be brought to him next morning. Like his father before him, he preferred to keep his wealth about him, sending only twice a year to the Bank at Ipswich. With Clancy sitting on the bed while he brooded over his bags, he counted out a precious handful as tribute to the Church, Clancy fighting him, with Bromewellian vigour, every inch of the way. The money (in Clancy's opinion) was destined to be spent on a pair of dashing grey geldings without which life at Lincoln's Inn was impossible to support with either comfort or dignity.

The Captain found it impossible to make Clancy understand (the great booby) that while one was bored to death by Mogus, still his Church stood behind him as a warning, and the warning had already been given. Like Saul he had been stricken blind in his wickedness. Like Saul he must make amends.

'He'll drink it,' declared the moody Clancy, swinging off the bed with his hands thrust into his empty pockets. 'That hardened old swigger has had more claret off Twigg than Redonda ever has! He'll drink it or else bury it in his asparagus bed!'

But this was the last gesture of a beaten army, firing off blank because its real ammunition has been expended.

Nevertheless, Clancy did more during his brief stay at home than merely stock the larder with game, deplete the cellar and dispute over money matters with his father. He was as fond of the old man as his fundamentally selfish nature permitted him to be, and it was at his instigation that a famous eye-doctor, visiting just then in Woodbridge, was induced to come to Redonda and make an examination of the patient.

This gentleman declared himself unable to do anything for Captain Bromewell. The sight was ebbing slowly away from the bleared eyes, bluer than ever in their blindness. The most the doctor could promise was that the irritation in them which still sometimes troubled him, would pass.

Since he happened to be on the spot, he had, too, a look at the eyes of the French Prisoner who — on account of continual poring over columns of figures and small mechanical parts, was becoming subject to strange headaches. The doctor prescribed glasses for him and — while he did not waive the question of a fee — announced heartily that that would be all right, he would collect it from M. Otto, the representative of the French prisoners in England — with whom he had already had dealings in London.

Clancy considered this the greatest joke. He alone amongst the gang he had brought down with him believed Vandervoord to be what he said he was — a Netherlander.

'He'll go to collect it and get nothing for his pains!' he chuckled.

'I wish I thought so, Mr. Bromewell,' Vandervoord replied with a half-grin, half-sigh, 'but on the contrary I fear he will be paid promptly. I am well known to be a Frenchman at M. Otto's headquarters!'

There were days when living was farcical to him, not worth the effort — situations not worth explaining, inventions and calculations not worth the making; times when the whole European situation, revolving as it did perpetually around the movements of Bonaparte and his invading armies, seemed to have been brought about and sustained solely to keep him — Vandervoord — in a state of continued ignominy, suspense, frustration. 'Look at the map of Europe and you will see nothing but France!' Bonaparte was to boast later, with awful truth. She sprawled there, a great hairy bear with the tricolour cap upon her head, fattening at will upon the frightened States about her — the Prussians, Bavarians, Hanoverians, Austrians, Sardinians, Romans, Spaniards, Swiss, Neapolitans, Poles, Belgians, Flemings, Dutch. When she was hungry, she snapped here or there — bit off the heads of dukes or priests or petty princelings, landgraves and stadtholders, with one paw upon the limp body politic to keep it in its place. When she was thirsty she drank blood. *Look at the map of Europe and you will see nothing but France.* And the head of France — the bear's head — faced towards England, as the same map would show.

Three things served to depress Vandervoord at this time besides his headaches, not yet alleviated by the glasses (which was not strange as he continually forgot to wear them); the continued foolhardy optimism of the people he lived amongst, concerning the danger facing them across the North Sea (a danger so much more vital since Bonaparte himself had just been appointed to the command of the army 'against England'); incongruously with this, a sudden revival and multiplication of the old childish rules and regulations, paper-signings and oath-takings, concerning himself — as if he were the only possible source of danger; and thirdly, a letter from a man at the Netherlands headquarters in London, of whom he had never heard before, stating that M. Elesius had gone home on urgent private business, that he, the writer, was not acquainted with any previous particulars of M. Vandervoord's case; that search in the files had proved fruitless and that — if M. Vandervoord would be so good as to write it all down again, supplying full place and date, and get two responsible persons to witness his account — one of whom should be a Justice of the Peace — it was just possible that something further might come of it; that further — wishing to be really helpful — this gentleman had mentioned the business (so far as he understood it) to M. Otto at the *French* headquarters, who had replied that, with international affairs in the state of flux in which for the moment they unavoidably were, he regretted that he saw no prospect of M. Vandervoord the *Belgian* prisoner being able to take out French naturalization papers *as requested*; but advised him to be patient meanwhile and to supply further reasons of his request, preferably in duplicate.

This confusion worse confounded, the inevitable development (or so it seemed to Vandervoord) of writing to any Government department, no matter to what country it belonged, contributed still further to his general sense of frustration and disgust. In the evenings, when Clancy and his friends wanted Vandervoord for cards and wine, and song — he was often not to be found. Once he was missing for three days, coming back unshaven and without an appetite from some orgy in the fishermen's quarters at Slaughden Quay, about which — though still quite civil — he would say nothing to anyone.

The punishment of such an offence, if known, would have been at the least the cancellation of his parole to Redonda and a renewed incarceration. It was concealed from the Captain without too much difficulty, but it could not be concealed from Spens who — seeing a fine opportunity for venting the full force of his long-pent-up jealousy towards the French Prisoner, threatened to disclose everything. Harriet bought him off by allowing the agent, as a sop, to go his own way in an important farm matter.

They had come to a tussle more than once, since her father's illness, over the way Redonda farm should be run. In the early autumn Harriet had desired the ploughboys to plough in old seaweed on the newly-turned acres, while Spens, suspicious of this new and untried manure, declared that it would 'wholly pison the land', and countermanded her instructions. Harriet in turn counter-manding his, had had the extreme pleasure of passing Spens as she rode beside the first dripping tumbril of seaweed on its way, by her orders, to replenish the very fields he had declared it would poison. That particular victory had lowered his authority in the eyes of Redonda as much as it had heightened hers. He could not afford many repetitions of it, and yet appeals to the higher court of the Captain were, he knew, fruitless. Spens was getting old. That was his sentence and his doom. Any ambitions he had once cher-ished of turning yeoman-farmer on his own account had been quashed by Enclosure and by the rapid rise in land prices since the War. Now the most he could hope for was to stick on at Redonda for as long as he could, putting as good a face as he could on his own ever-diminishing authority.

But the French Prisoner's unexpected defection played for once right into his hands. On a certain leaden November afternoon Harriet met Spens standing triumphantly on the edge of her turnip-field (for in Spens' eyes it became hers the minute after she had mucked it with seaweed).

He did not stand as a good farmer should, astride of the rows (shortage of labour had prevented the crop from being lifted, as yet), but planted his feet smack upon the turnips, crushing them under his heel. He could afford such a gesture of contempt.

It was a long tussle and cost Harriet more than she would have paid for anything else in the world but Vandervoord, for it cost her her dignity and authority. Vandervoord, under Captain Bromewell's direction had evolved amongst other things a mechani-cal flail — a machine which he called jokingly the Iron Man — which would thresh more grain in a shorter time with less labour than Spens had ever dreamed of. It was the latest toy he had made and the finest, heaviest stack of corn had been put aside for its initiation. Yet that afternoon in the turnip-field Harriet gave the stack back to Spens for threshing in the old way, in the Great Barn, and went back to tell her father that the Iron Man had broken down and was not yet ready for use.

Her father took the news more philosophically than Vander-voord. Indeed, it comforted the old man, as he sat in his chair downstairs before the fire, to hear the steady ceaseless rhythm of the flail as of old, beating out the grain from the chaff in his Great Barn — the money from the waste material. He had the first sack of grain brought in to him and sat there, sifting the richness through his fingers as the hours passed, smiling as he listened to the seasonable music of the flail. It was Redonda's contribution to the sound of coming winter as surely as the cry of plovers and seagulls, flying ever more inland, was the contribution of sea and sky.

Vandervoord was affected differently. He did not protest, as Harriet half-feared he might, at the postponement (she regarded it as no more) of the employment of his invention. He was stony silent, unmoved as the Iron Man himself. Harriet, more disturbed by this than by any angry outburst, assured him the whole affair had been on his behalf, for his benefit. He assured her in his turn, that he did not care, it was of no concern to him whether the Iron Man was used or not — whether his pump-mills or his seed-drills were used or not — it was of no concern to him whether the whole of Redonda (or the whole of England for that matter) chose to submerge itself, like Dunwich, under the waves, or even whether he was swept under with it. Which last made her cry out:

'And *me*?' What of *me*?'

To which he replied, the words breaking out of him in a sudden torrent, as surprising after his long silence and indifference as must have been the sudden flow of water from the rock under Moses's staff:

'Cannot you understand, Harriet, that we are solitary! Each one of us is solitary! We are born so and die so, fundamentally we live so — anything else is a stupid delusion —'

'Oh Van, we are *not* solitary! We are together! You and I are together, we have each other —'

For answer he unclasped her hands from about his neck with a gentleness more dreadful than any thrusting repulse would have been. After that, and especially after Clancy's departure for London once more, he went less and less to the Cabin, more and more to the rough quarters at Slaughden Quay where, report had it, he was his old cheerful self always, always in demand, always gay, always welcome, always the centre of bustle and attraction.

He was drinking too, so heavily even in that time of heavy drinking that it was a conundrum how he could manage to carry it, or find the money to pay for it — cheap fiery smuggler's stuff though it was. Once Harriet, stealing late at night past his old workroom at the back of Redonda's stables, saw him sitting there by lantern-light, looking at his hands thrust out over the table before him, which were trembling ceaselessly as poplar leaves, which tremble as they breathe. He was staring at his hands as if they had betrayed him, had committed some unspeakable offence that condemned him to some intolerable punishment which nevertheless must be endured. She saw him take up a small pair of calipers in his right hand and some fragment of mechanism, of the nature of clockwork, in the other, and set out to bring the two into conjunction (as she had so often seen him do, with such consummate dexterity). It was apparent that such conjunction was almost as purposeless as would have been the conjunction of a spray of poplar-leaves criss-crossing another spray.

He gave a groan at the sight, which Harriet heard even through the closed window, and uttered an exclamation in his own language which could have been only: 'My hands! My hands!' Then he dropped his head upon his closed arms over the table and lay there, absolutely still, except that he beat the knuckles of his clenched fists continually upon the table, as if he were thrashing the misery out of himself as the flail threshes the grain out of the chaff.

The sight was so dreadful to her that she could not go in, could not even bear to watch it but hurried away, to sob into her pillow half the night and to hear his words 'We are solitary! Each one of us is solitary!' echoing, crowned with heavy meaning for the first time, as long as she lay awake.

The next morning he was the same as ever, except for the new reserve: gentle and polite with her, faintly amused at her obvious solicitude and concern for him. She thought: *if I reached out my arms now I could hold him close to me — and yet he would still be as far off as the Americas!* And wondered idly why the word Americas should ever have come into her head; perhaps only because they were the last word in remoteness.

Yet still, pathetically anxious to misunderstand what would

perhaps have been too hard to bear if understood, Harriet excused him, saying to herself: It is our cruel circumstances, it is the war, it is because we have to disguise what we feel for each other in the presence of everyone else — it is Spens, it is the affair of the mechanical flail, it is the stupidity of those foreigners in London who muddle all his correspondence up; it is his worry about his own country and relations; it is because we cannot marry yet, it is because he desires me physically and is tormented for want of me. And she laid in wait for one of his now-rare visits to the Cabin; then took him to her with the wanton violence of the North Sea swallowing up, to the point of obliteration, its own coastline — without pause, without pity or respite — striving to drive out, to thaw with the warm conspiracy of bodily nakedness, those cold arctic wastes between her and his spirit.

Believe that it has to be — or there is no reason in life at all; believe that she had to learn that hardest lesson of all — that the loved creature may be close at hand, may share the same bed, even the same breath; and be no more attainable or within call than the far, far distant or the long, long dead. Here, though the invading tide of your love may rise, kissing the brow, the eyes, the mouth that is so dear and sweet but will tell nothing, the hands that clasp only each other, feel only each other — still you are walking only on the dead coast, swallowing up only the dead coast, whilst the live spirit, loved long since and lost awhile, fails evermore to return.

CHAPTER XIX

HEARTS OF OAK

In Rehearsal
THEATRE ROYAL OF THE UNITED KINGDOM
Some dark foggy night about November, will be attempted by a strolling company of French Vagrants, an old Pantomime Farce, called
HARLEQUIN'S INVASION
or the

DISAPPOINTED BANDITTI
with new Machinery, Music, Dresses and Decorations.
HARLEQUIN BUTCHER BY MR. BUONOPARTE
from Corsica
(who murdered that character in Egypt, Italy, Switzerland,
Holland, etc.).
The other parts by
Messrs. Sieges, Le Brun, Talleyrand, Maret, Augerean,
Messina and The Rest of the Gang.

In the course of the Piece will be Introduced a Distant
View of
HARLEQUIN'S FLAT-BOTTOMED BOATS
warmly engaged by the
WOODEN WALLS OF OLD ENGLAND
To Which Will be Added (by command of His Majesty,
and at the particular request of all good Citizens)
The Favourite Comic-Tragic Uproar of
THE REPULSE
OR, BRITAIN TRIUMPHANT
The parts of John Bull, Paddy Whack, Sawny MacSnaith
and Shone-ap-Morgan by Messrs. NELSON, MOIRA,
ST. VINCENT, GARDINER, HUTCHINSON, WARREN, PELLEW,
etc., etc.
The Chorus of *Hearts of Oak* by the
JOLLY TARS AND ARMY OF OLD ENGLAND
Assisted by a Numerous Company of Provincial
Performers, who have VOLUNTEERED their services on
this occasion.
The Overture to consist of *Britons Strike Home, Stand
to your Guns, Rule Britannia* and
GOD SAVE THE KING.
*Satirical poster printed for J. Aspern by E. Macleish at
2 Bow Street, Covent Garden. Price 2d.*

As time went on, the behaviour of the Alde down by the Shearings
grew more amenable. The outline of the Shearings themselves took

on a recognizable shape and the river became (as Vandervoord had prophesied it would) subject finally to the influence of the tides. The current could be seen moving under its dun-coloured surface, combing the long hair of the drowned grasses with strong invisible hands now,this way, out to sea — now inland, as the tide flowed in. But the surface above the current remained strangely unruffled. Even in a strong breeze which brought the seas dashing up the shingle, uprooting anchors and tearing the bottoms out of small boats — or in an east wind that hammered the heather flat and tore branches off the pine and fir trees in its frenzy — even then the water in the Shearings still stayed unruffled, protected (as it was) by the last high bank of shingle along the dunes.

Nobody liked the piece of land known as the Shearings, but since it bore nobody any malice so long as they let it alone, and since — unlike Bonaparte — the water in it seemed at length to have settled down and showed no sign of desiring to extend its frontiers, gradually it came to be accepted as part of the landscape. People remembered a time when the Shearings looked very different from what they did now, just as they remembered a time before there was a lighthouse at Orford Haven, or a battery of powerful guns at Landguard Fort. That was all there was to it. Redonda's land, bordering the water there, was gradually fenced off to prevent the loss of livestock in the quicksands which occurred in parts of it, and for some time on holidays and Sunday afternoons, idle boys used to collect, sitting on the fence as boys will and throwing in sticks and corked bottles for the thrill of seeing their slow but inexorable sucking-down. Sometimes, too, men drunk enough to be valiant took the old short cut to or from Aldeburgh through the Shearings, and Harriet continued to use it whenever she had cause, despite all Vandervoord's protests, and perhaps to prove that here at least she had power and would not be gainsaid. Since the fencing-in of the land, she would have argued with him if he still protested (which these days he did not) that there was no longer any danger — except for a small strip of land which the Shearings preferred to leave looking like land but which was in reality bog, covered with sedge-grass. Over this treacherous patch, this mirage of sunny serenity, blue-green dragonflies almost as large as blue-tits loved to hover in Summer, weaving in and out of the reeds like shuttles—never less than two or three of them at a time; or else suspended in the sunlight in a dream as iridescent as themselves.

Over it, too, in Winter, ran the scarlet-footed moorhens, ducking and clucking as they flitted by, fearful of everything except the fearful ground over which they passed.

Once, only once, Harriet made a mistake here, seeking to cut off a corner by following the wake of a moorhen. She came home minus one shoe, her white stockings caked with yellow, evil-smelling mire to the knees.

'Oh, Miss Harry!' cried Susan, who happened to be visiting at Redonda and who had met her mistress as she came in — as she usually did — by way of the dairy; 'Oh, Miss *Harry*!' and her forlorn, shocked face showed that she guessed everything — not only the quicksands but the forbidden way of the quicksands, and Harriet's disobedience to that command and — who knows? — perhaps even the reason for the disobedience. Devotion can guess so much, blindfold, that the sharp-eyed but casual glance can never discern. 'Oh, Miss Harry, don't you goo fer to do it, I beg!' But which of all the unmentioned things Harriet was not to do, she meant — no one could tell.

Harriet, still with her heart thumping from her narrow escape, found relief in anger. Susan had clutched at her skirts in a gesture more impulsive than discreet.

'Let go of me!' cried Harriet, smacking down her hand sharply, and running upstairs to shut her door on everything except the vision of the Shearings and the clammy, dragging feeling that had wrapped itself in a second about her feet and ankles at that first false step. So *cold*, she kept saying, *even in summer* . . . and her teeth chattered. It was unbelievable that water could ever be so cold!

Whether anyone else ever knew of the adventure she could not tell. Sometimes she suspected that Spens knew — not only of the Shearings but of the fisherman's Cabin beyond it — from a sardonic way he had of glancing up at her whenever she set foot outside the grounds. He had never approved of her going about by herself, it was wholly unladylike, but since he was so disobliging and the farmlands had to be looked to, and to take a servant was a waste of the servant's time and a bore to her — she ignored his disapproval. Her father, she knew, believed she went with a servant or with Spens. It was not the only thing he was deceived in. If Spens had challenged her by taking the matter into the morning-room before her father, she would have met and beaten him there by pleading the exigencies of war. She was managing too well during such exigencies — and Spens too fumblingly — for any verdict but Not Guilty. Her turnips had done marvels on the 'pisoned land' while Spens' turnips, without the seaweed manure, were half the size and riddled with blackfly at that. Her wheat, sown by Vandervoord's new seed-drill, in land drained by Vandervoord's pump-mills, manured with rich silt out of the new dykes and ploughed with the new plough, was twice as thick in the row and strong in the shaft as Spens' wheat, as well as a better green. In everything the old order had failed, the new one had triumphed. Let him *dare* to take it to the morning-room — he would see who would win!

But these petty personal rivalries, as the larger rivalries between Northern and Southern England, the farmers and the manufacturers, Parliament and the services, Army and Navy, Church and State, sunk into sudden insignificance with the publishing of the Defence Act, calling out all brave men in the service of their King and Country, now in dire peril. Too late in the eyes of foreign realists like Vandervoord — almost too late even in the eyes of Mr. Pitt and his Government — England woke up and saw the huge shaggy bear's head with the tricolour cap upon it facing her across the Straits of Dover. She saw the evil-smelling jaws open and snap in her direction for the first time, after years of snapping — yes, *and* swallowing — in every other direction. Hearts of oak were invoked, and oaken hearts responded, sound to the innermost core despite the roughest exteriors. Differences were forgotten, points of dispute laid aside, crying evils, senseless cruelties forgiven with a magnanimity almost saintly in the breadth of its circumference — since now the matter was not one between oppressor and oppressed but between brother and brother. Gaunt, filthy children, shipped from the workhouse to the factories to work their fifteen hours a day or more, slept as they stumbled along the dark roads between the two prisons, dreaming of a victorious Britain, desiring and hoping

for no other. Seamen with backs still bruised from the floggings which were the chief discipline they knew, weakened by the abominable food served out to them at profiteering prices and by the vitiated atmosphere of living-quarters which would have disgraced a clean pig — such men rose up and cheered themselves hoarse when Nelson's flagship passed, crying 'God save our Nel!' Living symbol he might be of the authority which perpetrated such injustices upon them — but a bright and brave hope of the justice they still hoped to attain.

If this paradox is difficult to understand, so too is a rainbow, a shooting-star, a waterfall, icicle formations upon ferns in winter, flower-carpeted mountains in Spring, a lark's song, a rose's scent, love at first sight, and at last sight, and long after the loved object is out of sight altogether. Such things are not for analysis but for wonder and praise. Bonaparte did not believe in them, had not had time for their investigation, had never been hampered, more than half an hour or so, by any such thing, in the carrying out of his meticulously-planned and admirably executed Continental ambitions. Now the time had come when one thing only stood between him and the peaceful period necessary for the true renaissance of Europe, under the flag of the tricolour and the letter N — the British Fleet; the wooden walls defending the last citadel of liberty in Europe — not to mention the innumerable, uncountable small merchant ships, impudently plying to and fro over the seven seas despite his blockade, and carrying in their despicable holds (some said) three-quarters of the whole world's trade. Destroy the lion in his lair, the ships in their ports, whispers the letter N; manœuvre in your incomparable army way for numbers, advantage and position! Fifteen millions of people MUST give way to forty millions.

But across the Channel another letter N (for, unfortunately for him, there *is* another N) signals: *Never mind manœuvres. Go at them!* And they do. All England goes at them — the children in the factories, the seamen in the ships, the agricultural labourers growing the bread which is not theirs to eat, guarding the game that is not theirs to catch, driving the bullocks whose beef they will not by any chance taste — that Roast Beef of Old England whose savour nevertheless they celebrate in a song which roars from the taverns in perpetual and wholehearted defiance of Boney and his (so they say) diet of fried frogs.

Redonda, in that first fine frenzy of patriotism which swept the country in its hour of danger, set its house in order with the rest; the carpenters there turned from making scythe- and broom-handles, wheels and water-butts to the making of pikestaffs for volunteer foot-soldiers, and shutters for the windows of all those houses in the neighbourhood which, like Redonda, faced the sea. The smith ceased his labour on well-buckets and door-latches to make firelocks and pike-heads. Man-traps which had been set by gamekeepers to catch poachers were rushed to new positions to catch invading Frenchmen instead. Ditches were cleared, fences, barns and bridges repaired, all in double quick time to the tune of the drum and the fife. Flags, not resurrected since the days of Blenheim, now flew bravely from church towers, volunteers drilled in market-squares and on commons — ten thousand of them, all over the country — ex-smugglers turned sailors, ex-sailors turned secret agents, ex-service men of every sort reappeared in their faded regalia, much as a Red Admiral butterfly will do, which has wintered it in some wardrobe and reappears in Spring with cobwebs decking the edges of tattered wings.

And men like Captain Bromewell, who were ex-militia men and big landowners and farmers and Justices of the Peace all in one — were driven out of temper and nearly off their heads by the sudden spate of literature which descended upon them, all marked Urgent, all demanding instant answer — half of them cancelling the other half out almost before the ink of the laboriously filled-in answers were dry upon them. Yet still they poured in, drawing attention to previous *errata*, regretting that they had neglected to enclose enclosure now forwarded, or to attach Paragraph B; asking for duplicates, further particulars — providing further particulars themselves, longer and longer as the year wore on and the tension ever accumulated.

Even to a man who delighted in mental intricacies, conundrums, tabular statistics and the neat filling-in of lists, such literature became, as time passed, more and more of a strain. To Captain

Bromewell, who had always hated to take up his pen as much as to lay down his riding-crop, they were a bane from the first. He had grimly clung to his judicial duties, despite his blindness, until now — but with this paper invasion, as he called it, he saw no hope of catching up with his affairs at all. 'God in Heaven, Harry!' he used to exclaim to her, as they sat together late at night, struggling over some particularly difficult governmental document: 'Devil burn them up — how do they think of such things? Is there a special department for tormenting such fellows as ourselves. Tear it up! Throw it overboard!'

He persisted with a vague hope that the document that was torn up or burnt was somehow disposed of — despite constant evidence to the contrary. The reading-out of such papers became inevitably a sort of antiphon, Harriet supplying the quiet even questions and the Captain responding with loud spurts of derision, condemnation or despair. 'So they want to know how many indoor servants we have? God in Heaven, have them in, Harriet! Muster them here — count every toenail!' Or again: 'Have we told them about the barn set aside for volunteers' accoutrements till we're black in the face, or have we not?'

'I think this is some other department that wants to know, Father.'

'Devil burn the lot of them! Some other department! Tear it up, girl, tear 'em all up and hang them in the privies — that's all they're good for!'

Then there would be further instructions from Whitehall; an urgent communication from the War Office with a red seal and a special messenger, announcing that on such-and-such a day Colonel So-and-so would be at such-and-such to inspect the Volunteers, or the fortifications or signal-stations, and would every facility, etc., etc. And after colossal efforts had been made, ceaseless labours engaged on, a frenzy of involved organization achieved, only by superhuman expenditure of sweat and blood and tears — something would lamentably misfire. The muskets would not arrive in time, the semaphore would break down, the Volunteers would miss the coach, the Colonel would not arrive at all; or else he would arrive at some totally different place on some totally different day, in the drizzle, and be painfully surprised at the lack of enthusiasm, etc., etc. and the evident unreadiness of the preparations, etc., etc. And *that* would entail further filling-in of papers and explanations and apologies; and finally the muster of Volunteers for the Parish of Snape as notified in the June lists would have to be called in again and altered, since by July the numbers had changed completely — some having dropped out because the Colonel didn't come when he said he would, or because the muskets didn't come at all — or because men had got married; others joining late because they weren't on the spot earlier and could they particularly request that they always went on duty the same time as Tom Spurling because (tell-ee-for-why) that was the only reason they joined at all?

Between these two extremes — the laconic stupidity and stubbornness of the local population (rolling over and obscuring their bright enthusiasm as the local watersmoke rolled over and obscured their native heaths) and the appallingly verbose stupidity and stubbornness of Whitehall — Captain Bromewell and his fellow-landowners and militia commanders moved like men confounded. They met occasionally at their headquarters in Ipswich or Woodbridge and anathematized Whitehall and the local population to their hearts' content. Each one had a tale of muddling or incompetence with which to cap his fellow's. What they wanted here, they said, was a Bonaparte. *He'd* soon show 'em a thing or two in the way to get things done! And then ... lest such statements, overheard, should cause alarm and despondency in the heart of the girl who brought them their wine or the old man who cleaned their boots, they went at great length to retract them, pointing out with unnecessary heartiness that though days might be black, Old England had seen worse, we must all pull together, then we should weather the storm, and to hell with all foreigners, particularly Corsicans, who wanted to come over here and try their dirty tricks on us!

If his friends, armed with good eyesight, had their work cut out to keep abreast of their labours, on paper and otherwise, Captain Bromewell was doubly handicapped. Harriet served him as secretary as long as she dared — but sharing her father's opinion as to the worth of the papers and documents, and more than sharing

his opinion concerning the real worth of Redonda and its farmlands — she was not prepared to skimp the one for the other, no
matter how long it might take to attend to both. She looked very
tired in those days, and shabby — living as she did in her old habit
and riding-boots. She was seldom in bed before midnight, or up
after five. And the farm continued to prosper and she to love it
and take pride in it, no matter how Whitehall snowed fresh papers
down upon them, no matter how the war on the Continent might
be going.

No news they say is good news. There had been no news of
Clement and his family since they had moved into the neighbourhood of Berne, six months before — for the sake of Clem's health.
This silence had not worried his family unduly — Clement was
always such a poor correspondent unless he had some success to
record, and successes had been hard to come by in recent years.
But Bonaparte's latest aggression, the invasion of that Canton and
the occupation of Berne, boded no particular good. Once Sophy
had sent them a newspaper cutting — no letter with it, just the cutting
— announcing that Miss Sabrina Bromewell had won a prize at a
charity ball for a particularly tasteful tendering of a Handel *aria*.
Harriet had read this aloud with distaste. Her father heard it with
amusement and some pride in his only grandchild.

'The chit! It seems only the other day that Clem wrote to us she
was in short frocks! And now before she's in her 'teens she's dazzling
'em!'

'Showing off,' Harriet commented.

'If you had a fine soprano, *you'd* show off too, my girl — but you
never had a voice — no more than a corncrake.'

'Fat, Guzzling, Little Slug,' said Harriet, sounding every word
with capital letters. 'Yes, she will have just the figure for a singer!'
(She had gone once in her life, against her will, to an opera with
Sophy, and it had confirmed her in her previous opinion that operas
were rubbish.)

There were, therefore, inquiries to put through to Whitehall — and
to the assiduous Marsham — about Clem; there was the bull, Bromewell Beauty, to be sold and a grant of money made to Clancy out
of the profits from it; to Clancy, who wrote cheerfully that he now

belonged to the Devil's Own — the newly-formed corps of Inns of Court Volunteers, and that he was consequently in desperate need of funds for uniform and various other unspecified items. There were three carpenters and the smith to be loaned from Redonda to the Military Commander at Orford Castle — and other men to be found in their place; there were (and this went particularly against the grain) papers to be signed testifying to the worthiness and incorruptibility of one Captain Twigg, who had proffered his services to the Admiralty as officer commanding the newly-formed corps of Sea Fencibles — a collection of fishermen and boatmen as cunning as himself who, it was proposed, should take over a force of armed barges in the River Stour. There were local volunteers still to be enlisted, instructed, drilled — arms promised to them, uniforms found for them, funds raised for them, ammunition requested for them; there was an encampment to be prepared, and a redoubt and an arms dump; there were maps and charts to be drawn, copied, corrected; there were High Authorities to be billeted, and their servants and horses; there were proclamations to be read in public and exhibited on the parish notice-board. There were the free meals to be organized, once a week, for the *really* indigent and starving — out of Redonda's stocks and on Redonda's premises. And always and above all there were papers to be signed as Justice of the Peace, Assizes to attend, cases to be heard, judgments given — all this in addition to the strenuous, steady and successful management of one of the largest farms in the eastern counties.

Small wonder that the strain of all this told on both Harriet and her father. Try as they would to cope with it, to face it and, in the true family spirit, *not to be beaten* by it, come the four corners of the world in arms — eventually they had to admit failure. They must have help or break.

There was one obvious choice — the French Prisoner.

Harriet named it, as casually as could be compassed — bringing forth a torrent of exclamations from her father.

'Are you mad? This is Government work!' stubbing the papers with his forefinger, 'Military work!' stubbing again, 'Secret work! D'you think I should be allowed for a minute to employ a foreigner?'

She tried again, for reason's sake — not for love's — or so she told herself:

'He's on our side, Father. You know that.'

'So he says, but it's never been proved and never *will* be, if you ask my opinion!'

'He's extremely neat with a pen and with figures — and he reads well — '

'Tchah! Don't waste my time and your breath, Harry. It's not the slightest use.'

Suddenly, as if one second of piercing vision had been vouchsafed him through his bandages, he sat up straight and said:

'You've not lost your head about the fellow, have you?'

She answered as Vandervoord himself might have answered — obliquely and laughing:

'Whatever makes you think of such a thing, Father?'

'I don't know.' He threw himself from side to side in his chair uneasily, as if trying to shake off the supposition. 'But if I thought so, that would be the last straw on the camel's back. Damn it, I'd give up the struggle altogether — '

To which again she answered — with a strange pang of pity for him as he sat there, blindfolded, corpulent, very tired but still aggressively, eagerly alive and on the defensive: 'I can't *think* how such a notion could have got into your head!' Which again was true. She could *not* think, for certainly nobody about the place, having guessed the truth about her and Vandervoord, would have dared to bring it to these quarters.

But he had *not* said (as on one occasion, fearing just such a situation, she had thought he would), that he would get rid of Vandervoord. Circumstances being what they were, the French Prisoner was too valuable for that. In the absence of the smith at Orford he made — it turned out — quite a passable smith; in the absence of the carpenters he made a very good carpenter (though he kept off the very roughest work for the sake of his hands). Handy at everything, there was nothing he would not set going, or improvise, for Captain Bromewell's advantage.

Vandervoord, indeed, had come to resemble that useful article on any farm — the furzebranch, which may be stuck into a weak spot in the hedge to prevent stock breaking out, or children breaking in; that will clean the chimney, or sweep the path, or do to set the broody hen on, or to light the bonfire. Get rid of such a treasure? Not likely. Besides, wasn't there some commandment about not turning the stranger from the gate? It was to be hoped he had remembered the text right, for then by keeping Vandervoord he would be suiting his own personal convenience and Scripture too.

The bull Bromewell Beauty sold in Ipswich for a hundred guineas, to Spens' chagrin (who would have been surprised at fifty) and Harriet's triumph and delight. She had gone to market with Spens on purpose to witness what she knew would be his discomfiture. The price was the highest ever paid for a red-poll bull in that market and a tribute to her father's genius in judging and breeding, but it had been Harriet who had stuck out for a reserve of eighty-five guineas with both auctioneer and agent against her. The bull was to go to the North. Spens, who had hand-fed him as a youngster, felt the usual brief pang at parting with a fine animal. Harriet, patting her capacious leather pocket with the hundred guineas in it, felt no pang at all.

Meeting Vandervoord accidentally on her way home afterwards, she told him of this, commenting scornfully on Spens' foolishness. 'At any moment,' she said, 'I expected him to burst out crying, he looked so woebegone — '

'He was fond of the beast. You weren't.'

'Indeed, I was! I admire anything successful. Beauty was a triumph for us, but he has brought *this*' (jingling her pocket) 'to Redonda, and that is what I care about!'

'And this?' he had asked, waving his arm towards Farley Spinney — Farley Woods by rights now. The timber had just been sold by Captain Bromewell to Admiralty contractors and at that very moment a gang of woodmen were busy there with saw and axe, bringing the green giants crashing down, lopping off their limbs, binding their bodies with chains of iron to bear them, captives, away.

'And this?' he had asked, as if to say: 'Do you feel nothing about this, either?'

They had dismounted at the edge of the spinney, on the edge, too, of an afternoon bright but chilly with forebodings of Winter. Bright as the sunlight, chilly-pure as raindrops, a robin sang from the heart of the wood, now here — a pause — now there, as if he continually altered his point of vantage the better to observe the intruders below. The two horses, at reins' end, were busy cropping the short grass about Harriet's and Vandervoord's feet. Perhaps a minute passed before Harriet answered him — with her eyes upon the scene before her, not upon him.

'What do you expect me to feel? Because I am a woman do you expect me to burst out sobbing because we have sold those trees? I wish you could learn, Van dear, that I am a farmer by instinct, not a sentimentalist! Yes, of course I loved them — as long as they were necessary to Redonda; while there was still room for them to grow and sense in their growing! I love every stick, every stone, every leaf and grass about the place — you know that! Haven't I often told you that as a child I used to resent the very fowls picking round the door because I feared they were eating up Redonda and that one day they would eat it all away? But I am not a child now. I have more sense.'

There was a warning cry from the edge of the wood, and a scurrying sound. Looking up instinctively, both Harriet and Vandervoord saw the topmost boughs of one large oak tremble uneasily above the other foliage — as if they still could not quite believe what was coming to pass below. For a minute or so there they trembled, turning a little this way and that, leaning momentarily towards another oak for consolation, towards an ash for advice. And then the groan — the breaking heart of the tree as it surrendered, still with noble slowness, crying *a-a-a-h*! as it descended, crashing dead to the ground with the ruin of all its lower limbs, already lopped, about it.

To Vandervoord the incident was deathly. The head of the fated Marie Antoinette, suddenly severed and rolling towards him, could not have made him momentarily more aghast. It symbolized the crash of his own early hopes, his promising start in Java, the idiotically (for Fate *was* idiotically malevolent) sudden death of his father, necessitating his recall from that country; the sea-battle, the capture of his vessel — and all the subsequent imprisonments, frustrations, humiliations and waste. Waste, waste, *waste*! he said savagely, silently; and the oak tree, leaving an echo of shivering leaves still behind it, still protesting in the vacated air, echoed waste, waste, *waste*!

'Five pounds for that,' assessed Harriet: ' — and there are forty or fifty such to go! Yet you want me to pull a long face and say what a shame it is to fell such noble trees, I *know* you do!'

'*Nom de Dieu*, I don't *want* you to do anything, Harriet! Years ago — before you were ever born, possibly, I schooled myself to give up *wanting* people to do things — it only resulted in their doing the exact opposite!'

'It isn't as if Father and I arranged it entirely for our own sakes either,' she went on, almost as if she had not heard him. 'We consider it our duty to let the Admiralty have the wood — our duty to the country, for that matter! It so happens that it pays us well, but the timber was ready for cutting — if it had not been them it would have been someone else who bought it. I can't understand you, Van,' she went on, turning her back on the scene of their dispute and looking sulkily at him, 'it isn't as if you were mad about country life yourself, you have often enough told me that your place is indoors with machinery — not out of doors with grass! I have never heard you so much as mention Farley Wood before, and yet now, because we have sold some of the timber in it, you pretend to be broken-hearted —'

'Observe,' he announced quite quietly to the bright, cold landscape about them, 'the Farmer speaking.'

'What of it?' she flashed; 'is it such a shocking thing to be a farmer?' Her hand was still outstretched along the top of the fence beside them; he turned and laid his own upon it with an urgency he had not shown, it seemed to her, for months. When he spoke it was still very quietly.

'Listen,' he said, 'I think what you have just said explains the immense difference between us; it is why we always fight. It is why we can never be at peace, never happy! I agree country life is not for me — my place is in a workshop. Nevertheless, when I saw and heard that tree crashing just now, I saw a living thing killed in its prime — a living spirit, Harry! And *you* call it timber! Even while it was still growing, still alive, it was timber to you. And Spens, too — to-day he was sad to see the bull go; he remembered it as a calf, or when it was sick and he had to stay up with it — or the first day it was turned out to grass. To see it go to another owner cost him a pang for which I respect him. But to *you* the bull was merely a handsome carcass on four legs, bred by Captain Bromewell of Redonda and worth a hundred guineas but not one tear!'

'You are talking very stupidly,' said Harriet, as lightly as she could. But the situation was not a pleasant one — she would change it. She kicked out at the skirts of her habit and turned about, pulling crossly at her horse's head and beginning to walk on, up the long avenue, towards Redonda.

'On the contrary,' he replied, but more lightly — falling into step beside her as he fell in with her tone of voice; 'I am talking very much to the point. I am seeing very clearly for the first time what I should have known all along — that I am worth just as much to Redonda — and to you — as the timber was, as the bull was; and when I, too, have served my purpose I can go!'

She could think of nothing better to say to this amazing travesty of the truth than, again: 'You are talking very stupidly, Van' — still hurt in her pride at his criticism of her success over Bromewell Beauty, yet mystified as well that this lover of hers, whom she grieved always to feel bound to her only by the slightest and most tenuous of threads, could yet make a declaration suggesting she should ever want him to go! — signifying surely (by contrast) that *he* would want to stay . . . Or did it? What precisely *did* such a statement signify — and why must it be that sentences that matter in one's life so vitally (hardly more than half a dozen or so in each life at most), must disappear and be swallowed up past answering, just as fast as trivial chatter?

Since she didn't answer him except by this repetition, he went on speaking with the same unusual urgency:

'Listen, Harriet. Will you prevail on your father to let me go? You *can* do it, if you will — and only you can do it. There is nothing more for me to work on here — nothing that any able-bodied man cannot do if he puts his mind to it. I can be transferred, if your father agrees, to some other place, somewhere else. It would be far better.'

She would have liked to have said in her bitter shock and grief:
'Is this what all your vows have come to?' — but then he had never
made any vows. She would have liked to have said: 'But you promised me — ' — but he had never promised her anything either. That
much, at least, she must concede him. Of course there had been that
ceremony in the Cabin when, hands meeting above the Bible, they
had pledged each other *Set me as a seal upon thine heart and as a seal
upon thine arm. For Love is strong as death, jealousy is cruel as the grave.*

Cruel as the grave, said their horses' hoofs, plodding obediently
along behind them up the avenue. *Cruel as the grave, cruel as the
grave, cruel as the grave.*

She could not answer him. The tears were streaming down her
face so that she was half-blinded by them. He went on, more
gently, more like his old self (cruelly, cruelly like his old self!):
'I am thinking of you, my darling, as much as of myself in this. It's
no good, as you see, between us. It doesn't go. I have stopped doing
any good work, yes — I did some at the beginning, I'll admit that —
but lately it's been clumsy, cheap stuff. It doesn't go.'

She stumbled over a stone then and nearly fell. Immediately he
was tenderly near her, catching her arm at once, helping her up and
supporting her on her way with a most damnable solicitude. She
would like to have said: 'You would push me over a precipice with
the greatest satisfaction but because I merely stub my toe on a stone
you are all helpfulness and kindness!' but the tears prevented her.

Cruel as the grave, cruel as the grave, cruel as the grave went the
horses' hoofs, plodding onwards behind them with cheerful
inconsequence.

Vandervoord went on holding her arm, speaking to her, but
because of the hoofs, and the thudding in her ears born of the ache
of constraint she had set on her throat to stop sobbing aloud — and
again perhaps because she could not bear to hear any more, because
what he said was always worse and worse — Harriet could not hear
him.

By now they were approaching the quarry on the left of the
avenue; the quarry which, as long as Harriet could remember, had
supplied the sand for Redonda's kitchen and dairy floors. Its
entrance, before it shelved steeply down into a yawning yellow gap,

was beaten as fine and smooth by recent rain as the sands of the seashore.

When they reached it she stopped suddenly with an impulse she could not have explained in words — much less controlled. She bent down and with her free hand (he was still holding her left arm as kindly as he might have an old lady's), she reached down her riding-crop and with its horn tip she wrote on the smooth surface of the sand the words *Harriet Vandervoord*. Once done, she felt a great sense of release; it said all that need to be said by her and no more.

Vandervoord followed her painful tracing of the letters; then he dropped upon one knee in the sand and, after a gesture of compassion towards her, as horrible (to her) as his earlier solicitude had been, he rubbed out the second word with the palm of his hand.

It vanished into the sand as if it had never been.

At that the dumb crying ceased and she burst into a storm of passionate weeping, her arms rigid beside her, the tears coursing down her face unrestrained from her closed eyes — sobs choking her frame — almost stifling her.

'Ah *no*!' he said, his arms about her, comforting her, his handkerchief dabbing at her wet face as kindly as a nurse might comfort a child. 'Ah no, Harry darling. Don't! Don't!' and — as she persisted — he said with a note of real despair: 'I warned you, didn't I? I said that those who loved me were always unhappy! Believe me, Harry, I did my best to avoid it — to avoid you. I said that it would never go!'

The ludicrous repetition of a phrase indifferently adapted from another language, jarred on Harriet almost more than anything that had gone before. To strike him with her whip was not worth the gesture but if it had lain in her power just then to strike him dead, she would have killed him without compunction.

As soon as she had collected enough disciplined breath to speak, she said: 'Don't say any more, Van — I beg — I implore you. I am very tired' — shaking her hair back, still with shut eyes, and putting up, very slowly, one trembling hand to replace a strand of it which, in her grief, had broken loose. It was difficult to achieve — as if it too were no longer to be controlled or influenced by her, but in the end it was done.

The fumbling, slow action smote Vandervoord. He found himself thinking: *So this is what she will be like when she is old*. Knowing so well that he would never see her then — would long, long have escaped her. . . .

From Farley Wood there came the creaking uneasy sound of another oak stirring upon its severed foundations; then the pause, as before, the fearful conference in the foliage, the cruel, irrevocable crash. He heard it, and died again within himself — and the unhappy queen died again with him — and his youth, his ambitions and hopes, even love — which should have been strong as death but was only cruel as the grave.

Tears must momentarily have blinded his eyes too. He had to take his glasses off to wipe them clear. When he could see again distinctly Harriet had her back to him, and was obliterating the remaining name in the sand with her foot. Her breath still came unevenly, piteously at odds with itself as a sobbing child's.

'Let — it go — after — the other,' she said, 'that far — at least.' And again, 'Come, we must go up to the house.'

CHAPTER XX

AFFAIRS COME TO A HEAD

O, if thou knew how thou thyself dost harm,
And dost prejudge my bliss, and spoil my rest;
Then thou wouldst melt the ice from out thy breast
And thy relenting heart would kindly warm . . .

W. ALEXANDER

FREAK weather is a feature of the climate in a country at war. That winter in East Anglia was no exception. The gulls flew inland, far up the Alde and the Stour to new feeding-grounds, as if they renounced the coastline for ever. Herons and curlews forsook the swampy stretches of the same rivers to join the rooks over the ploughed fields. Huge seas running in the Channel and the North

Sea kept up a continual pounding of the coast, piling up ramparts of shingle in unexpected places as grim monuments to their destructiveness — smashing small craft like matchwood and spitting the splinters contemptuously back again upon the beaches; gnawing away fiercely at the earth cliffs and swallowing up the human habitations upon them as, underpinned, one by one they fell into the waves and were sucked back in them and swallowed up in them, only to be regurgitated later on in pitiful scraps of flotsam stranded amongst the seaweed and wreckage of fishermen's boats upon the exhausted shore.

For everyone who lived along this part of the coast the Winter was accompanied by the never-ending thunder of waters, now near, now far; by cunning inundations of water flooding up silently at full moon and rendering the lower floors of the fishermen's cabins uninhabitable, and drowning the cattle and sheep. The wind blew continually from the East or Nor'-east, bleak and powerful, urging on the raging grey-green waters to fresh depredations, scudding across the gleaming beaches to scour them clean of every impediment; threshing away at the pines and fir trees which stood, wise ancients that they were, with their backs to the tempest, their leafy arms curled about their heads like those of a man out in rough weather.

There was one thing about it, the people told each other, shouting to each other to be heard above the tempest and the pounding roar of the waves — Boney could never invade in *this* weather! And they kept stout shutters up over their windows to break the force of the wind just as much as to douse the lights within from Boney. That was outside. Inside the house the larder was even barer than before. Bread and meat — fats of every kind — were scarcer than ever. Fish was not to be had, for the sea had swallowed up much of the remnant of the fishing fleet — nets, boats, crews and all, while the rest of it was about other business, whenever it was possible to put to sea.

And still, despite the stormy season, the English frigates went about *their* business, overloaded in the holds below, over-masted and over-canvassed above, but ever pitching onwards with their brave heads well down to wind and weather, King's Enemies and Acts of God — their masters and crews making a virtue of danger and turning it, with consummate skill and courage, to their advantage. All through that furious winter they carried on, in merchant ships and naval vessels, both sound and rotten, riding those unbroken white horses with the lightest possible touch on the bridle and the gentlest, cunningest pressure from the heel — Nelson and Duncan, Jack Tar and Captain Twigg. And trade went on, and goods were delivered, and the sinews of war grew slowly stronger as the days lengthened and the cold strengthened and the tempest at last died away.

It was always called a tempest in East Anglia; perhaps because the inhabitants recognized nothing so mild as a storm. When it ceased, giving place eventually to a calm sky streaked with ragged clouds, the people came outdoors again, shaking mats and rugs in the wan sunshine and drying their damp belongings. Farmers began to repair the fences broken down by the wind; a few fishermen, too, patched up old boats and set off shakily upon the now docile waters to drop a tentative net.

It was hardly strange that in such circumstances — which absorbed their full attention, the ordinary country folk could not be much interested in a new alliance, concluded by Mr. Pitt on their behalf with Russia, Austria and Turkey. Bonaparte had invaded Turkish territory by invading Egypt. The head of the bear had turned aside, for the time being at least, to tear a hole in the flank of yet another nation before resuming its concentration upon Great Britain. The Russian Fleet, encountering the British Fleet upon neutral ground during exercises in the Mediterranean had found it convenient and suitable to agree with the champions of liberty about the wickedness of French aggression. If the Russians had havered before such agreement — which to do them credit they did not — the matter was clinched for them by the Battle of the Nile. The onlooker sees most of the game and on this occasion the military might of France's brilliant general was obscured from the Russian view by the white sails of Nelson's squadrons going in to the attack and cutting up the trapped French fleet like mincemeat.

The onlooker sees most of the game and nothing succeeds like success when it comes to making an ally; nevertheless, the Russians had more sober grounds for joining the new Alliance against the

French. Seeing Bonaparte frustrated in the West (inexplicably) by the island of Great Britain, frustrated in the South by Austria and by the British Mediterranean Fleet, frustrated in the North by transport difficulties — she knew still that the conquering hero must go on conquering or collapse, because that is the rule of war; knew that water, rising to flood level and encircled by a thick wall, as France was encircled by hostile nations, will always find a way in the end through the weakest spot in that wall. The water had not yet risen to full flood level; it was merely making inlets here — as in Malta and at Alexandria, or splashing over dangerously there — as on the right bank of the Rhine; at the same time quietly but effectively isolating the Swiss mountains and the Italian Alps and bogging the flats of Belgium and the Netherlands. But this was all nothing — so far, a mere trial of the strength of the Grand Army, a sharpening of bayonets for a real offensive. The road to Russia still lay open, could not (by reason of geography) *help* lying open — and water will always find the weakest place in the wall.

So it was that Russia joined the champions of Freedom, and it would have been a wonder if, despite the scurry of diplomatic activities in the Capital cities concerned, any of the country population of England saw any particular cause for rejoicing in the news, since they had so much else nearer home to absorb their attention, including the problem of finding two good meals a day.

Surgeon-Lieut. Fiske was married to Miss Mogus in the Spring as arranged, in London, and the Bromewells of Redonda contributed a cask of wine and a couple of dressed fowls for the occasion — all well matured. The rectory was shut up shortly afterwards to allow of Mr. Mogus paying some prolonged visits during which he might hunt down and capture a female relative to take his daughter's place; and the Clerk read the church lessons very tremblingly before Captain Bromewell, afterwards to be horribly reproved for faulty enunciation. (The Captain had become a constant and critical church-goer since his affliction.)

He was almost as hard-worked as ever, since a satisfactory successor to Harriet — in a secretarial capacity — proved impossible to find. Those who could not read or write were already fully employed about the place; those who could had been drafted off to the towns. There remained the Clerk, hard of hearing and stumbling of speech; Spens, who was so slow that the Captain complained that squitch-grass came up between his sentences; Harriet, who had not the time to spare from her other work, and the French Prisoner.

One can tell much from the eyes. Perhaps it was because her father's were still hidden behind bandages that Harriet could never be sure whether he had forgotten that suspicion he had once entertained of an intrigue between her and Vandervoord; whether it had vanished as suddenly as it had come, or whether, beneath the surface, it still lay brooding. At all events she lacked the courage to bring the matter to the test. She did not suggest Vandervoord as assistant again, and whether her continued silence about so obvious a choice kept his suspicions alive or whether the Captain had dismissed them from his mind on her first disavowal was not to be known. At any rate, he made no effort to employ him so but by using Harriet, Spens and the Clerk in different shifts of labour, he managed to exclaim and confound his way through each full day.

Vandervoord was left, as he had been ever since the 'Emergency', to fill the odd place about the farm when wanted and — when not — to employ himself over his own interests and inventions. He was forbidden (much to Spens' delight) to use the Cabin again, and the Andersons' old donkey was sent to bring away his precious bits and pieces from the Fortified Area. He was also advised against visits to the taverns on Slaughden Quay, though a man (as the Captain knew) must have his amusements and must take them where he can find them — provided he is not a prisoner of war.

He did not cease to visit the taverns — a fact of which Harriet was bitterly aware. Each week he did less and less at Redonda, drank more and more down at Slaughden Quay. But she was impotent to do anything about it, and Spens knew that, too — and was pleased at that. It was good to get even with my fine lady — however devious the method! He did not envy the French Prisoner any more. Since this rival had fallen from favour with the Captain, Spens' envy had died a natural death. Indeed, if Vandervoord had been suddenly removed at this point, half Spens' grim enjoyment would have been reft away with him; for it lay (as in certain cold natures it has a way of doing) almost more in appreciating the ill-fortune of others than any good fortune befalling himself. So nowadays he appreciated the silent clash between Vandervoord and Harriet, the sense of chafing frustration and uneasiness which hung in the air whenever one or the other of them, or sometimes (happiness!) both, happened to cross the agent's line of vision.

No, Harriet could do nothing about it — not as yet. But she could and did refuse (as Vandervoord had known she would) to make any application to her father for his transfer to some other place.

One fine May morning the Captain, tempted by the weather, had his hunter brought to the front steps and prepared with Spens to visit certain outlying districts of Redonda. He accomplished his purpose but at the same time caught a chill on the lungs from the bleak wind that had been blowing all the while. He took to his bed on his return, sweating with fever and anger — and some fear. Here too, for all he could tell, was Retribution — the Writing on the Wall.

He took to his bed, roaring out for Susan Shattuck.

In the old days, whenever the boys or he had been ill (Harriet too, he supposed, though on thinking it over he could never recall a time when Harriet had been really ill) it had been Susan who was delegated to the sick-room and whose hands had both ministered and soothed. So now, nothing would do but that Susan Shattuck must be sent for and must come and nurse him as of old.

Susan, when approached for this purpose by the goosefeather girls — long in the tooth now but still 'girls' to Redonda — prevaricated, wept, begged to be excused, pleading her widowhood (Anderson had not long survived the coal-mines), the baby, anything she could think of. But the Captain had never taken No for an answer from anybody. He sent Spens next, to smoke her out as once he himself had smoked her mother out, nearly thirty years before.

Spens returned with that sideways smile and look that was both his defence and attack. 'She's in pod agin,' he told Harriet. 'Reckon that's why she 'on't come!'

Harriet paused in her task of weighing out the kitchen goods, putting her hand to her back to lessen its aching. She had only recently come in from superintending operations at some distance from the house; she had not sat down since she rose that morning. It was now five o'clock in the afternoon.

'Have you told my father?'

Spens jerked his head sideways briefly, in a gesture which meant Not yet, but my word won't there be a shindy when I do! And how *you* will dislike that, my fine lady, since she's your favourite — and how *I* shall enjoy that, since it's to your disadvantage!

'You are not to tell him,' said Harriet. She finished weighing out the flour with great deliberation, and locked both it and the salt away. (If she did not, in its heavily-taxed state, it would, she knew, be stolen.) 'I will tell him myself.'

If she had not been so tired, a trifle of shame at Spens's news might have visited her; but weariness these days had come to blunt the edge of every emotion — which was its one blessing. She had not seen Susan for months — somehow had always missed her on her occasional visits to Redonda's kitchen. She had not asked after the child or condoled with her about Anderson, or done a thing more than remember to set aside in the dairy the cream and eggs which she had promised her each week — and which she seldom forgot to do; sometimes, perhaps, when she was particularly busy, but not often.

And now Sukey thanked her for the cream and eggs by being, as Spens inelegantly expressed it, 'in pod again'. It was really too vexing! Particularly as the child could not possibly be Anderson's. He had been gone, poor brute, too long.

But her father would have to be told, there was no gainsaying it. She climbed the staircase very slowly, trailing one finger along the woodwork as was her habit, to make sure that the housemaid was thorough in her polishing.

'It's no use, Father. Susan is stubborn and won't come. She's expecting.'

'You mean she's in pod again?'

Harriet bit her lip. That he should repeat Spens' identical expression boded no good.

'Devil take the woman,' said Captain Bromewell faintly, collapsing back amongst his frilled pillows. 'That's no reason! It's a reason for not going to heaven — it's not a reason for refusing to do her duty here by nursing me!'

Harriet came nearer, took up a pillow-frill between finger and thumb, feeling its crispness to see whether the new laundress, like the housemaid, was making a good job of it. Always in the back of her mind these secondary considerations persisted, no matter what moved in the forefront; always there were the things in the house to be seen to — and in the dairy and on the farm; things growing, changing, needing to be replaced.

'Have you seen her?'

Her? Who? She was miles away. 'Tch! Susan, Harry! Have you seen her?'

'No. Spens went, as you told him. She cried and said she wouldn't come.'

The Captain breathed heavily. 'She'll come,' he said, 'if I have to get off this sick-bed to fetch her!'

'But Father — there's not only her own objection. There's the child.'

'What of it? It's an idiot, isn't it?' (It was wonderful how he never forgot or mislaid, in his sharp old brain, any fact relating to his work-people.) 'You can get someone else to mind it. *I* need her more than it does!'

His voice shook for a moment, and he plucked at the sheet with one hand. 'It's too bad that when I'm ill, when I make a perfectly reasonable request, everybody is out to obstruct me!'

'We are *not* out to obstruct you, Father! You shall have her if you want her. I thought that you would not want her, seeing —'

'Well?'

'Seeing she's in her present condition,' finished Harriet lamely.

Controlling one's breath these days, thought the Captain, is just like putting one's horse at a fence in the thick of the hunt. You put him and you put him and it's too damned high and he's fallen there before once; you put him and you put him, dragging him on with your hands and knees, dragging him back when he tries to shirk it — the brute won't go, the hedge is too much for him, then *whack* —

over! and all to do again at the next hedge. That's how difficult breathing is.

The problem became portentous, the hedge ever higher, the hunter ever less willing to attempt the jump; and Harriet stood there babbling about morality! If Susan came, the hedges, he knew, would cease to rear themselves up so gigantically, she would soothe him and smooth the pillows and hold the glass without spilling it as Ivory invariably did; yes — and she would wipe up all the horrible humiliating messes he made too, without making him feel in any way humiliated — just as she used to do in the past.

Mr. Mogus would say she was an adulteress. So, strictly speaking, she was. But Mr. Mogus, God be praised, was in Wiltshire, and in any case there is no sense in being Pharisaical about things. Damn it all — above all he *needed* her — if she had had fifty bastards he would still need her, providing she had not lost her sick-room skill.

'She is a bad — wicked — woman,' he said at length, very slowly, making — as it were — three separate jumps of it on a very uncertain mount. 'I shan't speak to her when she comes. I will write it down on a slate —'

'But Father — your eyes!'

But he had made up his mind. By not speaking to the sinner he would conserve his precious breath and satisfy his conscience — both at one stroke.

'Non-sense,' he said, again very slowly; 'non-sense, (like that) 'I shall write large. Single words. Food. Chamber-pot. Water. She — can read — I hope? Or what did she — live so long in this house for?'

Yes, she could read. Single words, anyhow, written large. She had not been Harriet's companion for so many youthful years for nothing.

That, Harriet could see, settled the matter for him. He had no doubt she would come. He sank back on his pillows, concentrating all his efforts now on the problem of breathing with the most advantage and least expenditure of labour.

Slate. Pencil. Sukey. It was Harriet's business to provide all three. Tired as she was, she went downstairs again, pulled her old red cloak off the chair in the hall where she had dropped it, limp as herself, half an hour before — and went out to the stableyard for a conveyance.

It was typical of her, as it had been of her father, that there was no doubt in her mind that Susan would come. They desired it, they had never either of them taken No for an answer when the power lay in them to compel Yes. They were not going to take No now.

The ride in the wagonette was short but full of birdsong. Sprays, bowers, blossoms of song hung in clusters over her head as she rode — from blackbird, thrush, starling and through them all the *coo-roo coo-roo* of the wood-pigeon who all day long had not ceased his hoarse, urgent love-making in the depths of the wood. She thought, *It is May. They have been singing all day. How is it I have not heard them until now?* And knew that she had been too busy, too utterly tired for the ear to hear or for the heart to be lifted up or the tongue to praise. *Sweet birds*, praised her mind now. *Sweet, sweet birds! Singing and building round Redonda all day long. Just as they always did in play-time, in May-time; just as if there were no trouble here at all . . . And if I could be out in the meadows now I should hear the best of all, the wildest, freest of all — the lark, singing high in the sightless distance above his nest, dropping like a stone with a heart of fire, as the smooth flints upon Aldeburgh beach, if you broke them, have a heart — an inner secret heart of crusted quartz.*

So, through the liquid almost luminous notes of Spring evensong, through lanes heavy with hawthorn scent, and glistening with the evening dew, she came at last to the cabin by the Smithy.

She did not move to get out of the wagonette, for Susan had heard its approach in the distance and came forward to meet her.

Spens was right. She was indeed far gone in pregnancy, though this was not what shocked Harriet; it was the gauntness of her face, the enormous size and depth of her brown eyes, ringed (it would almost seem) with bone instead of flesh. Without moving her arm from the side of the wagonette she sat, staring at her old servant, and Susan, mute, motionless by her gate, stared back.

They looked at each other — motionlessly, compassionately — two tired women, with the bright bubbling birdsong of May, which has never heard of weariness or of anything except beginnings, spilling itself all round them all the while — falling faster than the dew, shining more brightly and shimmeringly than the diamond-points of dew in the heart of each tiny rosette in each spray of mayflower.

In years gone past, at the different stages when young Harriet Bromewell had ever desired anything, it had been Susan's pride, very often, to have been able to put the desired object into her hand almost before she had opened her mouth to demand it. The old perception did not fail her. She knew what Harriet had come for now, and that there was no possibility of refusal.

'Oh Susan, you must come at once,' began Harriet. 'Bring the baby, it shall be looked after. He won't have anyone but you and he says you are a bad wicked woman and he will not speak to you, you are to read what he wants from a slate.'

It was like her not to attempt to cajole; to let one know the worst from the first. But there was a sure way to Susan's heart too, which she did not scorn to follow.

'He can't see at all,' she continued. 'His eyes have to be bathed with oil each day because they get so sore and he says Ivory hurts him. And now he is ill as well, and says he can't breathe — his lungs hurt him when he breathes —'

All this time Susan did not take her eyes from Harriet's face, from the well-loved face — reading such change there that it wrung her heart even more than the account of the sick man. She had (as her mother had had before her) the steady unwavering gaze of certain country-bred people — as if the object looked upon were being learned by heart, or could yield up richer information about itself the longer it was observed.

So it was she gazed at Harriet, desiring deeply to know what could have brought about such change in those features which were as intimately familiar to her as the features of her own child.

The longer she gazed the larger her eyes seemed to grow, the thinner her face. Cows that are in calf, Harriet knew, achieve an attenuated look about their masks and snouts — as if all the purpose of their life were concentrated for the time being in their swelling sides. The head and muzzle appear to shrink as the belly enlarges. But there was surely more to Susan's case than that!

A dreadful suspicion assailed her.

'Susan, when did you last bring your basket for the goods I laid aside for you?'

'I 'an't 'ad no goods, Miss Harriet, since last toime I saw you —

'But I *told* you, Susan! I told them I would put the things aside each week for you! The brown pullet's eggs and the jug of cream. I told you to call for them each week!'

Someone had blundered. Anger filled her, and a humiliating recollection as well of those weeks when, contrary to promise, she had *not* remembered . . . Had Susan come during one of those weeks and, finding herself forgotten, gone away again discouraged?

'That's roight, Miss Harry. I come and brought your mended things. But they 'an't never told me of no goods — '

No. Someone had *not* blundered, someone had thieved and should be made to suffer for it! Her back ached as if a knife had been laid, sharp blade against it, and were slicing it open with a most delicate and precise malice.

'Ah well — never mind now. We've no time for it now. Fetch your things — and the child — '

At least she will be better fed, she comforted herself, when she's back at Redonda. From the look of it she's starving.

Driving back again through the hawthorn lanes, with the shower of birdsong thicker than ever in the twilight as if the full orchestra knew that it must soon end, *crescendo*, its chorus of triumphant praise — Harriet said as in duty bound to do:

'You *are* a wicked girl, you know, Sukey. Who is it this time?'

Susan was silent, absorbed (or pretending to be) in the as-silent boy in her lap. He was a big boy now, nearly two, but he lay back against his mother as if he were still helpless, letting the bushes flicker past his eyes without making any effort to take in the picture — or any other part of the surprising scene.

'You know, I suppose,' said Harriet, 'that my Father could turn you off for this and put you on the Parish?'

Even that dread threat drew no response.

'It's extremely silly not to tell me, Susan. I can well understand you being ashamed — for it *is* a shameful and disgusting state of affairs and the last thing I should have expected of you, knowing the advantages you had at Redonda, and how gently you were brought up there . . . But I can't see you righted if you don't tell me. You really are enough to drive one to distraction! You starve and say nothing — you break the Fifth Commandment and say nothing —'

Susan muttered then, chin resting on her baby's unheeding head, something about not wanting to get anyone into trouble. . . .

'But you are *in* trouble, Sukey! It won't help you if others keep out of it; which they shan't, once I catch them!' But whether she was thinking of the thief in Redonda's larder or of Susan's partner in adultery was not clear; perhaps of both.

Still her servant was unpersuaded, dumb.

Harriet sighed: 'Very well. You always *were* a mule for obstinacy! But if the man comes hanging round Redonda, I shall soon discover him and then, I warn you, Susan, he shall hear just what I think of him, and shall get what he deserves!'

Clattering into the darkening stableyard, she jumped down first, flinging the reins to the stable-boy and turning to help down her doubly-burdened companion.

Standing thus, with her hands momentarily under Susan's elbows, some generous impulse made her exclaim, despite her weariness, despite the common-sense that told her Susan had no real say in the matter at all:

'Thank you for coming, Sue, it will please him.'

The tired eyes smiled into the tired eyes.

'That's for you, Miss Harry, that's not for nawthen else. If *you* fare to want me —'

But that was too much — an intrusion.

'Why should I want you? Why should I want anyone? It's for the Captain, you know that very well! Now go into the kitchen and have a solid meal for once in a way. I am still angry with you, you know, for being such a fool about the goods I left for you!'

Next morning there was, as the kitchen staff put it, 'forever of a shindy' over the matter of the stolen rations. The culprit was discovered, scarified, and handed over to the Parish authorities for summary punishment. The culprit implored to be kept on at any price, fearing starvation more than the constable — begging to be whipped, docked of a year's wages — anything. But Harriet was adamant. The culprit had taken good food meant for Susan, week after week, month after month. Let her starve now if need be! Redonda would not harbour her. And she was dismissed from mind almost as speedily as from service.

Under the odd monastic silence that ruled in Captain Bromewell's sickroom, he very slowly improved. The doctor was loud in praise of the nurse's attentions, the patient continued to say nothing, except in large print on a slate. He still breathed with difficulty and required constant attention even at night and — for the first time in his life — to be told of the business of the day began to distress instead of to satisfy him. More and more he left things to his daughter, devoted more and more time and attention to the crafty tussling with his lung-trouble, manœuvring for position against it with dogged persistence.

But large affairs cannot be so handed over, nor great decisions delegated, nor important documents signed *per pro*, without some sort of power of attorney, and this, perforce (in the absence of his sons) devolved upon Harriet.

Mr. Marsham came down to arrange it, bestowing it upon her as gingerly as he had bestowed everything since that first unlucky kiss. She took the gingerliness as a compliment — but not so his renewed friendliness with Vandervoord.

It disgusted her. While she was busy, even until late at night with unending papers, the two men would sit in the dining-room below her, drinking Captain Bromewell's wine and discussing matters which did not interest her and could *never* interest her — not even if she understood them which, thank God, she told herself, she would disdain ever to try to do!

Spasms of trembling fury possessed her at such times, sitting alone up in her room, surrounded by papers, while the murmur of their conversation and confidential laughter, together with the odour of their coffee and tobacco, drifted idly upwards. If she listened (which she disdained to do; had she not more important things to do — *work* to do?) she knew they would be talking of Bonaparte, always of Bonaparte, drawing plans of campaign on the tablecloth with knives and forks and salt-cellars, the horse-radish sauce shall-we-say representing Bonaparte, *this* France, *that* Russia, *this* Naples, *that* Sardinia, and if he goes *there* we shall certainly come *there*, my God was there never to be an end to this endless talk about Bonaparte — was life ever to be again as it used to be — no sinister letter N directing it?

Vandervoord appeared not to see her these days, except as a stranger whose abilities he respected but whose friendship he had no desire to gain. As soon as Marsham had departed for London again she dressed ship for action and ordered him to come to her, the full authority of her father upon her.

It was the same room in which she had first seen him, standing in the same way before her father, extremely respectfully and attentively and yet (as she had felt from the very beginning) with a fundamental contempt of them both, and of anything they could do to him.

Looking across the desk now at his hands, clasping one another loosely before him (she would not look at his face; to look at his face unloosed a whole flood of tenderness in her, made her eyes well with tears whose proximity she had never suspected) Harriet informed him of the position. She had her father's authority behind her; behind them both the authority of the Military Commandant and the Lord Lieutenant.

'You are not to go any more to Slaughden,' she informed him.

His hands moved a little, the fingers flexing and stretching as if they had taken her command between them and were handling it, testing its strength and integrity.

'You persisted in doing it,' she went on, 'when Spens advised you against it. You persisted in going when my father spoke to you about it. After the letter from the Military Commandant you still went, determined to flout us all —'

'And what will you do to me if I persist still, as you call it, in "flouting" you?'

She hesitated. It was a trial of strength that for once in her life she did not accept with gusto. Her voice trembled.

'I shall have to inform the Military authorities.'

'Don't be a little fool, Harry! What is all this farce about? I asked you, months ago, to get my release for me. You refused. Do you suppose I am still so anxious to stay here that I am frightened by your threats? I shall go to Slaughden when I please and drink there as often as I please, and you may tell the Commandant *what* you please; the result as you know will only be to enable me to get away from here — in one way or another — it really does not signify — '

The drowned man lying upon the beach with his lips gagged with seaweed, she thought, must have struggled a little before he drowned — must have fought for his life, as *I* would, as my father would . . . but Van does not fight, he slips down, he *invites* the waves to drown him; if one were to lean over the side of the boat now, imperilling one's own safety, reaching out an arm — both arms — to him, most desperately trying to save him — he would shake them off.

Do not look at his face, his most dear face. Do not even look over and beyond his head because in doing this you cannot avoid seeing his head and loving it, and his shoulders, and the neck round which the arms wrap themselves so naturally, as if they have come home at last; round which even now, at this moment, they ache beyond words to be.

She said aloud: 'I hate you and I love you. I am in most deadly pain for you. When I wake in the mornings the pain is ready waiting for me, it wraps itself as heavily as lead round my heart; there is only one second of consciousness each day that I can be happy in — before I remember. . . . Oh, is it so with you, Van? Is it so with you?'

My darling, said her mind. *Speak to me. We have been so close together in joy, have been so much part of each other. Is it credible that being now in this mortal distress, we cannot be equally close together in pain?*

'Don't — ' he said. '*Ma Mie* — my dearest — don't.'

The desk was no longer between them, her arms were round his neck again, strange homecoming that should have been so sweet and dear — and which held, she found, precisely no significance at all.

She said, 'You don't answer! As long as I have known you I have been asking you questions — and you have never answered!'

'Perhaps because there *is* no answer,' he replied. 'Have you thought of that?'

No, she had not thought of that. There was always an answer, even if it was one that one didn't want — one that had to be denied, fought against, contradicted —

'I beg of you,' he said, 'don't try to hold me, Harry darling. There is a devil in me — you must have learned it by now — that won't allow me to be held. It was what I was afraid of, from the first — when I begged you so incautiously not to come near me! I knew it could only end in our destruction —'

Some fearful hint of what he had once been through, at some time in those past years, those lost, secret, *separate* years of which he had never told her, made Harriet's heart even heavier here, although that had hardly seemed possible.

'You don't want me to lose my reason, I am sure,' he went on quietly. 'I haven't my freedom, as you have. At least leave me my reason! It is not such an easy thing to retain, you know — it is lively, restive — the thread that binds it is very slender —'

'I won't try to hold you — I would never try to hold anyone that hated me!'

He sighed. 'If you can say that it shows how little purpose there is in my trying to explain myself —'

'Do you love me, Van? Only say if you love me!'

For answer he pressed his lips swiftly upon her forehead, laid his cheek upon her forehead, framed the old *Je te veux! Je te veux!* with silent lips, but did not speak.

There was a pause, long enough for three generations to be born, to suffer, wither and die. Finally Harriet began again, quietly:

'What do you want to do? Where do you want to go?'

'Away — God knows where. Wherever I am sent, I suppose.'

'Is it — is it because you are cross with us for not letting you go with Captain Twigg?'

'Twigg? Which was he?' ... No, apparently that was not the reason — at least no cause for jealousy *there*!

'And if the Authorities do *not* send you away?'

'They will do if you ask them. You know that.'

Yes, she knew that.

'And — if I *don't* ask them? Forgive me, Van! I am trying not to be stupid, I am trying to speak plainly and tell you everything.' Her voice trembled again. 'There is — a — a possibility — there is a danger — Oh, you know what I am like; it may be that however much I am convinced *here*' (touching her forehead) 'that I should do so — down *here*' (touching her heart) 'it may be otherwise.'

'You mean you won't tell them?'

'I mean that I may not be able to. . . . Oh, don't despair of me, Van! I will think and *think*, I will try to see what you mean, the justice of it — yes, quite dispassionately — Don't despair of me!' she begged him again.

It was not the way the interview should have ended, with a plea from the hand that wielded the power, to the powerless one. But had any single interview with Vandervoord ever conducted itself according to plan, according to sense, according — above all — to desire?

'Very well,' he conceded (the powerless hand relenting, commanding the hand that wielded power), 'I believe you, and that you will try. I know it is very hard for you, my dearest, who have always had everything your own way — or turned it into your own way — it comes to the same.'

He bent again and kissed her again, briefly.

'And, while you are thinking,' he said, 'forgive me, or try to! I know that I must seem so very cruel to you, who would not — God knows — if he could help it, hurt a single hair of your head — '

That night, Harriet woke in the middle of a hideous nightmare, screaming loudly, so loudly that the noise brought Susan barefoot to her bedside before she was properly awake.

Speaking thickly, quickly, she said — not knowing what she said or to whom she said it:

'Oh — he is going, he is slipping, slipping! I can't hold on to him any longer — there is too much water in the boat — '

'*Sh — Sh*,' soothed Susan, holding Harriet in her arms so firmly that the waters receded in the face of this loving pressure and support, and the boat ceased to rock, turned instead (in jerking sequences) into her own familiar bed. . . . 'He 'oont go, my darling. He 'oont go and leave you, ne yet the child. He must love the child!'

CHAPTER XXI

LOUISA, AND SOME MORE LETTERS

> Quoth he, Most lovely maid
> My troth shall aye endure,
> And be O be thou not dismayed
> But rest thee still secure.
> My love shall be the same,
> It shall ne'er, shall ne'er decay,
> But shall shine without all blame
> But shall shine without all blame
> Though body turn to clay.
>
> *Old Song*

THE tide in the affairs of men — that auspicious tide that had swept Bonaparte's army on to victory after victory ever since it had first marched under the Republican banner, began — though not to recede — at least to move a little more slowly and laggingly after the Battle of the Nile. Taking Fate by surprise as it were, and attacking her in the flank whilst she was engaged in a frontal attack upon him, the chief actor in all these events deserted his overseas army and arrived back in France — solitary, but with such an aura of personal power and absolute self-confidence that the court-martial which would surely have been meted out to any other commander in such circumstances not only failed to materialize but the Government which would presumably have authorized it collapsed before him. He had landed — if not a defeated, then at least a stale-mated and (one would have supposed) almost a dis-graced, Commander — on the shores of France; he had deserted the flower of the French army in the moment of its need — that army which he had promised to lead into the most fertile places in the world, there to find glory and riches. At home, he found the French armies also sensing that the tide was at repletion-point; they had been pushed back a little in Germany and in Italy; their strategy had begun to include (for the first time) plans for retreat and retrenchment in cases of necessity — though still, and always, *pour mieux sauter*. Yet a certain Corsican general, having left his own forces besieged in Egypt and returning to find the other armies (whose strategy had been as much his as the Army of the Nile) almost equally at a disadvantage, was no more embarrassed or imperilled by these circumstances than by any other circumstances yet shaped by History. Despite them, almost in a day, he made himself sole master of France.

News of this *coup d'état* — so ominous and so utterly unexpected — did not disturb Captain Bromewell and the other John Bulls like him nearly as much as Mr. Pitt's new Income Tax — which had reached the portentous and hitherto unparalleled proportion of ten per cent. That the tax was designed chiefly to enable His Majesty's Government to finance a successful war against a country which did not approve — in theory — of even one per cent private capital, and would certainly tax them infinitely more grievously if it were to win — was the last thing that occurred to these gentlemen. They were, together with the manufacturers in the North and the Midlands, the New Rich of that generation — and to have their just profits milked away from them in such unheard-of proportions called forth almost as much outcry and commotion as if the enemy had already landed at Dover or Harwich. The aristocracy, milked similarly, made less outcry — but then practice they say makes perfect, and generations spent in giving financial aid to their king (even if sometimes not the rightful king) and country had given the gentry plenty of practice. It is the freshly-calved heifer that kicks over the bucket, not the experienced old cow.

Meanwhile, emissaries did not cease to pass between the belligerent nations — with France ever more ready to talk peace as she saw, ever more clearly, the crying need for a breathing-space in which she might consolidate the gains she had already made; and Britain ever ready to listen to proposals, even while she never ceased to go on girding her tardy armour about her. Ten thousand volunteer troops drilled in London alone, in addition to over five thousand red-coated regulars and two thousand horse. It was to the sound of their trumpets and the tramp of their feet that Pitt listened, more than to the protests from the farmers and manufacturers. *Fifteen millions of people must give way to Forty!* And the French ex-general Doumouriez, refugee and military adviser now in a country he had once himself prepared plans to invade and conquer, wrote from the centre of its tolerant safety:

> I will not speak of the particular defence of London, for I refuse to believe that an enemy could ever get near enough to the Metropolis, when the whole of England was up in arms, when patriotism was firing one of the bravest nations in Europe; and when that Nation was fighting for all it held most dear and sacred.

When Bonaparte's latest peace offer came, it was, therefore, repelled with scorn; and Income Tax was still ten per cent, and Volunteers still went on drilling — with one musket between every four men — and the conditions of life for the average island house-holder became, as invariably they do in wartime, progressively but very slowly more irksome and harder to endure.

Captain Bromewell was not up and about again before Midsummer. Susan had been brought to bed of her second child as unobtrusively as possible and had continued to nurse him and it in shifts. This time it was a normal baby but its father remained, as Susan had intended he should, a mystery. So long as it was kept out of earshot of the Captain (together with its brother), that was all he cared about. He had other matters to interest him just then, than the problematical fathers of Redonda's bastards.

If he could have known that his daughter Harriet was in precisely the same shameful condition as his sick-nurse had been, Captain Bromewell might very well have been shocked at this juncture out of his renewed absorption in agricultural and county matters. It was a piquant situation for all but those immediately involved; the daughter of a wealthy farmer, brought up to consider herself, if not genteel in every respect, at least superior in every respect and to every situation; who had been superior, too, in the past, to suitors who had always been, in the eyes of gossiping neighbours, much too good for that hoighty-toighty creature; who had travelled abroad finally to find a partner equal to herself and (not discovering

any such paragon) had returned to Redonda like the Virgin Queen
— its queen — despite the fact that her father and brothers were the
rightful owners and heirs; a girl who had led poor Mr. Spens a
disgraceful dance, for ever countermanding that knowledgeable
man's instructions and thinking she knew better; who had not
hesitated to insult the rector about his geese and to endanger his
daughter's life on the right-of-way; whose habits were so violent
and so arbitrary that only the other day she had thrown out poor
Mary So-and-so for the most trifling offence connected with a
parcel in the larder; who had whipped that poor Susan Shattuck
for being in the family way and injured the unborn child thereby;
and who was, finally, bringing her poor father's hairs in sorrow to
the grave by dint of the life she led him and her bullying dictatorial
manners and her way of considering herself superior to everything
and everybody in the whole born world. How are the mighty
fallen and the weapons of war perished! Such neighbours, only too
anxious to avoid encounter with the redoubtable Miss Bromewell
in the past, now went out of their way to meet her in the highways
and byways, to be able to say they had seen her in her shameful
condition and to report with smacking lips how sadly changed she
was.

Nothing could better exemplify Harriet's innate authority,
through the whole course of her life, than the fact that though at this
time she had the whole of the surrounding countryside against her —
each one of the neighbours anxious to make as much mischief out
of the situation as possible and bring as much unpleasantness to her
— there was not one among them, man or woman, who dared to
visit the house and disclose the truth about his daughter to Captain
Bromewell. Not a servant, sniggering behind the balustrade from a
safe distance as her mistress laboriously passed, would have given a
single word of evidence against her, if she had been called summarily
into the Captain's presence and bribed or bullied there to tell
what she knew. Even if death could conceivably have been the
penalty for remaining silent, still they feared Harriet worse than
death, and that her calm implacable revenge would pursue them in
the hereafter, as effectively as now her just criticisms pursued them
and found them out in every quarter of farm or house. They did

not love her, had indeed no cause to; but there were many amongst them who would have said, as Kent said of King Lear, that there was that about her that they fain would serve — the quality of Authority. That quality did not diminish in their eyes because she was in that 'shameful disgraceful' condition in which Susan Shattuck had been; rather, it added a new and terrifying stature to her authority — that she could do even this thing — she, Miss Bromewell — she, a lady belonging to a powerful and proud family — and still surmount the situation. Even the famished wives of the outlying tenants and labourers of Redonda, coming once a week to the newly-instituted Free Dinner served out by Harriet in the Great Barn, took the bowl from her hands with a bobbed curtsy still to her position as 'the lady', and not as the Benefactress of the place. Such is the power of personality.

So it came about that the servants attending at the Bromewell table came to behold Harriet sitting at its head, silent, brooding, *enceinte*, while her father, blind as that Justice he so frequently symbolized, sat opposite her, declaiming (while he cracked his walnuts) against the state the country was coming to, particularly its neglect of Scripture and of the stern moral qualities which had been commanded of us — as cold and solid and heavy as the stone upon which Moses had first received them. No wonder, he was wont to say at the fifth glass, that we had to suffer the tribulations of war — for our house was built on sand, divided against itself, a whited sepulchre and so unprepared that inevitably the Strong Man had come (as prophesied) to despoil it. Furthermore, Armageddon and the Third Flood (for the First was what happened to Noah and the second to Louis and Marie Antoinette) — yes, the Third Flood was undeniably upon its way towards *us*. It would roll on inexorably, overwhelmingly, separating the sheep from the goats, the wary from the blind, the saints from the sinners and delivering them all up, on the crest of an abominably high wave, to the Judgment Above.

Anxious at this stage to miss no door, however humble or obscure, through which he might conceivably enter and be saved, Captain Bromewell began to show hospitality to wandering non-conformists, Wesleyans and non-Wesleyans — heartily despising

their (to him) essential common-ness but not disdaining, nevertheless, to kneel with them and be prayed for — and to command the
indoor staff also to kneel and be prayed for — lest even this procedure might find grace in the sight of the inscrutable Lord. He began,
too, to take an intense interest in prognostications and prophecies
of all sorts, calculations from inspired schoolmasters revealing
when the war would end, to the exact day and hour; interpretations
by gypsies of reputedly royal blood, of the Book of Revelation
and the inner significance of the Beast and the numerals 666. Then,
too, if he could persuade one of the wandering ministers to stay a
day or so with him, he would enlist their good services as temporary
secretaries whilst he made endless dispositions, memorials, suggestions for pamphlets, even a Tract for the Times, built round the
word *Repent!* On another occasion he would invite a couple of
distressed French émigrés of the Roman Catholic persuasion (of
which the country at that time was receiving a continual trickle)
and would allow them to turn the morning-room into a temporary
Oratory; not actually going so far as to ask to partake of their
services conducted there, but sitting just outside the half-closed
door, hands crossed on the stick between his knees and taking it all
in — so as to be able to plead in the hereafter (if ever accused of
having been blind in *that* particular direction) *My spirit was willing
but my flesh was weak.*

Through all these alarums and excursions at Redonda, Harriet
remained hostess; calmly, indifferently accepting and making
provision for the various and varying guests, as completely confident
of her ability to prevent awkward questions emanating from them
to her father as she was of her ability to control the curiosity and
malice of the servants. Neither failed her. Extraordinary as it may
seem, she survived the visitors — all of them — sending them on
their way finally with no word vouchsafed as to whether she was
maid, married, widowed or the Whore of Babylon. Authority
could do no more — not even when Bonaparte wielded it.

But the strain upon bodily fibre, no less than upon personal pride,
was intense. If Susan had not been there — not beside her but
nevertheless within reach — all those endless months, possibly she
could not have borne it, must have broken down and given way.

But as Susan had been the first to inform her of her condition, so she was the last to leave her in it. She did not leave her, in fact, and yet was never too much present — sleeping at night in Clement's old dressing-room, where a crib had been put up for the elder child. It was at the end of a passage and so out of earshot of the Captain's bedroom, though within reach of the smallest sound from Harriet's. Harriet's nightmares, off and on, continued, despite that infallible cure, the flint with a hole in it, which Susan had threaded through and hung over the bed-head.

As to Vandervoord, what can be said of the reactions of that changeable and unpredictable creature? He had received her news with elation, he was really (though Harriet could hardly, after his recent behaviour, credit it) pleased and proud. He wanted to tell the Captain of it, the village of it, the world of it — talked of everything in the world in connection with the child-to-be except of that marriage between its parents which would have a little amended but not cured the blot of its illegitimacy. He was sweet and tender to Harriet again, calling her again *Ma Mie*, begging her to take care of herself, for all their sakes, to sit down and take things easy — to consider, not the (to him) inconceivably dreary details of farm management but the immensely exciting promising future of the child. *Shall not thou and I, between St. Denis and St. George, compound a boy, half French, half English, who shall go to Constantinople and take the Turk by the beard?* Well, the boy was compounded but the future remained to be planned for him — a brilliant future, an engineer's future in a world built of steam and steel. 'Think of it!' he said, taking off his glasses the better to see her (he still had the delusion that he could see better without his glasses for everything except reading, although he had come to need them for all occasions), 'he will be free!'

Loving him for his enthusiasm, and for the surprising innocence of his appearance when he suddenly, as then, removed his glasses (as if a child peeped out from behind the mask of a man), Harriet's heart smote her that he should still be chafing so under his parole. But he did not — it appeared — mean that at all; tossed her condoling words aside swiftly, almost contemptuously: 'I mean he will live in a free world, Harry! A new world, a new century, for

honestly I think we are in the death-throes of the old, and a good thing too. He will be free to think for himself, and to plan for himself; no imbecile restrictions and savage superstitions to wear him down, no soul-destroying pressure stifling him — '

Was Marriage an imbecile restriction, a soul-destroying superstition? These forebodings Harriet, who would have fought a lion single-handed in the desert any day, was too much coward to discuss; and it did not seem to occur to Vandervoord that she would want to discuss them, or indeed that they had any relevance to the subject in hand. This — although she had reproved him for formulating the idea of telling her father, and he had replied: 'Oh yes, of course he won't want to have a *foreign* grandchild, will he? That wouldn't do at all! By God, I hope he is a real *square-head*, Harry, like me, and that he will embarrass his grandfather by his appearance every time he looks at him!'

At another time he would ask, as if with the engaging concern of a friend interested (but by no means intimately) in Harriet's day-to-day worries and problems: 'How long are you going to keep it from the old man? Are you going to spring a surprise on him?'

How easy it should have been to reply to that, 'Only as long as it is a disgrace and shame to him and to the family name. Make a runaway marriage with me — to Ipswich, Norwich — anywhere where I may conveniently get back soon enough to superintend things here — and I will tell him the minute we return — yes, *and* make him proud of it, as surely as my name is Harriet Vandervoord!'

But her name had only been that in her dreams, in the sand, and she could not bring herself to say it, ever.

Vandervoord had always been so fond of children, too. He would let Susan's slow, simple-minded Tommy come into his workshop next the stables and muddle about amongst his things, while Spens or any other adult was positively forbidden to enter at all, much less to touch a tool on his table. He would pick up the lumpish boy in his arms and hold him, calling forth whatever feeble spark of curiosity and vitality was in him with the utmost nimbleness and fanning it to almost normal flame. This naturally made him Susan's devoted admirer for ever, but did not please Harriet.

'I can't think what attracts you in the boy,' she said once, and again: 'I wish you would not call out to *me* when you are playing with Tommy. I am trying to see him as little as possible; I don't want my own child to be a lunatic!'

'Oh Harry,' he protested laughingly, 'he is *not* a lunatic! He is wiser than most of us. It is just that he does not excite himself, as we do, over trivial affairs —'

Did she scent reproof in that, or was it just that she was becoming, in these ever more trying days of pregnancy, more and more sensitive and suspicious?

Watching the boy utterly absorbed in fitting a nail that Vandervoord had given him into a hole in his bureau, Harriet exclaimed: 'He can't even talk yet — and his nose is dirty. Pah! I don't want to look at him any more! I can't think what you see in him —'

'Freedom,' said Vandervoord; 'he is *free*! He is not bound, as I am, to sit here waiting for the war to end, and for some fool in an office to sign a paper at last granting me something that *he* has never lacked; he is not bound, as you are, by a never-ceasing round of employments. The clock does not touch him. War does not touch him. Love itself does not touch him — have you noticed, Harry, that he cares no more for his mother than for any of the rest of the servants? That he will go as readily to any of them, when *they* call, as he will to her? And *that*, you know, must be the greatest freedom of all!'

'If *my* child went as readily to strangers as to me,' Harriet replied, should not call it free, I should call it unnatural —'

It was typical that in conversations she invariably said My child, My baby — never Ours; that in conversation he said Your child, Your baby; she out of a pride that did not dare to claim a link that he ignored, he out of the inviolable separateness of his own nature. Whichever of them spoke it was always Harriet's child, Harriet's baby — a fatherless creature from the first, just as surely as Susan Shattuck's children were.

What became increasingly hard for Harriet to endure was the disparity between her knowledge of Vandervoord and of the rest of life. As her experience in agriculture had enlarged, Harriet had grown to tell from a single grain of barley the probable weight of a sack of it, the price of a comb or the yield of a field. From the behaviour of birds over ploughed land, or from the look or direction of the clouds, she could forecast the weather and ordain the day's labour accordingly. If a cow were due to calve, or a mare to foal, or a clutch of eggs to hatch — it was the mistress of Redonda who could foretell, better than any of the rest of them, the exact day and hour of the happening. *Perhaps*, she had once pitifully persuaded herself, *it will be like that with Van; it only needs patient application on my part, and persistence — and the knack will suddenly come*. He will present me with a problem and I shall work at it and puzzle at it and quite suddenly I shall pierce to the heart of his secret. I shall understand him as well as I do Father, or Clancy — as well as I once did Clement — and nothing that he can say or do in the future will be painful or perplexing any more because it will be *understood*.

Alas for Harriet! She could discern the face of the skies indeed but not the signs of the times. And the signs of the times were ominous.

From the moment when she had first gone to her lover and informed him of her condition, Harriet had considered herself released from the promise to 'think it over', or to reason herself into that frame of mind in which she would see (as he desired her to) the justice of his plea to be released from his parole at Redonda; and — devolving on that — from active intervention on her part to secure his transfer. Nor did he refer to the matter again, whether because he saw the futility of doing so, or no longer desired to, was — like so much else concerning him — not to be guessed.

Two incidents stood out during the time she went through, prior to the birth of the child. The first was an indiscreet call on her, in her bedroom, one night when he was drunk — to inform her that 'all of Slaughden' had just joined him in drinking to the unborn's good fortune; followed immediately by an avoiding of her altogether for three weeks and a subsequent urgent but inexplicable plea with her to bring about a miscarriage, since any child of his was doomed and bound to come to disaster.

The other incident was the arrival of two letters, brought to Vandervoord from the Netherlands by Captain Twigg — who, being considered too ungodly these days to enter the house itself, was entertained in the stables by Spens, who still remained in close friendship with the sinner. Harriet, recognizing the Captain's gig as she saw it standing in the stable-yard one day, saw, too, Spens invite Captain Twigg in — saw him, further, make a gesture to Vandervoord, shouting at the same time some sentence she could not, through the closed window, hear. But the unusualness of the circumstances brought her to a standstill by the staircase window and kept her watching. She was more surprised still to see Vandervoord accept Spens' apparent invitation, and, bending his head (in a gesture how reminiscent!) enter the stables with the other two and shut the door behind him.

The door was not more firmly shut against her than he was himself, next day. Twigg had departed again, Spens was furtively contrite, conscious of having started work late and of being (because of the bottle) unable to cope properly with it when started. Vandervoord was pale, silent, preoccupied.

To Harriet's natural inquiries, 'What did he want you for? What was it about?' he would not answer, said it was nothing — that being barred from the house the fellow naturally wanted company — with other equally lame and unsatisfying responses. He acknowledged the receipt of no letters, yet Harriet, going two days later into his workshop with some message for him from her father, lit upon them as it were quite by accident.

The day had been a scorching one. Vandervoord, busy still about improvements to his pump-mills, had gone down to the Shearings in shirt and breeches, leaving his old jacket hanging on a nail behind the workshop door. Harriet, seeing it hanging there and wondering idly whether in this heat he still carried the map about with him or left it in his jacket pocket, felt it to see.

The map was not in the pocket, but there were two letters, addressed in an identical spidery handwriting and written, so she supposed, in Dutch. Though they had been in his possession only two days they bore already signs of much handling, of folding and re-folding. Without stopping to reflect she took them out, opening them up and standing there in the dusty sunlight, peering down at those hieroglyphics which must have told so much and meant so much to him, after the years of silence — yet which told her precisely nothing.

A futile rage possessed her, a consuming ache of jealousy swallowing up every other emotion and shaking the crisp pages in her hand until they rattled, stirring the golden motes of dust in the apprehensive air. It seemed impossible that, desiring to read them so intensely — to know so beyond all words what was in the letters — the very force of her desire should not in some way prove translator and make all plain. Something was written here which had moved him tremendously — something which belonged to that other life of which he had told her nothing, *nothing* — though every moment of her life from childhood had been laid at his idle disposal if he so wished it, a book whose lock was in his keeping, which he might open and read at leisure.

Why, if they were not important, had he not told her casually of the arrival of the letters? Why, if they *were* important, had he not come to her at once, asking her to share in his happiness, telling her his good fortune and of the news contained in the letters and who the writer was, and what like? Whichever way she looked she bruised herself against these tormenting inquiries. Well — if *he* would not tell her, Twigg would tell her! He had been the intermediary — he at least could not withstand her demands!

But before she could formulate any plan for getting hold of that elusive Sea Fencible and secret agent, her pains had started and the child she had begun to think would never be born was at last upon its way.

How she survived the last dinner with her father she never knew, but go through it she had to, or else confess an indisposition which might lead to awkward inquiries.

Periodically, as the meal endlessly (or so it seemed) progressed, she had to rise to her feet and march about the carpet to cover her ever-increasing distress at the spasms of pain, until he asked her testily what the devil she was at, tramping up and down like a sentry? Immediately the walnuts were put on the table she left him to them, pleading urgent business with her papers upstairs; and upstairs she went, leaning heavily upon Susan, with the grotesque dignity of those great with child.

The child was born late next morning, in the same room in which she had been born, thirty years before. A midwife familiar about the estate delivered it and Susan took it and brooded over it with a wordless tenderness — that instinctive offering-up of joy and praise which issues forth from ignorant people on the birth of anything new into a world already old with sin and sorrow. It had long been arranged that she should be wet-nurse, thus relieving Harriet from a too-embarrassing tie. Harriet indeed had kept her well-fed with that purpose in mind, as well as from a natural desire to make up for past neglect and to see her old servant well done by.

It was a girl. 'Anyone can get a boy, it takes a man to get a girl,' quoted the midwife comfortingly as she plied the mother, chilled to the bone with shock and supreme effort, with warm drinks. Harriet, never having foreseen the possibility (like Vandervoord she had been sure it would be a boy) was filled with feeble resentment, so that she wept weakly into her pillow. She would not admit to disappointment — to do that was in some odd way to be defeated in the very first round by the whim of sex in her own child; but she refused to look at it when it was held up to her and complained feebly to Susan that 'the letters' were very hard to lie on, they were bruising her cheek.

'Did I make a noise?' she asked the midwife, and was relieved to hear No, nothing uncommon — and that all the while Sukey, as instructed, had been singing and banging about with a broom. No inquiries had come from below stairs; the worst crisis was over. If only Susan would take the tiresome letters away now she would get some sleep!

The midwife looked round-eyed at Susan, then commiseratingly at the fretful worn face of Harriet turning restlessly on her pillows. Sukey bent down and removed the imaginary letters with real care.

'See,' she said softly, 'you'll sleep now — you'll be off in slumberland in two minut's, Miss Harry.'

So the long deception was played out to its successful conclusion, and a life begotten, conceived and given birth to at Redonda, and by the mistress and the prisoner of Redonda, entered the world without the cognizance of the master of Redonda altogether. Fate had been kind in little things if not in great ones. Clancy (the one danger) had not been inspired to come home at any time during the pregnancy and Sukey's children, already on the premises, could be blamed for any wailings or cryings in the night.

A feverish cold, they said, kept Harriet in her bed for a week at that time. Captain Bromewell, led by Ivory, used to stump up to sit in her bedroom daily and complain for about a quarter of an hour, so reassuring himself of her slow convalescence. Susan attended her. There was no sign, in fact, of Susan ever leaving Redonda again after that compulsory return to the fold — a fact which suited everybody very well at that juncture — most particularly Harriet. But as soon as she could manage it, at the earliest possible moment, she was up and about again, paler than usual, youthfully slim once more — but essentially the same in her driving-power and dealings with the work-people — above all in her sense of authoritative control.

Had the baby been a boy it was to have been called Louis — a name of romantic and aristocratic associations to Harriet, possibly of something more to Vandervoord, for he had suggested it himself in one of his rare enthusiastic moments, and Harriet had been enchanted to fall in with the suggestion. They had never concerned themselves with a name for a girl, and this complete lack of interest showed itself again now, when, out of chagrin or laziness or perhaps both, it was decided merely to extend the original choice into the form of Louisa.

Even that, Vandervoord would like to have been able to withhold:

'Poor brat!' he had said, 'she should be left to choose her own name!'

'Since she can't be christened,' agreed Harriet, 'I see nothing to prevent her doing so when she is of age.' Meanwhile, the name of Louisa served well enough.

... It was no use: memory of the letters, more accurately of his concealment of the news of the arrival of the letters, still rankled with Harriet. She could not be one with him in gladness over her safe confinement, in admiration of the baby. The letters came between. They came even between the lines of her day-to-day correspondence — that spidery, indecipherable handwriting showering itself down, a clogging midsummer gossamer over her bold housekeeping writing and her farm accounts. At last she could bear it no longer. She accused Vandervoord:

'Van — you had letters from home. Twigg brought them to you. Why did you not tell me!'

It *was* an accusation, not a question. His face took on at once that secret guarded look she knew so well, and had learned to dread so deeply.

'Perhaps I knew you would find it out for yourself. Not much escapes you, does it?'

'But it was *unkind*, Van! I can't understand you! I know how you have longed for news from — from over there — at least I have guessed it. You might at least have told me, even if you don't want to tell me what is *in* the letters!'

'Why,' he asked, 'should I tell you what is in the letters?'

It was horrible, inconceivable, but he really wanted to know. It really seemed to him that an affair which must concern him so deeply should still be no business of hers. She tried again. (One must try again, or die.)

'After all we have been to each other,' she said, 'after my being so ill — after Louisa —'

'My darling,' he said, 'what is this, a conversation or a text for repentance? I have work to do'—he indicated his desk, his never-ceasing employments; '*you* have work to do — can we not agree to disagree over this matter? I shall never think as you do, not if we both live to be a hundred — which God in His infinite mercy forbid!'

Harriet burst out crying, 'Oh, why did I ever learn French!' she sobbed. 'Why didn't I learn *Dutch* when I was at Lausanne with Clement? Then at *least* you couldn't have tormented me about what was in the letters — I could have known for *myself*!'

He took her in his arms at that, amused and yet contrite — comforting her, loving her (as he could not help doing) in her natural, completely unselfconscious moments, when she gave vent to her feelings as instinctively as an animal does. He kissed her with great tenderness, stroking her hair, her cheeks, speaking sweet words to her.

'Never leave me, Van!' she cried, 'never, never leave me!'

And he: 'I can't see you, *Ma Mie*. Your breath has blurred my spectacles. Always when you have been to see me I have to take off my spectacles and wipe them,' and he did so now, looking down at her all the while still with that half-amused, half-contrite expression, as he continued meticulously to rub his glasses between his handkerchief folds.

She saw that it was no use. He would not answer. He would never answer. . . .

'Without your glasses,' she said, still catching her breath a little, 'you look as you did at the beginning — '

'Ah,' he answered, 'but how do you know how I looked at the beginning?'

It was a cruel thrust. 'I meant, of course,' she said lamely, 'at the beginning of your life here, with us.'

'Ah yes,' he agreed, 'the beginning of the Thirty Years War — '

'Has it seemed so long, Van? Half a lifetime?'

'Longer,' he answered, looking downwards at his spectacles as he still rubbed them between his handkerchief folds. 'Three lifetimes; four lifetimes, Harry. . . . Never mind, my love — you have done much to alleviate them, and who am I, a mere nobody, to complain at the fortunes of war? Why, they took my great-grandfather and tore his toe-nails and finger-nails out with red-hot pincers, and branded his tongue with a red-hot iron and bound a wooden post on his back — on the back of an old man, Harry — a respected burgher, a devout churchman, none better — and they marched him out of the town and tied him to that post and carved out his heart before his eyes — '

'Don't! Don't!' Harriet begged, covering her eyes.

'And there was a daughter of his,' he went on remorselessly, 'a simple sort of creature but harmless — much engaged with good works as your Miss Mogus used to be. When Alva's soldiers came, they were sure there was treasure buried in the house or, failing that, in the garden. They were on fire with greed for treasure — loot of every description. When my great-grandfather would not admit to having hidden any such treasure, they took this daughter of his — '

'Oh *don't*, Van! What is the use of telling me all this — such terrible things that happened such a long time ago — '

'But,' he replied (whether genuinely surprised or not, she could not tell), 'you have so often asked me to tell you things of my family, and about my country. I am telling you now. They took her, and they tortured her too, rather more subtly — shall we say— than they tortured my great-grandfather. You need not cover your ears — fortunately bad times do not last for ever, and even Alva's soldiers went away again after a time; but you know I am afraid she did not recover. She ceased to do good works for the poor — simple creature that she was — and the servants had constantly to watch her from that time onward, or she would dart out into the garden — Summer or Winter — and fall into the dirt on her hands and knees and claw at the earth like a dog, crying: 'Where is it? Where is it?', looking for that treasure that had never been there — that everybody *knew* had never been there; that they had tortured her to make her disclose.'

There was a pause, then:

'I don't know why you tell me these things,' she said, in a small, miserable voice. 'They have all been over for a long time now — I can't do anything about them — '

He took up her hands in his and kissed them.

'Brave, practical Harry!' he said (did he mock?); 'always active, always ready to *do* things — to be *at* things — What a wastrel you must think me, who talk so much and achieve so little — '

She murmured: 'I think nothing — I love you — '

His hands, shaped already busily about some piece of work, stayed still at that, letting her love lie between their open palms for a minute, like the gift of God that it was. Then a whistle outside the window attracted their attention. It was from a farm-lad, rosy, triumphant, standing there with a dead magpie dangling from one hand and another bird from the other.

Seeing Harriet through the window, he held both arms high, displaying his trophies hopefully. Harriet felt suddenly sick, ducked her head aside, asking Vandervoord:

'What are they? Are they both magpies?' remembering much too easily the superstition concerning magpies.

'One,' he said, 'is black and white; a large bird — '

'I know,' she said faintly; 'a magpie — '

'And one is blue, like the feathers you have in your hat — '

One for sorrow. . . . She turned to go.

'What is the matter?' he asked her. 'Surely they are both pests? You are not going to scold him for killing them?'

'No,' she said, 'but it is an omen. You know how foolish I am about omens these days — I who used to be so brave . . .' and she went out swiftly, back to the house without stopping on her way, and sending Spens, later, to settle with the puzzled boy.

CHAPTER XXII

MISS SABRINA BROMEWELL PAYS A SHORT VISIT TO REDONDA

> 'Sabrina fair,
> Listen where thou art sitting
> Under the glassy cool translucent wave . . .'
>
> MILTON

THE new century had not opened auspiciously for the country as a whole nor for Redonda in particular; the Spring had prolonged itself into a series of wan, vapourish months which made the land so sodden that even the new pump-mills were not altogether sufficient to drain it. The sheep had foot-rot. The best brood mare injured herself inexplicably and had to be destroyed. The grain-crops were so backward by June, and so weak in the stalk that the harvest, of which so much more had been expected than ever before, promised to be the poorest for years; while poppies and charlock and tall helmeted thistles, taking advantage as they always will of the dispirited depleted ranks of wheat and barley about them, hoisted their impudent colours all over the cornfields. Add to this that the daughter of the house had been brought to bed of a bastard, unknown to her father — and it required only the letter from Sophy to complete a picture of bad luck, if not of overwhelming misfortune.

Sophy's letter, which had been six weeks on the way and which arrived at Michaelmas, announced briefly that her husband Clement had succumbed finally to a galloping consumption, leaving her practically penniless; that she herself was being received amongst the good Sisters of the Convent of the Annunciation at Berne; that she was sending her daughter Sabrina back to England so soon as a suitable escort could be found for her. The child was to stay with her Lowndes grandparents in London but Sophy also bequeathed her — with due solemnity and the report of the dying Clement's acquiescence — to her grandfather Bromewell, who would surely see it as his duty, etc., etc.

Captain Bromewell accepted the letter in the spirit in which it had been sent. He grieved for his son Clement, for that promising young life cut off so cruelly; for his long exile from home. Though he had not given more than a passing thought to his elder son for months gone by, he sat now, for hours at a time, recalling Clement in his early days, chasing the elusive memories with the same stubborn persistence with which he had chased his cough.

He further commanded that Clement's old bedroom should be made ready for the arrival of the fatherless child — the orphan, as he persisted in calling her (for he had for some time recovered from his earlier curiosities concerning the Roman Catholic religion, and chose to regard Sophy now and henceforth as being quite as dead as if she were already below the ground).

In a sudden access of enthusiasm and generosity he went further, ordering that Clement's old room should be re-papered with a very fine Chinese paper (one of Captain Twigg's smuggled 'bargains' of the days of long ago, which had been kept against the day when it might be needed). This was rich in glinting swallows and in sprays of delicate grey bramble, which delighted the old man since, by running the tips of his fingers over the newly-papered surface, he could feel the remembered pattern below.

Standing there, snuffing in the smell of paint and paste, he was carried back to the days when he had newly come home to Redonda; when his wife's bedroom was newly papered with a fine paper . . . when the dressing-room . . .

'Leave Susan in the dressing-room,' he said to Harriet, jerking his head towards the small adjoining room, 'then she can look after the girl.'

'She can hardly do that, Father. She has her babies to look after — '

'Well, the place is large enough, isn't it? The children can, I suppose, be disposed somewhere else — out of earshot? Don't *make* difficulties, Harriet, they come quite fast enough without making 'em!'

'I'll see her about it,' Harriet promised, 'but I don't think she's fit.'

From the first she had no intention of allowing such an arrangement; Susan was fully employed already in nursing her (Harriet's) child, she was not to be turned over to minister to a fat schoolgirl who would not know good service even when she saw it.

Nevertheless, to avoid complications, Susan must be got out of the way — together with Louisa and the other two children.

'There's nothing for it,' Harriet told her. 'You must go back to Anderson's cottage. I shall make you an allowance for nursing Louisa and *this* time there won't be any risk of your starving! And if there is anything else that is needed, you are not to be a perfect fool, Sukey, you are to come to me at once. I can't put things right unless I am told about them!'

With butter two shillings a pound, a quartern loaf of bread 1s. 10d., candles unprocurable and even the now universal substitute of rush-lights hard to come by, Susan was grateful for the promised allowance.

'There's just one thing, Miss Harriet.'

'Yes?'

'I thought I'd have the milk for the two on 'em' — she indicated the sleeping infants, her own and Harriet's, lying close and warm as peas in a pod in the same cradle — 'but that's not there.'

'Are you sure?'

'Reckon so, Miss Harry. I feed the little girl first — and after that the boy — but that puckers its face up and looks at me wholly old-fashioned, and that cries and cries after. Reckon his little stomach's not full — '

'Or else wind. It might be that.'

'Ah no, Miss, and I'll tell 'ee for why. The little girl gets the wind, and that screws herself up and screams the place down till she's put roight agin. That's a different cry altogether — '

Harriet clicked her tongue in annoyance, going closer to look down at the babies; but her inexperienced eye could make nothing of such a superficial survey, except that the little Louisa, being five months younger than Susan's own child, was far smaller, and plumper and more compact.

It was aggravating news. All the plans had been made, right from the first, on the understanding that Susan's milk-supply would be ample for two. If she had had twins it would *have* to have been ample for two. Yet now she announced her incapacity, without apology, just as if it couldn't be helped. . . .

Harriet hesitated. Cow's milk, like everything else that year, was in poor supply. But needs must when the Devil drives.

'Very well,' she said, 'I shall send you down cow's milk two or three times a week for the boy. You are not to give it to *my* baby — you know that! You have undertaken to nurse her and you must do it. But the boy is old enough now, surely, to do well on cow's milk.'

She looked down at him again. They both did. He was a long, gangling infant, with a head bald as a patriarch's. He seemed to be engaged in a sleeping race with his much smaller companion in the cradle — for both of them were so intent in their unconsciousness — had an expression of such creased resolve. Louisa had the larger share of the cradle, although she was smaller, and this seemed to Harriet — and to Susan too — entirely suitable. After all, the child was half Bromewell, and as such entitled to the best.

When Clancy came again for the shooting, he brought his niece Sabrina with him. She had grown startlingly like her father as he had been in his 'twenties — more still like Harriet, even down to the colouring of dark hair and grey eyes. But she wore her hair short as a boy's in the fashion of the moment, clustered darkly round her small ears and impudent neck.

Impudent was the word that best expressed her, to Harriet's mind. Even the fact that the girl was a mirror of her own girlhood — a fact exclaimed on admiringly by all who saw her — served only to irritate Harriet as another piece of impudence on the part of her niece — a caricature rather than that imitation which is perfect flattery.

Naturally Sabrina delighted her grandfather. Her lively curiosity, quick laughter, the intensity of her exaggerated, schoolgirl emotions — *adoring* this, *detesting* that, *dying* for the other — were echoes again to him of his own daughter in her 'teens. The house was young again; Clement had never gone out of it, never been defeated by either life *or* death. Time was defied!

Spens became her slave. The dogs — who had cared previously only for the Captain or for their adored Clancy — were also her slaves. The aged Ivory would do anything for her, excessively badly, and delight to hear the sweet tones of her reproof. The goosefeather girls and their cronies of kitchen and poultry-yard congregated in groups to see her come down dressed in her childish finery for dinner — imparting a roguish Continental brilliance to that otherwise solid meal by sheer force of gesture and laughter. Harriet, dressed sedately in slate-coloured wool beneath a Paisley shawl which had belonged some years earlier to her Aunt Hannah, carved the portions for the household in silence, frowning down over her knife and fork while the chattering, tinkling minx Sabrina bounced on the chair between her and the Captain, facing her uncle Clancy, and making *moues* at him from behind her wineglass; recalling, to both her infatuated male companions, in a thousand nostalgic and characteristic ways, the dead Clement as brother and as son . . .

'I thought you said she was fat,' said Vandervoord one day — watching from beside Harriet in his workshop the younger Miss Bromewell's triumphant home-coming after the daily ride with Clancy — with the dogs thronging about her, the groom grinning at her, her very pony seeming unwilling to leave her.

'So she was,' Harriet replied. 'She has grown up, that is all! Do you think her pretty?'

'She is very like you.'

'That's no answer!'

'I wonder,' he went on, still watching the girl as she dominated the stable-yard, keeping all in a bustle about her, 'what she is like when she is in a tantrum. Have you ever seen her in a tantrum?'

'No, and if I do she will pay for it! I don't intend to have any spoilt child tricks here. Sophy has spoiled her abominably. Clement *knew* she would!'

'And yet your brother Clement was, after all, a Bromewell. Do you mean to say he *permitted* the spoiling?' (Again, was he mocking, or really wanting to know?)

'He wasn't well,' said Harriet, 'he was dying. How *could* he stop it?'

'Nevertheless she is a very charming child,' said Vandervoord, bending again over his calculations. He appeared to forget her, to forget even Harriet, as soon as the tip of his pencil touched the paper — just as usual; a circumstance that was comforting to Harriet, since it was habitual with him. Here was something at least, that belonged to the old Redonda, before Sabrina had ever invaded it!

It was not, after all, the girl's liveliness that most disquieted Harriet. It was not (to do her justice) Sabrina's good looks and universal popularity. It was her insatiable curiosity regarding Redonda and everybody in or about the place; she must *know*, she must be *told* (and this too was in character).

As she went like a brisk wind through the old house from top to bottom, examining its few pictures (Who is that? Where is that? Who painted it? When?), its *objets d'art* ('Is there anything at the bottom of this vase, Aunt?' I am *sure* I heard a tinkle. Do you suppose somebody has hidden something in it?'), its views from the windows ('Who lives there? Why? Is that a short cut? To where? How old are those trees? Did Grandpapa plant them? Ah — there is my pony! How much did my pony cost, Aunt?'), as this ceaseless stream of inquiry flooded out of the girl, disturbing loved old associations without replacing them by loved new ones — Harriet could willingly have wished her deaf and dumb, or even afflicted like Susan's Tommy, with no interest or curiosity in life whatever. She hated to answer, but she had to answer — knowing that if she did not, Sabrina would go elsewhere for satisfaction, and this would have been too humiliating.

It was no time at all, of course, before Sabrina had ferreted out the presence of the French Prisoner. That Harriet had done her best to discourage her, that he himself had proved as elusive as a butterfly, only added pleasure to the final cornering and capture. She came in to dinner that night glowing.

'Oh, Uncle *Clancy*! she said, 'I have been talking to that *romantic* man, M. Vandervoord!' He has been showing me the most wonderful things in his *toy*shop, as he calls it — '

'And you, I suppose, are out to break his heart, you minx!' Clancy answered. At thirty-five he was already rotund, rosy, the perennial bachelor, the perfect foil to a dazzling niece.

'She may break his heart so long as she don't break his implements,' said Captain Bromewell. He was very pleased with his retort, and laughed longer than any of the rest — so long that he began to cough.

'And he told me about his pump-mills down by the Shearings,' the breathless girl went on, 'and how he has a scheme for diverting the river to supply power to drive a saw in the pit in Farley Wood — '

The names come so pat off her lips, thought Harriet jealously, *she might have been born amongst them, and have lived here all her young life.*

Captain Bromewell ceased to cough. The plan for the sawmill was the very latest inspiration of the French Prisoner's. It had not been put on paper yet, nor yet discussed, except with the Captain. Harriet herself had not heard it so much as mentioned.

Fine grounds for jealousy here, for more than one Bromewell!

Clancy alone did not care. What was it all to him except grist to the mill? He held up his claret glass to be filled again by Ivory.

'That fellow must have been worth his weight in gold to you, Father,' he said. 'Damned if I ever saw a place so changed — you wouldn't know the Shearings! When Clem and I used to go duck-shooting down there — '

But nobody wanted to hear about the duck-shooting except Sabrina, who wanted to hear everything, to miss nothing.

The Captain was not, of course, going to admit any nonsensical weight in gold. He was not a farmer for nothing.

'He's been useful enough, considering he's a foreigner,' he admitted, 'but that's only one side of the story! Some of his gear has been expensive, *very* expensive — and I have an idea he could be more economical if he cared to. But that's the way of human nature. If it's not your own property — be damned to it! Use it as carelessly as you like — YOU don't pay for it!'

It did not seem to occur to the old man that neither had he paid the French Prisoner; no, not so much as a brass farthing, in the whole time of his sojourn at Redonda.

The matter of the sawmill continued to rankle ... He hated to reprove his darling, but still —

'Don't pester the fellow, will 'ee, Sabrina?' he said, 'or he won't get on with the scheme, perhaps. I should like to start it, this Winter.'

Then Sabrina *must* see the fortifications. Nothing else would content her. What, be wintering here, right on the East Coast, with Boney just across the water — and not be taken to see all the exciting plans going forward, and the soldiers drilling, and the Sea Fencibles in their armed barges, and the new Signal Station at Orford and — above all — the new Martello Towers, seventy-four of which were being erected all round what the Romans used to call, in *their* day, the Saxon Shore — with their great circular walls *nine feet thick*, just fancy, and a powder-magazine below and observation posts above ... Nothing would serve but that Uncle Clancy *must*, positively *must*, take her to see the fortifications; which — being an army man himself and the son of his father — Clancy was certainly enabled to do.

She went, she saw, she conquered. She came back with ecstatic descriptions of all the sights she had observed on sea and shore. 'And Mamma used to say I should be bored to death here!' she incautiously let out, once; 'that a dull farm was no place for a Mam'selle educated abroad. But she didn't *know*! Why — I have seen more exciting things here this Summer than ever I saw before. Even London is dull to it!'

What sweeter music ever fell upon the ears of a doting grand-father; what harsher discord upon the ears of the Mistress of Redonda? — the speaker of the sentiment being oblivious, needless to say, of both the effects she had produced.

'Oh yes, and at *Aldeburgh*, Grandpapa,' she went on, 'I saw the identical fisherman's cabin that M. Vandervoord told me he used to work in when he was busy designing the pump-mills. I think it is a perfect *shame* that you took it away from him — such a *nice* little house all on his own!'

This cosy, Robinson-Crusoe aspect of Vandervoord's cabin-life had certainly never occurred to his employer. The warm rush of sympathy in Sabrina's voice thrilled him to a slight shame.

'You don't understand, my pet,' he said, 'I was not *allowed* to let him go on using it. It came within the Fortified Area, and foreigners, especially prisoners of war, are forbidden to approach the fortifications — '

'But you are a Justice of the Peace, Grandpapa! It was on your land! He is on parole to *you*! If *you* gave him permission to go on using his little cabin, *nobody* could have prevented it! After all, he was working for *you*, and working for this country — '

The identical arguments Harriet had used, on just such another occasion — and still every bit as unanswerable! Sabrina went on, brimming over with the quaintest compassion for the ill-used Vandervoord:

'He told me he used sometimes to sleep down there, and that the sea came so close up beneath his window that sometimes he felt as if the next wave would break in and engulf him — '

She had that romantic respect towards the sea and its antics of any person who has lived long inland.

'The more fool he,' responded Captain Bromewell, seeing no romance in it at all, and continuing to crack nuts with a blind dexterity born of habit and a determination not to be beaten in this any more than in anything else: 'That would have been a mighty useful service to me, wouldn't it — *and* to the country — to go and get drowned and waste my time on an inquest, and the parson's on a funeral and everybody else's on idle gossip!'

'An inquest, what's that?'

'Finding out how silly people came by their deaths, Miss. *That's* what it is!'

'Oh, Grandpapa, how *gruesome*!' She shuddered her bare shoulders deliciously, and Clancy groaned in mock resignation, saying that *Now* he supposed she wouldn't rest content until she was taken to an inquest and allowed to view the corpse.

Sabrina's joyous laughter tinkled amongst the glasses. Of *course* she must go to an Inquest, but meanwhile she was not to be distracted from her present sympathies — 'And I think you are a dreadful *cruel* man about the cabin, Grandpapa, and I am all on *his* side, and not at all on yours!'

Ice tinkling upon ice could not have sounded more coldly to Harriet. As soon as she could conveniently do so next afternoon, she sought out Vandervoord in his workshop, accusing him breathlessly —

'You let her come in and waste your time, your precious time! You *like* talking to her!'

'Certainly,' admitted Vandervoord, laughing at her furious onslaught; 'I like to see my rival —'

'Rival!'

'So she is, Harriet. Ever since she arrived Redonda has had no more time for me! I may perform all my old tricks—' he made a rueful grimace — 'but the crowds don't gather any more, they are all agog round Miss Sabrina!'

'At least you have *her* sympathy and *her* admiration,' retorted Harriet. 'She was boring us all at dinner last night with stories of your ill-usage over the business of the fisherman's cabin —'

He did not notice the satire, if satire there was, but only replied surprisingly, putting the tips of his long, clever fingers together:

'It was certainly a very useful place.'

Useful! The shrine of their first kiss, first endearments, first consummation of their love for each other and delight in each other; the scene of that solemn compact between them a hundred — No — a thousand years ago — with the Book and the Key ... *Useful!*

'And she talked of plans for a sawmill,' Harriet went on; 'you had never told *me* of any sawmill!'

'Didn't I?' he said, again surprised. 'I am *desolé*. Allow me to show you.' And he pulled the desk drawer quickly open to take out some drawing.

Harriet covered her eyes. 'No, *no*,' she said, 'I don't want to see it. You know I don't understand such things! I only meant it would have been kind to tell *me* first, not her — '

At that he shut the desk drawer again swiftly, sighing a little. '*Harriet*,' he said, 'Harriet, Harriet, *Harriet!*' as if no word, except her own name, could be trusted to contain the full weight of his fatigued reproach; as if he could not even be bothered to rebuke her in greater detail, since the same sort of scene between them had already occurred so often in the past, so profitlessly — and might, for all they knew, be destined to occur just as often in the future.

But desperate wounds require desperate measures, as has been said. She sat down, for the first time in her life, in his chair, at his desk — looking up at him to say quietly:

'You were quite right when you said she was your rival, Van — but you did not go far enough. She is mine, too — and our child's.'

It was the first time, too, that she had said Our Child.

He was politely puzzled.

'You will never speak out, you know, so I have to. God knows, already I've had to do so many unwomanly things — one more or less won't hurt! Listen for a minute. You know what Redonda means to me, don't you? Every stick and stone in it, every blade of grass, every ear of wheat! You have often teased me about it, but you said yourself that it was beyond curing. Mr. Mogus used to call it my Idol, my Golden Calf. Well, if I *have* bowed down to it, I have worked and slaved for it too, *and* done good by it — nobody could deny that!'

He assured her, gently, No, nobody could deny that.

'Very well, then. I did it gladly, *all* of it — because I loved it. You love your pump-mills, love triumphing over inert matter — water, earth, gravitation, just as *I* triumph over climate and war and labour shortages and foolish, sluggish workpeople. We have *both* worked for Redonda!'

He agreed, Yes, in a way that was undoubtedly true.

'Understand this,' she went on. 'Some who work as I have worked have had an incentive. They are working to an end — what is it the Bible says? To enter into and possess the land. But I never *could* possess the land! There was Clement before me and

323

though he didn't want the land he wanted the value of it and my father would have been doting enough to see that he got it! After Clement there was still Clancy — their children (if they had any) before me and *my* children ... Do you begin to see what I am trying to say?'

She gripped the arms of his chair tightly, seeking support and strength from their strong firmness.

'Clement is dead, Van,' she said, 'Clancy is a bachelor still and it does not look as if he intends to marry. He used to say he would marry for money, but now there is money and to spare — and he does not need to! And my father is resigned to it, now. He said so, last night. He said he will be happy in his grave, to think of me keeping house for Clancy here, an old bachelor and an old spinster together.' She beat upon the arms of the chair. 'He says he intends to have Mr. Marsham down here again to alter the will, Van; that he intends to leave Redonda jointly between Clancy and me *for our lifetime* and after that it is to go to Sabrina. Do you understand? When my father dies, when Clancy dies, I hold it only in trust! It will be for Sabrina to inherit — not for me, who have laboured for it as none of them has ever laboured. It will be for *her* — not for Our Child.'

There was a pause; then he said, shifting his position a little:

'I am not very well acquainted with English Law — but surely a bastard —'

'A *love-child*, Van!'

'Very well, then — a love-child, cannot inherit?'

He might have been raising some obscure legal point, to while away an idle half-hour, instead of discussing something vital, personal to them both as their heart's blood.

'I haven't had much more time than you have,' Harriet answered, 'to study the Law. I've been busy with other things. But there is such a thing as helping to remove, just a little, the stigma of illegitimacy — not much, but just a little. It is done by the parents marrying.'

Now, if ever, said her heart, thumping steadily against the back of her chair, and pulsing painfully in her constricted throat, *Now, if ever, he will declare himself.*

But there was again only a listening silence — a silence not to be endured.

'If I were able to go to my father,' she said, speaking with pain because of the dryness of her throat, 'and say to him, "This is my husband, and this is our child. We could not tell you before and no doubt things have not been done as you would have wished — but surely wartime excuses many things? This is our child, *your* grandchild — born at Redonda and part of Redonda — '"

She could not go on. Vandervoord laid a hand upon the back of her chair.

'But as you say, there is Miss Sabrina,' he said. 'No amount of church ceremony will do away with her, will it? I am very much afraid you will have to haul down your colours, Harry darling, and make the best of things, for Miss Sabrina starts with several advantages over our little brat. She is astoundingly pretty, she is Clement's child, the child of the eldest-born, she has already won your father's heart and she was not born out of wedlock. What can you put against that?'

It was as if he had played an ace against her king, in a game that bored them both but which it yet satisfied them, in a sense, to finish.

She answered with another question.

'What then? I am to look after the place for her, I suppose, until she is ready to inherit it?'

He made the slightest gesture towards her.

'Nobody could do it better.'

'Christ in Heaven, Van, can't you pity me? Can't you help me? I am speaking to you out of my heart's blood and all you say is, Nobody could do it better!'

The trembling in her voice set up at long last a trembling roughness in his — as the violent speeding-past of some frigate, full-sailed, will rock any other craft in its creamy wake.

'I have told you before and I tell you again,' he said, 'do not expect me to make life tolerable for you! I cannot even make it tolerable for myself; how should I be able to do it for you ? — '

'By taking my hand when I hold it out to you, Van! By pitying me when I am in distress! Oh!' she cried to the unresponsive silence, leaning back exhausted in the chair and closing her eyes, 'I feel as if

I were drowning in front of your eyes, reaching up my arms to you — and you will not even lean down to attempt to catch hold of me —'

'If I touch people,' he replied, still remotely, from a thousand, thousand miles away, 'I only harm them. By touching you I have given you nothing but great misery — and a bastard. I have desperately incommoded your life. If I had never come here, you would never have missed me — you would have been happy —'

'But you *did* come,' repeated Harriet, 'and I *have* been happy — and now I am most desperately *un*-happy. Can't you help me, Van? Can't you help me, my dearest dear?'

The light was now fast fading from the room; he made another helpless, hopeless gesture, raising his arms a little and then letting them drop again; and he whispered something she did not hear. Her last hopes died with the light.

As the weeks passed, Sabrina became increasingly familiarized with Redonda, and increasingly desirous of helping Harriet and her grandfather with its administration. It amused her to dress up and pass amongst the poor of the parish, gathering curtseys as thick as cowslips, and compliments with the first and last greetings of the day. It is amazing how the mere sight of beauty can alleviate, temporarily at any rate, suffering and distress; so these poor people, suffering as all the lower classes in the country were suffering then under the cruel and ever-increasing stresses of war, still beamed to see her bright face coming, and lost some of their cares in hearing the care-free lightness of her step.

All the same there was some vexation, even for her. 'Oh, Grand-papa!' she said one day, reporting to him after some such Lady Bountiful tour, 'they called me a Pharisee! I am not a Pharisee, am I?'

He laughed. 'You don't understand their lingo yet, Sabrina. They mean Fairy when they say Pharisee in these parts. They meant you were as pretty as a fairy — and so you are! So you are!'

He could not see her, but he did not need to see. Beauty was in her voice, her gait, the scent of her garments, the feel of her rounded arms about his neck.

Another such Lady Bountiful excursion led, inevitably, to the discovery of Susan Shattuck's cottage, whither she went to deliver the extra milk.

'She has a dear little fellow with a red nose,' she reported, ' — and twins, a girl and a boy. The boy is *twice* as big as the girl, Grandpapa, but Susan says it is often so . . .'

'Nobody told me our Sukey had twins,' said the Captain. But it was not an affair of much importance in any case.

Harriet, who might have been supposed to have more interest in such woman's talk as Babies, was, Sabrina found, even more discouraging. She did not want to be bothered with talk about the unusual twins, nor even to be told that the little girl was a duck — so lively and smiling — but that the boy seemed to be poorly, he just lay still —

'All Susan's children are like that,' said Harriet, biting off a thread determinedly. 'The first boy was a perfect log.'

'But the little *girl* isn't a log, Aunt! She smiled when I called her by her name and almost held out her arms to me — '

'I really think it would be better if you gave up some of these visits of yours, Sabrina. Heaven knows what you may catch in the way of fevers or worse. They live like pigs — '

'But they are so pleased to *see* me! It would be horrid of me not to go when they are so pleased to see me!'

'They are only curious,' replied Harriet, 'like someone else I could name.' And again she bit off, almost vindictively, the length of thread from the sheet she was hemming.

It was just as hard for her when the name of Vandervoord came up — as it inevitably did — for discussion.

'He is very romantic, isn't he, Aunt? He is not really *handsome*, but then myself I don't care for those out-and-out Apollos. But his circumstances are so strange, and it must be so dreadfully sad for him (though I know everyone here is as kind as can be to him) to be separated so long from his friends and his home. Do you suppose he is married?'

'You might try asking him, Sabrina.'

'Oh — I *have* asked him! It was one of the first things I asked him, but he only laughed! It would be *too* sad if he had a wife and children pining away for him at home!'

'It would indeed,' said Harriet. But the Inquisition was not yet over:

'Do you suppose he is *really* not French? That he *is* Dutch, as he pretends to be?'

'I don't have any opinion. If he says he is Dutch I have no reason for believing he does not speak the truth.'

'On the other hand,' said Sabrina, cocking her curly dark head on one side and staring into the fire, 'he is quite certainly *listed* as a French Prisoner, because I looked up his papers in Grandpapa's desk.'

'That was very naughty of you!'

'Ah *no*, Aunt!' The curly dark head bent sideways again in mock contrition, dropping itself, for a moment, on to Harriet's knee: 'But I had to know! Didn't you — don't you ever feel like that? That there are some things you simply *must* know, or die?'

Without waiting for or expecting an answer, she went on:

'All the same, he speaks French with a most *undistinguished* accent — as no Frenchman I ever heard speaks it. There is another thing that occurs to me —'

'Really? You are very prolific of ideas, to-night!'

'I don't know whether I ought to mention it.' She dropped her voice mysteriously. 'But I think you and Grandpapa and Uncle Clancy should have it in mind. He *might* be a spy!'

'So he might . . . Any night now,' concluded Harriet, with more bitterness than even her dark words warranted, 'we may all be murdered in our beds!'

Sabrina's suspicions of Vandervoord, however, died a speedy death. He was too entertaining a companion to be distrusted, too obliging with his time and his tireless fingers, which constructed for her, quite effortlessly it would seem (while she babbled away to him) the usual riot of ingenious toys.

. . . It was the cornelians, the old story of the cornelians, which precipitated the crisis. She had been visiting Susan Shattuck again, nursing one child whilst Susan washed the other and listening, as she loved to do, to stories of Susan's childhood at Redonda. She no sooner heard of Harriet's and Susan's youthful excursions in search of those semi-precious stones on Aldeburgh beach than she must do it too. 'Come too!' she begged.

Susan could not come because of the children.

Uncle Clancy would not come because it was a tame game; he could buy her better trinkets at Ipswich any day.

Harriet would not come because she could not spare the time.

There remained the French Prisoner. 'I should have been enchanted,' he said, 'but you forget the beach is out-of-bounds to me.'

'You mean you cannot even *walk* down there with me, for half an hour, to look for cornelians?'

'Not even for half a minute,' he said, enjoying her dismay.

She took it exactly as Harriet would have done at her age.

'What nonsense!' she said, tossing her head. 'First of all they take away the cabin from you, and now they won't even let you accompany a lady —'

'It is the law,' he said, 'and ladies, even pretty ones, must obey the law —'

'Oh no, they must not! They will *change* the law if it suits them!'

So they wrangled together, laughing, he laying a wager of his single remaining shoe-buckle (the silver one) that she would not be able to get permission for him to join the cornelian excursion — she vowing, just as assertively, that she would not only achieve permission for that but would get his cabin back for him as well.

'If you could do *that*,' he commented, 'I should indeed begin to believe you could work miracles.'

Harriet had been disturbed by Sabrina's report of the children's condition 'up at Andersons'. She went to investigate on a certain leaden November afternoon, when the black hawthorn thickets each side of the lane were trimmed only with rows of raindrops, and dun-coloured sparrows sat hunched amongst the twigs like so many dead leaves.

She found Tommy, as usual, playing (if it could be called playing) with a small wooden horse (a Vandervoord product) in the puddles outside the cabin door. He did not look up as she passed. That was usual, too.

Inside she found her own child fat and flourishing in Susan's lap, and its foster-brother lying, as always, in the cradle, but this time more quietly than ever. Susan looked anxious.

'That won't suck any more,' she said, 'and that won't sleep, that just lays there, poor morsel, waiting for the end, fare to me. What should I do, Miss Harry? You know what they say — Children and Chicken is always a-pickin'. Well *this* one picks!' she said with mournful pride, nodding down at the robust Louisa, 'but *that* 'ont look out for itself at all!'

Harriet took up the recumbent baby's hand in her own. It was burningly dry. A pulse in the patriarchal head fluttered ceaselessly like a moth against a window-pane.

But he was not 'silly', like Tommy, only ill. There was a recognizable intelligence in the gentian-blue eyes which focussed themselves now, despite the fever, on Harriet's face. Where and who was his father? What mysterious legacy of health, talent, temperament had he bequeathed this scrap, this morsel?

'*This* 'un,' went on Susan, dandling the crowing Louisa, 'cries when she see me give that little old baby the bottle. Let me try *her* with the bottle, Miss Harry dear, and nurse him myself — that might fare to be more hongry then —'

'You promised me faithfully to be wet-nurse to my child,' said Harriet. 'Are you going to break your word to me?'

The whole world was trying to break its compact with her these days. Well, she would fight for Louisa against the world!

She had no intention of seeming cruel to the sick baby. She was merely standing out for her rights, for Louisa's rights, and Susan knew it. Susan lived on her charity, all three of them lived on her charity and she sent cows' milk in addition. Was it much to ask that Susan should abide by her part of the bargain?

Susan was beaten. She ducked her head a little, kissed the top of Louisa's head and repeated, in extenuation, that she only thought that might be more hongry, then . . .

'Has he been christened yet?' Harriet asked.

'No. The clerk he was passin' moine this week, and he looked in, and reckoned that weren't hardly wuth it.'

Hardly worth it, blinked the gentian-blue eyes of the baby, up into Harriet's eyes. No good making two bites at a cherry, when one final bite will do.

'Well, I'm sorry for you, Suke, and sorry for the child too,' said

Harriet. 'But you promised me, you know — and you wouldn't want to hurt Louisa, would you?'

That certainly was the last thing Susan wanted.

'Very well then,' concluded Harriet. 'We will continue the way things are. He may pick up,' she said, looking out of the window, 'when we get some good weather again. When the Spring comes — so much may change!'

'Yes, Miss Harriet,' answered Susan, hopefully as ever, 'and the dear Lord knows best what to do with His own.'

Does He know best, wondered Harriet, driving back slowly through the sad lanes, between the silent birds in the rain-decked thickets; can it be that He knew best when He sent Van here in the first place? Yes, and put it into my heart to love him, and made such a coil of trouble for us all? How can 'trouble' be 'best'?

Perhaps that was what remained to be seen — and suddenly it would all become clear — gloriously clear and comforting. No more letters to come between; no more Sabrinas; no more locked lips in answer to cruelly vital questions. Spring comes. The small blunt-nosed flowers nuzzle their way through the warm, breathing earth, the green bursts out of the hawthorn boughs, the birds will not, cannot, stop singing because of their endless, irrepressible joy . . . And when Peace comes (will it, Oh will it come with Spring?) we shall look back upon this time and laugh, and wonder that we should ever have distressed ourselves so. We shall be at *home*, at Redonda; he and I and our child, together for evermore.

She arrived back at Redonda to discover that Sabrina had prevailed upon her grandfather to give the French Prisoner back his fisherman's Cabin; permission to keep his things there; permission to use it for work.

'I *told* him I could do it!' she told Harriet exultingly; 'see what he had to hand over to me as his part of the wager!'

The silver buckle lay glinting in her hand; the buckle that had been on Vandervoord's dusty shoe the first time Harriet had ever set eyes on him, in her father's morning-room.

Harriet hurried upstairs and, in the privacy of her own rooms, was violently and painfully sick; so sick, and in such pain, that she had to take to her bed and stay there for three days — deprived by

331

cruel accident of the thing she wanted most in the world just then — the chance of communication with her lover.

When she could bear it no longer she sent Bess, her new little maid, over to his workshop with a note, reading: 'I forbid you to go to the Cabin. H.'

It was not judicious. It might be termed suicidal, but it was the only motion, at that time, of which she was capable, and she could not be upon the rack without moving — that was too much to ask.

She lay for hours waiting for an answer to the note; an answer which she knew (in her heart) would not come; that *could* not come. Did she deliver the note, she asked the servant.

Yes, it had been delivered.

And what had he said?

He had taken off his glasses and looked at her and said Thank you, there was no answer.

There *was* no answer except, of course, that he went to the Cabin. She saw him going to the Cabin, for she had had her bed (as when she was a child) moved close to the window, and from her window her view commanded all the wide expanse of landscape that lay seawards. Now that the leaves were off the elm trees she could see people passing up or down the long avenue, and where the path branched off by the old way, the short cut via the Shearings, down to the beach.

She saw Vandervoord going that way, two or three times — an ever-diminishing figure through the mist intent about its own employments; sometimes he carried gear, sometimes not. He never looked up towards her window — not even on the occasion when Sabrina also happened to be there; he did not seem to hear her impetuous hailings.

She turned to Harriet with chagrin.

'I wish I knew what he *did* down there, now I have got him his old Cabin again!' she said, and later — recurring to the subject without warning after the most earnest conversation about the proper width of lace on a *berthe*: 'Even after I got him his old Cabin, he hasn't remembered about the cornelians. He has never said again that he will come with me to look for them; he just laughs!'

If you are acting, Harriet said to her niece, silently, *You are doing it extremely well. Your mother could act, too. I have seen her deceive your father dozens of times over quite trifling affairs. She enjoyed deceiving, it was second nature to her, and now she is deceiving herself, or the Convent sisters, or even God, who knows?*

But you *shall not deceive* me. *I shall be equal to you, because Van matters to me much more than ever poor Clement did.*

When Harriet was up and about again, and busy again about the farm and on the estate, she said to herself, *They will deceive me much more easily now, but they will try to arrange so that I never see them together. What a fool they must think me!*

And — to be sure — she never saw them together.

If she mentions the Shearings, Harriet said to herself, *it means that she is past deceiving, she has reached the brazen stage. She will not tell me directly that she is going to the Cabin as his mistress, but she will talk about the Shearings, to break it gently to me.*

If she talks about the Shearings, as surely as God is my witness, I will kill her, though how I don't yet know.

So Sabrina talked about the Shearings one day; how Vandervoord's pump-mills — so she had heard — had first inundated them; how the quicksands had swallowed up a bottle which Vandervoord had given her the previous afternoon to show her the power of the quicksands. But that had been from the beach side, the other side of the fence.

'It is a great pity, in a way, about the Shearings, isn't it?' she asked her aunt, 'because Susan tells me that the short cut to the beach used to be down that way — that was the way you and she used to go as children. But no one can use it any more.'

'What nonsense,' said Harriet. 'Sensible people — not nervous fools like Susan Shattuck — still use it. You have seen Vandervoord using it — '

'Ah yes, Aunt! *He* uses it, but then he says *he* can do so safely because he knows exactly where the danger lies! But that it isn't safe for anyone *else* to do it, because nobody else has studied the water as he has done, in that part. He said he had the greatest difficulty, at one time, from preventing someone else from using it every time they went to the beach — and long after it wasn't safe to be used any more by anyone but himself!'

'When I have occasion to go to the beach — or to Aldeburgh for that matter,' Harriet heard herself saying, quite calmly and clearly, 'I always go by the Shearings and I always shall.'

Sabrina studied her aunt with admiration.

You are overdoing the admiration, Harriet told her silently, *just as you have been overdoing the innocence, and all the other things*.

'Is it really possible — ' began Sabrina. She was looking out of the window of Harriet's room again, away towards the coast, and towards the pewter-coloured gleam of those tidal waters. Her eyes were dancing mischievously.

You are thinking, said Harriet — again silently — *that it would be great fun to thwart this man who has warned you so carefully against the Shearings. Yes, I believe for once in a way you are sincere. You are really put out with him about the cornelians. If you can persuade me to tell you the way, you intend to visit his Cabin, by way of the Shearings; to pop your head suddenly in at the window (there is no glass, you will be able to do so quite easily, and the woodwork will be smooth to your touch as a bone) — and to show him triumphantly the direction you have taken. Then — while he is still limp from shock at your disclosure and relief at your safety, when you have him off his guard, as it were — you intend to demand that long-promised stroll on the beach, looking for cornelians — with kisses as additional amusement. How sad that there will be no kisses, and no cornelians either!*

'I am surprised,' she said aloud, as casually as possible, 'that a girl of your courage and high spirits, Sabrina, that a *Bromewell*, should allow herself to be warned off a perfectly usable path because an attentive foreigner has qualms about it. If English girls are so ready to take orders from abroad, Bonaparte may find it easier to invade than he thinks — '

Sabrina stiffened a little but smiled all the same. 'He is not really *attentive*,' she confessed with the divine candour of youth, 'but he *is* afraid for me; he told me he wouldn't wilfully let his worst enemy go by that way — and *I* am not his worst enemy, am I?'

Harriet smiled. 'I see he has certainly scared you out of your wits about it,' she said.

Bromewell dared Bromewell — a challenge that was not to be refused.

Drumming with her fingers on the windowpane, and with her head held very high, Sabrina said: 'Oh, I *knew* he was being an old fusser about it! I *told* him I was sure it was safe enough! If *he* could use it — *I* could use it —'

'Provided, of course,' said Harriet, 'that you employ your common sense. It cuts off about three miles on the road, I believe — but then, of course, I never go by the road.'

Sabrina turned, ran to Harriet and knelt by her chair, eyes shining. 'Tell me how to get there by the Shearings!' she said.

She did not say, *To the Cabin*, but they both knew she meant *To the Cabin*.

Nobody ever asked more prettily for execution; though it is not really execution, Harriet found herself thinking, absolutely dispassionately, it is more like suffocation.

She leant forward. 'Well, you know how, directly you come to the wooden bridge across the Alde, past the barley-field,' she began, 'there are the reed-beds, just inside the palings? In the summer months they are full of dragon-flies, but at this time of year only the moorhens are there; you may see them running across, between the reeds, as you approach. . . .'

CHAPTER XXIII

POST-MORTEM

> Cruelty has a human heart
> And Jealousy a human face;
> Terror the human form divine
> And Secrecy the human dress.
>
> The human dress is forgéd iron
> The human form a fiery forge;
> The human face a furnace sealed
> The human heart its hungry gorge. — BLAKE

VISITATIONS seldom descend singly. Soon after the news of the tragic accident which had befallen the visitor to Redonda, came stories of a new outbreak of smallpox at Snape, the adjacent village. This was attributed to various causes; by the inhabitants to the fact that the Plague (otherwise the smallpox) had been caught by the paigles (otherwise the cowslips) in a certain field years earlier, during a previous visitation; that a child at Snape had recently gone into this forbidden field and brought back one of the plague-stricken paigles (the fact that these particular paigles had crimson blotches on their petals was evidence sinister enough), and so all unwittingly had laid the whole village once more under the scourge. On the other hand, the local midwife and Wise Woman attributed it to the fact that a certain Snape labourer, having served the Duke of Norfolk too well (otherwise got more than a little intoxicated) on market-day, had allowed himself to be inoculated against small-pox whilst in that condition and so, by contravening God's law as anyone could see, had increased the disaster tenfold. The over-worked doctors and clergy and magistrates were not so certain, being inclined to attribute the outbreak more to a combination of a wet Spring, damp and dirty living-quarters and the diet of perpetual pease-pudding which had reduced the whole labouring population's resistance to disease.

Be that as it may, the smallpox, although not invariably fatal, spread in the district insidiously, attacking here a little and there a little — sometimes taking one member of a family, sometimes laying a whole street low. Inevitably it reached, and invaded, the environs of Redonda, and at one of the busiest times of the year, when threshing and stacking were once more in progress.

This year the Iron Man was allowed into operation. Spens had said it would not work (he pronounced this judgment hopefully in turn about all Vandervoord's improvements and was invariably confuted). It worked excellently and speedily, but even so and despite the shockingly poor harvest of the previous year, there was still plenty of corn left over and to be threshed by the old way, by hand. So short was the labour for this that Harriet herself on one occasion had to take a pitchfork and lend a hand in the rickyard.

She herself escaped the smallpox, as she escaped (in the course of her life) most illness. She said herself that she could not afford to catch it, and the household in general escaped — perhaps because it had fared better and lived more cleanly than most of the labourers round about. But the cottages round the outlying farmlands were ravaged by it, and Susan Shattuck caught it and was for some time made very ill by it — so that the blacksmith's wife had to come in and look after the children.

As she had children of her own to care for as well, it was some relief when the ailing Anderson infant died — for this made one charge less, and — as the harassed but kindly woman told Susan — since the Lord had marked him for His own from the start, he might goo by the way of the Plague as well as any other way. Infant he had been born and as Infant he was buried, anonymous to the last.

It was difficult to tell to what extent Susan Shattuck grieved over the loss of her second-born. She had been so ill herself, and her always plain face was now so pitted with the disease that to Harriet, looking down upon it, it seemed to be as solemn as a deserted battle-field, which inspires feelings of awe and compassion in the be-holder but cannot feel these emotions itself — cannot indeed feel anything of what it looks like.

Harriet had been sure all along that Susan would not die of the smallpox, because to die of it would have been to break her word to *her* — Harriet — and to desert Louisa — both unthinkable acts. Susan did not die of it and Louisa, like her mother, did not catch it; and the crazy Tommy caught it and was not interested at all, nor even much incommoded as far as anyone could see.

By summer the peak of the disease had been passed; Susan was up and about again; the rest of the convalescents were up and about again, and only the peppery scars on their faces remained to show (as the marks of an ancient plough will still show across meadow-land) what stresses they had once endured and survived. More and more of the men of military age were being conscripted and borne off for land or sea service. More and more the elderly and the women were called in to supply their places on the farm or in the fields.

There was a very obvious place for Susan Shattuck. The Officer of the Parish had been called up and since a Watchman was needed in his place, to go his rounds, the choice fell at once upon Susan. Whatever the smallpox had done to her it had not affected her sharp eyesight, which had been a legend in Redonda in childhood, when she had been able to pick out distant objects such as birds' nests or feeding rabbits for the Bromewell boys, almost as if she had had a telescope to her eyes. It had been the only quality they valued in her; it had not diminished.

Her duties were, as soon as it was dark and after she had put the children to bed, to patrol the lanes and byways of Redonda and make sure that no streak of light escaped from any habitation; that no bonfire still burned after dark; that no lantern carried by cow-man or shepherd exceeded a certain brightness — light enough to guide his steps but not to serve as beacon to the enemy. She was provided with a tall staff with which to beat out bonfires or rap on offending shutters, but carried no light herself. She did not need it. Like Harriet, she knew every inch of the ground where she had been born, and lived all her days, and could have walked it blindfold — as, in effect, on moonless nights, she did.

Following up a certain bobbing lantern one evening, a lantern that exceeded a legitimate brightness, she found herself tracking the French Prisoner on his way back from the Cabin.

'Oh, Mr. Ford!' she said (she never had been able to compass his outlandish name), 'I didn't know that was you, sir! I'm after you for that old loight!'

'Why, it's Susan,' he said, recognizing her much more slowly than she him by the light of the offending lantern.

'Yes sir, and you must douse your loight if you please, or I shall get into trouble — '

'We shall *both* get into trouble,' he corrected her, 'and that would not do at all. I am sorry you had to follow me, through all that mud; it must have flared up without my noticing it; I assure you I am usually *very* careful!'

He turned it down to a mere flicker, and they walked on side by side in silence, he marvelling continually at the absolute confidence with which the woman stepped out beside him, forward into a pitch blackness that would have baffled him to a standstill had he been alone.

'Have you been working down at that old place all day, sir?'
'All day.'

'Lord save us! Ain't that cold, Mr. Ford?'

'There is a chimney, you know, Sukey, and I get a little fire going; there is plenty of driftwood lying about on the beach. You would be quite surprised,' he went on, 'at how comfortable I can make myself.'

She sighed, marvelling. She had peeped into his workshop at Redonda in the past and been awestruck by the array of implements, the neat figures and diagrams lying upon his desk, which produced eventually such stupendous results. He was always so clean and tidy too, with his papers. She had never known any other man able to keep such order — and not many women either.

'How is the little Louisa, Susan?'

'The little owd dear, she's lovely, Mr. Ford! That walked yis'day, as sure as I'm walking beside you now, that held out her arms and I called "Come, my darlin', come to Sukey," and that came, saying "Sue! Sue!"'

Soo! Soo! mocked a barn owl, swooping past them soundlessly out of the darkness, but shaking the heavy layers of cold in the winter night, so that the stillness round the walkers was thrown into invisible ripples as a pool might be. Their route led them past the smithy. Before the door of her home Susan stopped and said:

'You'll step into moine and see her?'

Just as he had vouchsafed no reason for asking after the child, so now she did not elaborate her invitation. It was natural for him to ask, natural for him now to accept the invitation.

'Mind your head, Mr. Ford, if you don't moind, sir!'

He ducked his head and went with her into the Cabin.

It was the first of many such visits 'up at Anderson's', after her evening rounds were over and his day's work was done. He took to going there, quite often, instead of to the taverns at Slaughden, and was the better in health for it, and his work too. He had become interested, and had interested the Captain so much, in the idea of a saw-mill that should be steam instead of water-driven, that he had obtained permission to go into Ipswich from time to time to consult with a man called Fulton — an engineer there who had studied with Cartwright and was now opening up a promising manufactory on his own account. He went half a dozen times in all, into Ipswich, quite unattended, and came back and worked incessantly in his Cabin; sometimes sleeping there, sometimes returning to have a late supper with Susan and sit before the fire in her cabin and hold the sometimes sleeping, sometimes wakeful Louisa on his knee.

They did not talk much of anything at first except the baby; how beautiful it was, how healthy, how fearfully and wonderfully made, how increasingly intelligent and sweet-tempered — how like —

'Do you reckon she favours her mother, Mr. Ford?'

Look up, baby. Smile, sleepy baby, smite the heart with the likeness between the bud and the rose!

But Susan did not know how deft he was at avoiding a direct question; he only laughed and said:

'Better favour her than her father!'

His spectacles fascinated Louisa. She was always reaching up to those pinkly-glistening discs (with the firelight dancing upon them) and trying to touch them.

Yes, it was normal to talk of the child, and about how long the war would last, and whether that old Boney still meant to invade us. ('Reckon he does — they say that's got foive hundred thousand men over the water waiting — th'owd besom!'); about the faint-heartedness of our Allies who, defeated in a couple of battles by French armies reinvigorated by their returned Commander-in-chief, had most perfidiously deserted from their Coalition with us to sign a separate Treaty with *him*. ('Reckon he thinks *that*'ll pause us — that we 'oon't goo on, without them, but there — those ould foreigners don't know Old England, do they, Mr. Ford?')

In some odd way she absolved Vandervoord altogether from being a foreigner, crediting him, in her perfect wholehearted innocence, with an outlook upon international affairs as English as the name she had so kindly read into his own. It amused and touched him, it was so unlike any other treatment ever accorded him. And yet, in a way, she had, too, a most delicate touch with him, despite all her country crudities, and never once intruded into those silent and secret places of his spirit where neither she nor any other human being might ever venture. This was company without familiarity, intercourse without contact, a *via media* after his own heart.

It was soon clear that nothing pleased Susan so much as to be able to praise. When she had exhausted (even for her) Louisa's praises, she passed naturally on to other beautiful subjects, loved long since, perhaps, and lost awhile.

But not so very long since. Not long ago at all, in fact, there had been poor Miss Sabrina Bromewell.

It was natural, sitting in the firelight, to praise this lovely being who had burst so suddenly upon Redonda and who, after illuminating it a while with her presence, had been snatched away to meet her death so cruelly in the quicksands in the Shearings.

Susan did not — as Vandervoord had a little feared — dilate as everyone else did, upon the dead girl's likeness to Harriet. To her nobody could be like Harriet. She did not draw conclusions about the temporary nature of happiness or beauty, the vulnerability of life, the inevitability of death; concentrating instead, as plodding ignorant people will, upon the actual drama of the moment — the last appearance, words, direction of the fated Sabrina.

It appeared that Susan, coming up to Redonda 'that very day' to return some of Harriet's mended linen, had met Sabrina bursting, bright and breathless, out by the dairy door. The girl had seized Susan exultantly by the shoulders and kissed her, saying that she was going to do it, she was going to show him how little she cared for his warnings! (Here Vandervoord groaned.) She was going to walk down to the beach by way of the Shearings and — what was more — she would bring a reed in her hand to prove it — one of those handsome tasselled reeds that grew where the moorhens built their nests, and nowhere else . . . When he saw the reed in her hand — the triumphant plume — he would *know* that she could not be dictated to! That she had dared to defy him.

Susan repeated this *verbatim*. She had thought about it so much since, every word, every glance, every gesture. She could not make a mistake.

She insisted that she tried to put the girl off by every means she could think of; that Sabrina had only laughed, tossing her head back and saying that her aunt told her that *nervous* people were always saying such things; that it was perfectly safe really 'for folk with their wits about them'; that it cut off (as Susan knew much better than she did) 'about three miles by the road'; finally, that her aunt *invariably* went to the beach by way of the Shearings, and if her aunt could do such a thing in safety, why not she?

Susan had tried to say, without appearing 'saucy' (perennial problem of the lower classes), that Miss Harriet Bromewell had been born and bred there, that she knew every stick and stone, that she *could* not make a mistake — but that it was different for a stranger.

She had not added that nobody had ever been able to stop Harriet from doing anything that she wanted to do — though she may have implied it, as she did now to Vandervoord. But she did not, even now, breathe one word of criticism of Harriet, much less of condemnation, who had so casually (it would seem) let her own brother's child run into mortal danger. She pitied Harriet from the bottom of her pitiful heart, for having laid upon her conscience — quite by accident — a most awful load of responsibility in this affair, the memory of which she must bear about with her to the end of her days.

Above all, she did not say who the 'he' was — the man whose anxious endeavours to protect Sabrina from the danger of the Shearings had first roused her determination to meet and overcome them. She knew what everybody else knew — that the French Prisoner from his Cabin had heard the cries for help — Sabrina's cries — that he had risen from his seat once or twice because (as he had testified at the inquest) there was 'something human', he thought, in the sound; but that when he went out into the little ragged garden at the back of the Cabin he had seen so many gulls wheeling about in the air over the Shearings, and making such a raucous clamour, that he had come to the conclusion that all he had heard was just that — the gulls crying, nothing more.

So of course she had not been discovered until she was long overdue at Redonda. Then the hue and cry had been raised, and search made of that sinister spot, which had been (all the same) so slow to yield up its prey — keeping (for some grisly satisfaction of its own, no doubt) one of the dead girl's small bronze leather sandals as souvenir.

Susan had particularly noticed the sandals. They were such ridiculously fragile things in which to go walking in English country; built (no doubt) for pavement promenades in the elegant Swiss town where Sabrina had bought them — not for East Anglian mud and sand. But she had been wilful about the sandals as she had been wilful about everything; they were the height of fashion and perhaps — who can say? — there was someone upon whom she wished to make an impression.

Who can say indeed, echoed Vandervoord, but his thoughts were not in the words — were in the dairy at Redonda — hearing Sabrina telling Susan of her intention, and that she was going because her aunt told her to go; that it was perfectly safe.

'Tell me again,' he commanded Susan (after all, when Horror loomed up as hugely as here it did, one may as well turn as much illumination upon it as possible), 'what Miss Sabrina told you Miss Harriet said about the Shearings.'

'She said to goo on till she come to the bridge,' repeated Susan obediently, looking straight into Vandervoord's eyes as if it helped her to remember this part (which however she had by heart), 'and then she would see the reed-beds alongside the water. That was full of dragons in summer (*in the habitations of dragons, where each lay, there shall be grass, with reeds and rushes*) and Miss Sabrina would know, toime she reached it, owing to she'd see the old moorhens skitterin' in the reeds to git away from her —'

Ah — but there was a last chance — a faint chance but how indescribably merciful is the fact that there is a chance at all! Harriet might have been warning Sabrina *against* the reed-beds. If you go *that* way, she might have said, you will be lost.

Speaking with infinite hesitation (which Susan all the same did not perceive) he said, feeling his way gently:

'Miss Harriet — was warning her *against* going that way? By the reed-beds?'

Susan's brown eyes opened wider, gazing surprisedly into his.

'Oh no, Mr. Ford, sir! Miss Harry she told her to take that way, owing to that was the shortest cut of all! Bothers me' — she went on, turning to gaze into the fire — 'however Miss Harry come to goo so wrong there. Reckon she was flummoxed with Miss Sabrina's questions or Miss Sabrina took her up wrong ... As for me, *I* couldn't set her roight — the poor mawther! I've not bin down by the Shearings, not since the water come there! I darsn't! But that's what *she* say — to goo on till she come to the bridge — '

'No!' shouted Vandervoord, rising suddenly to his feet, crashing his fist down upon the little deal mantelshelf so that everything upon it rattled and one of the children in the next room whimpered in its sleep.

'Mr. Ford, sir!'

'Don't tell me again, Susan! Don't tell me again — once is more than enough!' and groaning, and beating his head with his fists he strode up and down the small room, up and down, up and down, breathing so heavily and with his eyes staring so through his glasses that to Susan it seemed as if he might at any moment fall down in some fit.

She stood silently watching him, twisting a corner of her apron as his substance and shadow passed and re-passed her in mortal distress. Her complete bewilderment at the turn events had taken put the match to what was already smouldering within him, so that it burst into blinding flame.

'Are you really such a fool,' he said, speaking roughly for the first time in all her experience of him, 'that you don't see what you have just told me?' He came close up to her, seizing her by the wrist above the hand that still held the apron. 'Your mistress *murdered* her niece!' he went on. 'She knew as well as any of us that the way by the reed-beds was the quicksand! She directed that poor child — God help her! — straight into it as much as if she had walked beside her all the way —'

'Mr. Ford, sir — you don't know what you're saying!'

'It is *you*,' he contradicted her, 'who have not known what *you* have been saying! Well, now you *do* know. I have told you! What merciless joke of Fate's was it that prevented your giving evidence at the inquest? As surely as I stand here, it would have hanged her!'

He was referring to the fact that Susan had not been called at the inquest. She had been sickening even then with the smallpox; there had been plenty of other witnesses, who had seen the girl on her last walk.

The baby Louisa began to cry in the next room.

Susan let her go on longer than it was her wont to do — longer than she had ever let a child cry in her life. Then she went in the darkness of the room and brought out the sleepy child and held it out, with stiff arms, to Vandervoord.

'Kiss her farewell,' she said. 'You can't never come here ne more, Mr. Ford. I 'oon't have them here that can talk such things of Miss Harriet!'

He took the child from her without looking at it, lifted it so that he might lay his cheek momentarily against its cheek, keeping his eyes still upon Susan. The wailing had ceased, the baby lay still, blinking contentedly down into the firelight.

'You know quite well that what I have said is true,' he said finally. 'But I see how it is. You would rather be wrong — with — with *her*, than right with the whole world. She may commit even murder —'

'She sinned in another way before that —' said the woman surprisingly, 'but that's not for me to judge her, ne yet you!'

'Ан! — you *admit* she sins, then? You admit she is not a paragon!'

This intimacy, this vivisection almost of the soul and body of Harriet was the more appalling to him, following as it did upon all the delicate tender discretion of the past. She was as close, vital, vulnerable between them at this point as her own child was.

'I admit nothing,' Susan declared. 'You'll not niver get me to say nothin' about my own dear mistress. Say farewell to this blessed babe o' yours, Mr. Ford — and goo!'

He went. It was a final departure. As final, he knew, as Susan's decision to say nothing, admit nothing, that might implicate Harriet more than she had already been implicated by the death of Sabrina.

She had been so composed at the inquest. A little pale, perhaps — but in the circumstances how natural! She had admitted at once that she was to blame; that she had pooh-poohed the idea of the danger in the Shearings to Sabrina; had told her niece that she herself frequently went that way.

Had that been quite wise, she was asked?

And she had admitted in a very low voice and after some hesitation that No, it had *not* been wise, it had been most foolish of her. She saw that now, only too bitterly —

That was all. The rest of the evidence, including Vandervoord's own, had been hurried over as much as possible, to avoid adding further grief to a family already so heavily afflicted. If anyone was to blame it had been he — whose ears, hearing those 'human sounds' should have been (Public Opinion considered) a little sharper — who should not have been so easily persuaded, against his better judgment, by the crying of the gulls.

The inquest had been the last occasion on which he and Harriet had stood up together in the same room. Thronged though it had been with people, they had been conscious only of each other. He had been staggered then (remembering the natural grief and shock of the occasion) to feel the same physical urge welling up in him, reaching out hungrily to her — despite the occasion, despite everything. Harriet was there and he was impelled towards her, silently and on a full flood, as she towards him, however little she cared to show it. With the throng of people between them, their mutual waves of physical desire loomed up, reared themselves and raced onwards towards each other, over the heads of the spectators, clashed in a glorious mounting music of green spume and foam, died in the moment of supreme fusion — fell apart and were sucked back and away from each other, faint, exhausted to the last point of exquisite lacy attenuation.

All this without (needless to say) any of the spectators having any notion of what was happening — conscious only of the subdued but still dignified figure of Miss Bromewell and of a Captain Vandervoord (he had somehow become a Captain in the early stage of the proceedings and no amount of accurate addressing of him later by the presiding authorities could then un-rank him in the eyes of the populace) — of a Captain Vandervoord then, who was obviously very upset by the disaster that had overtaken the young lady, positively *desolé* over his unfortunate mistake about the seagulls. . . . Nothing more, nothing less.

Clancy had gone back to town. To stay on at Redonda after the tragedy left him — as he insufficiently put it — with a bad taste in his mouth. (Though normally of short memory, he could never forget, now, how he had teased Sabrina about wanting to be taken to an inquest.) He would not even stay long enough to take the affair of arranging the funeral off his sister's hands. (His father had been prostrated.) So Harriet had arranged for the funeral, and the Lowndes grandparents in London had sent down Floral Tributes so enormous and of such an everlasting nature, that reproach by flowers had never been better said. They did not attend, themselves; they, too, claimed to be prostrated.

Sabrina was buried in the churchyard at Snape at Harriet's particular request. Their own churchyard was visible from her bedroom in winter. The gravestone bore the inscription:

SABRINA HARRIET BROMEWELL
1784-1800
'THOU BROUGHTEST ME UP
OUT OF A HORRIBLE PIT
OUT OF THE MIREY CLAY . . .'

It was believed for a long time by the big folk round about that the Reverent George Crabbe, the poet, had had something to do with the choosing of so harrowingly appropriate a text. So she was buried, and ceased gradually to be talked about, and once a week, when Susan went to put flowers on Infant's grave in the churchyard adjoining Redonda, she made the pilgrimage to the Snape churchyard afterwards and did the same for the dead Sabrina.

The winter passed, slowly, and the month of March brought two important events. The Prime Minister, conscious of a general feeling in the country (and in the King too) that he was waging war in kid gloves, holding up the war effort, failing to take the initiative against an enemy who took the initiative everywhere and always, from force of habit — in short, conscious of incommoding instead of invigorating and directing the Government — resigned. Fate, as Vandervoord might have said, was so tickled by this circumstance that she immediately murdered (by proxy) the Russian Czar — thus removing a monarch who had been lukewarm at the most towards Mr. Pitt and Great Britain, and instituting instead a new King, who was passionately Anglophile — thereby powerfully altering the whole course of subsequent events. Pitt, having gone out of power like a lamb to the slaughter, came back to it a very lion of energy. Like many other great leaders he was clairvoyant. He did not see an end to the War—the most dangerous that Great Britain had ever engaged in — but he saw that the arrival of a new Czar had once more shifted the ever-shifting Balance of Power in Europe and that for once the scales had tilted, albeit ever so slightly, towards our side.

The Battle of Copenhagen, Nelson's victory in the North as much as had been the Battle of the Nile in the South, followed soon after. This tilted the scales of power yet a little more. The Treaty of St. Petersburg, between Great Britain and the Czar of all the Russias, was yet another sign vouchsafed. Occupied Europe raised its dejected head a little, began to hope just a little, to mock (on dark nights and from round street corners) members of the illustrious Armies of the Republic.

About this time that gallant Sea Fencible and late smuggler, Captain Twigg, made his third and last attempt to seek a reconciliation with his old partner, Captain Bromewell. And Captain Bromewell, being by this time bowed with the shock and grief of his grandchild's death and excessively weary, gave in finally to his importunate pleading. There were still, he felt, vast sums of forgiveness and forbearance to be made up on his account before he could depart this life and go before his Maker with a clear conscience. Twigg should be the recipient of both.

Captain Twigg, however, hardly noticed the favour. He was bursting with self-importance, commissions from the Government, and with a very dirty sheet of parchment with a long seal dangling from it, signed by My Lords of the Admiralty, and congratulating him on something or other — conspicuous gallantry, remarkable seamanship, the skilful carrying out of an Important Mission, Captain Bromewell really couldn't say which it was for sure — most of the phrases seemed to crop up in the conversation with Everybody's Friend, and more than once. But he was being so undeviatingly and concentratedly forbearing that these trifles passed by, unheeded.

The head and sum of it all, however, turned out to be that Captain Twigg was still after the French Prisoner. There had been an Expedition to the Netherlands in the previous year, which had failed ignominiously — entirely owing (as Captain Twigg explained in voluble detail on Captain Bromewell's counterpane) to the fact that *he* had not been in command *here* so that he could not advise that so-and-so fellow *there*; and there hadn't been nearly enough thought given to the project, ne yet cash — and talented men — real seamen — had been employed merely as *pilots* — leaving gold-laced landlubbers and the army, as usual, to turn the expedition into expensive failure.

But mark his words, he said, jabbing painfully upon Captain Bromewell's knees through the counterpane; things would be blowing up again before long. Watch the Netherlands! Watch the Dutch! Old Boney moight think he had them in his pocket, like everyone else, but look at the way their parleyment kep' breaking down, why they were just *making* trouble, fare to him — and Boney would be wholly sorry — before he'd finished — that he ever had anything to do with 'em. There wasn't of course open rebellion but *he had his informants*. Things were going on that would very much surprise Captain Bromewell. *Underneath*. Trust me, he said, we have a way o' knowin' these things!

But (there was, it appeared, a But), there would be *more* ways of knowing these things if a few more chaps that spoke the lingo could be procured. Frenchmen there were, ten a penny — but Dutchmen, no. Name Your Price, he generously invited Captain Bromewell. Fair's Fair, he's wuth a bit to you but reckon the Guv'ment'll pay it!

He had got so much into the habit of talking in inscrutable ciphers that it was some time before his old companion caught up with his purpose.

If it had not been for the lassitude which had overwhelmed him ever since the disaster in the quicksands, Captain Bromewell might have enjoyed nothing more than a verbal tug-of-war with this plausible old rascal — the French Prisoner functioning as rope between them. But all zest and vitality had gone out of such encounters, since for him the spirit of Vitality itself — once called Sabrina — had been quenched.

Worse still, any pleasure he might have had in retaining the French Prisoner had been quenched too, since, if it had not been for him and his infernal pump-mills, the Shearings would never have been inundated, his darling would never have been drowned in them.

Mistaking the old man's silence for the first stage in a crafty piece of bargaining, Captain Twigg began again to state his case.

'Oh, go *away*, Twigg, you stink of mackerel,' said the Captain, waving a feeble hand. 'Go away and ask the fellow yourself. It's nothing to me whether he goes or stays, it's of no consequence at all.'

Impossible as it may seem to relate, Vandervoord refused to consider the scheme at all. Twigg was dumbfounded.

'You hain't a grudge against me?' he hazarded. 'I fare to bring you those letters, didn't I?'

'You did, my good fellow, and I'm everlastingly grateful to you — but I can't join you. I'm engaged at present.'

'*Engaged?*'

'I've a piece of work on, a contraption of my own. I can't leave it half-finished.'

'But — you don't get *pide* for that, sir, do you? Captain Brome-well don't pay you?'

Vandervoord smiled, shook his head.

'Then why the devil can't you leave it, same as any man would?' and Captain Twigg spat into the fireplace with contemptuous precision.

'I don't know, Captain. I don't — I assure you! I'm a fool, I suppose. I've begun it, it's progressing, it's interesting — well, yes, it has wonderful possibilities, really astounding —' He broke off. 'But that won't interest you —'

Captain Twigg scratched his head.

'I never, in all my born days,' he said slowly, 'expected to hear a man say, when offered his freedom, No, lock me in agin, I've grown to fancy my chains!'

'Ah yes, but you must consider, Captain, in the realm of pure mathematics there *aren't* any chains!'

All that Captain Twigg could think of this was that Well, really, it was wonderful the way he had picked up the lingo. All the same, it wasn't natural. No man ever gave a more unnatural reason for wanting to stay in a place; to work without pay!

'Fare to me,' he said slyly — rushing in where angels — where

Sabrina herself — had feared to tread. 'That the *Reason* was in those letters I brought ye! *And* she was such a fine one, too, though gettin' on a piece. You should have seen her face when she handed 'em to me — took out of her bosom,' he went on, with a mournful gesture, removing his own grubby hand out of the top of his waistcoat. 'And handed 'em over, and said "thank you", I suppose it was, in her own lingo — and was off again —'

Vandervoord's face was a blank wall. Everybody's Friend became aware that, for once, he had overdone the friendly touch.

'No offence intended,' he said lamely, then — more hopefully — 'You'll think it over? It's the chanst of a lifetime, sir!'

'I have already told you,' said Vandervoord, 'that I have other work on hand; urgent business here, that must be attended to. You must consider the matter closed.'

'The *Cap'n* won't stop you, sir! He leave it to you, he says. Reckon it's up to you to say —'

'What is for M. Vandervoord to say?' inquired Harriet. She had come into the room without their hearing her and now stood between them, looking seriously from one of them to the other. It was the first time that she and Vandervoord had met since the inquest.

Captain Twigg opened and shut his mouth without saying anything. Vandervoord answered for him:

'It appears that your father is willing to release me from my parole so that I may, if I like, join an expedition to the Netherlands —'

She raised her fine eyebrows a little, replying coolly:

'And you are going, of course —'

'I have been making my apologies. I have work on hand that cannot be left —'

The surge of joy that flooded her heart and flushed her cheeks at that, making her blush like the girl she once had been, was succeeded by a surge of pain. For *this* reason — for *work*!

They stood looking at one another, ignoring the visitor. Baffled by the sense of inexplicable hostility hovering about him — whether between the two of them or between each of them separately and him he did not care to investigate, Captain Twigg made his hearty adieux. They hardly noticed — it would seem — his departure.

Disgruntled and disappointed, deeply wounded in his newly-set-up pride as a prominent patriot and a man who succeeded in all he undertook — he said to Spens when he got outside:

'There's something I don't fathom about those two — '

Spens winked, a slow lugubrious wink, raising and lowering the blinds of a salacious peep-show.

'Oh, it's *that* way, is it, bor?'

The blinds were lowered again and Spens nodded twice, portentously.

But even the fascinating thought of an *affaire* at Redonda could not entirely distract Twigg, just then, from the humiliating remembrance of a man — a prisoner of war, forsooth! — who had refused his offer so that he might stay at Redonda and do work that he wasn't paid for.

'Somebody's crazy in this house,' he said heavily, coming down the stone steps and giving the little leaden figure of *P'tit-P'tit*, at the side of them, a malicious kick with his gaitered leg before swinging up into the saddle. The statue tottered on its cracked base and fell over, lying there, looking wide-eyed into the gravel. Spens made no effort to replace it, after the visitor had bidden him a reserved farewell and moved off at a slow trot down the avenue. It was a little God of Love or some such disgusting thing. Let it fall!

CHAPTER XXIV

THE HUNT IS UP

> . . . But a stirring thrills the air
> Sounds as of joyance there
> That the rages
> Of the ages
> Shall be cancelled and Deliverance offered
> from the darts that were . . . — HARDY

THE recent victories of the British, diplomatic and otherwise, had given Bonaparte pause. These interruptions to his grandiose plan for consolidating the whole of Europe under the single flag of the Tricolour could not be permitted to continue. They were trifles in their way, compared with his territorial and political victories, but still they had their effect upon the subject peoples — who would not, it appeared, willingly embrace Liberty, Equality and Fraternity at his hands so long as they still had hopes of having Liberty without the other two. And Great Britain was the stumbling-block, from his point of view. So long as Great Britain continued, from just across the Channel, to open her arms to French emigrants and to allow her Press complete freedom to publish libellous and lying statements about himself and the Republic — so long, too, as the British had the power to undertake innumerable annoying little raids on the French coast on dark nights, there to land spies and traitors and so disseminate their frivolous propaganda and encourage hopes which they would never in any circumstances be able to fulfil (for how could a nation of shopkeepers undertake the liberation of mankind?) — so long as any of these things happened, then just so long the development of his own strategy was interrupted and his beneficent plans for the reorganization of Europe must remain, perforce, a scheme on paper, nothing more.

The weary conqueror must have sighed. He had most certainly to deal with this final adversary sooner or later. Once before he had thought the time ripe to concentrate his attacks upon her; but his star had — most strangely — directed him and his Armies to Egypt instead. He had withdrawn his invasion troops then from Brest and Boulogne, and had broken up, for the time being, his immense concentration of barges and transports there. Now, once again, it would seem that his full attention must be directed towards England; that indeed, he could not hope to settle anything — not even the appointment of a tame Republican to the smallest Bavarian bishopric or to the most insignificant postmaster-generalship in, say, Utrecht or Flushing — until he had once, finally and for all time, settled with her.

Invasion-flotillas had their uses, even when inactive. They could be used for bargaining. The more or less continual exchange of Notes which persisted between the two Embassies of Great Britain and the French Republic would contain references to these

M

flotillas — friendly or otherwise — references which must in due course have their effect in any peace settlement. The British secret agents, drifting in on to French soil on one moonless tide and out (if they were lucky) on another, would be sure to report on any strange sight. Let them report! So much the more would the English know that he meant business, this time; so much more in the way of ultimate reparations and humiliations he would be able to extort!

So Bonaparte began once again, in this weary war, to collect together his invasion forces, to enlarge the fortifications and batteries protecting Calais, Brest and Boulogne, and to concentrate there, once again, his stores of food and of equipment, together with his fleets of barges and troop-transports. The letter N was borne aloft once more on a banner, and the signposts of Boulogne were newly-painted with the words 'The Road to London', pointing with their wooden fingers across the Channel.

From the other side of the Channel the letter N replied, and in answer to the renewed threat of invasion, Nelson was appointed to the supreme command of the North Sea squadrons, over a patrol of waters reaching from Orford Ness to Beachy Head.

This was the big news — the kind of news that stirred London in general and Wordsworth amongst his mountains in particular — the select bluestockings and the French émigrés at Norwich and the ordinary man and woman in every part of the Kingdom. November was to be the crucial month. People remembered from the time old Boney was trying to scare them before, that the experts had all been agreed about the month of November — that season of mists and rolling water-smoke and of a special — so it would seem — malevolent tide all its own.

Long before November, therefore, the coastal areas began once again to prepare themselves, even more thoroughly than before, for the final crisis. The issue of firearms was still lamentably insufficient, so that in the smithies up and down the country the Bible verse was inverted, with ploughshares beaten, if not into swords then into pike-heads, and other peaceful agrarian implements turned as swiftly as might be into weapons of war.

There was, naturally, an increased spate of Government instructions to Redonda (as to other large establishments) at this time; more forms to be filled up, more questions to be answered in duplicate; plans were initiated and furthered, once again, for concealing valuables, driving cattle, and burning crops in the event of the worst coming to the worst; all of which had to be memorized, experimented with and improved upon; extra parish relief had, in addition, to be undertaken; extra self-denying ordinances accepted; a stricter watch on windows and doors after nightfall had to be kept, and a fuller report sent in to the authorities concerning stray visitors in lodging-houses or persons observed acting in a suspicious manner at or near any fortified area.

With this renewed pressure of work — quite apart from the farm management — Harriet coped, as always, steadily and efficiently. She could have wished, however, that it had not fallen upon her (after receiving instructions from the Lord Lieutenant) to request Vandervoord to return to her the Military Pass which had allowed him to pay those visits to Ipswich 'upon the lawful business of Captain Bromewell, J.P., of Redonda'. It was inevitable, in the circumstances, that the interview should remind him of that previous one when she had tried to take away his privileges.

This was the second occasion on which they met, after the Inquest. Once again it was in the morning-room.

Harriet held out the Lord Lieutenant's letter across the desk towards him, saying:

'You see, it is a mere matter of form. They have to take these precautionary measures and I am afraid you are included with the rest of the — the visitors. It may not be for long — till December at most —'

He stood holding the letter for a very long time, looking down at it. Still looking down, at last he said to her:

'You could, of course, if you cared to, get me an exemption from this.'

He struck the letter lightly, contemptuously, with the back of his hand, and went on composedly: 'But of course I do not expect it of you. You have always resented my visits to Ipswich. You have visited Fulton and tried to persuade him against receiving me —'

She cried out hotly, 'That's not true!'

355

'You don't deny,' he said, 'that you have at any rate called upon Fulton? And questioned him about me?'

It was absurd that, because it was his voice speaking to her—his very dear voice—she should feel a shame concerning a visit she had a perfect right to make — had been in fact instructed to make on her father's behalf, by the Lord Lieutenant, so as to confirm the French Prisoner's reports of his activities at Ipswich. But now, since he considered this to be a shameful act, the colour of shame flooded her cheeks.

She said, trembling a little: 'I went because I was advised to. I found him full of praise of you —'

He smiled, an extraordinarily bitter smile.

'And that struck you as surprising?' he said.

They might have been two people who had never been joined by anything except animosity in the whole course of their acquaintance.

'Oh, Van!' she heard herself crying brokenly, 'must it always be like this, whenever we meet? It isn't bearable! I beg of you to believe me, I had no hand in that (she indicated the letter) at all. When it came my heart ached, because I knew how you would resent it; because I knew I would have to enforce it and that you would think—just as you *have* done and without any, *any* justification, Van! — that I was glad of an opportunity to incommode you —'

He did not answer. Instead he fished deep down into his pocket and produced the Pass, with the seal on it and the Lord Lieutenant's signature. He threw it down on to the desk before her.

'There you are,' he said. 'You have now taken my parole from me, and with it.the only employment which resigned me to this existence; resigned me to it so much that I refused Twigg's offer of liberty and a chance to return to my own country. Nevertheless I should be grateful, I suppose! You might have taken my life as well! You have at least left me that!'

Hardly understanding the full implications of what he said, because they were so fearful, Harriet answered:

'Do you really think it lies in my power to do that?'

'It lies in your power,' he answered, 'to do incalculable damage; it lies in all our power, *all* of us, to do the most horrible things to each other. The world is full, at this very moment, of people tormenting and making each other miserable in the most obscene ways! Dear God,' he exclaimed, 'we should have been born upon islands — each one of us, every one upon his own island! then at least there might have been a chance of real joy, of real innocence! As soon as we meet, we begin to kill each other — implacably, eternally to fight each other. Even loving is fighting — '

'No! *No!*'

'Yes, *Yes*, Harriet! Have you not learnt that from me, at least?' And he went across to the window and stood looking out of it, down upon the fallen *P'tit-P'tit* with his nose in the gravel, and down the leaf-drenched avenue of elms, with his hands clasping and unclasping behind him in restless frustration.

In a way it was some relief, though a poor sort. Until now he had always been so gentle, even in dispute with her; his natural good manners had rebuked her bad ones — even when the right was on her side for all the world to see. 'Oh!' she had once cried out to him in real vexation, 'you are always so sweet-temperedly in the *wrong*, Van, and I am always so bad-temperedly in the *right!*' To which he had replied characteristically, 'How can you be so sure you are right, *Ma Mie*?'

It was ten thousand, thousand years since he had called her *Ma Mie*. It was a million years since they had been anything but enemies to each other. And she loved him so much, so overwhelmingly, that even now the sight of his figure standing framed in the tall window moved her to a gesture of the utmost tenderness towards him; and her lips framed endearments which she lacked the courage to speak.

Even if she *had* spoken them aloud, she had the conviction that he would not have heard them.

But he *was* conscious of her, for he said, without turning round:

'How much longer are you going to keep me in suspense? Take it up, for God's sake, Harry — lock it in the desk, put the key of the desk in your bosom — make my humiliation complete! I can't prevent it and you know it, but if you have a spark of mercy left in you, hurry, hurry!'

She did just as he said, took up the Pass, folded it, locked it away

357

in the desk drawer, and put the key back where she always wore it, on a chain round her neck and tucked into the bosom of her dress.

When his ears told him this procedure was completed, Vander- voord turned and came back to the desk.

'Am I at liberty to go?' he asked, 'or have you some other treat in store for me!'

'I would almost rather tear my tongue out than tell you,' she said. 'But — they have put sentries on the fortifications again, and my instructions — in the present emergency — are that nobody from Redonda, *nobody* — not even I myself — may go any longer on to the beach there, or use that Cabin — '

He was always incalculable. So now he answered quaintly:

'The Lord of the Manor's Right extends to above the ebb of the tide.'

It was a catch-word he had learnt from Clancy. At one time it had been his amusement to learn, parrot-wise, certain legal phrases and judgments from Clancy's law-books, and to roll them off his tongue at appropriate moments. This had served for mirthful occasions, but now it was not meant mirthfully and Harriet knew it.

She answered seriously: 'Yes, but not in war-time, Van. None of us has any rights now, if the Military Authorities choose to over- ride them.'

'So,' he said, 'it seems that we are to be hedged in by restrictions of every sort. Would it be permissible, I wonder, for me to go into one of the barns and hang myself from the rafters there, or is that also against the regulations?'

Harriet answered: 'Believe — you *must*! — that I shall do every- thing I possibly can to make all this less irksome to you. I will send a tumbril for your things at Ipswich — '

'Don't be a fool,' he said, 'I am not going to have that precious apparatus shaken to bits in a tumbril!'

It was the kind of reply she would have endured from nobody else in the world, and he knew it.

'Will you tell me then,' she went on quietly, 'what — '

He broke in with 'Oh, let it be! Leave it to Fulton. He will take care of it. One day — who knows? — he may even gain some profit by it, when the world has come to its senses again — '

'But it isn't fair that *your* work, *your* inventions should benefit someone else!'

'No?' he replied coolly, without looking at her, 'I don't think that your father has been of the same opinion for the last seven years!'

It was a cruel thrust, but to-day he was giving no quarter.

'At least,' she attempted miserably, 'you will let me fetch your things from the Cabin — '

He half shrugged. 'Fetch them if you like,' he responded, 'throw them into the sea if you like. It's of no consequence. There is always Slaughden — '

'You know perfectly well, Van, that Slaughden will be out-of-bounds as well.'

He pretended to be surprised at that too. 'Indeed!' he said, 'well, well — how one lives and learns! At this rate, unless I am very careful, soon everything will be out-of-bounds except your bed, Harriet.'

It was utterly unlike him; a great tiredness swept up over her, causing her to renounce the whole wretched struggle between them, and she dropped her head down silently upon her crossed arms on the desk. The tears pressed themselves slowly out between her closed lids, as if saying, *You see? You knew we would have to come*, and began tracing a way they knew well, a *via dolorosa*, down the side of her cheek and on to the hard desk.

She felt a hand resting lightly upon her bowed head then, and passing tenderly, exactly as it used to do, over her smooth hair; and heard him saying in a whisper:

'No, no, my darling; that was unwarrantable. Since we must hurt each other we must — but not in that way — '

Perhaps it was a dream. She had fallen asleep out of her great weariness, and had dreamed it. Had, at any rate, dreamed the endearment.

When she opened her eyes, he had gone.

What he did with himself or how he existed during the weeks that followed she hardly knew. Captain Bromewell was ill again, requiring constant attention, but too weak to insist on Susan's ministrations — which was fortunate, since her hands were already full. With superintending the attendance upon him, and the affairs of the farm — particularly the Michaelmas sowings (which were to be done on a new system, under her orders), and dealing with all the new business that besieged her owing to the Emergency, Harriet was literally too tired to know or care much what had become of him. Surely he had not, after all, dared to disobey her (and so risk his life) about Slaughden? There was no evidence, one way or the other, to show.

She took to going down to Susan's cabin whenever she could spare a moment, to see the child. She had begun to love it as she had once supposed she would never be able to love anyone except its father. Drawing comfort from its occasional ludicrous likenesses to him (a brief pencil sketch foreshadowing a portrait in oils) — and comfort from the pleasure that Louisa began to take in her company, somehow the weeks passed by. They went neither slow nor fast, they were timeless . . . But she was hurt that Vandervoord himself had not seen Louisa for weeks. Though he might have grown tired of *her*, surely he should love his own child! Surely he was not so unnatural as to hate his own child!

Nor could Susan supply a proper explanation of his behaviour.

'But you saw him last!' persisted Harriet, 'what did he say? Did he *say* he was not coming again?'

Susan shook her head.

'Didn't he love her?' asked Harriet, putting out her hand to the baby; who, after a beaming pause, leant forward suddenly with the most artless and perfect benevolence, and took hold of Harriet's fingers. 'How could he resist her!'

According to Susan, it seemed that he loved her, true enough. She couldn't say more.

The notion dawned upon Harriet that he was pervertedly visiting the sins of the parents upon the children; he was punishing Louisa by not loving her and wanting to see her — just as he had punished *her*. He was thrusting Louisa out of his life as he had thrust Harriet — because he feared that if he did not, this morsel, this scrap, might in some way entwine itself about his affections so that he could never escape. Was *that* the way he thought of it? Well, if he did, he should see she was not beaten yet. If she could no longer fight for herself, she could fight for her child.

'If he won't come to see *her*,' she told Susan, 'you must take Louisa to see *him*.'

'I can't do ut, Miss Harry. Not if you asked me ever so!'

'What do you mean?'

'Please don't you ask it of me, Miss. I'll send her to see him if you say so — but I'll not take her. I'll not speak to him!'

Harriet gazed at her, amazed. That the docile Sukey should turn so passionate at such a request was inexplicable. She could not fathom it at all, nor could she extract further explanations — only a bursting into tears and a request Please, please to be let alone.

'Very well, since you're so obstinate about it — but it's not very obliging to me, is it?'

And she went slowly home through a drift of rattling Autumn leaves, to the house that should have been a home to come to — that should have sheltered her husband and child — and which held only a sick old man.

Nevertheless, she still loved it, most passionately, looking up now at its massive brick through the burnished trees and thinking to herself: *Mine, mine, mine — and Van's and Louisa's! One day, when all this muddle is straightened out and there's peace again, and rest again, then Redonda shall come into its own!*

It was absurd that, under her surveillance, Redonda fields should bear more wheat and more roots, her cows yield more milk, her sheep more wool, her poultry more eggs, her pigs more bacon, her meadows more hay — and yet that her own life should still be barren amidst this richness. It was absurd that here not a stick or a stone should be out of order (she must speak to Spens about that gate-post in the five-acre, that needed attention) and that her own life should have such woefully hungry patches in it. That's what they called poor soil, here; the sandy soil of the coastal regions — 'hungry land'.

The thought came to her that it might be as well to pray that this state of affairs might be changed; not that *she* should be changed, but that the things that happened to her might be. 'I am getting pious in my old age, like my father,' she thought, smiling a little grimly. There had been a time when her father, like God Almighty, could move mountains for her. Well, he could not move *this* mountain . . . There still remained God Almighty — or so Mr. Mogus claimed.

She was glad Mr. Mogus was still away. She would go to the Clerk and get the key of the church, as though she were attending to some ordinary Parish business — the flowers for the Altar (how long since she had bothered herself about such things!) or notices to be put up in the church porch concerning the Parish.

She made her way towards the church, across the right-of-way. The churchyard was grey-green, full of tussocky grass and tall, dried kexes, with fallen horse-chestnut fronds lying upon it, like large flecks of solid sunlight scattered indiscriminately over grass and graves. Someone had cut a late crop of hay amongst the gravestones and the wheelbarrow, with the rake and scythe still lying athwart it, stood under one of the half-stripped trees. There was a bitter smell of bonfires in the air, mingled with the dank smell of old leaves — too old to be this century's, thought Harriet — harking back possibly to centuries long ago; it was natural that they should loiter between the gravestones from year to year, and be overlooked by the gardener.

Standing quite still in the hazy sunlight, feeling it warm upon her head and the back of her neck, Harriet heard voices. The sound came from a building along one side of the church — a secular extension, as it were, in which coffins sometimes had a brief resting-place, and where the gardener and gravedigger kept their tools.

There was laughter mixed with the talk. Harriet stiffened. In the Rector's absence it was the business of a Bromewell to see that order was kept on these premises. Laughter did not signify order.

She walked on, into the churchyard, and went up to the out-building.

Afterwards she could not have said whether it had been a surprise to her, or whether she had expected it all along. There was a long trestle-table standing down the centre of the room, upon which sat Vandervoord, one leg dangling, while he chipped with hammer and chisel at a small headstone. The gardener (for he it was) stood beside him, looking at him, hands on hips — not quite laughing, but ready to be extremely diverted by the next remark that should fall from Vandervoord's lips.

Harriet paused on the threshold, uncertain. The whole situation seemed so irregular; and yet — and yet . . .

Before she could decide anything, Vandervoord had felt her shadow cross the doorway, had looked up and seen her.

This was the third encounter between them, since the inquest.

He slipped off the table with slightly overdone respect. The gardener dropped his hands to his sides as if surprised stealing apples.

'Have you come to tell me,' said the beloved voice, 'that *this* is forbidden too? Don't tell me that *this* is forbidden! It is such an innocent pursuit, I assure you — and on these premises too . . . After all, a man must fill the time somehow; or does the Lord Lieutenant — ingenious fellow! — suspect that I have erected a signal-station in the belfry?'

The gardener had slipped away, cat-like, embarrassed as much by Vandervoord's irreverence as by Miss Bromewell's silence. They heard the wheelbarrow go creaking hastily away to some distant part of the churchyard.

Oh, Van my darling, said Harriet's heart, *how long it is since I have seen you — light of my eyes, and joy of my heart!*

Aloud she said, 'I had business — at the church — '

'What — *you*? Business at the church?'

' — and I heard voices — '

'And wishing of course to know, you came round to see. Very natural!'

She stepped in, a little more closely to him; came up and stood by his side, as if ignoring his comment.

'What is it you are making?'

For answer he gestured down at the table. On it lay a small rough headstone for a grave, from which Vandervoord's hammer and chisel had already begun to wring out the cold delicate pattern of a scroll, overlaid by the wings of a bird. She reached down her hand and touched it, feeling the residue of chipped stone flowing beneath her fingers. She had little taste in such things, but to her it was beautiful since his hands had wrought it.

'I didn't know you could do this sort of stone-work, Van.'

'Is there anything,' he replied lightly, 'that I can't do?'

She sighed. 'I begin to doubt it! What is it for?'

'A grave, Harry. A little — little grave!'

'A child's grave?' A morbid thought struck her, 'Van!'

But he had begun to chip at the stone again, seating himself side-saddle upon the table, cocking his head on one side the better to lure the flowing lines of the scroll out of the granite block.

'Since you won't be content till you know, I will put you out of your torment,' he said ' — but it was intended for a surprise. Have you seen Susan's baby's headstone?'

No, she hadn't. She had been busy . . .

He interrupted her: 'Do. Go and see it. It is the poorest thing, a rough lump of granite—no bigger than the hunk of cheese a farm-hand eats for dinner — or *used* to eat! She comes every week to tend it, and put flowers on the grave. And she goes on from there,' he said, 'to Snape, to do the same service for Sabrina's grave.'

He did not trouble to give her a courtesy-title. Perhaps the dead have no need of such things.

Chip, *chip*, *chip*, went the chisel, cheeping like young birds in a nest. Vandervoord bent down over his work and blew upon it, breathing into it the breath of life, scattering the clogging dust.

'When I had finished this,' he went on (since Harriet said nothing), 'I intended offering it to Susan to replace that rough memorial. Poor child, it had little enough in life and was meanly served, too, in death. It cannot care now, one way or the other — but Sukey will care —'

Yes, Sukey would surely care — would be proud and grateful beyond expression. Infant would have the finest headstone in the whole of the churchyard — since *he* would have made it! . . . Yet, still, there was an incongruity, somehow; for Van to be doing such a thing at all (he used to say in the past that hammering ruined the hands for fine work, destroying their fine sensitivity). And now his hands were covered in stone-dust, and his nails cracked, she could see, with the finger-tips roughened from contact with the granite . . .
Add to this that Susan herself had been in a frame of mind utterly antagonistic to him. Yet here he was doing her a favour — and confident that she would be glad of it!

'Are you so sure,' she could not help asking, 'that Susan will be grateful to you?'

'Why should she not be?'

'I saw her to-day,' said Harriet. 'I have just come from her. I wanted her to bring the baby to see you —'

'My dear Harry, how could she do that?' he said, stopping in his hammering, surprised enough for a minute to look at her. 'The baby is dead! You see me here carving its headstone!'

The cold, pure pattern of the scroll climbed upwards, winding itself invisibly, icily round Harriet's heart as she looked and listened. There had been a time when he had said, 'At least leave me my reason,' and, further, 'the thread that binds it is very slender' . . . Had the thread snapped? If it had *not* snapped (and no lunatic, surely, ever worked so deftly) how could he possibly be so cruel, even for a moment, as to forget the very existence of his *own* child!

In that moment she began to hate him — still without knowing it. Not intermittently, but steadily and stealthily.

'You are not thinking of what you are saying,' she said. 'I meant our child, *your* child —'

'Of course, to be sure, *our* child,' he repeated, like a lesson chanted.

'— and she would not bring her to see you! You have done something — absurd though it seems — that has offended Susan; without meaning too, I am sure,' she amended, 'but these ignorant creatures, you know, take offence very easily —'

He seemed to be surveying the scroll with unusual interest, summing up all its possibilities. He did not say anything, but he whistled quietly as he looked at his work.

The problem remained unsolved, insoluble. Susan, who was never offended at anything, had yet taken offence at him; he, the sweetest-natured, best-mannered man who ever walked the soil of Redonda, had nevertheless returned her earlier hospitality with rudeness and — worse still — utter neglect.

The memory of Louisa's gesture — the leaning forward with a straight little back and taking hold of her mother's hand with that artless, perfect benevolence, giving all of her beaming self in the gesture, came again to Harriet.

It was cruel, abominable, that a father blessed with such a daughter should be able to desert her! That he should prefer to sit here instead, gossiping with gardeners, and wasting his time and talent on a gravestone for a little bastard. . . .

'If you would think a little more of the living child,' she said, her lips trembling, ' — and a little less of the dead one — '

'Yes,' he resumed, just as if she had not spoken. 'She goes on to Snape churchyard and pays the same tender service to Sabrina in *her* grave; every week, rain or shine, in burning heat or bitter frost. I believe she prays for her soul, too — hoping (so she once told me) that the young lady might give an eye to her baby in Heaven, since it died so young and will need a nurse there. These ignorant people, as you say, have the most grotesque fancies. . . .'

It was not to be borne. Harriet could not remember leaving him, or whether she said any more to him or not — because the next thing she remembered was walking homewards again, with the sound of his industrious chipping diminishing slowly behind her.

No, it was not to be borne. If he himself had been capable of arranging the whole incident for the purpose of humiliating her, it could not have been better managed. Tears filled her eyes — as so often these days — but this time they were tears of pure rage. He had humiliated her — and Louisa with her — and Redonda with them both! He cared less for the Mistress of Redonda and the child (his own daughter) who should one day inherit Redonda than he did for a dead love-child of Susan's — who was better out of the way in any case since it would have been sure to grow up sickly and so be a burden to itself and to the Parish.

He did not only insult her with this over-solicitousness for the dead baby. He enlisted Sabrina's ghost upon his side, too. Well — he should see that she was not afraid of him or of ghosts either! He should see . . . The blackest most poisonous thoughts filled her heart — so black and horrible that they moved with hooded faces, jostling each other. Somehow or other — she did not see how as yet — she would repay him with interest for having served her so!

Just as she had once, so long, long ago, willed for the world not to end, so now she willed (it was too tempestuous and impatient to be called praying) for the War not to end. If the War ended (for better or worse, in victory or defeat), Vandervoord would be a free man, escaping both her and retribution. So it must drag on — for years if need be — until the perfect punishment had been awarded to him who had punished her so cruelly all this last year and more. A year? She could not count the period in weeks and months — knowing only with Shakespeare in his sonnet that it was 'A Hell of Time'.

The punishment, she found herself saying as she walked, *is death. The punishment is death, is death, is death. Nothing less pays a rich enough ransom; nothing else will serve to wipe out the memory of all that he has done to me and mine. He must die, so that his child shall have no memory of his past, and no fear of a future in which he may suddenly reappear to bring woe and doom to her as he has done to her mother!*

Mingled with this hooded thought was the thought of his dearness; how sweet he was, how companionable, how entertaining, how gifted beyond words with his head and his hands. These sunny love-thoughts lay athwart the black revenge thoughts as the coarse golden fronds of horse-chestnut leaves lay scattered, here and there, over the grey-green tussocks of grass in the church-yard.

O Van, O my heart's love, say it is not true! Come to me once, again, as you once came! Love me as you once loved me! Set me as a seal upon thine heart and as a seal upon thy arm, for love is strong as death, jealousy is cruel as the grave!

Cruel as the grave-stone you carve for Susan's dead child; cruel as your neglect of my living one!

From that time onwards, though she did not in any way neglect any of her everyday employments, Harriet began to consider how best she might achieve her purpose.

You still want your own way, Clement had said, long, long ago, *and would I believe commit murder to get it.* She had wanted her own way with Sabrina. (*Beware, Van! Beware, my darling, my most devilish lover!*)

And now, as if to make up for the poor harvest, there came a month of perfect Michaelmas weather, bland, sunny, with that particular golden quality in the sunshine and in the intense blueness of the skies over the stubble fields that belonged to no other season. Even the North Sea seemed to have fallen under the same pacific spell, lapping at the shore for once with lover's kisses instead of with wailing and gnashing of teeth. Bonaparte's Weather, the Boulogne troops called it over the water, associating, as so often, the sunny days with the ruler of the hour. Bonaparte's Weather, agreed the English, preparing afresh the beacon-masts, the watch-houses and the wonderful new invention of the semaphore tele-graph by which means messages could be sent from Yarmouth to the Nore in no more than five minutes. Zero Hour was approaching once more, as it had done in previous years and would — for all anyone knew — do many times again. So let watchfulness be redoubled and the whole Nation stand on guard!

Dear God, prayed Harriet, *do not let the Invasion come — for in the confusion Vandervoord will escape. Ah, Father in Heaven, do not bring the War to an end, do not allow the negotiations to come to anything, for in the Peace which would follow Vandervoord would escape too!* So single-minded was she in this infatuation of desire that the suffer-ing or otherwise of millions of European inhabitants meant less than nothing to her. Bonaparte himself was nothing (at this juncture) but a puppet manipulated by a God into movements which mattered only in so far as they affected her or Vander-voord.

She began to be craftily attentive to possibilities — no matter how small — for tripping Vandervoord into some fatal indiscre-tion. There had been rumours of an enemy landing-party in the Yarmouth area; a shepherd-boy had sworn to seeing lights sig-nalling from the Moors at midnight; a sailor on leave, tipsily indif-ferent to King's Regulations, had been shot for walking into a forbidden area. Surely with all these rumours flying about, and with the Volunteers and Sea Fencibles so nervily on the defensive — and with Vandervoord himself as indifferent to danger as he had always been — it should be possible to trip him — having no part herself in his punishment beyond a rejoicing that he had been finally rewarded for all his sins of omission and commission.

Whether such concentration of passion and purpose made her light-headed or not, she was not sure, but she began after a time to have the suspicion that Vandervoord understood these intentions of hers perfectly well; that he was as amusedly indifferent to them as he had been to all the intentions of her whole life, fancying himself able to parry any blows she might deal him with one hand behind his back.

They did not meet again after the encounter in the churchyard. The days continued golden, and her implacable purpose continued. The fox may avoid the path where it scents human footsteps — but sooner or later it errs, and pays for that error with life. The partridge which can lie so close and still in the stubble, betrays itself finally by the brightness of its terrified, unwinking eye. When the snow comes, the hare in its form is not safe any longer; when the tempest blows, the leaves are blown away that sheltered the hedgehog in the hedge-bottom; when the corn is cut the rabbits must run for it — though they crowd in, to the very last minute, invisible in the innermost ranks of wheat.

But he was making a fight for it — yes, she must admit that! From all accounts he went no more to the forbidden area of Slaughden Quay. He did not attempt to approach the Fisherman's Cabin again, whether by road or by the Shearings. He broke no bounds to get again into Ipswich (as she had hoped he might) to inquire after his beloved machinery. Fulton had been once to see him, and had been closeted with him for two hours in his workshop — but there was nothing culpable in that. He seemed determined, indeed, at this period to perform the part of a model prisoner of war, and to mock her impotence in being able to prevent his achieving this ambition. Once a week he had to report to a Military Headquarters which had taken up permanent residence in the neighbourhood. He did so promptly to the minute — returning as promptly and winning the inevitable whole-hearted regard of all the men there with whom he came into contact. His name indeed became a byword for good behaviour, and colonels whose duty it was to deal with him and others used to remark that if everyone gave as little trouble as the Prisoner at Redonda, everything would go a great deal more easily, mark their words. One Colonel became so interested in Vandervoord that he offered of his own accord to write to M. Otto to reveal to him that there had been some misunderstanding and that the man classified as a French Prisoner was — strange to say — not of French nationality at all.

Perhaps the most certain evidence of Vandervoord's unfailing good manners lies in this: that he thanked the man who made this offer just as warmly as, through the course of time, he had thanked all the other thirteen, fourteen, fifteen — what was it? — he had long ago lost count and so, he was sure, had M. Otto — always supposing that gentleman had ever kept count. Whether the Colonel ever wrote or not, he neither knew nor cared. The procedure seemed by now to belong to some long-closed chapter in his life; it could help him as little as the carved headstone he had just finished for Susan's baby, could help the baby.

In mid-September Mr. Mogus returned to his rectory, and paid a visit of long-delayed condolence to his old neighbour Captain Bromewell. He was in time to hear Captain Bromewell's views on the Machine as the Beast and the number 666 in Revelation, and to learn that, if strength were given him, the Captain proposed to devote a whole new pamphlet to this subject and to rouse the people of England to their common danger. He was particularly violent on the subject of pump-mills.

On Mr. Mogus afterwards describing this interview to the doctor, the doctor declared that that final harangue about the Machine and the Beast was sufficient to account for the Captain's death, which took place later that same evening. His heart had given way, the doctor said, under the constant strain of his abuse of the pump-mills. He had long been warned against any undue excitement but it was the doctor's opinion, strictly between ourselves, Mogus, that no Bromewell ever born took kindly to advice, heh?

This not too friendly comment might be taken very well as an epitaph for the Captain, for it certainly described him better than the eulogy later inscribed on his headstone.

Once more Clancy could not come down to Redonda for the funeral. It cut him to the heart, he declared in a letter to Harriet, but really urgent business had called him down to Wiltshire; and since we cannot do the dead any favour by pulling long faces about them, and since in any case a hardworking lawyer and Volunteer deserves some relaxation, would Harriet pack up and send down *by the very next London-Norwich coach*, the very handsome rook-rifle that the Captain required no longer and which, in his lifetime, had been as untouchable to Clancy and Clement as any *tabu* to any aboriginal.

The funeral service went off without any hitch. (*Practice*, Harriet might have thought grimly to herself, *makes perfect*.) And the first day her father's coffin went out of the house, Harriet arranged for the baby Louisa's cot to be brought in. The King is dead. Long live the King. As head of the house undisputed (in Clancy's absence) she had her own furniture moved into her father's room, and Louisa's and Susan's things were to be put in her old room — with the inevitable Tommy relegated to the dressing-room — at least until he reached the bird-scaring age, which could not now be long delayed.

There remained Clancy, even if he was absent; and what was to be done about Clancy when he returned home eventually — at least to share possession. But there was no use in worrying oneself over problems which had not yet arisen, especially since another, still very much present, remained to be solved.

Harriet could not grieve for her father. He had stood for a power opposed to her power (when it came to marriage) and the going down of such a power was not an occasion for grief. Age went out of Redonda and youth came into it — her lovely girl, her Louisa! The very walls must rejoice, as much surely as the ground rejoices to feel the fresh green spears of grass pushing their way, in the Spring, through the dried dead tussocks of last year's grass.

Whilst the mistress of the house attended the funeral, the servants scrubbed and polished with a will. Something portentous was afoot! The furniture was to be shifted as soon as the big fires, that Harriet had ordered to be got going, had aired the bedrooms. Later the same day, Susan and her precious charge and their furniture were to be brought over in the wagonette.

But at midday Susan was already at Redonda — eyes burning, hair flowing, utterly distraught. It was some time before she could talk coherently at all, she had run so fast, she said, and all the way. She carried dire news.

It appeared that, just after she had given the children their breakfast, she had gone down her bit of garden to hang up some linen which had been in soak overnight. She put it a long way down the garden, she added, because she was afraid of Tommy's dirty little fingers. (It was not her linen, it was Harriet's.) When she came up to the house again Tommy was seated, as he had been before, by the doorway in the sun — but Louisa, whom she had left in her crib, had vanished. Tommy said The Man had taken her. He meant Vandervoord, explained Susan — almost unnecessarily, since there was only one man in the world for Tommy.

In Louisa's place, in the crib, was the Letter.

She held it out now with a hand trembling from distress and exertion, to Harriet.

Harriet took it with surprising calmness and broke the seal and unfolded it just as calmly. It had been addressed on the outside simply 'Harriet'. It was very short.

My darling,

Through the help of kind friends a chance has come for me to reach freedom. I am taking that chance, and taking Louisa with me. Do not fear, I love her as much as you do and will — God help me — do her less harm than, despite yourself, in the course of time you would be bound to do. Think kindly of her if you cannot do so of me. For what has happened in the past, I am *desolé*. For the future — Oh Harry, I hope! I hope!

Mention us both in your prayers, if you ever pray. You will never find me.

JAN VANDERVOORD

She found herself folding it up again tidily, back into the same creases from which it had been unfolded; and heard herself saying aloud to Susan:

'I suppose he is making for Portsmouth.'

'To *Portsmouth*? Oh, Miss Harry — not with my blessed baby!'

'Be quiet!' shouted Harriet through Susan's storm of frightened tears. Inside, her mind went on quite calmly. *Of course, Portsmouth will be the place; that is the word that has been hidden in the back of my mind all these weeks; that is the clue I am seeking. In this jigsaw puzzle it is the vital piece with the dagger upon it, and it will sink into his heart.*

She wasted no more time on Susan. In a sudden whirlwind of activity she had enlisted Spens, the best team of horses, the fastest vehicle in the stables — and was off to Bury (without waiting to change out of the black clothes in which she had gone to the funeral service) in search of someone suddenly become indispensable to her — Captain Twigg.

Spens swore he would be there, and was as good as his word. He was run to earth in his old haunt of the Blue Goose, and brought, at once, breathless and flattered, to the private room Harriet had engaged, at the best inn in the town.

The French Prisoner had escaped, began Harriet without preamble. She had watched him carefully during the last few weeks and had become convinced that he was working as a secret agent for the French Government. There had been the incidents of the light signalling from the moors at Yarmouth, of the rumoured enemy landing-party. He was implicated in both. In proof of her statements as to his sympathies, Harriet further added that when captured he would be found to have upon him a most detailed map of Portsmouth harbour and all its fortifications — the penalty for owning which was death.

Twigg could only nod in agreement to all this. She gave him time for no more. Harriet declared she had put the matter straightaway into the hands of the Sea Fencibles because she preferred that the reward should go to local men and not to members of the Regular Army — who might come from anywhere. She would pay all expenses.

'Spens will corroborate me in every detail,' she said.

Spens did so, with humble pleasure.

'Spens and I intend to stay here in Bury,' she said, 'until you can report his capture. He has also kidnapped a child.'

Spens could corroborate that too — with an additional wink of both eyes to Captain Twigg.

Captain Twigg congratulated Miss Bromewell on her promptitude. Could she help the Authorities further (here he puffed out

his chest) by supplying a hint, a clue, as to the probable direction
the fugitive had taken?

'He has probably taken the London road, *en route* for Portsmouth,'
said Harriet.

Captain Twigg thought no. Decidedly no. No enemy agent
carrying a secret plan or chart of Portsmouth's fortifications would
be so crazy as to head for that town.

'I assure you,' said Harriet, 'that it is just what he *would* do. You
do not know him as well as I know him!'

And she gave him the money for the journey.

She and Spens stayed six days and nights in Bury, waiting for
news — letting Redonda rot if it cared to. The hunt was up, the
hounds were in full cry and such music was sweeter to their straining
ears than any other sound on earth.

On the seventh day Twigg was back and had news for them. The
bells of all the churches were ringing so loudly as he told them —
celebrating the Peace of Amiens just concluded between Bonaparte
and Great Britain — that they had to shut all the windows and draw
the thick curtains across them to be able to hear above the joyous
din.

Captain Twigg had obeyed Harriet and gone to Portsmouth; and
nobody had been more surprised than he was, to learn that Harriet
had guessed right. He had come upon the French Prisoner almost
at once, sitting at breakfast in the Red Lion, feeding Louisa with
porridge from one hand and reading a newspaper with the other.

Twigg, with the dignity and assurance of an armed guard lent
him by the Garrison — had searched the French Prisoner; had come
at once upon the map of Portsmouth Harbour and had forthwith
made all the motions of arresting Vandervoord with the sternest
warnings of what lay ahead.

'Speak louder,' said Harriet. 'I cannot hear you because of the
bells. Speak louder. What then?'

What then? Why, then M. Vandervoord had laughed hearty,
and had asked him why he did not learn to read; then he had waved
the newspaper which announced the Peace Treaty, in large print,
right in front of his face. That had wholly flabbergasted the Sea
Fencible; he was not sure that he was not flabbergasted still.

Then? What then? Why, then Vandervoord had invited Captain
Twigg to dismiss the puzzled soldiery (which he did) and to sit
down and have some coffee with them (which he did, having been
riding all night like a fiend). Besides, it was the last chance, seeing
that M. Vandervoord said that in half an hour he and the child
(to whom, it appeared, he was father) were boarding an American
merchantman which would be leaving on the next tide. He was
going to America to work with a relation of that Mr. Fulton in
Ipswich — a man who had ideas about all sorts of things, fare to him,
including a boat (Mr. Vandervoord had obligingly drawn designs
on the tablecloth for him) which could be submerged for eight
hours at a time.

Captain Twigg had been so interested in the possibilities of such
a craft, both for legal and illegal purposes, that — if Harriet had
insisted — he would have admitted that he had not pressed the
second charge — that of kidnapping the child. But (he said in part
extenuation) the little mawther was so happy with him, 'that was
laughin' all over her little old face' — that there seemed no doubt
that he was what he claimed to be, her father. Was that so?

Certainly, Harriet agreed, he was the father. (Spens, Spens, can
nobody stop the din of those horrible bells?)

Well then, said Captain Twigg loudly, still trying to shout down
the hysterical joy of the bells. Well then . . . there seemed no more
to say. The merchantman had sailed as arranged, on the next tide,
with the Vandervoord passengers aboard. He couldn't rightly
say for where, he found the Portsmouth harbour folk wholly old-
fashioned when it came to providing information. But the beer!
And the lights that night! And the bells ringing their old hearts out!
Long, he repeated fervently but incomprehensibly, might they all
live, Miss Bromewell, to repeat the day!

Afterwards Captain Twigg used up a considerable portion of the
expenses in celebrating the Peace all over again at the Blue Goose
with Spens.

'Fare to me,' he said, 'we got to make the best on it while it lasts,
bor. That ain't ne more than a fair-weather Peace! Time Winter
come, that'll bloo up to a tempest, sure as eggs are eggs!'

Nor, truth to tell. did the prospect seem at all to dismay him.

CHAPTER XXV

THE WHEEL COMES FULL CIRCLE

Bright golden moon, that now art near to thy setting, go
thou and salute my lover, he that stole my love, and that
kissed me and said 'Never will I leave thee'. And lo, he
has left me, like a field reaped and gleaned, like a church
where no man comes to pray, like a city desolate . . .
Therefore I would curse him, and yet again my heart fails
me for tenderness, my heart is vexed within me, my
spirit is moved with anguish . . .'

Chants Populaires de la Grèce

To get back to the house was the thing. Yes — to get back to the
house, even the desolate house which could never be a happy house
any more.

The avenue had never seemed so long; she was not yet half-way to
the sandpit, and the sandpit was only half-way to the house. Harriet
stumbled along, looking straight before her, seeing nothing, feeling
the great, tiring pain of what had befallen her and the smaller, cunning pain of the gravel pressing upwards through the thin soles of
her shoes.

It was stupid to walk in such shoes; they were indoor slippers, the
very ones which, in her furious haste, she had neglected to change
when she first went with Spens to Bury. And — coming home
again, she had not been able to sit still in silence any more, but had
jumped down at the entrance gates and made her way alone (or
begun making it) up the avenue to the house.

Somebody else, too, had worn the wrong shoes. Sabrina had worn
the wrong shoes. But — God in Heaven, it cannot have hurt so much
to have been softly invited within the marshy land there — I will not
say quicksand — it was always marshy there, long before the pump-
mills, whatever they say — it cannot have hurt as much as the gravel
pricking up into my insteps, and under my eyelids, seeking out the
tenderest parts of my being . . .

An odd thought flickered in her black mind for a moment — like the last flame of a fire before the fire subsides into a breathing, steady and obscure smoke: *If it were snowing now, I should be leaving tracks of blood along the avenue.* But it was not snowing. The steady rain of the morning and early afternoon had ceased, but there was still a feeling of wet weather about — rain over the sea perhaps, for the gulls were flying inland — and she was conscious that the elm trees about her were still weeping (after their habit), still letting the rain-drops drip from their branches in mournful susurration, saluting her as she passed.

Van had wanted them down, always. He admired their beauty but he could not live at Redonda (hadn't he said it?) unless the big trees shadowing the drive were polled — he would feel a prisoner ... But no, that was not accurate. Dear Christ, that was far too definite a thing for Van ever to have said! What he had said was '*Any*one would feel a prisoner' and 'If *I* were living at Redonda', not 'When I live at Redonda' ...

It was not that he thought they were dangerous, only that they made him feel shut in. He had wanted them cut down — and yet the trees in Farley Wood ... but then who ever expected consistency from him?

At least you are safe now, she said to the elm trees, *now you will never know axe or saw.* Only Act of God or of His lieutenants the East or Nor'-East winds would ever lay them low, now. They were reprieved, for a little, from terrible loss, from grief, as she had not been reprieved. They should be grateful.

The elm trees made the only sound in all the stillness, an inter-mittent quiet sobbing dispersing itself over the landscape. Occasion-ally they spattered their tears in big, heavy drops down upon Harriet's head as she passed beneath. She put up her paisley shawl over her bowed head, to ward them off. She was bowed certainly, half against the cold unmerciful evening with its afterthoughts of rain, and half with the weight of her intolerable burden of anguish. *Desolé* was the word. She saw it suddenly as a woman bowed and middle-aged as herself, dressed in the green of a dying leaf, and travelling for ever up an unending avenue towards a house which could never be reached and which (even if it were reached) held nothing but emptiness for evermore.

377

Emptiness for evermore. It was not to be borne! Clenching her fists tightly into the cold palms of her hands, Harriet screamed as she trudged, unheard and unheeded. This quiet, self-controlled creature — this 'haven of peace' as Van had once called her, screamed now like a trapped beast or a beast in labour. Nothing ceased but what was lovely or hopeful; nothing lasted but the unendurable, and that lasted for evermore.

Still bowed low, with no cessation of her trudging struggle up the avenue; with the feel of the wet gravel by now close against her instep and her wet skirts clogging her ankles as she walked, still with clenched fists, still screaming against what had happened to her (now soundlessly, now aloud, but always unheeded and unheard) Harriet continued her pilgrimage towards the house. Certain inescapable facts and memories lashed her in the face as she travelled, together with the raindrops; the fact of Van's escape, with Louisa; the fact that he had ever been born (or she for that matter); the fact that Redonda was waiting for her coldly, stilly, mocking her with its memories; the fact that the elm trees wept too; the fact that the whole purpose of her life, which she had been building up with such patient and insect-like application, had proved as futile, finally, as the labours of insect or a bird; as a bird that, losing one nest and the eggs in it, builds another, and yet another, and yet another — never ceasing its hopeful labours in the face of continuous disaster and yet, for all that, steadily deteriorating with each endeavour, like a small machine running down and wearing out . . .

First the triumph, the round, downy nest, with the breast feathers lovingly sacrificed to it, and the brood of six blue eggs. Then — sudden death or damage or thievery — and the next nest and brood — and the next; finally the bird half-crazed and wholly exhausted, sitting without hope upon eggs that would hatch fledglings just in time to be killed by the first frost; fledglings in a nest that was no more than sticks piled rakishly together, and a tuft of sheep's wool, dragged off the nearest bramble.

Sheep's wool. That reminded her. Farley Field needed fencing again, for judging by the tell-tale tufts of sheep's wool in one of the gaps, many of the beasts had worked their way through there into the wood and must be damaging the bark of the young trees within.

THE WHEEL COMES FULL CIRCLE

She must see to it, see to it, see to it (saying the words to fit the slow
trudge of her feet; fence for the sheep, fence for the sheep, fence for
the sheep — and suddenly stopped in her tracks, arrested by the
grinding thought that there was no sense or purpose in seeing to
things any more. Seeing to things had been for Van and her (perhaps not at the moment but in the future — oh yes, in the future!);
it had been for *their* life — not for hers alone. To go on now as she
had always done would be to ape that hen-bird who, with her
precious first nest destroyed, still senselessly, fruitlessly, piteously
builds and builds, and lays and lays without knowing why or where-
fore, only that she must do both, or else die.

. . . A bird's nest in Winter. Yes, soon the Winter would come, and
those little houses of feather, twig, sheep's wool and horsehair, which
had been hidden all the Summer, would begin to disclose themselves
in the stripped trees and hedgerows like a species of large Winter
flower; most delicately etched against a skyline the colour of pewter
— the small dark solid shapes that were the flower-nests, the great
thin traceries of the trees and bushes that held them.

Clancy had always thought an empty bird's nest a grievous sight.
(It was odd that she should remember a casual remark made by
Clancy, twenty years earlier, but the grief-stricken mood brings
such thoughts winging home to itself, however huge the intervening
span of space and time.) Harriet thought them sad, too. As a
practical creature and a farmer-to-be, she had, even then, deplored
their uselessness. There they were, their purpose over, finished with
— so rake them out, plough them in, store them up as matter for
bonfires — do *something*, not just leave them scattered over the
countryside, hundreds and thousands of little houses each one as
important and individual as Redonda — and now deserted and forlorn.

A presage of snow to come weighed down upon her eyes and
shuttered them down, the heavy snow of a short day in mid-Winter,
the kind of day that no one ventures out in — except the necessary
horseman and the shepherd. With tears still coursing from her shut
eyes down her cheeks, and in cold little rivulets by her ears, Harriet
yet had the most curious and premonitory sensation of oppressive
snow, bearing down upon her eyelids — much as the icy weight of
it must press upon and bear down the tender twig-framed nest. . . .

379

> . . . Be left more desolate, more dreary cold
> Than a forsaken bird's nest, filled with snow
> 'Mid its own bush of leafless eglantine . . .

Desolate. There was no escape from the word. (Which are coldest, the ankles or the cheeks? The one from the earth's tears, the other from mine? Will there ever be warmth in the world again, will the end of the avenue never be reached?)

The elms kept up their pitying susurration as she passed them. All over the park she could hear them — some weeping singly, some in groups of twos or threes — like giants gossiping with their heads together about the frantic human being travelling so slowly below them. Desolate. *Desolé*. Redonda should be re-named. *Desolé* was the only possible designation. If Van had given her nothing else for the house, at least he should give her the name for it — he could not avoid doing that! There was both irony and sense in that!

By now she had passed the sandpit, had passed the gleaming holly-bush where once she and Susan had sheltered from the tempest hundreds — thousands of years ago. The pain of the gravel pressing against her soles was now almost as hard to endure as the pain in her heart and spirit and whole body. With her teeth clenched, Harriet still could not keep herself from screaming; the sound of the screams came out grindingly and grudgingly like the short gasping cries of a woman in labour — Yes, she was in labour indeed and striving hard, hard for her grief to be born. Yes — she concluded, if I could rid myself of it in one mighty spasm — this terrible and unspeakable horror that has happened to me — even if it splits me asunder and leaves me spread-eagled and dying on the road here — at least I shall be free of it! If I died of it, if I went to Heaven or Hell — yes, even there, whatever else had to be endured, at least this anguish would be left behind.

Oppressive upon her cold eyelids the thought of the snow to come, the endless, empty Winter opening upon a Spring flowering for all but her; cunningly persistent the pain of the gravel below her and this thought sidling in at a cranny of her relaxed mind: *The worst horror — the one I have not dared to think of yet, is that this is always to be with me, is never going to end*. What is there of this to be considered in detail before each night and its nightmares comes to relieve me? Hopes abandoned, pride shattered, dreams frustrated, ambitions obliterated — all these will torment me until I die; but these are secondary. The grief itself, the solid unspeakable lump — the monstrous birth that Van has forced upon me, will remain for ever. I must bear it and yet I cannot bear it. I cannot die — and yet I cannot live and endure it.

She reached a spot where an elm had fallen, three winters ago. They had not been able to spare the labour to saw it up just then, so had sent a man and a horse-team with chains to haul it to the side of the road. There it lay now, the grass grown long round about it, and as Harriet drew level with it, some small creature (a squirrel or a bird, she could not have said which) started out of one of its crannies, surveyed the scene around with a bright eye and with-drew again swiftly into its dark, chosen home. The year was ending, the Winter's night drew near, but *something*, living within there, had a heart of joy, of hope, that nothing could touch.

The snow will come; the snow may come and pack that cranny, and suffocate whatever inhabits it — but the hope will die with it, as the sound fruit of the nut ripens in the kernel; but I am an empty husk.

Hearing a hail in the distance, she looked up (she had been trudging onwards with her eyes fixed upon the drive), and saw Susan running towards her from the house. She felt neither surprise nor resentment. (What emotion should she ever feel again but pain and grief?) When Susan had reached her, she came forward swiftly and seized her wet mistress by both her elbows, feeling their rigidity through the sodden shawl. Harriet did not look up or pull away from her. There was in any case a kind of urgent authority in the other's hold which would not have been gainsaid. The grey day looked down with the last flicker of light from between its dying eyelids upon the two small shapes of these bowed women — bowed both against the cold and the wet, in the middle of the long drive.

'Come up to the house, Miss Harry — and be warm!'

'He has gone,' replied Harriet, through chattering teeth and with infinite difficulty, as if they were the last words she could find strength to utter. 'He has gone, and he has taken Louisa, and I hate him for ever! Nobody is ever to speak his name again — do you hear? Nobody! Never again as long as I live — or as he does!'

Still the bowed intent shapes faced each other, bent towards each other like the sheaves of corn in a stook. The moment seemed to go on for ever. The teeth chattering in her head would not cease — nor yet the firm grasp of Susan's hands under her elbows.

'Come and be warm,' repeated Susan. 'You are perished with cold — wholly perished. You must be made warm!' With a gesture of infinite tenderness she released Harriet's elbows, folding her instead close to her bosom. There is no lightning and no thunder now but the gesture, and the emotion that inspired it, come full circle once more out of the eternal spaces whence they have been waiting since that day, long, long ago, when with exactly the same gesture and tenderness the younger child had caught the elder one and held her to her breast.

'Dear child,' said a voice Susan's and yet not Susan's, 'Dear mistress. Dear child.'

With her face bowed, muffled against Susan's breast, against the strong, stout beating of her heart, Harriet said: 'You lost your own child because you nursed mine. I made you starve him. And now we have lost *both* — do you hear? — *both*?'

Susan's arms enclosed her like bars of iron, strong and loving bars; there was no getting away from them. The bitter angry words seemed to slip through these bars and wing away like hideous birds — far, far away until they were no more than a speck . . . Yet they were only the precursors of a whole aviary of evil creatures, compact of sick malice and despair, forced upwards in her and beating with their noisome wings insistently against her brain and her mind and her heart.

'You are kind to me,' said Harriet, 'because you are so soft you have to be kind to somebody! I've ill-used you in the past, I've forgotten your very existence; I did not care when your child died and I do not care now! If he had left me *my* child I should have taken her from you as soon as she needed you no longer, without a thought, and if you had ever hurt so much as a hair of her head — even accidentally — I should have killed you — '

'Hush, Hush,' said Susan, pressing her close, warming her with her unheeding, inhuman loving-kindness.

'I should have killed you, do you hear!' cried Harriet, '*As I killed Sabrina!* Do you know that? I suppose you are so soft, and such a fool that, even now I have told you, you do not believe me — ' and she began to cry again with great, tearing sobs.

'Be quiet,' commanded Susan, pressing Harriet's head down into the warmth and darkness of her bosom, against the triumphant beating of her heart. And again she repeated with great intensity: 'Come and be warm, and let me change your wet things Miss Harry, dear. Come and be made warm — '

And they began to walk, so entwined, on towards the house.

A great lassitude came down upon Harriet and her head went heavy, suddenly, upon Susan's shoulder. It was not fitting that she should be seen walking so, up her own drive, but it did not matter any more. Nothing in the whole wide world mattered any more. Numbed, frozen, careless, but more utterly weary than anything else (as the shock of great grief is mercifully the most wearying thing in the world) she stumbled onwards.

Susan began to sing as they went — snatches from the jingles they had carolled as children, swinging from the boughs of the same elm-trees or picking from the same clumps of paigles, or searching for pharisees down wells and springs in the same park. Tunes that had sung their sweet flutelike way into memory before Van had ever come into her experience, and which now remained after him.

She closed her eyes completely, leaving the direction of their steps entirely now to her companion. She could imagine Vandervoord standing in the bows of the ship with the child in his arms, with his eyes and his whole mind looking ahead towards the thought of America and wrapped up in that thought as completely as he and the child were now wrapped up together in his travelling cloak. She could imagine his hands busy about the child, tucking it in more securely, adjusting one of its dangling shoes; hands that were never to touch her again in tenderness, or desire, or even in common friendship. And again, with the last remnants of accumulated force and bitterness welling up in her both together, she cried out, 'I hate him! I hate him! I hate him!'

At that Susan, speaking with a voice not like her own at all, but with the authoritative timbre of one familiar and yet unfamiliar to Harriet (as if a blue and scarlet angel out of one of the coloured plates in her Bible had suddenly opened his mouth and spoken with words that were swords), said:

383

'You love him. You will always love him and the child. We will both love them, however far they go from us. Our love will wrap them round like a cloak in the cold days out there and in the summer it will be cool as water on their foreheads —'

'To love him always,' answered Harriet, without surprise or difficulty and brushing aside the mention of the child as if it did not exist — so much is the lesser swallowed up in the greater — 'would be intolerable and you know it!' The blue and scarlet angel, speaking through Susan's homespun, *must* know it, knowing all things — 'It is because I loved him that all this has befallen me!'

'Love him more,' went on the remorseless, yet tender voice — 'Not hate him more! If you love him you go after him and are with him — and yet not with him; if you hate him, you are tied here to this place and this time and there is no escape. I tell you this because I love you more than I love him, or my own children, or your child; because nothing that you can do will stop me from loving you, however hard you try. Send me away from you; send us all away from you! Still you cannot send my love away from you. You cannot cease to be dear to me, and the apple of my eye —'

The words that were swords clove their way through Harriet's spirit, shining with terrible blinding majesty. 'Oh whither,' cried her wordless spirit in response, 'shall I flee from Thy Presence? If I descend into Hell Thou art there!'

And she stumbled, falling upon her knees at the foot of Redonda's stone steps, beside the fallen statue of the boy with the flute.

In an instant strong arms were again about her, helping her up; not clad in the blue and scarlet array of that angel-companion she had fancied in her delirium, but comforting ones, clad once more in homespun.

It was not fitting to be helped up her own steps. It was not fitting to be borne upon the wings of an angel or the devotion of a friend. And she was so tired she could not tell which was which any more. One thing only she knew. There was a century, perhaps ten thousand centuries, of pain to be worked out — part and parcel of an autumnal landscape backed by a desolate house — part and parcel of her inheritance.

Helped and supported by Susan's arm, Harriet went up the steps, and into her inheritance.